THE SINGING

ALSO BY KATHERINE GENET

The Wilde Grove Series

The Gathering

The Belonging

The Rising

The Singing

Wilde Grove Series 2

Follow The Wind

The Otherworld

Golden Heart

Wilde Grove Prayer Books

Prayers Of The Wildwood

Prayers Of The Beacons

Wilde Grove Bonus Stories

Becoming Morghan

The Threading

Non-Fiction

Ground & Centre

The Dreamer's Way

The Singing

KATHERINE GENET

Wych Elm Books

Quotations from The Wildwood Tarot on pp299-302 used with permission. The Wildwood Tarot, copyright Mark Ryan and John Matthews. (Welbeck Publishers Ltd UK/ Sterling Publishing USA.)

Wych Elm Books

Otago, NZ

www.wychelmbooks.com

contact@wychelmbooks.com

ISBN: 978-0-473- 56306-6

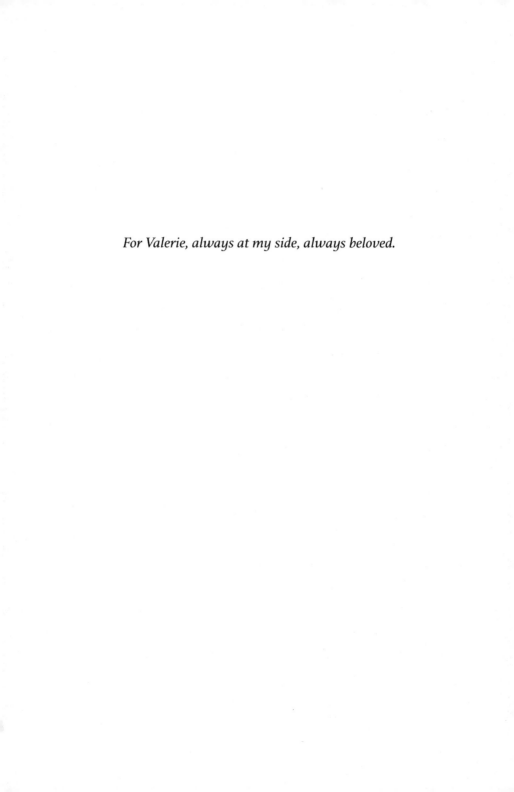

For Valerie, always at my side, always beloved.

1

I AM GRANDFATHER OAK, THE KEEPER OF THE WILDWOOD.
If you venture far enough into my realm I will know of
your coming, and eventually, you and I will meet. I stand in
a clearing, my branches heavy about my crown, and we will
gaze upon each other, and perhaps, if it is appropriate, if
you are willing to learn and follow the ways of the Wildwood, I will gift you with an acorn, a seed from which to
grow.

But for now, the Lady of the Grove, who is also a Lady of
the Forest, dreams. Her visions ripple through my woods
like the wind, and I capture her seeings in my leaves. They
shiver with tension, droop with the despair of her dreamings, and I know I must go to her.

For dreams are permeable and the worlds are
connected, as are thus we all.

I find Morghan of the Grove and step into her dream,
and in doing so, create a space in it where she can see me.
Where we may speak.

Where I will be able to remind her of the way the wind ducks and dives, of the way the tree grows, of the flowing of sap, of the singing of a bird, the soft slither of a worm, of the moon burnished between branches.

The space created becomes a room, and I – I fashion legs for myself, long and lean, and a torso that bends, hands and arms, a man's head, hair a bushy halo of leaves and twigs. The transformation makes me shiver as though the wind tousles my leaves, and I smile.

The still-dreaming Morghan slaps her hands against the window, calling for those out there in her dream to stop, to stop the nightmare.

I speak to her, and for a moment, my voice is still that of the forest – the bird, young and featherless in its nest, the tapping of twig against branch, the bell call of leaves in a silvered breeze. I clear my new throat and the hum and buzz of my voice becomes words.

Morghan turns, looks at me, her face soft and slack in surprise, and then she recognises me.

'Grandfather Oak,' she says, and I laugh and laugh and laugh and sweep my arms out to draw her over to sit with me. I stoop against the dirt ceiling of the room I have fashioned.

Morghan sits, and I fold my long limbs onto the seat opposite her.

'What are you doing here?' Morghan asks, and looks out the window again, where her dreaming is interrupted.

'Your visions tumble and blow through my woods,' I tell her. 'I come to speak to you because of them.'

She glances out the window again, where terrible things

are happening, where flesh, soft and vulnerable, grows bruises the colour of plums, and wild red blooms.

Morghan, Lady of the Grove, Lady of Earth, Sky, and Sea, of Life and Death, shakes her head. Her fingers are splayed against the table between us. She glances down at them, curls them into fists.

'How?' she asks, and for a moment I think she means to question how we are where we are, how I am there with her in this fashioned space, this room in the middle of a dream.

But of course not. This is not her question. This, she has taken in stride.

'How do I stop it?' she asks, with another glance outside at her dream. 'All the time, all over the world.' Her shoulders are tense with the question, and I shake my head.

'You know the answer to this,' I tell her, and she tips her face back, her eyes closing for a moment.

'Remind me,' she says, and I see the white line of her throat move as she swallows.

I shake my head, unused to the flexibility of this form, and the twigs in my hair rattle against each other. 'You do as you always must.'

She looks at me, for we both know.

As do you.

'You continue to dig your roots deep.' In my voice is the echo of the rabbit burrowing down into the soil.

'You continue to spread your branches wide.'

She nods and breathes, shoulders straightening. Her hands unfurl, like buds upon a branch.

'You grow your acorns,' I say, and I think of all the acorns I have gifted to those who venture into my Wildwood, seeking the heart of things, finding me, finding themselves.

'And you shake your branches so that the acorn may fall, and begin life anew,' I finish, for there it is, the entire cycle, what we all do, what we can do.

What we must.

Over, and over again. Lifetime to lifetime. Season to season. Sunrise to sunrise.

Breath to breath.

Morghan touches the silver oak leaf and acorn that hang from a chain around her neck, along with the egg that is a gift from her Goddess, and she smiles.

'Come now,' I say, and look up from the diner table to the waitress bringing our milkshakes on a tray. 'I have taken the liberty of ordering for us.' I wink at Morghan, who looks at the tall glasses placed on the table. Hers is brown, the colour of soil, chocolate.

Mine is green, chlorophyll, for I am a tree, after all.

We toast each other and laugh and laugh and I reach out over the table, extending a twiggy finger, and touch her chest.

To remind her.

To remind all of you.

Dig deep. Spread wide.

2

ERIN TOOK A SLOW BREATH AND TRIED TO GATHER HER WITS about her. They were a little frayed with nervousness, and she breathed into and through the feeling, looked down at Fox by her side.

She'd come so far since Morghan had set her the gardening task. Even further since she'd come to Wellsford in the first place – that seemed such a long time ago, she could hardly fathom it.

And now. Now, she was ready, she thought, to venture beyond the gates of the garden. This was the next step, Morghan had told her. Erin turned and looked back at her imaginary garden. It was barely recognisable from the over-grown jungle it had been just weeks ago. She'd been coming here every day, armed with pruners and trowel, determined to bring order and discipline to the unruly beds.

It seemed to have worked. Erin had to admit that she felt steadier, sturdier. Well planted. Well-tended. She stifled a giggle at the gardening terms, but it was true. How something like imaginary gardening had managed to have this effect on her, on the way she felt, was still a mystery.

But it was true.

She had tended her garden, and in her waking day, had made decisions, pruned her thoughts, always asking herself if what she was doing, thinking, saying, belonged in her garden. If it would grow strong and true.

And in doing so, Erin's imaginary gardening had turned into visionary gardening. And now she was ready to take what Morghan had said was the next step – to go through the gate and out into the Wildwood. Someone would be waiting for her there, Morghan said.

The spirits would become her teachers.

She shouldn't be nervous, Erin chastised herself. After all she'd already been through – Kria and the loch, watching Morghan help Blythe – this next part should be a bit of a doddle.

But the spirits becoming her teachers? What, exactly, Erin wondered, would that entail? Who would it be? It didn't sound...safe. Not entirely. Why couldn't she just continue what she and Morghan were doing every day?

But Morghan said she had to do this too. This was following the Ancient Path. As far as it would take her. If she wanted to take up her calling, this was what she did. She had to step out into the Wildwood and do it with just Fox by her side.

Erin winced and looked down at Fox, who stared up at her with narrowed eyes, as though she'd heard what Erin was thinking. Erin rubbed sweaty palms against her skirt and grimaced.

'Sorry,' she said. 'That was phrased badly.'

Fox's eyebrows rose as though she wanted more.

'I'm just a bit anxious, that's all.'

Fox flicked her ears and got to her feet, trotting towards the gate as though she'd run out of patience. When she got to it, she turned and eyed Erin steadily.

'Okay,' Erin said, walking along the path on legs that were the teeniest bit unsteady. 'Here we go, then.' She huffed out a breath. 'Out into the Wildwood.'

Really, she thought. She oughtn't to be so worried. After all, Morghan did this every day. Even Stephan – he went back and forth, Bear Fellow meeting him to teach him about the plants and their healing properties. Erin put her hand to the gate and steadied herself, pushed it open.

Perhaps that was why she was so nervous. Stephen had told her, wide-eyed, his first meeting with the great Bear God, and how he'd squirmed around on the ground like a worm, practically soiling his trousers before he'd got himself under control.

Of course, she'd already met her Goddess. Perhaps she'd see Elen of the Ways again today. That wouldn't be so bad now, would it?

Erin shivered, imagining the gaze of the shining, antlered Goddess settling upon her once again. She swallowed, remembering.

But Fox trotted towards the trees, the white flag of her tail waving. Erin followed it, gritting her teeth, then taking long, slow breaths to keep herself present and steady. She knew that in her waking reality, her body stood beside the well in the garden behind Ash Cottage, but she wasn't really there with it. She was in spirit, going off on an adventure.

'That's right,' Erin said out loud. 'An adventure into the

Wildwood. People have been doing this for hundreds of thousands of years.

'I've done this before.'

The sound of her own voice calmed her, and she steadied in her spirit form, slipping between the trees and looking around herself with unexpected, bright-eyed wonder.

'Wait for me!' she called to Fox.

Fox flicked a glance back at her but didn't slow her pace, and Erin found herself picking up her skirts and breaking into a run, ducking in and out of the trees, thick branches laden with green leaves, to follow.

'I said wait for me!'

Fox stopped, a grin on her face as Erin ground to a halt behind her, cheeks red, her hair come loose about her shoulders, bits of leaves and twigs in it.

'Wow,' Erin breathed. 'What is this place?' She turned and looked back at the forest that sat like a thick curtain behind them, then gazed again at the sudden broad lake, where the sun, angled low in the sky, set the lapping waves glittering with diamond sparkles.

Fox gazed out over the water with Erin for a long moment, then turned and set her dainty feet over the stones of the shore and followed it in its wide curve. She turned her head and checked that Erin walked behind her. There was much to do, to learn. To become.

The lessons couldn't start soon enough.

Erin lifted a hand and squinted out over the water. There was an island in the middle of the lake, and she shook her head briefly at the vision of it.

'That's not, um, Avalon, is it?' she asked, shaking her

head even as she asked the question. Of course it wasn't. Avalon was just a story.

This was real.

Besides, it wasn't big enough.

There was something familiar about it though, and with a jolt, Erin remembered the lake in Morghan's personal Otherworld place. This wasn't the same one as that, was it? Hadn't there been a small, conical island there as well?

She had so many questions, but with each asking, each desperate desire to know, she felt herself tremble, the vision around her waver slightly, and Erin discovered that she needed to relax, to go along with the experience. Too much struggling with it, questioning, was dragging her back to her body again.

It was a delicate thing, she realised, this walking in the Otherworld.

Fox stopped at a place where the beach widened, became a fat crescent of pale stones, wet at the edges by the tongue of the lake. There was a tree, growing from the ground under the stones, and Fox sat down patiently under its branches, and looked at Erin.

Erin's eyes widened, and she gazed at the golden pears hanging from the laden branches. Tentatively, she reached up a hand and touched one, then, following some inner imperative, she plucked it from the branch and lifted it to her lips.

It was sweet, and juice ran down her chin. She ate it all, even the pips, Fox waiting silently for her to finish.

Before leading her down to the shore where she stopped and looked again at Erin.

'Okay,' Erin said, the taste of the pear still sugary against her tongue, and she looked out over the water, frowning when she spotted something under the gentle waves. A dark shadow.

There was a rope tethering the shape and Erin leant down, dipped her hand under the water and grasped the rope, tugging at it, feeling resistance. She pulled harder and the dark shape moved, rose towards the surface, the water rushing from it, and Erin's face broke into a smile.

It was a boat. Of course it was a boat!

She hauled it towards the shore, a long, low-slung canoe, and Fox leapt nimbly into it, running to the bow to sit looking expectantly at the island. Erin coiled up the rope and threw it into the boat, then clambered in to sit on the miraculously dry plank seat across the middle.

The boat floated out over the water and Erin leant slightly to look over the side, down into the water where shadows darted and flashed, coming closer, then swimming away. She sat back up and inhaled, concentrated on her breathing for a moment as the island came closer and closer. The boat ground against its shore and Fox jumped out, turning to wait for Erin.

Erin wasted no time, picking her way onto the shore, wondering briefly if she ought to tie the boat to something, so that they could make their way back when they were done doing whatever they'd come here for. But the rope was at the wrong end of the boat, and she stared at it for a moment, biting at her lip, then shrugged. There was nothing to tie the boat to, anyway. And the island was not very far from the shore.

If she had to, she could swim to it. Something snuffled at her shoulder and Erin jumped, giving a little squeal. It was a horse, the colour of milk, its eyes like pale toffee. It snorted and nibbled at her shoulder again, then turned and ambled away, Fox falling in behind it.

What was this place, Erin wondered? Boats that moved themselves, horses that lived on tiny islands.

She breathed deeply and smelt woodsmoke. It made her squint up towards the top of the hill that was the entire island, then hurry after Fox and the horse. A path spiralled up around the hill and Erin walked along it, feeling the warmth of the sun on her head.

She rubbed nervous palms against her skirts.

There was a shack on the top of the hill. Erin stared at it only a moment before turning her head towards the figure beckoning her.

'Come,' the old woman said. 'Come sit down.'

Erin drifted over to the white-haired crone, astonished at the sight of her. She sat on the stool across from the woman. Between them, a cooking pot hung over a fire.

'Who are you?' Erin asked, her voice little more than a croak. She hadn't known what to expect, coming here to the Wildwood, but if she'd had to guess, it wouldn't have been this.

The old woman stared across the fire at her, then sniffed.

'Manners are the first lesson you're needing then, I see,' she said, and for a moment, her voice sounded of wind and wave, of far-off dreamings and seeings.

Fox turned her head and glared at Erin, white tail tip twitching.

Erin bent her head immediately. 'My apologies,' she said, and she took a breath. 'I am Erin.' Another quick breath. 'Erin of the Grove.' She risked a look at the figure hunched on the stool opposite, skirts bunched around, thick fingers clasped in front of her. The woman stared at Erin, eyes shrewd and bright in her creased face.

'May I know your name?' Erin asked.

The woman pursed her lips. Shook her head. 'No,' she said. 'My name is not important.'

Erin's eyes widened. She'd not expected that answer. 'Then what do I call you?'

But the old crone merely sniffed and reached for a bowl and ladled something into it from the pot hanging over the fire before sliding a spoon into it. She got up from her stool and waddled over to Erin.

'Eat this,' she commanded, holding out the steaming bowl.

Erin looked dubiously at it. 'What's in it?'

'Take it,' the woman insisted.

Erin took it. Fox looked expectantly at her.

'But what's in it?' Erin asked again.

The woman was back on her stool, looking Erin over. She blinked her pale eyes. 'Why are you here?' she asked.

Erin licked her lips, holding the bowl. What was she supposed to answer to that?

The woman looked at her, brows raised, waiting.

'Um, Fox brought me here,' Erin said.

Fox's head drooped.

Erin took a breath. 'I'm seeking,' she said.

'Ah.' The old woman perked up. 'What are you seeking?'

'I don't know,' Erin admitted, feeling her shoulders slump.

How was she supposed to know? She had no idea what she was doing.

'I'm following the pin cushion,' she said, then swallowed.

The old woman tossed back her head and laughed raucously. It was the sound of ravens and crows crying harshly to each other. She smiled widely at Erin. 'You have met my sister, then?'

Erin frowned. 'Your sister?' she asked uncertainly.

'The Yaga, of course.'

'Oh.' Erin shook her head, even though it seemed to swim on her shoulders. 'No,' she said. 'I've only heard stories of her.' She blinked, looked again at the old woman. 'She is your sister?'

The old woman raised her shoulders in an elaborate shrug. 'In a manner of speaking.' Her white hair bobbed around her head like floss in the low sunlight.

'Well then,' she said, thrusting her chin at the mug in Erin's hands. 'Eat.'

Erin looked down at the food in the bowl. She sniffed it cautiously, but it smelt only like the lentil stew her mother had made years back, during her vegetarian phase. That had only lasted a week before Erin's father had put a stop to it. She grasped the spoon in a hand that shook a little.

Weren't you supposed to avoid eating when you were in the Otherworld? Erin frowned. Or was that only when you were with the Fae?

'Are you one of the Fae, then?' she asked, spoon between her fingers.

The old woman tossed her head and laughed again, thumping her hands against her thighs as though Erin had said something enormously entertaining.

'No,' the old crone said at last, her laughter wheezing to a stop. 'Now eat it.'

'But why?' Erin asked, unable to help herself, even while lifting a spoonful of the thick stew to her lips. Her mouth watered, and she tasted it. Swallowed the stew down.

'Because you're too skinny,' the old woman said and laughed again.

Erin glanced at Fox, but she just twitched her ears and watched as Erin scraped the stew from the bowl and ate it. It was rich and flavoursome, better than anything Veronica had made, and Erin was surprised to find she'd eaten it all in just a moment.

'Thank you,' she said, holding the empty bowl.

'Ah,' the old woman said. 'Already your manners improve.' She nodded in satisfaction. 'Now ask your questions.'

Erin's brow rose. She had a lot of questions. Was the woman serious?

But the old woman sat placidly upon her stool, nodding her head gently, and Erin swallowed, searching her mind for a question to lead with.

'Who are you?' she asked.

The woman shook her head, swept her arms out in a wide gesture. 'I am the crone who sits at the top of the hill, red-faced from her cooking pot and waiting to answer your questions.'

'Is this some sort of puzzle – a riddle?' Erin asked.

The woman's eyes narrowed. 'A riddle?'

Erin guessed not. She tried again. 'Why am I here?'

'To ask your questions.'

Erin bit back the retort that came to her lips. She was asking questions.

Obviously not the right ones, however. She leant back on her stool, gazing around for a moment at where she sat, the bowl and spoon still on her lap. The ground underneath them was worn to dirt, and the cooking pot blackened with age and use. The shack was little more than a lean-to, and for a moment, Erin wanted to get up and go and look at the things she could see piled in its shade. They were just shapes and she squinted at them. Bedding, maybe. More cooking things.

Questions. What questions should she be asking?

'Why a pear?' she said, the words falling from her lips before she even knew she'd meant to speak. 'Why a pear, and a white horse – and the boat, what about that?'

The old woman sat back and regarded Erin steadily.

'Good questions,' she said with a benevolent nod. 'But not the right ones.'

Erin's heart sank. Was this what it was to be like, here in the Otherworld? Everything in symbols and riddles? She thought furiously.

Then cleared her throat.

'What wisdom do you have for me?' she asked, feeling herself flush with the temerity of asking.

But the crone beamed and reached into her pocket, pulling out a clutch of bones, stones, and twigs, which she threw down onto the ground beside the fire, bending over to decipher their message.

'Ah, yes,' she said, leaning forward to pluck up three of them and pass them over to Erin. 'Welcome,' she said, and for a moment, her voice was the rattle of rain, the gusting of dust. 'Welcome to the path of initiation.'

Erin's brows rose. The path of initiation? She reached out and took the stones and twigs from the old woman, blinking and looking down at them to find that they were etched with symbols.

'These are runes,' she said in surprise.

'Of course,' the old crone said. 'Do you not work with those?'

Erin nodded, closing her hands around them. She cleared her throat. 'Where does it lead?' she asked. 'The path of initiation. Haven't I already done it?' She thought of Kria.

The old Goddess leant back, a smile on her face.

'Well,' she said. 'Each lifetime has its own initiation, one which leads you into the heart of the world, and your place in it.' She laughed.

The old Goddess bent forward, still chuckling.

'Where else would it take you?'

3

ERIN EMERGED BLINKING BACK INTO THE SUNLIGHT OF HER garden. She lifted her hand and opened her fingers, the lines visible across the skin, her empty palm.

She had carried the stones back with her, hadn't she? The runes?

For a long moment, she was perplexed that they weren't there, and then she gave a shaky laugh. Of course they weren't there – this was the waking world. She was back in the garden at Ash Cottage. She'd not been able to bring them back across with her.

Except she had, hadn't she?

She remembered the symbols, which runes they'd been.

Erin tipped her head back unable to believe the journey she'd been on. She'd done it – properly done it. Stepped across the borders of the world, stepped outside her garden, and walked in the Wildwood, just like Morghan had told her to.

Her face creased into a wide smile, and she lifted her

arms in a glorious stretching to the sky. She gave a little shimmy of joy.

She'd done it. She'd really done it.

'You're looking awfully pleased with yourself.'

Erin opened her eyes, then, suddenly dizzy, lurched to the side.

'Whoa, steady on,' Stephan said, rushing over to steady her before she ended up in the onion bed. He caught her and then had to catch his breath. Touching her was like getting an electric shock, minus the discomfort.

He still wasn't used to it.

But he liked it. A lot.

Erin grinned up at him. 'I did it,' she crowed.

Stephan set her upright, reluctantly, and kept a hand on her to stop her from wobbling. 'You need something to eat and drink,' he said.

Erin rolled her eyes, took a step, and flung her hands out to steady herself. 'Yeah,' she giggled. 'I guess so. And I need my runestones.' She nodded. 'I had the most amazing time, Stephan.' Then she laughed again. 'Even though I don't have a clue what any of it means.' Her eyes widened. 'I have to draw it all – that's what I have to do. Wow. Yeah.'

Stephan shook his head, grasped Erin gently by the elbow, trying to ignore the little shock of pleasure, and led her into the glasshouse and sat her down at the table.

'I'll go get everything you need,' he said. 'You sit tight and then you can tell me all about it.'

Erin beamed at him. 'And by the way,' she said.

He raised his eyebrows.

'Hello sunshine,' she said.

Stephan grinned at her. 'Hello yourself.' He leant over

the table and touched her lips with his, closing his eyes with the sweetness of it.

Erin wrapped her arms around his neck.

He shook his head when they drew apart. 'I am still not used to being able to do that,' he said. 'I thought for a while there I'd have to move in with you to get close enough to kiss, what with all the lockdown restrictions.'

Erin's eyes widened. 'You weren't thinking that!'

'Believe me, I was too,' Stephan said. 'I had the date ringed on the calendar when restrictions would ease.'

Erin nodded. That date had come and gone finally, and Erin suddenly remembered what else was planned for today. She glanced around. 'Did you bring your stuff?' she asked and felt a sudden rush of exhilarated anticipation.

Stephan nodded, looking at her. 'Yeah,' he said. 'Toothbrush. Change of clothes.' He cleared his throat. 'Is it weird, doing it like this?' he asked suddenly.

'Like what?'

Erin gazed up at him. He was so handsome, she thought, the way his eyes were so blue, and how they went all sort of unfocused when they looked at her, and she liked the way his hair curled around his neck too. He looked sort of like a Grecian god.

He shrugged. 'You know. Planned, and all.' He grimaced. 'You know, usually you'd just kind of fall into bed spontaneously...' He trailed off and shrugged again.

Erin forced herself back to earth. 'Yes,' she said. 'I know.' She looked up at him, and the sight of him set her fizzing again with buzzing, dreamy excitement. Then she narrowed her eyes, pressing a hand flat to the table to ground herself. 'Wait,' she said. 'Something's different.'

Stephan raised his hand and stroked his chin, grinning at her.

Erin's eyes widened, and she laughed, clapping a hand to her mouth. 'You shaved it off!' She shook her head. 'You didn't have to, you know. I was getting used to it.'

'Nah,' Stephan replied. 'I like it better like this, I think,' he said. His hand crept to his hair and tugged at it. 'Wanted to get this cut too, but haven't made the trip to Banwell, yet.'

'You're gorgeous,' Erin said, getting up and placing her palms on his smooth cheeks, smiling into his eyes. 'The most beautiful, wonderful creature I've ever met.' She felt light-headed again and laughed unsteadily. 'Maybe I'd better have that cup of tea and something to eat, though, before I kiss you again. I already feel like I could keel over.'

Her hands felt wonderful against his skin, but Stephan nodded, backed away, looking at her. He'd memorised her every feature, as though he were the artist, not her. He knew every expression by heart now – how she got two little lines between her eyebrows when she frowned, how she bit her bottom lip without even knowing it when she was thinking hard about something, how her cheeks flared with colour when she lost her temper, how her mouth trembled when she felt uncertain and lost.

He blew out a breath. 'Yeah,' he said. 'I'll go get everything. You sit tight.' He nodded, backed out of the glasshouse.

Stephan stood a minute in the garden, barely seeing the beds he'd been replanting, simply lost for a long moment in the sensation of Erin's hands pressed against his skin, the feel of her lips on his own. He swallowed, swiped up his overnight bag, and let himself into the house.

'Burdock!' he cried, bending down to give the dog a good pat and rub. 'Here you are, boy!'

Burdock wriggled in delight, then scooted out the open door into the garden. Stephan paused a moment, letting the weight of air in the cottage settle about him. How many times had he stood in this kitchen? A hundred? He shook his head. Probably a thousand.

Teresa's plants were all still in their pots about the place. Erin had hardly changed anything about the rooms, except to set up a small study in one of the rooms upstairs. Otherwise, it was still all Teresa's plants and furniture and artwork and books. All still like it had been. Stephan glanced towards the door and shook his head.

'You wouldn't mind, would you?' he asked, speaking to Teresa. 'You wouldn't mind about me and Erin, would you?'

He waited for a moment, head cocked as though to listen for an answer, then drew in a breath.

Of course she wouldn't mind. She'd be glad, he thought, for the both of them.

And she would have understood too, the bond they had.

The bond that went back lifetimes.

Stephan shivered, standing in the warm, dim kitchen. He could feel another aspect of himself just under his own skin, as though they shared sinew and blood still. He felt the other's anticipation overlaid with his own, his other, long-ago self's desire for Erin, and the woman she'd used to be.

Macha.

She'd used to be Macha, long ago, when they'd known each other.

That was the life he remembered most sharing with her.

Perhaps because they were both in the same place now as they had been then.

Stephan gave himself a little shake. How long had he been standing there, daydreaming? He was supposed to be making tea. Erin needed it – she'd been travelling into the Wildwood. Stephan roused himself and reached for the tea blend he'd made, months ago now, to ground the drinker after travelling.

Teapot and cups on the tray, and what else had Erin needed? Stephan cast around the room, frowning.

Runes. That had been it. He walked through into the little sunroom on the side of the house and picked up the bag of them from the desk in there. For a moment, he weighed them in his hand, then turned and went back to the kitchen, picked up the tea things, and carried them out to the glasshouse.

'Ah,' Erin said, falling upon the teapot and pouring the fragrant liquid into her cup. 'Are you having some as well?' she asked, teapot poised over the second cup.

'Yeah, won't do any harm,' Stephan said, and nodded. Might do him some good, actually. He felt a little…floaty. Untethered, almost. He looked around the glasshouse, at the grape vine that twined its way up one side, large leaves dark and veined. His gaze shifted to the potting bench, then back to the glazing. The sun was out, summer golden, sifting through the glass and falling in shafts upon the dirt floor.

'Are you all right?' Erin asked. 'You look like you need this more than I do.'

Stephan shook his head. 'I'm fine,' he said. 'Really, really fine, for that matter.' He looked over at Erin, at her heavy red hair loose about her shoulders, at her clear, flushed skin, her eyes the colour of the autumn forest. 'Everything just seems...more...than usual.' Stephan shook his head. 'I guess it's all the excitement, you know, but everything seems sharp, and I'm just really present.' He blinked. 'And happy. I'm happy.'

Erin's face blossomed in a wide smile. 'I know exactly what you mean,' she said, and glanced around at the building before looking back at Stephan. 'I feel it too,' she said. 'I feel like I could see the very warp and weft of your shirt, if I wanted to, and I feel like I could look at the sunlight and, I don't know, see its molecules bouncing.' She laughed. 'I don't even know what molecules are, but you know what I mean.' Erin breathed deeply, and the air filling her lungs tasted of soil and leaves and sunshine and joy. Her eyes widened.

'What?' Stephan asked, reaching for his tea, and wishing he could reach for Erin instead, that the day was done, and the night was ready to be theirs.

'I don't know,' Erin said. 'Do you think this is kind of what it's like for Morghan all the time?' she asked. 'You know, how she can see the web, and everything is brighter and more, kind of, there?'

Stephan thought about it for a moment. 'Maybe, yeah,' he answered.

'I mean,' Erin carried on, warming with enthusiasm to the idea, 'this is what she's been trying to get me to do, sort of.' A frown flitted briefly across her face. 'To sharpen my focus, to see through my skin, she says. Walking in spirit as well as body.' Erin narrowed her eyes, thinking about it. 'She says it happens spontaneously to us, our senses flaring like this, when we're excited or suddenly super interested in something. Or when perhaps, we're going on holiday and everything suddenly feels good, like the world is a big, wonderful place. Bigger and more wonderful than it usually feels.'

Erin fell silent for a moment, looking across at Stephan, feeling the breath in and out of her lungs, feeling like the blood coursing through her body had suddenly turned to gold and that her world was gloriously precious.

There was a lump in her throat when she got up from her seat and stood in front of Stephan, reaching for his hand.

'What is it?' he asked, looking up at her pink cheeks.

Erin shook her head. 'I can't wait,' she said.

For a moment Stephan was confused. 'Can't wait for what?' he asked stupidly.

Then understanding dawned. 'Oh,' he said.

He took her hand.

BURDOCK GAVE THEM A REPROACHFUL LOOK WHEN THEY closed the door on him, then sat down for a moment, listening to the murmurs behind the bedroom door. He yawned and went back downstairs. He had a marvellous chew-bone on his bed, which had been moved in front of the window where the sun slanted in, and he reckoned that giving it a good gnawing was just the thing he wanted to do right now.

On the other side of the door, Erin and Stephan reached for each other, and for a moment, Stephan felt the long-ago man he'd been sigh and murmur as he echoed Stephan's movements, his hands drifting over warm skin, searching out secret places, listening for quickening pulses, sighs.

He closed his eyes as Erin's kisses drifted down his neck and his arms tightened around her waist. Her bed was soft under them, and so too was the warm earth and summer grass, and when he sought her lips, he tasted Macha's as well, felt the strength of a thigh stretched out under his, the shifting movement of welcome, the soft calling of his name in his ear, his name, Finn's, his name, Finn's.

And he knew he was home again.

Erin tugged a blanket up over their cooling bodies and rested her head on Stephan's chest. She could hear his heartbeat and closed her eyes to listen to it, letting the deep metronome surround her.

'Is it still beating?' Stephan asked. 'Because I'm pretty sure that amount of energy should've killed me.'

'It's still beating,' Erin assured him, smoothing her fingertips over his warm skin. She smiled. 'Skipping a few beats, though.'

She felt his laugh through his skin. 'I wouldn't doubt it.'

Erin lifted her head and slid up the bed to look into his face. 'Did you feel them too?' she asked.

Stephan nodded. He knew exactly what she was talking about. 'Macha and Finn – yeah,' he said. 'I did.'

Erin grinned suddenly and flung herself off him, to lie, limbs loose and careless on the bed beside him. 'It should have been weird,' she said. 'But it wasn't.'

In fact, she thought, besides being mind-blowingly amazing, it was also refreshing to know that Macha could let her hair down and be something other than the single-minded, one-step-ahead, pushy other-life-Erin that she usually was.

'She loved you – or Finn, I mean – so much,' Erin said, wonder colouring her voice. She blinked and stared at the ceiling, before rolling onto her side and tucking herself under Stephan's arm.

'How many lifetimes do you think we've been together?' she asked. 'Morghan says most people we know in one lifetime we've known in others, and there are some super-close connections that just occur over and over.'

'We're definitely one of those,' Stephan said. 'I've got a feeling that we've been together an awful lot.' He cleared his throat. 'You don't mind, do you?'

Erin stared at him in surprise. 'Mind?' she asked. 'Why would I mind?'

Stephan looked pained. 'Well, I don't know. Only, now we've found each other, I guess I can't imagine ever, you know...'

Erin's hair tickled his bare chest when she shook her head. 'I don't know. What do you mean?'

'Ever being apart, I guess,' Stephan said, feeling his face grow warm. 'There's not going to be anyone else for me. Just you.'

Erin looked at Stephan, at his wide eyes, his colouring cheeks, the hope and vulnerability in his gaze. She shook her head wordlessly and lifted herself onto his chest, her hands cupping his face.

'Just you,' she whispered. 'Just you and me.' She pressed her lips to his, and the world exploded again around them, swirling with the energy that was their coming together, again.

'You feel that?' Erin asked, her voice low, urgent.

Stephan nodded, unable to take his eyes from hers. 'I feel that.'

She smiled again, feeling him stirring against her, his skin hot against hers, his breath quickening as she swung a leg over him, and took him inside her, sinking down onto him without taking her gaze from his.

They smiled at each other, and Stephan wrapped his arms around her, sitting up, holding her to himself, her skin slippery silky against his, and they moved together, slowly, rhythmically, and the room spun about them, the world spun about them, and their hearts beat together, and there was only themselves, the two of them, their quickening breaths, and the energy of their connection burst from deep inside them, from their roots, and rose up in them, strong and fierce and making them cry out together.

'Only you,' Erin said again, holding him to her, closing her eyes finally, feeling her heart thumping against her ribs, her skin slick against his, her hair a heavy tangle down her back.

4

MORGHAN SLIPPED QUIETLY OUT THE DOOR, STEPPING barefoot onto the lawn and lifting her face to breathe in the sweet scent of the summer afternoon in bloom around her.

A bird lifted its beak and warbled in the warm light.

Morghan walked across the lawn, letting herself think briefly about how she had walked this path before, as Blythe, then she pushed the memory away, a smile on her face. Blythe was rescued, had rested and healed, then rejoined the soul family, as she had been supposed to. That job had been done and done well.

Now, there were other tasks.

She was on her way to visit Grandfather Oak.

Morghan patted her hand absently to the small bag she carried, slung on a belt around her waist, to the offering she had tucked in there. She thought about her dream.

How unexpected it had been to turn from what was happening in her dream – which, she knew, was a dream about the world, its sickness, its strife – to see Grandfather

Oak standing there, a man, tall, thin, his hair bushy with leaves and twigs. Her lips curved again in a smile.

Even after all this time, she thought, she could still be surprised.

Grandfather Oak's small clearing in the Wildwood was hushed, the trees singing in low, soft voices. Morghan stood on the edge of the circle of trees and looked for a long moment at the large and venerable oak tree in the centre, before lowering her head in graceful acknowledgment.

'Grandfather,' she said. 'I come to bring you my thanks, for your visit last night.' She stepped forward with her smile wide now, and reached into her bag, drawing out her offering and placing it at the foot of Grandfather's trunk. She touched a finger to the small twiggy figure's torso, remembering how Grandfather Oak had reached across his diner table and pressed the tip of his finger to her chest. Leaning back on her heels, Morghan touched the spot on her breastbone, remembering the great jolt of energy that had catapulted her from the room Grandfather Oak had fashioned and back into her own bedroom, scrabbling to sit up under the covers, shaking her head in amazement at what had happened.

'I am blessed in your care and attention,' she said, remembering the first time she had come to this clearing, seen the massive old oak rearing up from the ground, his craggy limbs spread wide. She'd been young, on her own, and not used to the winding paths through the Wildwood, which had seemed to lead every which way. Even so, she'd gazed across the dim clearing at him and known, deep inside herself, who she was looking at.

Grandfather Oak. King of the Wildwood. Father of the Forest.

She'd gone to him then and lifted her hands to touch the rough bark of his skin, and instead of pressing her palms to his wooden flesh, she had stepped inside him.

And inside him it was dark and warm, and she'd lost her own shape, had become part of the old oak tree, part of the forest, part of the magic. After what may have been five minutes, or an epoch, she found herself back on the carpet of the forest floor, an acorn in her hand.

A gift. She'd been given a gift by the King of the Wildwood.

And so her adventure had begun.

'And goes on,' Morghan murmured.

'Dig our roots deep,' she said, on her knees at the bottom of the tree. 'Spread our branches wide.' Morghan blinked and sighed, finished the thought. 'Let the storms of the world only serve to shake our acorns free so that they might take root and grow.'

She'd taken that first acorn and carried it with her for several months, knowing instinctively she was supposed to plant it but not knowing where or when.

In the end, she'd planted it in the Otherworld, in a spot she'd picked instinctively, following nothing more than her intuition. But it had been right, and the tree that had grown from it was strong and beautiful. When one walked in the Otherworld, intuition was everything. It was important to walk there with the confidence to follow the paths one's kin took one on, and to let that inner, instinctive knowledge shine.

These were the lessons she was busy teaching Erin,

coaxing the girl towards readiness for her own travelling in the Wildwood, for the work she had to pursue there.

Morghan sighed, her breath light as the breeze, and gazed up at Grandfather Oak. Touched her fingers to her chest, her heart, then pressed them against the tree, in blessing and in gratitude. She closed her eyes.

And heard the lapping of water.

She shook her head and opened her eyes, unsurprised to find herself in her own small part of the Wildwood.

Morghan took a long slow breath, tasting the scent of the water, the rich loam of the earth, the flowing sap of the trees, and she looked out over the water, then behind her at the woods clustered close to the shore. Her fingers reached to touch Wolf's thick fur and she nodded to herself.

'Here,' she said.

Wolf looked up at her, amber eyes glowing.

Snake rustled between the dark ferns and slithered sinuously from the greenery and over Morghan's feet. He was heavy, his head a flat, blunt wedge that looked back towards the trees.

Hawk landed in a hushed rush of feathers upon Morghan's shoulder.

'Hello everyone,' Morghan said softly.

Hawk brushed her cheek with a wing, then settled back down.

Morghan turned her steps through the woods that sighed with a quiet breeze. The nest where Blythe had lain was empty, the blankets gone.

'Amara?' Morghan called, but the big cat didn't come. Snake quickened upon the ground, heading for the fence.

'Clarice!' Morghan said, surprised at the sight of Clarice

there in her space, fingers linked like claws through the wire mesh fence. 'Clarice. How did you get here?'

Clarice turned and shook her head. 'The Queen sent me,' she said flatly, and there was something in her expression that Morghan couldn't read. 'She told me to go a different way than usual, and this is where I ended up.'

Clarice glanced back through the fence at what lay beyond it, hulking and shadowed. 'What is this place?' She shook her head and her long white hair rippled like a curtain against her cheeks, and she pressed her palm to her heart. 'I can feel something here,' she said. 'In my heart. What is this place?' She gestured through the fence at the house. 'I mean, what specifically is that place?'

Morghan stepped closer to the fence and gazed at the half-burnt house. Why, she wondered, had the Queen sent Clarice here? To underscore what was here, of course, Morghan understood. But why? For whom – herself or Clarice? She gave a small, dry smile. Both of them, most likely.

'It is not supposed to be here,' she said. 'Not like this, anyway. Not in this state.'

'Obviously,' Clarice replied. 'Whose house is it?' She blinked her pale eyes. 'Or was it, I should say.' She cleared her throat, and rubbed her palms against her dress, suddenly nervous and not knowing why. She shook her head. 'Wait.'

Morghan closed her mouth around her answer and waited.

'Am I going to want to know this?' Clarice asked.

'The Queen sent you here.' Morghan said it as a statement, not a question.

'Yeah. But that doesn't mean...' Clarice's voice trailed off, and she cleared her throat again. 'Do you ever get used to Them running you up against things?' she asked.

Morghan laughed. 'No. Yes. Maybe,' she said.

Clarice narrowed her eyes and shot a glance at Morghan. 'That doesn't help,' she said. Her gaze turned back to the house, looking up at the remains of a child's bedroom, the bedclothes singed and blackened and flung about the room as though a whirlwind had gone through there.

'There's something else,' she said. 'That the Queen did.'

Morghan looked at Clarice and waited. It was something important, she could see. Clarice was even paler than usual, her lips pressed together in a bloodless line.

'The Queen has told me I am banned from the Fair Lands until after the solstice.' Clarice paused.

'And not the summer, but the winter solstice.'

Morghan's eyes widened. 'What?' she asked. 'Why?'

Now Clarice's expression turned wry. 'That,' she said, 'the Queen did not feel disposed to explain.'

Morghan was quiet for a moment, then reached out and touched her stepdaughter lightly on the shoulder. 'Perhaps it is a good thing,' she said.

Eyes narrowing, Clarice shifted slightly out of reach and shook her head. 'How could it possibly be a good thing?' she asked. 'All my friends are there. I spend more time there than here.' She shook her head again, more violently. 'I don't see why she would ban me from her world. I don't do any harm there.'

Morghan tipped her head slightly to the side, knowing she could guess several reasons, all of which might be

correct. Or none of which. She didn't voice any of her specu-
lations, however.

'You have friends here too,' she said mildly. 'And work
you could do, alongside the rest of us.'

But Clarice didn't answer. Her gaze had swung back to
the house on the other side of the chain-link fence. She
shrugged a stiff shoulder and lifted her chin towards the
house. 'She wants me to know about this place though,
doesn't she?'

Turning, Morghan looked at the house. She'd had weeks
to ponder it still being there, the meaning behind it.
Because of course there was meaning. Here in the Otherworld, all was meaning and purpose.

She hadn't counted on stumbling upon Clarice here,
however. That was a surprise.

But the Queen obviously considered it of benefit, for
one reason or another, and Morghan knew she would bend
to the Fae's wishes, for the Queen's gaze was longer and
broader than her own, and the vows between them were
old, but inviolable.

Morghan looked through the fence at the house. It was
an incongruous sight, in amongst the lush greenery of the
forest. She sighed. 'It's your mother's house,' she said.
'When she was a child. Or my version of it, anyway.'

'My mother's house?' Clarice turned to stare at the
burnt-out structure. 'Where...' Clarice cleared her throat.
'Where she lived with her father?'

'Yes.'

Clarice turned back to stare at Morghan. 'But you and
she fixed all that, didn't you? And you helped her, you know,
get herself back together.'

'I did,' Morghan said. And she had, she thought, remembering the little girl she'd found hiding in the wardrobe of this very house, how she'd coaxed her into trust. Brought the shard of Grainne back to her, so that she could find wholeness and a measure of peace.

'And everything was all right, then, wasn't it?' Clarice said, then winced. 'I mean, better, anyway. Mum was much better.'

'Yes,' Morghan replied and gestured at the house. 'This isn't still here because that didn't go well, because your mother didn't finish her healing as much as was possible.'

Clarice narrowed her eyes. 'Why is it, then, if it's not about Mum?'

There it was, Morghan thought. The crux of the matter. 'I thought to begin with, that its presence here meant I hadn't given up my anger towards him, Grainne's father.' She blinked up at the house. 'But I have done so. I feel nothing towards the man but a sort of weary sorrow for him.'

'My grandfather,' Clarice said with a shudder. 'I'm glad I never met him.' She wrinkled her brow. 'Did you? Meet him, I mean?'

Morghan shook her head. 'Not in this lifetime.'

Clarice's gaze drifted back towards the house. 'I don't know how you're supposed to reconcile a man like that,' she said.

'By taking the long view,' Morghan said distantly, staring at the scorched wood. 'By realising that they are a soul aspect adrift, disconnected, and that that is a terrible way to be.'

'Yeah,' Clarice said. 'But he hurt her. A tiny, defenceless

child.' She shook her head. 'I try not to think about it, or all the other crap things that happen in this world – of which there are far too many.'

'There are indeed,' Morghan agreed. 'Which is why we do what we can, where we are.' She turned away from the house and looked at her stepdaughter, whose ethereal looks made her into some sort of Otherworld sprite. But she was not that. She was human, flesh and blood and a beating heart full of love and hope. And fear. 'Why we nurture our essential nature, which is one of connectedness and grace.'

Clarice shot her a sharp glance. 'Do you say that for some particular reason?' she asked.

'I guess I'm just wondering why you're here,' Morghan replied. She waved a hand towards the house. 'I've pondered these last weeks on the puzzle of this house and have come to the understanding that it is an illustration – a reminder – of the need to constantly reassess the houses that we live in, the houses that we build.' She glanced at the building. 'The house is a symbol for so much about our self,' she said, her voice musing. 'When we dream of it, each room is often an illustration of ourselves, the state of our lives.'

Clarice was shaking her head. 'I prefer open spaces. I do not like rooms, and when I dream of them, it is because I am looking for the way outside.' She looked away from the house, unsettled, her skin prickling with something that felt like presentiment. As though she'd inadvertently said some-thing that went right to the heart of a matter she wasn't even aware of.

Or did not want to be.

Morghan didn't reply straight away. 'I do not know,' she

said slowly, 'but perhaps you are meant to find a lesson here for you as well.'

Clarice leant against the fence, turning her back on the house, even though she could still feel it there, cracked open and rotting behind her. 'A lesson for me?' She shifted her feet and crossed her arms protectively over her breasts. 'Why are there always lessons?' she asked. 'Why can't life just be about experiencing. Maybe even enjoyment?'

'It is about experiencing.'

'What about enjoyment, then?' Clarice's fingers dug into the flesh of her arms, and she looked sideways at Morghan's snake, who seemed to be peering unblinkingly at her from under the nearest vegetation. She was glad she herself did not walk with Snake. Snake was all business, all the time. She looked over at Morghan.

Why had the Queen banned her from the Fair Lands until Winter Solstice? She'd done it with no explanation, just picked her out of the crowd of courtiers, took her aside, and said the words without any preamble at all.

You are to return to your world and not come back here until after the Midwinter.

Not even the solstice, really, but after it. After midwinter's, which was – Clarice did a quick calculation – almost six months away. The dismissal cut into her like a knife, and she felt flayed open, helpless. She tightened the grip of her folded arms.

What was she going to do with herself until then? She couldn't think of a single thing. Everyone was busy – Morghan didn't need her. And besides, she really was more comfortable roaming the woods, crossing back and forth between the worlds, spending time on her own when she wasn't with the Fae. Clarice shook her head, and the goose-bumps were back, raising the hairs on her arms, the back of her neck. This was like being a kid again, she thought, not sure of anything, not knowing where in this terribly unfriendly world she belonged.

She'd solved that one though, hadn't she? She didn't belong in this world at all. She was half Fae, she'd decided, and there was home more than here.

Except now she was banned from the Fair Lands. Without explanation. Clarice shook her head and turned to look back through the fence – it was so out of place, this wire fence in the midst of this beautiful natural landscape. She grimaced.

'Why show you this house though?' she asked. 'Why not any other ramshackle place that needs to be torn down?'

Morghan looked at her. Clarice looked young again, vulnerable, a little lost.

She turned and gazed up at the house.

'Because this is part of my history, I think,' Morghan answered. 'We must always start where we are, with what we have.'

Clarice shook her head. 'I have just been banned from where I mostly am.' She trailed off, shrugged her thin shoulders, looked over at Morghan. 'And what do I have to start with?' She glanced back at the house. 'My foundations are about as poppycock sideways as that place's.'

'Do you think so?' Morghan asked. 'You are your mother's daughter, and mine,' she said. 'I cannot believe you do not have foundations that are not strong and true.' She took a breath and put an arm around Clarice's shoulders, drawing her gently away from the sight of the house.

'Perhaps the better question to ask is what have you built on top of them?' She smiled. 'We can think on it together perhaps, since you'll be spending more time at home.'

Clarice snorted. Shook her head.

Then sighed.

5

CLARICE STEPPED OUT INTO THE COOLING DUSK AND WALKED across the lawn, stopping to look at the line of trees and give a low whistle.

She waited, one hand tapping against her thigh before she took a deliberate breath and stilled her fingers. She whistled again.

Sigil came, silently, a glow of white wings in the darkening sky, and then a ruffle of feathers as she settled onto Clarice's outstretched arm.

Clarice stroked the owl almost as though she were a cat, then tucked the bird on her shoulder, so that if she turned her head, Sigil's wide eyes would be there, looking back at her.

What to do now, she wondered. The night was only just creeping over the hills and valleys, and there was nothing for her to do, nowhere for her to go. It was insufferable. How could the Queen have done this? Banished Clarice from what was practically her own home?

Clarice shook her head, felt Sigil's soft feathers against her cheek, the pale bird almost the same colour as her own hair and skin. She lifted her gaze. The same colour as the moon also, she thought.

This was her element. The night and the moon. She could cross the borders between the Grove and the Fair Lands without even thinking. She knew many of the paths like the blue veins that glowed under the milk-pale skin of her own hands.

Clarice shook her head, and Sigil stood up, stretching her legs in protest before settling back down in a huff of feathers.

Midsummer was close, Clarice thought, gazing at the moon sailing under a silvered cloud. The winter solstice was months away. Months during which she would do, what?

She had no answer for that. Morghan would try, she was sure, to engage her in the doings of the Grove, and of the village, but Clarice shook her head again at that idea. She was an outsider, always skirting around the edges of Wellsford life. Not for her, she thought, were easy lunches at The Copper Kettle, or evenings drinking and laughing at The Green Man, which would soon be open for business again.

She belonged out here, in the night. Flitting between the trees like some exotic moth, darting across to the Fair Lands and back again. She'd wandered into these woods when she was a child, little more than five years old, and had never really come back out of them.

Well, she decided. She would keep wandering. There were other places to explore than the Queen's lands.

Sigil still on her shoulder, Clarice paced closer to the

tree line, breathing deeply, centring herself, looking for the way to shift her vision so that she saw the spirit of the woods as clearly as the waking vision of trees and shadows and the small, scurrying animals that lived there.

And it was there, as it always was - the way into the Wildwood. Clarice sighed quietly in relief and lifted a hand to touch Sigil's feathers.

'Come on,' she whispered. 'Let's go for a walk.'

She stepped onto the path between the trees, turning her head to catch a glimpse of anyone she knew who might be passing that way. Surely her Fae friends would be out and about on such a clear evening?

The woods rustled with the murmurings and creepings of the small animals that lived there. Somewhere on a high branch, a bird opened its beak and gave a low, mournful hoot. Sigil turned her great eyes towards it but stayed otherwise still upon Clarice's shoulder.

Clarice peered through the shadows, searching for her friends. She wasn't the only one who liked to wander. In the Wildwood, in the in-between world, she often walked and talked with them. It was easy – only a relaxing and widening of the sight.

'Where are you?' she muttered, and Sigil chirruped softly against her ear.

Clarice shook her head. She walked further along the path, her body alert for the sense of someone with her.

And when one of the Fae appeared – finally – it was her body that knew of their presence before she turned to look, her skin prickling.

'Maxen,' she said, surprised, blinking in the dimness. 'I didn't expect you.'

The Fae man tipped his dark head in acknowledgement. 'You walk the borders?'

'The Queen will not let me into the Fair Lands,' Clarice said, and there was an edge of desperation to her voice.

'So, you creep along the edges, hoping for what?'

Clarice glanced over at Maxen, who she had known since she was a child. 'I belong there,' she said, her mouth set stubbornly.

'But you do not,' Maxen said, lifting his eyebrows at her.

'It is the only place I feel at home.'

They were both silent for a long moment. Somewhere in the woods a fox barked.

Sigil fluffed up her feathers, smoothed them down again.

'She didn't give a reason,' Clarice said. 'The Queen. She didn't give a reason.'

Clarice stopped walking, turned to look at Maxen. 'Do you know why she has banished me?' she asked.

He shook his head. 'I am not privy to the Queen's thinking,' he said.

Clarice looked down at her hands, the skin so white it seemed to glow in the dimness. She pulled her sleeves down over her fingers and looked up at Maxen.

'Can you take a guess?' she asked.

He shrugged, a smile appearing on his face. 'Can you?'

Clarice rolled her eyes. 'It's not fun when questions are answered with more questions.'

'Nonetheless, I stand by my enquiry,' Maxen said. 'Can you?'

'Can I guess?' Clarice asked, wrapping her arms around herself. 'No. To punish me, perhaps? Although I haven't done anything wrong.' She stared off into the forest.

'It should not be a punishment to live in the world you were born to.'

Slowly, Clarice turned back to look at him. 'But it is,' she said.

Maxen shook his head. 'What is the teaching?' he asked. 'To walk in balance, world to world?'

Clarice closed her eyes.

When she opened them, Maxen was gone.

The woods of Wilde Grove were all around her, the trees rustling slightly as they gossiped with the wind, and Clarice narrowed her eyes, looking into the dimness between their trunks, before lifting her hands to rub tiredly at her face and turning to walk back towards the house.

She stepped out of the trees and saw a figure strolling towards her.

'Clarice?'

It was Morghan, and she moved as silently over the grass as Clarice herself did.

'I'm here,' Clarice said, knowing full well that Morghan could see her.

Morghan stopped in front of her, smiling. She held out a hand and gently touched Sigil's feathers. 'Do you have plans for tonight?' she asked. Sigil's feathers were soft and warm under her fingers.

Clarice looked longingly towards the trees, to the path in there that would take her to the Fair Lands. She shook her head.

'No.'

Morghan dropped her hand and looked carefully at her

stepdaughter. Clarice's mouth was a tight line, her eyes distant, unhappy.

'What has happened?' Morghan asked. 'Did you try to go back?'

She meant to the Fair Lands of course, and Clarice knew she did.

'No,' Clarice answered. 'I just walked the borders.' She blinked, shrugged, turned to look back at the trees. 'Hoping to see someone, anyone I knew.'

'And did you?'

Clarice shook her head. 'Just Maxen, and he was as infuriating as ever.'

Morghan couldn't help her laugh. 'What did he say?'

He told me it is not a punishment to walk in the world I was born in.' She turned her eyes, flashing with sudden anger, on Morghan. 'But it is a punishment to be banished to it,' she said.

Morghan regarded her for a moment. 'Was that all?'

'Oh no,' Clarice said. 'Of course not – he reminded me that it is our task to walk in balance, world to world.'

'As it is,' Morghan said.

'Yeah, well, that's the bit I have a tough time with.' Clarice stuck her hands in her pockets so that Morghan wouldn't see them clenched into tight fists.

'Walk with me,' Morghan said, turning and taking a few steps before looking back at Clarice. 'Please?' she added, smiling.

Clarice stared at her for a moment, then ducked her head in the gathering darkness and followed.

'I've something I think will help you,' Morghan said.

Clarice shot her a suspicious glance. 'Help me?'

Morghan nodded. 'I've been giving this some thought. Mostly pondering upon the fact that the Queen sent you back upon a path that would take you straight to my private place in the Wildwood, and to the remains of that house.'

Clarice touched her cheek to Sigil's feathers. 'What about it?' she asked after a minute.

'Well, it is meaningful, wouldn't you say?'

'Nothing's ever an accident, when the Queen is involved, so I suppose so.' Clarice followed Morghan alongside Hawthorn House, wondering where they were going.

'Indeed,' Morghan said. 'But I keep coming back to the image of a house.' She stepped out from the shadow of the manor and crossed over a stretch of lawn to take a path into the far gardens. She led Clarice down the winding path until they reached the tiny cottage that sat in a circular garden at the end of the path.

Clarice stopped beside her and looked around. 'I haven't been here for years,' she said. 'Not since...' She blinked. 'Not since Mum, you know?'

Morghan nodded. She knew. 'Not since your mother passed.' She smiled at the tiny cottage. 'This was her space. Where she painted and drew and wrote.' Morghan paused. 'And dreamt.'

Clarice looked at the small building. It was only one room, but there was a sweet entranceway, a mullioned window, and the miniature cottage had a steep tiled roof, as though it didn't know it was only tiny. 'There's smoke coming from the chimney,' she said.

'Yes,' Morghan said. 'I've cleaned and cleared out the space for you to use.'

'Use?' Clarice turned and stared at her. 'What for?'

'It came to me in a bit of a flash of inspiration,' Morghan said. 'Here is a connection to your mother, and thus to your ancestors and your soul family. I think you need that.'

Clarice shook her head slightly and Sigil stretched for a moment up onto her legs, then settled. 'I do?' Clarice asked.

Morghan looked at her, eyes soft with love. 'I think so. Your connection with the Fae is not enough. You need the guidance and companionship of your own spirit kin.' She smiled. 'I think you will find them here.'

Clarice couldn't help it, she barked a laugh. 'What, are they packed away in the cupboards or something?'

Morghan continued to look at her.

'Fine,' Clarice said at last. 'Sorry.' She huffed out a breath. 'I guess I need something to do, while I'm in banishment.'

Morghan looked at her a moment longer, then turned back to smile at the tiny cottage. 'Dream work,' she said.

'What?'

'There are many ways to travel to the Otherworld,' Morghan said, then gave Clarice a crooked grin. 'Without disturbing the Fae. And there is little better a way to find your path through all worlds than by your dreams.'

'I barely ever remember dreaming.' Clarice shrugged.

'Then this is the time to work on it.' Morghan gestured to the little cottage. 'Sleep here over the next weeks. Make your sleeping and dreaming a ritual event, as they used to do at the Delphi Oracles and other places. The world has a long history of dreamers, and I think it might do you good to become one of them.' She turned and looked at Clarice.

'You just never know what will happen,' she said.

Clarice was silent for a moment. 'Are my mother's things still in there?' she asked.

'Some of them,' Morghan replied. 'But I want this to become your place. Tend to it as your own sacred space. Come to it as a priestess and a seeker.'

She looked at her stepdaughter's face in the waning light, trying to read the expression she saw there.

'Will you do it?' she asked at last.

Clarice swallowed. 'Why do you want me to?' she said at last, knowing she was answering a question with another question, but doing it anyway.

Morghan inclined her head. 'Because Maxen is right. You must learn to walk in balance. And you must learn to walk in this world.' She smiled. 'A strong house built on solid foundations is necessary to the success of that endeavour. Your dreams will tell you what you need and how to do what is necessary. They will also introduce you to your kin.'

She nodded. 'So, I ask again. Will you do it?'

Clarice glanced at her stepmother. When Morghan spoke like that, asked questions in that way, there was no room for a flippant answer. Whatever was spoken in response had consequences.

She looked at the tiny cottage, remembering her mother standing in the doorway, smiling out at the sunshine. She remembered herself, playing in the garden, a wide sunhat shading her face as she skipped along the paths, gathered flowers and pretended to make spells with them.

'Yes,' she said, her mouth dry. 'I will do it.'

Morghan beamed at her, reached out and touched a hand to her shoulder.

'Wonderful,' she said. 'Begin tonight, and may the

Goddess bless you in your dreaming.' She left her hand on Clarice's shoulder for a moment longer, then turned and slipped back the way they'd come.

Clarice stood where she was, listening to her heart thumping behind her ribs.

6

Clarice nodded, took a breath, then lifted Sigil from her shoulder. 'I'm going inside now,' she said to the bird. 'You can go fly and hunt. I'll see you in the morning, tuck you in.' The small joke fell flat under her nervousness, but she shrugged. 'Off you go,' she said.

Sigil spread her wings and launched herself from Clarice's hands, her horny toenails digging in for a brief moment before she was on the wing. Clarice stood and watched her fly, a bright streaking of feathers in the sky, the colour of the moon. She would see Sigil in the morning, for the bird would be back in her small owlery to roost and sleep for the day.

Clarice turned back to the cottage, not knowing what to expect once she stepped inside. For a moment she frowned, berating herself for dithering on the doorstep like this, as though she were just a clueless kid. She wasn't. She might not be strictly in balance, but she walked the worlds, and she could do this.

Dream. She could dream.

Nodding, Clarice stepped under the tiny stone porch and saw that Morghan had left the key for her, swinging from the doorknob on a piece of ribbon. Mouth still dry, Clarice took the large skeleton key and held it in one palm while she turned the knob and drew the door open.

It was warm inside the room, flames blazing away in the open fireplace that took up much of one end of the rectangular room. There was a small stack of logs beside it, and Clarice breathed in the smoky scent of the wood, then reached out with her hand to grip the door frame.

The scent reminded her of her mother. Of when her mother had set a match to tinder and fed the flames in this very fireplace. Clarice shook her head. Scent was such a strong reminder. She looked around the rest of the room.

There had used to be a large table at the other end, Clarice recalled, spread with a mess of paints and brushes, cameras, and stacks of the boards on which her mother would make her collages. The table was gone now, replaced with a small, tidy desk. Clarice closed the door softly behind her and walked over to the desk, touched her fingers to the camera that was there, then looked around at the walls.

There were Grainne's collages. A startling mix of photographs, words, and natural objects such as leaves and bark. Clarice stared at them, then walked slowly over to one that hung over a narrow bed that was also a new addition to the room. Ghostly under the encaustic wax was a photograph of herself, a misty sprite wavering between the trees. She blinked at it, putting a hand to her throat that was thick with emotion.

Clarice gazed around the rest of the room. It was different, and yet still recognisable in her memory as the place she'd run in and out of as her mother worked. But Morghan had been busy. It was clean, the floors swept, and the bed, the new desk, an old-fashioned washstand with bowl and jug – they hadn't been there before.

Beside the camera on the desk was a hinged box, the lid closed, and a thick, blank-paged journal, with a fountain pen lying neatly next to it. Clarice walked back over to the desk and ran her fingers over the embossed leather cover, then opened it. Morghan's handwriting was instantly recognisable.

Dream the threads of your life, outwards, inwards, world to world to world.

Clarice shivered despite the fire, and let the journal fall closed. The logs in the fireplace crackled and shifted with a gentle rustling. She turned to the box, plain, black-painted, and undid the latch, lifting the lid.

Morghan had thought of everything, Clarice saw. She touched a finger to the candles, bowl, and jars of herbs, and picked up a small stash of fabric, turning it over in her hands before replacing it in the box next to thread and needles.

Obviously, Morghan intended her to make a ritual of this. Clarice hoped there were instructions somewhere in the box, then shook her head. She could figure out what she needed to do, if she put her mind to it. It wasn't as though spellwork was completely foreign to her.

Living was spellwork.

She looked out the window at the darkness that was now complete. Later, the moon would sail high across the sky, a waxing silver crescent, a boat across a sea of clouds and stars. Clarice took a deep breath.

Was she going to do this?

She'd already agreed to.

She pushed her hair back from her face. Morghan had asked her, and she'd said yes.

There was an outhouse behind the miniature cottage and Clarice went out to use it, then came back inside and stooping over, she unlaced her boots, slipping them from her feet and setting them by the door. She took slow, deliberate breaths as she moved, watching her hands calmly as they worked, her face relaxed, lips gentle as she let herself move into ritual space.

She knelt by the fire, picking up a new log and lodging it on top of the others.

'Bless me with your warmth and clarity,' she murmured, watching the flames lick over the wood, and taking a deep breath, tasting flame and smoke and wood.

A kettle sat on the brick ledge beside the fire, and Clarice picked it up carefully, hearing water slosh inside it. She carried it to the washstand and poured the hot water into the jug, then set the kettle back on its ledge.

Morghan had set out a toothbrush, wash cloth and a towel, and there was a clean robe waiting on the bed. By the light of the fire, Clarice removed her day clothes, washed herself with the warm water, aware that doing so was part of the ritual, part of the magic, part of moving into a different state.

Part of weaving the spell.

Part of singing.

When she was dried, Clarice padded over to the bed and

sipped the robe on, letting the creamy folds fall around her. She tucked her feet into soft, felted slippers and looked up at the painting hanging over the bed. There she was, the wax making her ghostly and fey, peering out from between the tall, white trunks of a quartet of birches, as though they stood like a gateway from which any moment she would turn and disappear into.

A smile touched Clarice's lips. She had often vanished through that gateway.

And now, here she was on this side of it, preparing to dream her way into all the worlds.

Wherever the gateway of her dreams would take her.

The candles spread their light like stars across the small room, and Clarice placed them across the desk, using it as an altar space, arranging them in two branches, instinctively echoing the birch trees in the painting. She reached into the box and sifted through the rest of the contents, holding one thing, then another, seeking what felt right, laying a scatter of dried petals and moss like a pathway between the candles.

Clarice held the image of the treed gateway and path in her mind as she worked. What would lie on the other side of this dream gateway, she didn't know, and didn't need to. That part would come when she lay down and slept. Right now, she created sacred space within the room, and within herself.

Sitting down at the desk, Clarice organised the pieces of fabric, the tiny embroidery scissors, and the needle and thread on the surface in front of her. She looked at them for a long moment, then dipped back into the box for a fabric bag filled with dried herbs, which she put to her nose to smell.

She smelled lavender, and something citrusy – lemon balm, perhaps. And the musky, sage and cedar-like scent of mugwort.

To smoke, she wondered? But there was nothing included in Morghan's box for her to use to smoke the herbs. She looked at the fabric and sewing things again. A dream pillow, she thought, then smiled.

No, more than that. She knew how Morghan's mind worked.

A pin cushion. To follow through the gate into her dreams.

A smile still playing around her lips, Clarice picked up the fabric and snipped two layers roughly into a circle, then set the scissors down and threaded the needle.

She stitched as neatly as she could, focusing on weaving the desire to follow her dreams into each stitch. When it was stuffed with the herbs and she'd closed the gap, she looked at it for a moment, then threaded the needle with red floss.

A red thread to lead her through the web, she thought, dipping her needle into the centre of the pin cushion, and looping it around the edge and back through the centre on the other side, then repeating this until she had made a star pattern all around the tiny cushion.

It was done. Baba Yaga's pin cushion to follow through the worlds. A web of red thread to lead her safely there and back. Mugwort to aid her memory. Lavender and lemon balm to calm her to sleep.

Outside the flickering light of the room, an owl called out, and Clarice bowed her head.

'Tonight, we fly in dreams, Sigil,' she whispered.

She took a breath. 'Tonight, we go through the gate and into the dreamworld.'

What she would meet there, she didn't know. What, or who.

Perhaps herself, she thought, looking at the picture on the wall again.

The bed was soft, the sheets smelling faintly of lavender. Clarice put the pin cushion under the pillow and slid in under the blankets, lying there, watching the fire and waiting for sleep to come.

And with it, her dreams.

7

Stephan leant over Erin's shoulder, relishing the fact that he could put his hand on her, feeling the round nub of bone, knowing the silk of her skin hidden under her clothes.

'I can feel you, you know,' Erin said, poring over the runes she'd spread out on the table.

'Feel me?'

'What you're thinking – what you're feeling.' Erin's heart beat more quickly and she looked over her shoulder with a smile on her lips. 'It's like a cloud all around you.'

Stephan looked back at her. 'Okay then,' he said. 'What was I thinking?'

'In words, I don't know,' Erin said, gazing up at him, every nerve inside her alive and singing. 'But it felt intimate and tender and lustful all at the same time.' She blinked, gave Stephan a kiss on his cheek, and looked back at her runes. 'Which is very distracting, so unhand me for a moment. It's stronger when you're actually touching me.'

Stephan snatched his hand back, but he was laughing. 'Have you ever had this happen with anyone else?' he asked.

Erin touched one of the stones with a fingertip. 'There hasn't been anyone else. Just Jeremy, really.' Her shoulders hunched as she thought of him.

'Him,' Stephan said, wrinkling his nose. 'Then your answer is *nope.*' He crossed the kitchen to check on the pie he'd made and slid into the oven. Simon had given him the recipe with a wink. *Guaranteed to please,* he'd said.

Stephan hoped so. Although he wasn't entirely sure he'd even taste the flaky pastry and rich, savoury filling. He was too busy walking on air, and he was pretty sure his taste-buds were out of action. He'd have to make the effort to float back to ground for the meal.

Erin turned around in her chair. 'I dreamt of him once, when I was with him,' she said, and the faint grooves were back between her beetled brows.

'Yeah?' Stephan said. The pastry was turning a beautiful golden colour. Just like it was supposed to. 'What sort of dream?'

'I remember waking up from it and thinking it had been awfully odd, at the time. Like more than just a dream, you know?'

Stephan reckoned he did know. 'Mind you,' he said. 'Most dreams are more than just a dreams, when you get down to it.' Ambrose had been getting him to pay more attention to them. Said it would help with the travelling to meet Bear Fellow, and well, everything, actually. He slipped into his seat at the table, gave Burdock a scratch, and did his best to resist leaning over the table to touch Erin again.

It was difficult. She radiated, glowed as though she were a star.

'So, what was it about?' he asked, blinking, and making an effort to plant his feet on the ground.

Erin shook her head. She hadn't brushed her hair since they'd dragged themselves from the bed, and it was, to Stephan's eyes, adorably rumpled and tangled. He closed his eyes for a moment, reliving the sensation of that thick hair against his skin, the touch of heavy silk, and shivered.

Erin rolled her eyes. 'There you go again!' she said. 'I can absolutely feel it when your thoughts wander away to...you know.' She narrowed her gaze at Stephan, heart thumping again, a wide smile on her face. 'Which it seems they do about every...' She pursed her lips, pretending to think about it. 'Fifteen seconds.'

Stephan sighed heavily. 'Yeah,' he admitted. 'Maybe ten seconds.' He gave her an innocent look and spread his hands out. 'I can't help it. You're like the sun, and I'm in orbit around you.'

'Hmm,' Erin said, but she gazed at him, feeling their energy reach for each other again, setting every cell in her body humming.

She shook her head. 'Stop,' she said. 'Or we're never going to be able to have a conversation again.'

'Or a meal,' Stephan said.

'Or anything, pretty much,' Erin added.

Stephan gave her a sly grin. 'Well, one thing...'

She shivered. 'Do you want to hear about my dream, or do you want to go to bed?'

Stephan stared at her. 'You're really going to ask me that?'

Erin grinned. 'True,' she said. 'All right. Anyway.' She cleared her throat and groped for the threads of what she'd been going to say. 'So, it was a bit weird, really. I was someone else, in the dream – I mean, I looked like someone else – and Jeremy was someone else too. I dreamt he was this rich, important guy, much older than me, and I was a bit...simple, I guess you'd say. I did everything he told me to, because he was in charge, I guess. There wasn't anyone else I could turn to.'

'Did you love him?' Stephan asked. 'The guy in the dream?'

Erin shook her head. 'No,' she said. 'I don't think so. I think I was a bit afraid of him, actually. But I knew I didn't have any choice but to do as he wanted. I was his wife, and I knew I couldn't get along in the world without him looking after me.' She blew out a breath and shrugged. 'Anyway, I think that was a past life dream.'

Stephan nodded. 'I think you might be right. And it would kind of explain why you were drawn to him in this life too.'

'Yeah.' Erin tapped her fingers on the table and Burdock got up and padded over to her. She buried a hand in his fur, and he sat down, leaning against her, warm and comfortable. 'I think it explains a lot. Why I was drawn to him in the first place, perhaps. Why I stayed with him, even when I knew we weren't really suited, and even though I felt trapped in the relationship.' She looked down at Burdock's liquid brown eyes and smiled. 'I'm much better off now, aren't I, boy?'

Burdock made a chuffing noise in agreement. He didn't know what they were talking about, but he knew his two most favourite people in the whole world were in the same place and that they were happy – the smells coming from them were complex and deep and wide and so very strong and made him almost delirious with joy. And that made him the luckiest dog in the world.

Stephan snaked his hand across the table and reached for Erin's, their fingers entwining. 'I'm glad you didn't stay with him,' he said. 'It makes my heart hurt that you were stifled like that.'

Erin frowned.

'What?' Stephan asked.

'I was going to say that it wasn't just Jeremy, but my parents as well, who made things feel that way. Or my mother, at least. Dad was hardly around, really. Always working.'

'But?' Stephan asked, sensing one coming.

She considered it. 'Well, if there was perhaps a past life connection with Jeremy, of all people, who really, I only knew for a few years, wouldn't there be one between my mother and I?' Erin shook her head. 'Or is that just rubbish?'

'I don't know,' Stephan asked. 'But at a guess?' He raised his eyebrows. 'Yeah?' He blinked. 'I mean no, not rubbish. Yeah, it might be likely?'

'Good grief,' Erin said. 'Nothing's as linear and straightforward as I used to think it was. It's like there are connections everywhere and so much more at work than I ever considered.'

'That's the web, I guess.'

She nodded and glanced at the runes again. 'If that's the

web,' she said. 'Then these are part of it too – these runes the old woman gave me.'

'All of it's part of it,' Stephan said. 'And I know I haven't been journeying for long, but I've already learnt that everything is something, you know? The pear, right? Why a pear, rather than say, an orange, or an apple?' He squeezed Erin's hand. 'There's a reason it's a pear, right? Just like when Bear Fellow shows me something, it's meaningful.' He coughed out a laugh. 'It's fascinating and exhausting at the same time – having to pay attention to everything. Ambrose has me keeping a dream journal and another journal for all the jaunts I do with Bear Fellow.' He shook his head. 'Every detail gets written down so I can try to figure out what it means. And the more I write down, the deeper I dream, and the deeper I go into, well, the heart of it all, I guess.'

'I've been keeping a dream journal for years,' Erin said. 'I don't know what much of it means, though, except for the ones that really stand out.' She blinked, thinking about the one that had led her to come to Wilde Grove. The doors, the letters slid half under them. If it hadn't been for that dream, recurring over and over, she might not have recognised quite what she'd run into coming here.

Erin smiled suddenly at Stephan.

'What?' he asked.

She shook her head. 'Do you realise how many of these conversations we've already had, sitting right here at this table?'

'These conversations?'

She patted Burdock, scratching under his ears in the spot he liked best. 'I don't remember life being this interesting until I came here,' she said. 'I never had conversations like this with anyone. Maybe occasionally inside my head, but that was a bit dangerous, because it made me remember how unhappy I was, and then of course, that made me sort of drift away from everything. Sometimes literally.' She found another smile and beamed at Stephan. 'Now everything is totally different, and the world is huge and so amazingly fascinating.'

'I'm glad you stayed,' Stephan said fervently.

Erin grinned at him. 'Wild horses couldn't drag me away now.'

Stephan smiled back, knowing he was all goggle-eyed and silly with love, but he didn't care.

'Shit!' he said, and leapt up from his chair, almost knocking it over.

Burdock stood up too and barked at the sudden rumpus.

'What?' Erin asked. 'What is it?'

But Stephan was already at the oven dragging out the pie and spilling it onto the benchtop. 'Thank the Goddess,' he said. 'I suddenly smelt it burning.'

'It's burnt?' Erin sniffed the air, but if it was even singed, she couldn't smell it.

Stephan shook his head. 'Nah,' he said. 'Got it just in time.'

'So, let's have a look at these runes, then,' Stephan said, plate pushed aside, wellbeing spreading through him like he'd lain down in a warm, fragrant bath.

Erin nodded. 'I'm sure these are the ones the old woman gave me. I would have sketched them as soon as I came back but...ahem.'

Stephan couldn't help his grin. 'But, me.'

'Yes,' Erin said. 'You, for sure.' 'And you. Me and you.'

'Yeah. That too.' Erin squinted at him. 'Now, back to the runes...'

'Yep.'

'Good.'

'Okay.'

Erin looked back down from Stephan's dancing eyes to the carved stones on the table. 'Now,' she said. 'I don't know what order they go in, because the old woman didn't draw them out of a bag or anything like I do. She just threw the whole lot down on the ground, sort of squinted a bit at them, then picked up three and gave them to me.'

'Right.' Stephan said, concentrating properly for the first time on the spread of three runes. 'Bugger,' he said. 'I hope like hell *Tiwaz* comes after the others.'

Erin shook her head. 'They're intimidating, aren't they? They freak me out a bit actually, I don't mind telling you. And since they're in no particular order – *Tiwaz* could mean the situation now, since, you know, I consider the last few months, and the changes I've made, to be a bit of a victory...'

'All right,' Stephan said. 'Remind me what your book says about them?'

Erin got up from the table and went to the bookshelf in the sitting room and found the book on runes straight away. She'd learnt her way around Teresa's books perfectly well now, and they felt just as much her own.

Erin tucked the book under her arm, squatted down to put another log on the fire, and gave Burdock an affectionate pat. 'You have absolutely the best spot in the house,' she told him.

He thumped his tail, took the pat, basked in the warmth from the fire, and felt very content in his soft bed.

'Here we go then,' Erin said, sitting back down at the table and flicking through the book. 'I'll start with *Tiwaz*.' She cleared her throat.

'Victory and honour comes when one grows into the life demanded by spirit, not heedless of the difficulties and trials along the way, but upright and full of the conviction that comes when one unfurls in balance with the universe.'

She closed the book for a moment and looked glumly at the stones. 'It's not awfully encouraging, is it?'

'Well, I don't know,' Stephan said. 'It does tell you how to go about it. Gaining victory.'

'Yeah,' Erin agreed on a sigh. 'It just doesn't say *don't worry; it's going to be a piece of cake.*'

'True!'

Erin looked back at the book. 'Anyway. The next one is... right, here it is.' She grimaced. 'I don't think I've ever drawn this one before.

'*Thurisaz*. The threats of the world seem to loom over you and their shadow looks vast and dark. Know however, that all problems must be dealt with in spirit before you can act in the world, and the spirit is bright enough to cast aside all shadow.'

Erin put the book down and gazed at the rune. 'Great,' she said. 'What's the other one?'

'*Isaz*,' Stephan answered.

'Okay.' Erin flipped through the pages. '*Isaz*. The winter landscape freezes. The wind howls across the ice. Know too, that if you are frozen, unable to act, that after the winter freeze comes the thaw, and new life is born from the time of cold and stillness.' She looked up and gazed over the table at Stephan. 'Why does this feel like a warning?'

Stephan shook his head. 'What else did the old woman have to say to you?'

Erin blew out a breath. 'She said *welcome to your initiation.* Or something like that.'

'Wow,' breathed Stephan. 'Not heavy at all.'

'Nope.' Erin sighed, slumped for a moment, then sat straighter. 'Well, at least we've some sort of warning, you know? Whatever is going to go wrong, or whatever trial is coming, then at least I know it's coming, right?'

Stephan nodded. He pointed to the runes. 'And you know the way to deal with it.' His finger moved to *Isaz.* 'For starters, bear in mind that winter is not never-ending, and in fact, a bunch of plants couldn't complete their growing cycle without that period of stasis.' He sniffed.

'And *Thurisaz?*' Erin asked.

'Well, this is pretty much everything we've been learning, don't you think? To step forward, spirit first, I guess. That if we're not fit and healthy in spirit, if we're not bearing in mind the reality even, of our spirit, then we're just mice on a...what are those wheel things?'

'Treadmill?' Erin said, pressing her lips together. She was biting down on the urge to whine – to heave a giant sigh and think about how unfair this was. To bleat that she'd been through enough already. Hadn't she been through enough, already?

But she didn't say any of that, and she thrust even the thoughts themselves away. She had, after all, everything to be thankful for. She had a secure place of her own to live, any number of fascinating things going on, and people around her whom she loved and trusted.

That, Erin decided, ought to make her certain of being able to see through whatever was coming her way next, if indeed something was.

And at least, her initiation wouldn't be anything like Kria's.

It couldn't be.

8

THE SHOP DOOR TINKLED AS ERIN PUSHED IT OPEN. SHE grinned at the sound and waved to Krista, Burdock scooting in past her.

'I don't think I've heard such a terrific sound for months as your doorbell,' she said.

Krista stood up from the proofs she'd been pouring over and smiled widely before bending slightly to give Burdock a good scratch behind his ears. 'You're right there,' she said. 'I was starting to worry we'd never open up again.' She looked fondly around her shop. 'It's not the same, working in here on my own – it's meant to have people bustling in and out, browsing and finding treasures.'

Erin tripped lightly across to the table and beamed down at the cards spread over the pitted surface. 'These are them, then?' She peered closer, scanning them one by one. 'They're amazing,' she breathed. 'The colours are really luminous.' Erin shook her head. 'I'm so glad you persuaded me to try using watercolours.'

'They've come up beautifully, haven't they? I really like the technique you've been using with them,' Krista said. 'I've a bunch of different envelopes for you to choose from, for the card selection, and then I think we're pretty much ready to begin selling them in the shop and online.' She paused and pointed a finger at one of Fox peering shyly from behind a tree. 'I've already had one person ask if they could have a larger print of this one to go one their wall.'

Erin glanced over at Krista, eyes shining. 'Really?' She shook her head. 'You're not having me on?'

'I would not lead you on about such an important thing,' Krista said, then burst into smiles. 'It's going to be wonderful,' she said. 'They'll be a hit; I know it in my bones.'

Erin blew out a breath. 'I'm a bit overwhelmed,' she admitted, looking down at her artwork spread over the table. These were her paintings, turned into prints and cards. For people to buy. And apparently, people wanted to buy them. 'I know it's been the goal all along, but really seeing that people are responding to what I'm doing – to my art, you know – it's just blowing my mind.'

'You've found your niche, all right, I think,' Krista said.

Erin frowned suddenly.

'What?' Krista asked. 'What's wrong?'

Erin shook her head. 'Nothing,' she said dubiously, then looked at Krista, at her clear, dark eyes. 'Well, it's just that...' She trailed off.

But Krista raised her eyebrows. 'Just that what, Erin?' she asked, her voice warm with empathy.

'It's just that, will I have time to do this?' Erin blurted, looking back down at the table covered in cards made from her artwork.

'What do you mean, time to do it?'

Erin shook her head again and nipped a tooth at her lip. Burdock came and pressed against her side. 'Well, I mean...'

Krista waited, but Erin had wound down into silence. Yet, there was obviously something on her mind. 'Look,' Krista said. 'Let's go into the other room and have a coffee.'

'What about the shop?' Erin asked, startled. She hadn't had any idea, coming here full of excitement, that she would suddenly find...this...on her mind.

'We'll hear the bell,' Krista said.

'Where's Minnie?' Erin asked.

Krista laughed. 'She had to go back to school, and you should've heard the fuss she made about it too.'

'She didn't want to go?'

'She absolutely did not want to go.' Krista led Erin into the next room in the little warren that was Haven for Books and made her way to the coffee machine. 'I had to talk her into it, in the end.' She brought two steaming mugs over to the table where Erin had propped herself onto a stool.

'All right,' Krista said. 'Tell me what's on your mind.'

Erin looked down at the table, ran a finger over a groove in the grain, shrugged, then looked across at Krista. 'It just occurred to me, is all, whether I will have time for all this.' She spread an arm around to gesture at the room, at the various projects that Krista had going on all the surfaces. The books she made and bound, the talismans she produced.

'Why wouldn't you have time for your art?' Krista asked, cupping the mug in her hands. The heating in the old shop was cranky and despite it being summer now, the temperatures in this part of the country were still a bit low for her liking. It was the one thing she hadn't entirely gotten used to. She'd have to have another poke at the boiler or see if there was enough in the budget for a new one.

But all that was just a fleeting thought, and Krista brought her attention to bear on Erin sitting on the other side of the high work table. She'd been radiant when she'd blown into the shop like a fresh breeze, and yet here she was, suddenly wilting.

Erin worried at the groove in the table again, shrugging her shoulders. She took a sip of coffee. 'It's just that, you know, training to be Morghan takes a lot of time.'

Krista's forehead creased in surprise. She paused before she spoke. 'You know you're not actually training to be Morghan, right?'

Erin's eyes were clouded as she looked at Krista. 'Aren't I?'

'Are you?'

Another shrug. 'Well, aren't I? I'm supposed to be training to be the next Lady of the Grove, right? Because I was Macha in another lifetime.' She squeezed her eyes shut and corrected herself. 'Because I am Macha in another lifetime, and she is part of the original Grove and now I'm me, and I'm here, and it all fits neatly together.'

'Do you not want the job?'

Erin shook her head. 'It's not that at all,' she said. 'Although some days I'm not even really sure I know what the job is.' She subsided into brooding silence for a moment. 'What I do know, though, is that Morghan doesn't have a business on the side.' Erin blinked. 'From what I can see, she doesn't even have any hobbies on the side. It's all Lady of the Grove all the time.'

Krista looked at her. 'How long have you been thinking this?' she asked.

But Erin shook her head. 'I haven't,' she answered. 'Or at least, not consciously, you know? I didn't even know I thought this way until I stood out there and looked at all the amazing cards we've made.' She stared into her coffee mug. 'I don't want to have to stop doing it, Krista,' she said. 'But you know – art takes time. I already have barely enough, what with working at the care home, and then keeping up with everything Morghan and Ambrose want me to do.'

She heaved a sigh and they sat in silence for a long minute. Burdock looked from one to the other, then lay down.

'Does she do anything else?' Erin ventured. 'Morghan, I mean?' She shook her head. 'I still don't have a real, true idea of what she does as Lady of the Grove.' She blinked. 'I mean, I know she does a lot of walking in the woods, and stuff.'

Krista couldn't help it, she laughed out loud. 'Okay, she does a bit more than that.'

Erin laughed too. 'I know. I didn't mean it to sound like that.'

'You know she has a job, don't you?' Krista said.

'What?' Erin was startled. 'A job?'

'Well, more like her own business, although even that sounds wrong,' Krista said. 'It was more of a calling, really – a bit like your art is for you, I expect.'

Erin was still having trouble with the image in her mind of Morghan popping off to work every day. 'What does she do?'

'She works with the dying,' Krista said. 'It used to take

up a good deal of her days. She worked with people in their own homes, and with those in the care homes and hospices, before the pandemic.'

'I didn't know that,' Erin said, shaking her head slowly from side to side. 'I did not know that.'

'Isn't that how she met Wayne?' Krista asked. 'You knew that though, right?'

Erin nodded now. 'Yeah, but I guess I never thought that happened because...' she snorted. 'Wow, am I an idiot, or what? Of course that's how that happened. God, it all makes so much sense, now.'

Krista watched her. 'So, you know, if the Lady of the Grove had time to basically work a full-time job, don't you think you'll have time for your art, and taking that in a solid direction?'

'I guess so,' Erin said, her face lighting back up.

'And excuse me for pointing this out,' Krista continued. 'But Morghan isn't old or past her best before date, you know.'

'I know.' Erin took a breath. 'Of course she isn't. I've been an idiot.' She looked across at Krista. 'I just really couldn't see it for a moment. Isn't that weird?'

It was Krista's turn to shake her head. 'You got afraid because you realised how much you wanted something.' She grinned. 'Happens all the time – the trick is not to get caught up in it, so you can see a way past the sudden mental block.'

'Well, thank goodness you were here to talk me back to sanity.' Erin frowned. 'You realise though, it's brought up an important point?'

'What's that?' Krista asked, taking a sip at her coffee, and hearing the doorbell suddenly ring in the other room as someone opened the shop door.

'Well, it turns out that I really don't know what the Lady of the Grove does.' Erin raised one eyebrow. 'Don't you think I ought to? I mean, don't you think I need to? Since I'm being trained for it?' Another thought occurred to her. 'What if I'm not even the right person for the job?'

Krista shook her head. 'You've only just begun. You can't know you're not the right person for the job, yet.' She looked through the doorway. 'Got a customer, I'm afraid. Hold your thought.'

Erin waved her away, and then followed her into the main room where she stood and gazed at the first proofs of the greeting cards they'd made from her paintings. They'd turned out better than Erin had ever expected they would, or could, and now she was drawn into considering them again, seeing where she could make improvements for the next lot, where she could turn in a slightly different direction and really work the medium for best effect. It made her itch to get back home to her sketchbook and her paints.

'Can I take a couple of these with me?' she asked, as Krista finished ringing up her customer's purchases and wandered back to the table.

'You can take them all,' Krista said. 'They're yours, after all.' She turned and picked up pile of envelopes. 'Take these as well and let me know which ones you want to go with.'

'This is amazing,' Erin said, grinning. 'And you really think people will buy them?'

'People are already asking to,' Krista said. 'You've got an audience for them. A lot of us out there love this mystical, mythical, folktale, nature thing you've got going on.'

Erin shook her head, but it wasn't in disagreement. Another thought occurred to her, like a bright lightbulb going off in her head.

'Wow,' Krista laughed. 'You look like you've just had a bit of inspiration.'

'You've no idea, Krista,' Erin said. 'I did my first journeying yesterday – my first, proper, planned one – and I gotta tell you, there's so much I could paint from it.' She thought briefly of the runes and their disturbing message, then pushed them aside. The old woman on her stool on her hilltop would make an amazing painting, and so would the horse, and the pear, and the boat, and the lake...

She shook her head. 'Thanks so much Krista, I'm absolutely bursting with ideas now.' She paused, putting the cards and envelopes into her bag. 'And thank you as well, for you know, arresting my silly fears.'

'They're not silly, Erin,' Krista said. 'And perhaps you ought to talk to Morghan properly about what being the Lady of the Grove entails.' She gave Erin a pointed look. 'I'm sure it's not a position for everyone, you know.'

9

Erin stepped out of Haven for Books with bemusement on her face. Not for everyone?

Perhaps she should have stopped and asked what Krista had meant by that, but the shop door had opened again, and a small stream of people had come in, their eyes shining to be allowed once more to go browsing in any shop other than a chemist and grocer's.

Maybe Krista had been referring to Selena. Morghan's aunt, as far as Erin knew, and the Lady before Morghan.

She'd left. Upped sticks and gone who knew where.

Well, Erin realised, Morghan probably knew.

Erin took a long, slow breath. Hadn't she thought this through before – Morghan wasn't Selena, whoever Selena was, and Morghan wasn't going to leave the Grove, and certainly not before Erin was ready to take her place.

That was, if Erin wanted to take her place.

She whistled for Burdock to come back from the alleyway he'd scampered down, and they crossed the road.

The Copper Kettle was open, and a little further up the street, backing onto the village square, was the Green Man. It would be open soon too – the grand reopening, everyone was thinking of it as – and Stephan especially was excited about it, and the possibility of being able to play live music again.

Erin looked back at The Copper Kettle. Maybe she should stop and talk things over a bit with Lucy, if she wasn't busy.

She shook her head. Krista, as usual, had been right. She needed to pin Morghan down about what exactly being Lady of the Grove entailed. But the trouble was, that every time she talked to Morghan, she didn't end up being much more enlightened than when she started. She only ended up with more things to do.

But what things they were! The world was definitely a richer place than it had been a few months ago. Which was ironic, really, Erin thought, giggling and watching Burdock stop at the top of the lane that led to Ash Cottage to see if they were going home. Ironic because back then, she'd had way more money in her bank account.

Now, she didn't even have a car.

Ah, but she had her cottage, and that was a constant thing of joy, even if it didn't have a gas cooker or anything. It had a snug fire and comfy armchairs, and a garden in which worked the most gorgeous man she'd ever met. Erin quickened her steps home.

THERE WAS A NOTE ON THE TABLE AND ERIN'S MOUTH TURNED down in disappointment as she read it. Then curled upwards again as she got to the endearment at the end, and the question as to whether he could make her dinner again that night. She grinned as she put the note back on the table next to the cards she and Krista had made from her paintings.

She took out her phone, texted Stephan a quick message saying yes to dinner, wondering vaguely why he hadn't used his phone to message her with the question, then deciding she didn't care – the note on the table was quaint and sweet.

Maybe, Erin decided, she'd take advantage of the quiet afternoon to go and see Morghan. They hadn't scheduled anything, but there was nothing to stop Erin from wandering up there and having a chat, was there? And while she was at it, she could have another glance at the well up at Hawthorne House. She wanted to try painting it, to capture that amazing swirl of colour, and perhaps even, if she could, the idea that the well led down deep into the womb of the world.

When she shut up the cottage again, calling Burdock to heel, she was all but quivering with excitement. Her paintings looked beautiful as prints. She had so much more she wanted to paint. Her travelling had gone brilliantly.

And of course, there was Stephan, with whom she'd knocked about Ash Cottage the day and night before like they were born to be together. Although really, she thought, feeling the colour rising in her cheeks, they had spent most of the day rolling around in the bed. But even when they'd sat by the fire chatting after dinner, it had been easy and lovely. More easy and lovely than Erin had anticipated.

She'd not been sure – still wasn't sure, not completely – how much she wanted to share her precious cottage with someone else, even if that someone was Stephan. When he'd remarked the day before about how he'd thought about moving in with her, she'd been shocked, even though he'd been joking.

But what would it be like, she mused, climbing up the trail through Wilde Grove, her sturdy boots on her feet, and the woods fragrant and green around her – wouldn't they want, sometime, to move in together?

Maybe even get married?

She'd been about to marry Jeremy, after all.

She wasn't ready for marriage.

Was she? Not even to Stephan?

'You are completely lost in thought, Erin,' Morghan said, materialising out of the trees, Burdock panting happily at her side.

'Oh! I didn't even notice you there,' Erin said, flushing as though Morghan could see the colour and trail of her thoughts. 'I was thinking,' she said.

'Yes,' Morghan smiled. 'I saw that.'

'Thinking's not a bad thing, is it?' Erin asked.

Morghan shook her head. 'Of course not,' she said. But she waved a hand at the woods around them. 'But you do miss out on a lot when you're doing it so single-mindedly.'

Erin had stopped walking, and now she looked around at where they were, and blinked in the summer-speckled light. She was at the crossroads to the stone circle. How had she come so far and not even noticed?

'I was thinking about the future,' Erin said with a self-conscious grin.

'Ah,' Morghan responded. 'And did you come to any

conclusions about it?' There was a mischievous smile on her face.

Erin wrinkled her nose. 'Um, only that I don't know what's going to happen in it?'

'No one does, do they? We only know where we are right now, and whether we're in the flow of our spirit or not.' Morghan gazed around at the glory of the day. The sun was shining again, after the last week's days of rain, picking out the lime and dark greens of the leaves, and the whole woods smelled of light and sap.

Shaking her head, Erin frowned and looked at Burdock nosing around the roots of a birch without really seeing him. 'Does being in the flow of our spirit have much to do with the future?' she asked.

'Everything, wouldn't you say?' Morghan replied.

'I wouldn't know. How does it, though?'

Morghan turned her gaze to Erin and smiled. 'Come,' she said. 'Let's walk while we talk, shall we? Unless you were heading somewhere specific?'

'I was coming to see you,' Erin said. She scuffed a booted foot in the soil of the path. 'I wanted to ask you something.'

Morghan's eyebrows raised. 'Oh?' She turned her steps and led the way along the path that would lead to the circle, then beyond, around the hills to the view of the far-off sea. It was a longish walk, but perhaps, if they were going to talk about the future, it would be a good place. She quickened her pace.

Erin hurried after her. Her muscles were fit from all the walking she did now, and she barely felt the strain as her stride lengthened to keep up. She was in better shape than she'd ever been.

'What did you want to ask me?' Morghan said, turning to look at Erin with a smile. The young woman was glowing, her energy flaming out around her in twining snakes of blue. Morghan's smile widened. The easing of some of the lockdown rules obviously agreed with Erin. With Erin and Stephan. Morghan wasn't surprised. Not at all.

But Erin's face had taken on a pensive look and the flashing blue of her aura dimmed slightly. 'I was talking to Krista today – she had the first proofs of the greeting cards we've made from some of my artwork.'

'That's wonderful,' Morghan said. 'I'd love to see them when you have time to show me.'

'You would?'

'Of course,' Morghan answered with raised eyebrows. 'It's exciting.'

Erin gave a tiny shake of her head and Morghan laughed. 'What is it?' she said.

'I don't know,' Erin said with a small giggle of her own. 'I guess sometimes I remember you're just a person.'

That made Morghan laugh louder. 'Of course I'm just a person. What do you usually think of me as?'

Erin shrugged, feeling her cheeks heat. Hopefully Morghan would just think it was the exercise making her flush.

'I guess, what with walking between the worlds, and your golden hand, and all the things you know and do, I guess I think of you as...*more*, that's all.'

'I'm only more in the same way we can all be more.' Morghan stopped walking a moment and turned to look seriously at Erin. 'In the same way you're learning to be more.'

They stared at each other, then Erin nodded.

'What was it you wanted to ask me?' Morghan said at last.

Erin made herself relax, take a calming breath, not chew on her cheek. 'I wanted to ask you whether, if one day I was to be Lady of the Grove, whether I'd still have time for my art,' she said. 'I guess.'

'You guess?'

Erin nodded. 'Yes. I mean no. That was my question.' She blinked rapidly. 'And also, kind of related, I suppose, what does leading the Grove actually mean, in practical terms?'

Morghan's reply was amused. 'As in time management?'

'Don't laugh at me,' Erin said, frowning. 'It's a valid question. I'm trying to get a lot of things sorted out in my head so that I know what I'm doing, and what it's best for me to be doing.'

'My apologies,' Morghan said, bowing her head slightly. 'Let's continue our walk, shall we? While we talk.'

Erin nodded and fell in beside Morghan, her nerves jittery. She clenched and unclenched her hands in the folds of her dress, trying to make them stop prickling with nervousness.

'It's not that I don't want to be Lady of the Grove, if it comes to that,' she said, rushing the words from her mouth. 'It's just that everything has happened so quickly and having time for my art is really important to me, and I want to make sure I won't have to give that up.' She brushed a strand of hair from her eyes. 'I'm just trying to get my ducks in a row, make plans for the future.' She shrugged. 'So I know what I'm doing.'

'Is the unknown future causing you anxiety?' Morghan asked.

Erin thought that was probably self-evident, but she answered anyway. 'Yeah,' she said. 'It kind of is.' She reached into her pocket and pulled out a hair band, tying her hair back off her face. 'Things are moving and changing, you know? And I want to know I understand and have an idea that I'm in control of it.'

'Well,' Morghan said, stepping ahead to where the trail narrowed. 'I can assure you that you will have time to pursue your artistic ambitions, depending on what they are.'

'What they are?' Erin questioned.

'Of course. You must choose for them to be in alignment with your path, particularly if you take up the role of Lady of the Grove.'

Erin's shoulders drooped, and they walked in silence for the next while, in single file, and when Erin glanced up at Morghan's back at one point, she had to blink, because for a moment, Morghan was once more Ravenna, and she was Macha, following along this very path.

'Huh,' she said, an involuntary exhalation of surprise.

'What is it?' Morghan asked, looking back at her.

'Macha,' Erin replied. 'I was Macha for a moment, following you. Ravenna, I mean.'

Morghan nodded. 'We have walked this path many times.'

Erin thought about her lovemaking with Stephan. For several breaths during it, she had slipped into Macha's skin, back and forth, Macha and Finn, her and Stephan. It had been dizzying, breath-taking.

She fell into silence, and they walked, following the sun over the hills.

The path widened at last, and Burdock bounded ahead, catching the scent of the sea keenly in his nostrils and a sudden wild joy coursed through his body. He barked for the others to hurry up.

For a moment, Morghan and Erin looked out over the far view, the diamond-studded sea, the dazzle of sun and wave, and listened to the far cries of gulls as they skimmed the boundaries between sand and surf.

'I must remember to talk to Seagull more often,' Erin said idly, breaking the silence. 'It seems wrong to forget her, after all she turned out to be for Kria.' She blinked and looked over at Morghan.

'Why is it so hard to remember everything?' she asked. 'To make time for it all?'

10

Morghan looked out over the vista, feeling the breeze in her hair, its salty touch upon her skin. She closed her eyes for a moment, soaking it up, drawing in the peace and beauty of the scene as though she could breathe it, could absorb it through her skin.

Not through her skin, but through her spirit. It felt like much the same thing.

Opening her eyes, she glanced gently over at Erin. 'This is the question we always ask ourselves,' she said. 'And keep asking ourselves unless we have the luxury in our lives to wander off permanently into the desert to become a mystic.'

'I want to be part of the world,' Erin said, one side of her mouth tucked down. 'I don't want to go live on the top of a mountain or something and just eat honey or whatever.' She held up a hand. 'Not that it's not a valid choice or anything.'

'For some, it's a very valid choice,' Morghan said. 'But not, I think, for most of us, although I do think regular spiritual retreats, even if you don't go away for them, are essential.'

Erin shrugged. 'So, what about the rest of the time, then?'

Morghan looked at her and smiled. 'You tell me,' she said. 'You already know – you've been doing it the last few months.'

'What?' Erin's eyes widened and she shook her head, then stilled. Then sighed. 'Daily practice,' she said. 'Making time.'

'Making touching spirit a priority,' Morghan agreed. 'Again and again through the day, in small ways, in bigger ways.'

'This is what you call living in the flow of your spirit, isn't it?' Erin asked.

Morghan's smile widened to a grin. 'It is indeed.' She stretched and looked up at the sky, at the bunches of white clouds like cotton candy. 'And within this daily practice, this living in the flow of spirit, what happens?' she asked. 'What do we find ourselves doing?'

Erin followed Morghan's gaze to the sky as though she'd see the answer to Morghan's questions there. But there was only sky the colour of Stephan's eyes, and brilliant white clouds. She puffed out a breath. Shook her head.

'I don't know,' she said.

'Then let us see,' Morghan said. 'Let us stretch and breathe and reach. Let us stand here and let our spirits soar.'

Erin licked her lips, nodded. Watched for a moment as Morghan's gaze drifted, lengthened, as she dipped her arms then reached for the sky again, this time with intention.

Erin joined in.

The movements were fluid now, almost effortless, from daily repetition. She reached for the sky, breathing deeply as she did so, letting her breath out as she lowered her arms, then moved them to each side, embracing the air, drawing her hands towards her chest, reminding herself to seek the world from her heart, and balance herself from her centre. She touched her belly lightly, imagining the cauldron of her spirit there, and felt her spirit flex, streaming outward into the brilliant day.

She exhaled again, and saw her breath flowing outward into the world, a link, an offering.

She reached upwards again, echoing Morghan's movements beside her. They could do this exercise with no movements, Erin realised suddenly, simply by seeking the sensation, the letting go, the offering, the flexing, but the movements were a good aid, a way of focusing.

She sank into it and reached for the sun, feeling its heat upon her fingertips, spreading throughout her, igniting her so that for a moment she burned magnificently.

Her arms floated down, and the fire was tamed with the warm flow of the water of life, and she was buoyed in for a long, slow moment that stretched to forever and back again before depositing her gently upon the ground.

She dug her toes in, grew roots, anchored herself to the world, spread her arms like branches to the sky, bridged both.

Erin opened her eyes and the view dazzled her. She could see to the horizon; she filled the space between hill and horizon; her spirit flowed outside the bounds of her body, and she spun and danced and laughed inside its glory.

'We are part of the world,' Morghan said, her voice like a bell. 'And we come back to our centre, stronger, surer.'

Erin flattened her hands against her torso, breathing in, feeling the strength of her core. This is where she needed to step from, she thought. This was where she ought to make her decisions. From the cauldron of spirit inside her. It overflowed.

'I understand,' she said, blinking in the sunlight.

Morghan smiled at her. 'You do?'

Erin nodded. 'What do we find ourselves doing?' she said, repeating Morghan's earlier question. She swallowed. 'We find ourselves being steady.'

'Yes.'

'And this steadiness, this...' She groped for the word. 'This... largeness... is where we make our decisions from, isn't it?' Erin glanced at Morghan and for a moment she would have sworn she caught a glimpse of a hand that glowed precious gold in the light.

'Yes,' Morghan said. 'This strong centre, this connection with spirit, this is what we let guide us. If we are unsure, we come back to this centre, and stand securely within it, and move with its overspilling flow, and know that while our path forward might be difficult, that society might not always be in flow with us, that we might not – might never – know more than a few steps ahead, we are not alone, we are strong, we are guided, by our kin, by our own knowing and seeing self.'

Burdock came and pushed his nose into Erin's hand, and she laughed, his nose cool and wet against her palm, his whiskers tickling. She sank to the ground and wrapped her arms around the dog and hugged him. He licked her face and she giggled, letting go of him and squirming away.

Burdock grinned and wandered off to flop down in the shade of a tree where Erin had set his portable water bowl, his tongue hanging out and tail thumping the ground.

'So,' Erin said. 'The trick to planning the future is what? – Not to plan?'

Morghan shook her head. 'That's too simplistic, and of course we need to give thought to what we want to achieve, where we want to go, and so on.'

'But we have to keep stepping into flow, right?'

'And make our decisions from that place, yes.' Morghan blinked. 'Brooding and worrying, although completely normal, unfortunately, do not help us. That is action and habit from our egos, not our souls.'

'So, it's important to make time for our daily practice.'

Morghan laughed, sitting down and leaning back, enjoying the peace and the beauty. 'That's why it's called a daily practice.'

'Okay,' Erin said, sobering and plucking at a piece of grass. 'But I think it would still help if you could explain more to me of what Lady of the Grove does?'

One hand shading her eyes, Morghan sighed. 'Well,' she said, remembering her first-time meeting Ravenna, and the Lady of the Ways bidding her enter the cave to teach those assembled there. 'She teaches.'

Erin groaned. 'I cannot imagine having to teach another me.' She shook her head, trying to imagine just that. 'It seems so unlikely, that does.'

'Why?'

'Well, that I'd ever know enough to do it, I suppose.'

Morghan gazed over at Erin, whose hair was a dark red blaze in the sun. 'Of course you will.' She turned and smiled up at the sky. 'I knew nothing at seventeen when I first came here.'

'Don't take this the wrong way, okay?' Erin shook her head. 'But I can't even imagine you as a seventeen-year-old.'

The remark made Morghan laugh. 'I was ignorant at that age and too arrogant to know it.'

'Arrogant?' Erin certainly couldn't imagine that.

'Indeed,' Morghan said. 'I was very full of the fact that I was the one Selena chose to train to lead the Grove.'

'She was your aunt, wasn't she?' Erin shifted slightly to look at Morghan, her voice deceptively casual as she asked the question. They'd not talked like this before, not really. She hoped Morghan would keep going.

'We were related, yes,' Morghan agreed. 'I still remember the day she finally came to collect me.' She sat up and looked out at the far line where water met sky. 'I'd not known her very well when I was a child – more by overheard conversations and the odd remark, than by having met her. My parents didn't want her to visit, which I remember thinking was crazy.' Her lips curled in a smile at the memory. 'Selena was exotic and different by reputation, and I was always dying to meet her.'

'You hadn't met her at all?'

'Once, when I was a young child. I'd fallen in love with her, then. I must have been all of four years old. She let me sit on her lap and she was surrounded by the most amazing colours. I remember trying to run my fingers through them.'

'You could see auras?' Erin was fascinated.

'Yes, although the talent faded as I grew, until it was

barely anything more than a feeling, an instinct. I had to work to bring it back.' Morghan looked around at the hillside clearing. Everything rippled in her vision and brightened as she relaxed and focused.

'Is that why Selena chose you?' Erin asked. 'Because of you being able to see auras when you were young?'

'She wrote to me about a year before I ended up coming here to live,' Morghan said, remembering. 'She wanted to know if I still saw them, and if I could do anything else.'

Erin shook her head. 'What did your parents think about that?'

'I didn't tell them.'

'What?' Erin's eyes widened at the thought of Morghan involved in any form of subterfuge.

'It seemed...private,' Morghan replied. 'We corresponded for that year before she came to get me.' She glanced over at Erin. 'Wilde Grove usually does go to members of the family, even if sometimes they are distant ones. Selena was not really an aunt; she was my mother's cousin. My name was not even Wilde. I took that on by choice.'

There was a sudden lump in Erin's throat. 'I'm not related to you,' she said.

'You probably are, actually, if we were to go back far enough. The Wilde family has been in this area for a very long time, and so has your grandmother's. There's bound to be some connection there.'

Erin's mind boggled with the idea of being related to Morghan, no matter how distantly. The thought swirled around inside her head like it was made of lightning. It made her dizzy.

'Wasn't there anyone else in your family who would have been more suitable than me?' she asked after a long moment.

'No,' Morghan said. 'Not in any of my direct relations. I have a brother, and he has daughters, and I did go to meet them not too long before you arrived here.' She shook her head at the memory.

'What were they like?'

Morghan shook her head. 'Not Grove material. It was disappointing. I was disappointed, although not surprised, that my brother had not brought them up with more of an understanding of our heritage.' She paused. 'One of the girls showed some interest in it, but she was drawn to the potential power of the position, and that's not how it can be approached.'

'Power?' Erin frowned.

'All positions of authority have some power attached,' Morghan said. 'Even when we wield it – when we must wield it – lightly and compassionately.'

Erin was dazed. 'I've not thought of it like that.' She swallowed. 'What exactly are the Lady's...responsibilities?'

Morghan drew breath to answer, then closed her mouth and frowned. Images from her visions suddenly captured her and she blinked against them. The storming sky, and beneath, the rough waves tossing boatloads of refugees towards the safety of the Isle of Healing.

The egg in the bell tower, shining its light over the village, like a beacon.

'I don't know,' she breathed at last.

Erin sat straighter, looked at her in consternation. 'What?'

But Morghan shook her head. 'Here's the truth, Erin. For centuries, while such knowledge and practice as ours was forbidden, against the law, the Lady's job was to keep the wisdom, to make sure it was passed on. Which is what I'm doing with you, and everyone in the Grove, to the best of my ability.'

'It's not against the law anymore,' Erin said, her voice low in the yellow light from the sun. Her skin prickled suddenly. This was not the answer she'd expected from Morghan – that she didn't know what the duties of the Lady of the Grove were anymore.

Morghan stood up, brushing the grass and soil from her clothing, and squinting over to the horizon for a long moment before sighing and smiling tightly down at Erin.

'Come,' she said. 'Time to be heading back.'

Erin scrambled to her feet, disconcerted by Morghan's sudden change of subject. 'I travelled beyond the garden the other day,' she blurted. 'Just like you said I would be able to.'

Morghan's brows rose, and she turned for the path. 'Well done,' she said. 'I knew it would happen – the next big stage of your training will be led by the spirits. Did Fox take you?'

Erin picked up Burdock's water bowl, emptied it and folded it back into her bag, then hurried after Morghan, grinning at the memory of walking in the Wildwood, in the Otherworld. It had been as enigmatic and amazing as she'd thought it would be.

'Fox took me to an island,' she said, falling in beside Morghan and feeling the warmth of the sun on her grateful skin as they walked in the open air before the woods closed around them again. 'On the island, I met an old woman,' she said. 'Who gave me some runes.'

Morghan nodded and smiled back at her. 'What did they have to tell you?'

'The three runes were Isaz, Thurisaz, and Tiwaz.'

Erin's words made Morghan stop walking and she bent her head, sifting through her knowledge for the meanings of the runes. When she lifted her head, Erin was gazing at her.

'They seemed kind of bad when I read their meanings in my rune book. Are they? I mean, taken together, they kind of sound like a warning or something.'

Morghan's lips twitched. 'Bad?' she asked. 'No.' She shook her head slowly, thinking. 'But a message? Yes. I expect so.'

She turned and stepped along the path again.

Erin stared after her, then hurried to follow. 'What sort of message?'

Morghan laughed and the sound was light on the sea breeze. 'The task is to grow in spirit, to live a life in balance, in wholeness, yes?'

'Okay,' Erin said. 'Yes.' She nodded. 'And that's *Tiwaz*, isn't it? About the honour in life coming from meeting the demands of the spiritual as well as the physical, right?'

'Correct. So, bearing that in mind, then, what does *Thurisaz* tell you?'

Erin's brow creased in thought. 'Stephan and I talked about this,' she said. 'But *Thurisaz* confuses me a little – what does it mean that all problems have to be dealt with in spirit before you can do anything else?'

'You must walk the path,' Morghan said.

'The path?'

Morghan waved a hand, and Erin blinked, thinking

again that for a moment, Morghan's hand had gleamed as though made of precious metal. She squeezed her eyes shut, then blinked them open. Her heart ached suddenly, and a joy that felt almost like sorrow welled up through her.

'What?' she asked, realising she hadn't caught Morghan's reply.

'This path,' Morghan said. 'The Ancient Path.'

Erin shook her head, frowning again. 'But what about those who don't know about the Ancient Path? What do they follow?'

Morghan stopped walking and looked at Erin. 'That's an interesting question,' she said, then paused, working out what she wanted to say. 'When I said that the Ancient Path must be followed, I meant it broadly, in the simple fact that the Ancient Path is the path of spirit, of connectedness, of compassion, of being blessed and sharing those blessings.' She looked at Erin's face, at her fiery hair and clear eyes.

'But your question,' she continued, 'brings another thought to mind.' Connections wended their way towards each other in the back of her mind, seeking to snap together.

'What?' Erin asked. 'What thought?' A frisson of sudden excitement shivered through her, as though she were about to see things shift and change course right in front of her eyes.

'*Isaz*,' Morghan said.

Erin frowned.

'*Isaz* shows us the winter landscape that sometimes we are destined to wander.' Morghan drew breath. 'The landscape that in some ways it feels like the world is wandering – the planet, the people, the illness, the suffering.'

She smiled across at Erin. 'But,' she said. 'Each of us, perhaps, can be the thaw?' She paused. 'My most recent vision is that we must all constantly build and rebuild our houses, our lives, with connection and strong foundations.'

Erin nodded slowly. 'The old woman also told me my initiation was starting.'

Morghan looked at Erin, joy suffusing through her. 'Ah,' she said.

'It's not going to be like Kria's, is it?' Erin asked, then flushed. 'No, of course it's not.'

'No,' Morghan said. 'It will have its own challenges – all of which you are equipped to meet.' She turned for the path again.

Erin followed her.

11

'MORGHAN!' WINSOME BLINKED AT MORGHAN STANDING ON her stoop, a smile on her face. 'I wasn't expecting you.'

'Are you busy?' Morghan asked. 'Too busy for a pot of tea and a chat?'

Winsome laughed. 'Busy at what, I wonder?' She shook her head. 'Busy has been sadly lacking these last few weeks. She shifted at the doorway, suddenly grinning. 'I'm going to admit it – I'm glad we can finally catch up sitting down, instead of roaming the woods.'

'I don't believe it,' Morghan replied, an impish gleam in her eyes. 'You didn't enjoy climbing around out there in rain, sleet, and snow?'

'You exaggerate,' Winsome said. 'But surprisingly, I like the option to stay in and be civilised.' She stepped back from the door and ushered Morghan in, then gave a strangled laugh. 'I almost checked to see if Mariah were peering through her curtains to see me letting you in.' She blinked, shook her head. 'No word of her, erm, physical whereabouts yet, I suppose?'

'You suppose correctly,' Morghan said, taking a seat at the table with a satisfied sigh. Things weren't back to normal – things, she suspected, would never be back to normal, if normal meant pre-pandemic, but it was lovely to be able to make one or two visits. It certainly made everything a bit easier.

Winsome went to the sink then turned around, electric kettle in her hand. 'Do you think she will ever be found?'

Morghan didn't even have to consider the matter. 'Her body, maybe,' she said. 'But we'll not see her alive this side of the veil, such as it is.'

Leaning against the bench, Winsome shook her head. 'It really happened, didn't it?' The whole episode with Blythe. Winsome shivered slightly. She dreamt of it; even weeks later she still did. Morghan's eyes as she looked across the crowd at her, noose around her neck.

'It did,' Morghan agreed and watched Winsome, the strain in the lines around her eyes.

Winsome jerked around, filled the kettle and put it on to boil. The cups clattered as she placed them on the table.

'How are your dreams?' Morghan asked gently, watching Winsome's pale face, knowing her friend suffered, had so since she'd lost her position as vicar. They had done a lot of walking together, after the initial euphoria of helping Blythe, but much of it had been in silence, soaking up the energy of the woods, hoping it would be a balm to their battered spirits.

Winsome lifted her shoulders almost to her ears and

shrugged. 'Put it this way – keep your all-seeing eyes away from the shoddy state of my aura.'

Morghan laughed. 'I shall not take even a peek,' she said.

Winsome gazed at her for a moment, then shook her head. 'Last night I dreamt I was here in the vicarage, but the building was practically rubble, and I was picking through the ruins trying to sort it all out – and take care of a couple young kiddies at the same time.' She shook her head again, then set to pouring the hot water into the teapot. 'Maybe it will be easier now that the lockdown is easing and we're all vaccinated, but honestly, I still don't have any idea what I'm going to do.' She put the pot on the table and slid into her chair, a frown making soft lines between her eyes. 'Or even who I am, anymore.'

It was true. Was she even anyone without the vicar's dog collar around her neck and a church to go pray in? She'd not found the answer to that question.

On the floor, Cù stretched out and yawned, then looked at her with unwavering eyes. Winsome blinked and looked away from him. She'd refused to go back to the cave with Morghan, or even to go to the little summerhouse temple in the woods behind the church. She'd stopped everything except the almost silent walks with Morghan because it had seemed necessary. But it hadn't worked. She still didn't know who she was, or what she was going to do.

'Have you restarted the soul midwifery course?' Morghan asked.

'No.' Winsome busied her hands with the cups and saucers. Then let them drop to the table. 'I've let everything come to a standstill, thinking that would help me figure out where I am.'

'Has it?' Morghan asked, her voice mild, interested, unjudging.

Winsome shook her head. 'No,' she admitted. 'I just feel more adrift than ever.'

'Being locked away with everything much at a standstill doesn't help,' Morghan said.

'I've had a couple phone calls from parishioners.' Winsome blinked, glanced at Cù, then away again. 'Ex-parishioners, I mean. Wanting me to come around now that we can do that sort of thing more easily.'

Morghan raised her eyebrows and reached out to pour tea into their cups. 'And will you?'

'I'm not their vicar anymore,' Winsome said. 'I've no right.'

'They're asking for you,' Morghan pointed out. 'Is that not reason enough in itself?'

But Winsome shook her head. 'Maybe it ought to be,' she said, pressing her fingertips to the hot cup until it burned. 'But I don't know what to say to them anymore, what to offer them.'

'The same as you were able to give them before?'

Another shake of the head. 'I've no authority, anymore.'

Morghan reached over the table and took Winsome's hands in her own, holding them for a moment without speaking, until Winsome's fingers cooled.

'You've the authority of one who walks in spirit,' Morghan said at last, not letting Winsome's hands go. 'You've the authority of compassion, friendship, caring.' She drew back at last. 'What other authority do you need? What other authority do they need of you?'

But Winsome shook her head, stubborn. 'It's not that easy,' she said.

'Why?'

Winsome clenched her hands into twin fists. 'I got their church closed.'

'Ah,' Morghan said, sitting back and picking up her cup. She took a sip, looking at her friend over the rim.

'I did it,' Winsome said, hearing the defensiveness in her voice and unable to help it. 'It was my fault – my fault entirely.' She sighed suddenly. 'I was too stunned, at the beginning, to realise. It took time to sink in – just how badly I had messed up.'

Morghan stared across the table at her. She could try arguing with Winsome, she knew. Could point out all sorts of things. Things she was aware of Winsome knowing, deep down, under the guilt. But guilt and shame were rarely conquered by simple reason. It took something else.

'Forgiveness begins with yourself,' she said anyway.

Anguish twisted Winsome's pretty face. 'How?' she asked. 'I've ruined things for so many people. Including myself.'

'You've not ruined things for anyone else if they're still asking for your support. You went where your heart and spirit led you,' Morghan said, unable not to say it. She put her cup down.

'Then my heart and spirit led me away from what I loved!' Winsome was mortified to feel hot tears at her eyes. She wiped them away. 'I'm so tired,' she said.

'Winsome,' Morghan said. 'They led you deeper into what you love. They showed you the mystery beyond the liturgy, beyond the form, the ritual.'

'I know,' Winsome said miserably. 'I'm sorry. I just can't seem to get myself together. I feel like I'm just a leaf being blown around in a strong breeze.'

Morghan smiled sadly at her friend's suffering, feeling the pinch of it as though it were her own. 'The breeze is the breath of the world,' she said. 'And the leaf dances in it.'

Winsome snorted a laugh. 'You,' she said, and shook her head. 'You always see everything so differently.'

'Oh,' Morghan said, her voice faintly ironic. 'I am often forced to. Our spirits ask much of us.'

Winsome's eyebrows made for her hairline. 'I'm listening,' she said. 'What is being asked of you now?'

'You are a wonderful listener, Winsome,' Morghan said, a smile touching her lips. 'That's why your parishioners are still calling you, needing you.'

'Maybe,' Winsome replied, pursing her mouth like she'd tasted something suddenly sour.

'Erin asked me today what the duties of Lady of the Grove are,' Morghan said, pressing a palm to the table and examining her golden hand.

'That seems like a reasonable question,' Winsome said slowly. 'Shouldn't she already know this though?'

'She was just getting things straight in her mind. She was concerned she wouldn't have time for her art, which of course is very important to her.'

'But she will, won't she?' Winsome asked. 'I mean...won't she?'

'Yes,' Morghan answered. 'Of course. Just as I make time for my death work – which Winsome, we must get back to now.'

12

W INSOME BLINKED. 'WE?'

'Of course.'

Winsome looked away, gazing blindly out the window. 'I...wasn't expecting that.' She swallowed, looked guiltily back at Morghan. 'I haven't been doing the course.'

Morghan shook her head. 'That's not going to matter, although I think it's a good idea to get back to it, don't you?'

But Winsome didn't answer straight away. 'I don't know if I can, Morghan,' she said.

'Why not?'

'I've...I've lost my confidence,' Winsome said. 'I'll be rubbish at it now.' She shook her head, pretended to laugh. 'I'm just a washed up and depressed ex-woman of the cloth.' She cleared her throat, got up and took a biscuit tin out of a cupboard, pried the lid open.

'Have a Hob-Nob,' she said.

'You've lost some of your confidence, Winsome,'

Morghan said. 'But you'll not be a burden, and you're certainly not washed up.'

But Winsome just shook her head, broke a biscuit in her fingers in half and looked at its crumbs on the table.

'Do you remember the house in my woods, Winsome?' Morghan asked, as though she'd just thought of it.

Winsome lifted her face, brows knotted. 'The burnt-out one?' She shivered slightly at the memory of it.

'Yes,' Morghan said. 'That one.' She leant forward. 'I've been wondering why it's still there. I dealt with everything I needed to deal with years ago now. I know I haven't gone to that place for a long time – but it's natural to miss those we love who have gone on ahead of us.' She paused, searching for the words to articulate what was on her mind. 'Nothing is accidental in the Otherworld, Winsome. Rather like our dreams, our visions and journeyings are filled with symbolism, and I believe that house being there after all this time is telling me it's time to rebuild.'

'Rebuild?' Winsome asked uncertainly.

'Right,' Morghan agreed. She tapped a finger on the table. 'On one of my travellings to the Otherworld, my goddess, and my Queen, they gave me a potion to drink – so that I would have a vision inside my journey – and I found myself riding a horse.'

Winsome thought immediately of the horse she'd met during her own travelling to the Otherworld. It had been glowingly beautiful. She'd wanted to ask Ambrose what it meant, it being a horse, but Ambrose was another thing she was avoiding. Winsome shook her head slightly and fastened her attention back on Morghan. The kitchen clock ticked, and outside the room, the day was still, the gathering clouds still on the horizon.

'And the horse carried me to a forest,' Morghan continued. 'The Forest of Lost Souls.' She swallowed, took a sip of tea, looked at the biscuit she'd taken from Winsome's tin. 'In the forest, I found the spirit of a lost child, and took her up on my horse with me. The child gave me an egg.' Morghan's hand went unconsciously to the small crystal egg she wore around her neck with the silver oak leaf and acorn.

'An egg?' Winsome's eyes widened, then she frowned. 'Why an egg?'

Morghan shook her head briefly. 'I've always associated eggs with the soul. They're an ancient symbol.' Her fingers warmed the egg around her neck. 'The child gave me an egg, and I took this egg and rode to a village, to the church at the centre of it.'

'A church!' Winsome squawked, interrupting. 'Sorry,' she said sheepishly, shaking her head. 'But a church?'

'Yes,' laughed Morghan. 'An old stone church, if I recall correctly.'

Winsome goggled at her but said nothing else.

'The horse took me right up the steps into the great, square, bell tower of this church,' Morghan said, picking up the thread of the story. 'And when we got there, there was no bell, and I leant over and placed the egg where the bell should have been.' She smiled slightly at the memory. 'The egg hung there, larger now, and it glowed.' Morghan shook her head. 'How it glowed, Winsome. When we reached the ground again, the egg hung still in the tower, spreading its light out over the village and everyone put down what they were doing and came out to look up at it.'

Morghan paused a moment. 'I had not been the only rider, and this was not the only bell tower, and not the only egg placed to shine the light of the soul from it so that the lost may be found, Winsome.' She swallowed again, feeling the movement around the sudden lump in her throat. She shook her head. 'This is what we're supposed to be doing, Winsome. All of us. Shining the light of our soul so that we each may see the way.'

She drew breath. 'This is why the Grove has kept the knowledge alive all these centuries. For now. For this time. To shine the soul's light.'

They sat silently at the table, the steam from their tea wafting softly upwards.

Winsome shook her head. 'All right,' she said. 'I agree – it's time to do something. The Lord knows this is a bottle-neck time for the world. We're all being squeezed under the pressure, and I'm not at all sure that everyone will make it to the other side at the rate we're dealing with it all.' She winced, thinking about the times to come, the climate crisis and the humanitarian crisis that would go alongside it. Her brow twisted into a frown and her fingers went nervously back to her cup. Hadn't this been her job too? To share the life of the spirit?

That's what she'd considered it to be, anyway.

Winsome glanced down at Cù, then cast her gaze out the window, remembering Reverend Robinson and his flock standing on the lawn waiting for her to help them. She swallowed, blinked, looked back at Morghan.

'But what's this got to do with your burnt-out house and rebuilding?' she asked.

'Ah,' Morghan said, and sat back in her chair for a

moment. 'What do you do when your house burns down, Winsome?' she asked. 'When part of your life is destroyed?'

Winsome's mouth turned downwards. 'Rummage obsessively about in the rubble, apparently,' she said, thinking of her dream.

Morghan reached over the table and captured one of Winsome's hands. She gave it a gentle squeeze.

'What is it necessary to do, Winsome?' she asked.

'Oh God, you're relentless,' Winsome said, shaking her head. But she didn't take her hand away. It felt like holding onto a lifeline.

'Fine,' she said at last. 'Rebuild. There. You rebuild.'

Morghan nodded. 'I think so too,' she said. 'I think we take our experiences – even those that are little but ashes – and our knowledge and wisdom, and we build ourselves a solid foundation, and a strong house, in a strong community, and in the middle of that community we build a church tower for the light of our souls to shine from.'

They were quiet for a long moment. Outside, a sudden gust of wind breezed by, playing the branches like drumsticks.

'Well,' Winsome said at last. 'That should be a piece of cake, then.' She blinked owlishly at Morghan. 'I'm free next Thursday, what do you say we do it then?'

'You're on,' Morghan grinned. 'I happen to be free next Thursday as well.'

Winsome rolled her eyes. Sank back into thought. Sighed.

'You're right, though, aren't you?' She gave a tight shrug. 'It's time, isn't it?' she asked. 'To do what we can from where we are?' A ghost of a smile appeared on her lips as she repeated Morghan's oft-said words back to her. She dropped her gaze to her teacup and picked up the broken biscuit, fiddled with it a moment.

'There are things we can do, aren't there?' she said, the words flowing from her mouth like a sigh. 'Building a right life, taking the ashes of our experience?' She shook her head. 'Hiding away from that fact doesn't make it go away.' She broke the Hob Nob into quarters. 'And we have an obligation, don't we?' She risked a look back at Morghan. 'In this time and place, wouldn't you say?'

'Yes,' Morghan said.

Just the one word in answer, because what else was there to say?

Winsome struggled against it even while she knew she agreed. What did Morghan say every now and then? Examine your resistance.

She couldn't do anything, her resistance said. She didn't know who she was anymore, where she fit, what she was supposed to be doing.

Except Morghan had just told her what she needed to do.

What everyone needed to do.

Winsome leant closer to Morghan, feeling like this conversation was something she desperately needed to hear, to let sink in. Because she did have skills that could help people, herself, the world. Maybe, in the end, she was just being indulgent, hiding away like this.

Her muscles tightened to a cringe at the idea.

Morghan sipped her tea then set the cup back down. Smiled at Winsome.

'I am in fact busy on Thursday,' she said. 'Now that some

of the restrictions have eased around where we can go and what we can do, I would like to get back to my work with the dying. I am seeing a new client Thursday afternoon.' She looked steadily at Winsome. 'Will you come?'

Winsome couldn't answer straight away. She looked down at the crumbled biscuit and her mouth was dry, her heart thumping against the ribbing of her chest. She wanted to touch her fingers to her neck again, feeling for the black and white collar.

But there would be nothing there. Just the soft, thin skin of her neck.

And under it, the pulse that was her blood pumping around her body. Flesh and blood and spirit, she thought suddenly.

That's what she was. And she could shine.

She could help others shine.

Did she need the Church to do that?

She didn't know.

'All right,' she said, and her throat was so dry as she spoke that it seemed the words scratched as she said them. 'All right. I'll come with you on Thursday.'

She nodded and thought about the fact that she had been wallowing in the wreckage of her own life.

Was it time to stop kicking the stones about, and rebuild?

13

Morghan wended her way back into the depths of Wilde Grove land. She kept her chin lifted, her breathing even and controlled as her thoughts drifted and swirled on the eddying breeze. The day smelt of rain coming, and the trees rustled their leaves in anticipation.

All things in their season, Morghan thought. The great wheel turns, and we build and rebuild. We shine, dim, shine again.

Constant effort, constant striving, teamed with joy. Joy in connection, in the breeze, the whisper of the trees, the scurrying and creeping animals in the undergrowth, in those who walk the path with us, human, animal, spirit.

She stopped walking and drew breath. 'Back to basics for a moment,' she whispered.

Back to one of Selena's first lessons. Selena had called it *the calling of power*, and made Morghan practice it daily, wearing a great circular path through the woods until she was at first exhausted, then later, when she had got the hang of it, exalted.

'Ah, the things you have seen us poor two-leggeds do,' Morghan murmured, reaching out to touch a towering beech tree. She laughed. 'This is our problem, isn't it? We run swiftly and think fast, and forget to sing, do we not?'

For a moment, she listened to the deep voice of the tree, as it hummed and sang, and communed with its Grove mates, and then she smiled and patted its solid side. 'As always, your wisdom awes and comforts me,' she said, thinking of Grandfather Oak and the gift he had given her of appearing in her dream, and then she turned back to the path.

There was no time like the present for a little communing of her own, Morghan decided, then laughed again. There was no time but the present, she corrected herself. And the present was large – so much more elastic than most people thought. It was large enough to hang whole lifetimes upon.

Just using the words *large* and *elastic* broadened Morghan's awareness, she was so comfortable with flexing her spirit in this way.

And as Selena had long ago taught her, she patted the tree once more and set her steps to the path. She walked, feeling the swirl of the moment all around her, alive and elastic – that word again. She walked faster, sinking into that peculiar state of focused relaxation that was required to spread her spirit out like wings, to put each foot down on the earth and reach for some of the energy contained in it. A smile came to her lips and stayed there as her body flooded and vibrated with a sudden, deep feeling of well-being.

She grew taller, broader, lighter, fuller.

She walked and walked and let drop away the aches and pains of the day, the uncertainties, the sufferings, the doubts – her own, and those she felt from the ones she loved. They fell from her as she let them go and scattered across the soil.

She walked and walked and with every breath became more present, her chest rising and falling, her knees bending, her ankles flexing.

And her spirit streamed out around her, and she walked and watched herself walking and saw the forest around her solid and shimmering. Her hands tingled and she looked at them and she looked at herself looking at them and she flexed her fingers, and she flexed her spirit and she smiled, present in this great, ongoing, never-ending moment of the world that took her and embraced her with its beauty.

Then she breathed deeply, in and out, moving swiftly, the movement helping in some way she didn't understand and didn't need to. Selena had taught her truly – it worked, and that was what mattered.

And she called in her power. She swelled and grew with the truth of who she was. What she was. What everyone was. And she shone. She felt herself shining. She walked, spirit embodied, shining.

And behind her she felt streams of others walking with her. All those aspects of herself who walked embodied, experiencing, part of herself, part of her soul. She felt them and acknowledged them with a wild smile.

This was who she was. One of many, an aspect of one.

Most she did not know, only felt their presence, nameless, faceless, but potent.

These were her ancestors as much as any bloodline she claimed.

But one, one of them she knew well, and her feet slowed, and the rest fell away until it was just the one, just the one standing behind herself, following her, walking with her.

Morghan turned, and she gazed at the woman she had once been, who she still was, in some way.

'It is an unexpected pleasure to walk with you again,' Catrin, priestess and sorceress, said.

Morghan stared at the woman she had used to be, the one who, years ago, had led her through the tangle and labyrinths of the Otherworld and reawakened her own knowledge in her, clawing through the worlds and across the centuries, and she shook her head. The one who was so close to her for so long that often it had been that they looked through the same eyes.

'Yes, it is,' she said, and smiled at the familiar face.

Catrin looked around, her dark gaze passing over trees and light and shadow and coming once more to rest upon Morghan. 'We had many adventures, did we not?' She blinked. 'Many journeys, much exploration.' She tipped her head to the side. 'You learnt well, once you finally realised that the greatest teacher is spirit.'

Morghan shook her head, a smile touching her lips. 'As I recall, you considered yourself my greatest teacher, with your reaching, and your cunning, and your conniving.'

Catrin's smile was wide, amused. 'And how did I manage it but with spirit?'

But Morghan was remembering the burnt-out house. 'We have forgiven him, have we not?' Morghan asked, thinking of the man who had hurt her Grainne and Catrin's. 'We have relinquished? I am right in thinking the house means something else?'

Catrin nodded her head, then startled Morghan by smiling again. 'I cannot speak for you, but I have let it go – let him go. All this time it took, but it is done.'

Morghan sighed. 'You let it go only after centuries and lifetimes of meddling.'

Another smile from Catrin, this time however, it was hard and fierce, and she took a step closer, the trees folding in around them. 'I did what I considered necessary to save and protect the one I loved, and to assuage my guilt over her death, and to gain her forgiveness for my part in it.' Catrin tipped her head to the side and narrowed her eyes, her skin a ripple of shadows in the dimness of the Wildwood. 'Whatever issues...' she hissed the modern word, '...you have, are down to you alone. I reached out for you, yes, and we did what was needed, helping Grainne knit herself back together so that she could heal and step from the entanglement with that man, as must be done in these cases, and when we were finished with that, I taught you to remember the ways of the Wildwood.' Catrin settled down. 'I have made my peace and dwell in it now.'

Morghan stared at her. 'So, I am correct in thinking the house in my place has another meaning.'

At that, Catrin tossed back her head and laughed. 'Why do you ask me what you already know, Morghan of the Forest?' She laughed again, then swung her gaze back to Morghan. 'What do you want of me?' she asked flatly.

But Morghan shook her head. 'Nothing,' she said. 'I did not knowingly call you.'

'No,' Catrin agreed. 'Although here I am, and why is that, do you think?' Her smile blossomed again. 'What times you live in, Morghan of the Forest.'

'Indeed,' Morghan said on a sigh. 'Times that ask much, I think.'

'All times ask much of us, Morghan,' Catrin retorted. 'But yes, it is time to wield your power.'

Morghan stilled at the phrase Catrin used. 'You were a priestess, sorceress, and warrior,' she said, narrowing her eyes. 'And look where that got you.'

For a moment, she thought Catrin, Iron-Age Druid, would argue, but the woman sighed instead. 'I was a woman of my times, Morghan,' she said. 'As are we all.' She gazed off into the trees, then turned back to look at Morghan. 'I fought for our lands, our people, our knowledge. And yes, I fought with magic on my lips and a sword in my hand – but what, my Lady Morghan, will you fight with?' Her stare was direct, deep. 'What will you wield when the world needs you?'

And then the forest rang with her laughter again. 'You inherited a lot of myself, as much as you would rather not acknowledge it.'

There was a breeze, a clattering of beads, the jangling of iron, and Morghan was once more alone, on the trail that led through the Wilde Grove woods to Hawthorn House. Morghan turned her steps in that direction, a hand pressed against her heart to feel the harsh thudding there.

What would she wield? What had she but the strength of her spirit, her experience, and her knowledge?

Her love for the world?

That was enough, she thought. There was nothing better.

A PALE FORM LURKED IN THE SHADOWS OF THE HOUSE, AND Morghan raised an eyebrow to it. 'Clarice,' she said. 'What are you doing?'

Clarice shook her head. 'Nothing,' she said. 'I'm in exile, remember?'

'Ah,' Morghan said. 'Exile. Do you hate this world so much?'

Clarice pushed her hair back from her face and stared at Morghan. 'I do, as a matter of fact – although don't get me wrong, I admire what you try to do with it.'

Morghan stopped and looked at Clarice, whose face glowed in the dimming afternoon. 'What do I try to do with it?' she asked.

'Live with it?' Clarice asked, shrugging.

Morghan looked down at her feet, clad in their sturdy boots, bits of forest mulch clinging to their soles. 'Live with it,' she breathed.

'It's a hard ask these days,' Clarice shrugged. 'I guess you're trying to change some of it too, what with the community gardens, the care home, all those things.'

'Build the change you want to see in the world,' Morghan said softly.

'Yes,' Clarice said. 'I suppose so. Although you know, change isn't easy, is it?' She looked around at the gardens and lawn of Hawthorn House. 'I miss the Fair Lands like I'm missing part of myself. It hasn't been long, and I'm already done with this enforced change.'

Morghan sat down on a garden bench and contemplated her stepdaughter, who saw her doing so and shook her head.

'What?' Morghan asked, smiling.

'You're going to give me some pearl of wisdom, aren't you?'

'I don't know about that,' Morghan replied. 'I was going to ask you how the dreaming is going?' She bent down and unlaced her first boot, her oak leaf, acorn, and egg chinking softly against her breast.

Clarice hesitated before answering. 'Slowly,' she admitted. 'I'm only remembering bits and flashes yet.'

Morghan nodded. 'It can take some time – and sustained effort and intention. But if you put that into it, I think you'll suddenly be surprised at what appears.' She smiled. 'Almost overnight, if you like.'

Clarice shook her head at Morghan's attempt at humour. She spread her hands over her knees and gazed at the pale moons on her fingernails. 'It's okay though, going through the ritual of it every night.' She thought of the candles, the gateway, the pin cushion. 'It helps me feel a little bit less restless.' She gave Morghan a sideways glance. 'I still wish I could understand why the Queen is making me do this. I feel like if I had a reason, I could get on with it.'

'You have been serving her,' Morghan said, a sympathetic smile on her lips. 'Perhaps she now wishes you to find where you can serve here. All lives must be lived in balance, in careful tension between one thing and its opposite, and you, as much as you would rather not be, are human, just as Maxen pointed out. You are part of this world. You go back and forth, but when you are here, you are not wholly present. I am hoping that your dreamwork will help with this. And perhaps enable you to find a way to be more of a bridge between the world of the Fae and this one.'

Clarice stared at her. 'How would I manage that?' she asked.

Morghan reached for the laces on her other boot and unpicked the knot. 'I do not know,' she said. 'There must be some way you can share your experience, your very unique experience.'

'That sounds like it would mean interacting with people,' Clarice said, and shuddered. 'That doesn't sound pleasant.' Clarice considered it. 'Besides,' she said. 'We're Druids, we don't go in for proselytizing.'

Morghan laughed and tugged off her boots. 'I'm not asking you to convert anyone,' she said. 'Only that you shine.'

Clarice opened her mouth to make some sort of retort, then closed it again when she couldn't think of one. Instead, she shook her head. 'You haven't been to see the Queen for ages,' she said. 'Go and ask her what this is all about for me.' She blinked, swallowed. 'Please?'

Straightening, Morghan considered it, then nodded. 'I owe a visit,' she said, thinking that was probably the truth. 'And I will ask while I'm there.' She gave Clarice a sideways glance. 'I don't promise that she'll tell me her reasoning.'

Clarice stared out over the woods, where Sigil would be sleeping in her owlery until dark, when she would wake and wait for Clarice to meet her. They would spend a little time together and then Clarice would go back to the small cottage that had once been her mother's, and prepare to dream her way back into life.

But she missed the Fair Lands. More than she had words for. It had been her refuge since her mother had died.

'She has to,' Clarice said, then got up and stalked away over the lawn.

'Clarice?' Morghan called, and waited until Clarice had slowed and turned to look at her.

'What?'

'If you're heading into the village, can you pick up a book I've on order from Haven, please?'

Clarice narrowed her eyes. 'A book?' she said. 'You read?'

Morghan stood up, shook her head. 'Yes,' she said, laughing with amusement. 'I read.'

'When?'

'At night,' Morghan told her. 'In the quiet and peace of my room.'

'Huh,' Clarice said, then turned again. 'I'm not going into the village.'

14

Winsome scurried down the street towards home, her shopping bag swinging from one hand, and made sure to turn her gaze away from Mariah's house – still sitting empty – and try not to think about what had happened to the woman. Perhaps it wasn't such a bad thing, spending your life dancing with the Fae, captive in their realm, only able to see your own as a shadow or a dream. Or perhaps it would drive you mad, if you weren't someone like Clarice who moved back and forth between the two as though she belonged equally in each.

Either way, however, Mariah's house sat empty and Winsome ducked her head so she wouldn't have to look in its blank, staring windows as she went past.

Winsome's free hand inched toward her neck. She was collarless, and nor was she wearing her pectoral cross. Nothing.

Perhaps, she thought, she didn't have to figure every-thing out. Who she was without her job, without the cross, and who she was when she was someone who had walked between the worlds, been told a story by a wild goddess from a world more ancient than that of her faith's.

Perhaps, she thought, all she needed to do right here and now was to be open to the opportunities presenting themselves. And take the path one step at a time.

She walked towards the vicarage, her thoughts still swirling and looping, and then stopping, she looked around for Cù.

Winsome had grown used to the spirit dog at her side, the looks he gave her, sometimes amused, sometimes reproachful, always seeming to comment in some way, a silent communication between them. Silent on his part at least. Winsome had taken to having waffling, one-sided conversations with him.

He wasn't there. She stopped in the middle of the foot-path, ignoring the other people on the street and shaded her hand, looking for the dog. She touched her chest, trying to breathe more slowly while she scanned the road. She'd discovered that the dog appeared more clearly to her if she lowered her centre of being from her head to her heart.

Sometimes that was a trick when her thoughts were a rowdy jumble.

Winsome opened her mouth to call to him, then snapped her lips together. People would think she'd lost her marbles if she stood there and called to an invisible dog. And while she was all for individuality and even a bit of eccentricity, that might be taking it a wee tad too far.

Cù was across the road.

Winsome stared at him, brow creasing, and she called mentally to him.

He didn't budge. Simply stood at the intersection and looked back at her, his tongue hanging out, big chest heaving as he panted.

Then he turned and trotted down the street away from her.

'Cù,' Winsome said softly, under her breath. 'That road leads out of Wellsford.'

The dog didn't stop. He didn't look back.

Winsome, unbelieving, walked across the road and down the lane after him. Where was he going? Not to Hawthorn House – they would simply have gone through the Grove like they had every other time. Ditto Blackthorn House.

Winsome shivered slightly at the thought of Ambrose.

Who else lived up this way? There was only Erin, Winsome thought – but why would her spirit kin be leading her there?

She followed, eyes fixed on the ghostly form of the dog, her mind full of questions.

None of which the wolfhound seemed inclined to answer.

When they reached Ash Cottage, Cù turned straight into the driveway and across the lawn to the front door where he turned and grinned back at Winsome.

'I must be insane,' Winsome said quietly to herself, shaking her head. 'Letting a ghost dog lead me about the town.' She stepped up to the door and shuffled nervously. Lifted a hand to knock, then lowered it, staring for a moment at the brass door knocker.

'It's a dog,' she said, and couldn't help her smile. 'Not just any dog,' she said, glancing down at Cù. 'A wolfhound.'

Her smile widened, and she grasped hold of the knocker and banged it a few times.

There was a deep woof from inside, and the door flung open.

'Hey, hello, Vicar!' Stephan's smile was wide and open. 'This is a nice surprise.' He wrestled Burdock, whose nose was sniffing the familiar sting of magic, eyes narrowed at the sight of the spirit dog, back inside and held the door wider. 'Come in, please.'

'Thank you, Stephan,' Winsome said, shucking her boots and stepping into the warm cottage. 'But I'm not a vicar anymore, you know.' Her hand crept back to her bare neck.

Stephan's face creased in concern. 'Yeah,' he said. 'I know. Slip of the tongue, I guess. I'm real sorry about what Mariah did. It wasn't her finest hour, that's for sure.'

Winsome winced away from that and let herself gaze curiously around at the cottage instead. It was so sweet and welcoming, she thought. Lots of plants, lots of books. It was the polar opposite of the vicarage, which was far too large for one person. And furnished with battered, mismatched tables and armchairs that had seen far better days.

'It was my own fault,' Winsome said, shaking her head and looking at the art on the walls. 'Is this Erin's work?' she asked.

'No,' Stephan replied, letting go of Burdock, who gave Cù the side-eye and went back to his bed with a huff and grumble. 'It's Teresa's – she was talented too.' He looked at Winsome, noticing her greyish, tired skin. Maybe he'd make her take home some of his tonics he'd been playing around with. She didn't look like she'd been sleeping too well.

'It wasn't really your fault,' he blurted.

Winsome looked away from the detailed botanic drawing of some flower she didn't recognise and gazed at Stephan, his earnest blue eyes. 'Yes,' she said. 'It really was. I followed you to the solstice ritual. I danced with you.'

But Stephan was shaking his head. 'Maybe you did, but it's the magic of this place that led you to. Part of you recognises it, belongs to it, I guess.' He shrugged and looked suddenly sheepish. 'I don't think you should blame yourself, when...I don't know, spirit led you.'

Winsome nodded slowly. 'Thank you,' she said. 'And perhaps, in some ways, you're right. It's hard to regret a lot of what I've seen and done the last few months.' She frowned briefly. 'Any of it, actually. Even though losing the position I loved so much has been painful.' She subsided into silence, amazed suddenly that she was talking so openly to a young man in his twenties. But she liked Stephan, she realised. His easy warmth, his openness.

They shuffled around the tiny sitting room for a moment.

'You should carry on anyway,' Stephan said. He shrugged. 'You know, with your blog and your prayer meetings and all that. You don't have to be a vicar to do that stuff.'

Winsome stared at him. 'You're the second person who's said that to me,' she told him, thinking of her conversation with Morghan the day before. Morghan hadn't said it in so many words, but it had been there, implicit.

Stephan shrugged. 'Well, it's true.'

'Perhaps no one would come,' Winsome said, unable to believe she was confiding such a fear in this young man.

'Maybe, but I think some probably would,' Stephan answered. 'And how would you know unless you did it?'

Cù was looking at Stephan intently, and then he swung his gaze around to Winsome, eyes narrowed to squint at her as though to say *are you listening?*

'I guess you're wanting Erin?' Stephan asked after a moment's silence.

Winsome blinked at Cù and frowned again. 'I don't know why I'm here,' she said. Then leapt in the deep end. 'I followed my dog here.'

Cù ducked his head and stared at the floor a moment before lifting his squinty gaze to Winsome again. She swallowed. Perhaps she was here just to hear Stephan say what he had.

Cù perked up his ears.

Stephan's eyes widened before his face folded into a frown. 'Your dog? I didn't know you had a dog.' He looked around the room, even though he was certain no dog had come in with Winsome.

'He's, erm, my spirit kin,' Winsome said.

That made Stephan's mouth fall open. 'You have a dog as your kin?' He blinked in amazement. 'That's so cool. What sort of dog?'

Smiling suddenly, Winsome pointed at Burdock. 'He looks just like Burdock, but his fur is a lighter colour.'

'Wow,' Stephan said, shaking his head. 'That's wonderful.' He turned quizzical. 'You say you followed him here?'

Winsome nodded.

'You'll probably be wanting Morghan, then,' Stephan said.

'She's here?' That was a surprise.

Cù yawned. Scratched himself.

Yes, Winsome thought. He'd brought her here to listen to Stephan. To have that very conversation.

Stephan pointed to the window overlooking the garden. 'She's out there with Erin. They're doing some sort of something.'

Winsome nodded, then looked shyly at Stephan. 'Are you still...training...with Ambrose?'

'Oh yeah,' Stephan said. 'We go up to the cave every week.'

'The cave?' Winsome grimaced. 'I went there with Morghan once.'

Stephan laughed. 'Bet that was an experience. Takes some getting used to, doesn't it?' He waved a hand in the air. 'All the history, the magic.' He blinked. 'I thought I'd just be a gardener, you know? It was enough that I was learning all about plants and their spirits from Teresa; I never dreamt it would lead me so far.' He paused, shook his head. 'And now I have the Great Bear teaching me all about the healing properties of plants, and I'm going to enrol in a proper course so I can treat people legitimately – the best of both worlds, you know? It's really exciting.'

Winsome looked up at Stephan, saw his face glowing with anticipation, with happiness over his plans, the prospect of helping and healing, and his words rang in her ears.

The best of both worlds.

'Are you staying in Wellsford?' Stephan asked suddenly. 'Only it would be a real shame if you weren't.'

Winsome took a breath, let it out. 'I want to stay,' she said, and nodded, finding a smile blooming on her face. 'I want to find a way to make it work. Maybe like you said, the best of both worlds.'

'Great! I'm glad. You were brilliant with Erin and Morghan. Erin told me she could never have gone looking for Morghan without you.' He dragged a hand through his curly hair. 'And really, it's all the same world in the end, isn't it? But I guess you ought to get your boots and I'll show you out to the garden, instead of blabbering away at you.'

Morghan and Erin stopped their twin pacing of the garden when Winsome stepped out of the cottage, and both of them smiled widely at her. Winsome felt something rise in her – a welling of emotion, of belonging, of *fitting,* and it was so strong that for a moment she couldn't do anything but stand there, a lump in her throat, and feel some of the weight of her depression lift, begin to disintegrate. It wasn't that she would have an easy road, making her way back into the fabric of life in Wellsford – she had no illusions about that – it was that it would be worth trying.

'Picking up the pieces,' she murmured to herself, remembering her dream of climbing through the rubble. She cleared her throat. Building something new, she thought.

She remembered Morghan's burnt out house. Building on experience.

Something even stronger, perhaps.

'Winsome,' Morghan said, coming towards her, face lit by the afternoon sun, bundled hair shining. She looked down. 'And Cù, I see.'

'You can see him?' Winsome asked surprised. 'I guess I never really thought about that – or asked you if you could.'

'I can see him,' Morghan agreed, then turned to Erin, gesturing her over. 'Can you see Winsome's dog?'

A frown puckered Erin's brow. 'Hello Winsome,' she said, then cast an uncertain glance at Stephan, who just grinned, then looked at Morghan. 'Winsome's dog?' she asked.

'Her kin,' Morghan said, inclining her head. 'He's right there beside her.' She looked over at Stephan. 'You ought to be able to do this too,' she said, then spoke to both. 'It's just a slight step to the side.'

Erin's brow wrinkled.

'Breathe,' Morghan commanded. 'Relax your awareness from your head to your heart and your centre and hold it there. Then, let it expand around you, knowing that if you do, you'll see more.' She blinked. 'Become a calm, strong, observer and see the unseen.'

Winsome couldn't help it. As soon as Morghan had told Stephan and Erin to breathe, she'd done it as well, letting herself sink into that glorious, relaxed state where she seemed both more herself and more part of the world than ever. Her inner vision sharpened, and Cù grinned up at her, and she could see the bristly hairs on his face, his surprisingly long eyelashes.

'Oh,' Erin breathed. 'I see him – he looks like Burdock.' She smiled, her lips lifting in delight, then turned to scan the garden, looking for a glimpse of red fur. Her smile widened. Fox sat delicately twitching her ears by the gate, as though ready any moment to slip through and away.

'It's funny,' she said. 'It's not like real seeing, is it? It's kind of...' she floundered, trying to hold onto it.

'It's like a seeing and a knowing at once,' Stephan said,

looking at the garden, his plants, seeing their bright spirits glowing softly in the light.

'And it's hard to hang onto.' Erin said, blinking as her spirit-sight faded.

'It's like a muscle you need to work,' Morghan agreed. 'Which is what you must do, several times a day, every day, until you can do it at just at a thought.' She smiled. 'It is another way of walking the worlds. One everyone can and should do. Imagine what the world would be like if we could even just sense a little the spirit and consciousness of everything around us, not to mention those who walk with us as companions and those with whom we share the land, all at just a flex of the spirit.'

Everyone in the small group was silent for a moment as Morghan's words sank in.

'Is this what it's like for you?' Erin asked at last. 'Do you see like this all the time?'

Morghan considered her answer. 'I used to see like this only through effort, just like I'm asking you to do,' she said.

'Then what happened?' It was Stephan who asked, but Erin and Winsome nodded, looking at her.

'I touched the web,' Morghan said simply. 'Ravenna showed it to me, allowed me to see the truth of it, the way we usually cannot from within these bodies.' She sighed, smiled slightly. 'And now, I only have to remember, and it is right there. The web.'

Morghan paused, tipped her head to one side. 'But I have practiced a lot over the years,' she said. 'It's part of my communication with the world, my communing with it. It allows me, just as it will allow you, to see the reality of a tree's spirit, to hear their song, to see what steps beside us in the woods, to greet the fairy without having to travel to the Otherworld.' She pursed her lips in thought for a moment. 'It is the way to walk in spirit, to become re-attuned to the depths of our world, and to realise with whom we share it.'

Winsome frowned. She already saw the unsettled spirits of the deceased, and she saw Cù. 'Are there a lot of others we could see like that?' she asked, not knowing if she fancied the idea or not.

'No one is *other*,' Morghan said. 'We are all spirit, and some of us are spirit and flesh.' Her face softened. 'But yes, there are many, because everything has spirit.' She lifted her hands in a delighted shrug. 'The world teems with spirit, glows with life. It is a constant dance, to which we have mostly forgotten the steps.'

Winsome wanted suddenly to learn the steps. When it was put that way, she thought – who wouldn't?

'How did we ever lose sight of this?' she wondered out loud, her voice low with regret.

'I can answer that one,' Stephan said. 'We forgot.'

Erin nodded. 'We became materialists.'

15

WINSOME LET HERSELF INTO THE VICARAGE – EX-VICARAGE, she reminded herself – and stood in the kitchen, the door closed behind her, and realised that she was practically vibrating.

She tipped her head to the side, trying to determine why she was feeling this way. It was almost energetic, as though somehow, she'd plugged herself back in...

She shook her head. How long was it since she'd felt this way? Since before Mariah and Julia had overplayed their hand and got her and themselves into a fix.

Julia. Winsome stopped short in her thoughts and drew in a long breath, let it out slowly and shook her head.

'We need to do something about her,' she said to Cù.

Her spirit kin made no answer.

She shook her head. 'Not something about her,' she corrected. 'Something for her.' Winsome frowned over the realisation of what she was considering and drew in another deep breath.

'Nothing hasty,' she said, and this time she was speaking to herself, sternly. Just because excitement thrummed through her body as though she'd grasped hold of a live wire, it did not mean she should act blindly.

Mindfully. Winsome drew another breath. She needed to act mindfully.

Oh, but she was filled with ideas suddenly, half-baked plans, *possibilities*.

She sank down at the table. And wasn't that a relief? To feel like there were possibilities in her world again? That there were things she could do, things that would be of value?

Winsome leapt back up, went banging into her study and poked the power button on her laptop. She drummed her fingers impatiently on the desk, then noticed what she was doing and snatched them up, flattening her hand against her chest instead.

More deep breaths, reaching for calmness, her lips tickling with a hint of a smile.

The walk home from Ash Cottage should have gotten rid of some of this excited energy, but it had only built the more she'd thought about what she could do. What she was now determined to do, even if she got no response for quite some time.

She had an inkling though, that maybe some of the Wellsford people would respond. If she was brave enough to reach out to them.

Was she brave enough?

Perhaps Morghan, sitting at her kitchen table, had been right – it wasn't necessary to be a vicar to help the village. Perhaps no one would need her to be.

Perhaps it was only needed that she be resourceful, steadfast, determined, and with a vision for what they wanted, needed.

Community. Growth.

Winsome licked her lips. 'Strong spirit, willing flesh,' she murmured.

The old laptop had powered up at last, and Winsome clicked onto her email.

She should write to Dean Morton and ask whether their plans for the church and vicarage had been finalised yet. It had only been a couple months, and the Church was not known for moving swiftly on anything much. But Winsome wanted to know what was happening, so she could be prepared. If that was possible.

There was a new email from the Dean and for a moment, Winsome squinted at it, thinking she must be seeing things, that she wasn't reading things properly because she'd just been thinking about the Dean, but there it was. Sitting in her inbox like a little time bomb.

She clicked the email open, her face arranged into an anticipatory wince, and the excitement in her stomach turning vaguely acidic.

Winsome's gaze flung itself over the lines on the computer screen, and then she frowned and made herself read it more slowly.

St. Bridget's would be formally de-consecrated the next month and the process for deciding what would happen to the building would begin. It was likely that it would be sold, conditional on planning considerations. Most likely would be available only for commercial or community concerns, rather than available for conversion into domestic housing.

Winsome couldn't imagine the old church being turned into a home. She read the rest of the email, sliding into her chair, and pressing a hand to her mouth.

The vicarage would continue to be available for her to live in for a period of one year, if she so wished, and then it would also be sold.

The words swirled around in her head, and Winsome pushed herself back from her desk and got up. She hesitated a moment, then opened the desk drawer where she'd put the church keys. They were right where she'd left them and she stared at them for a moment, not knowing what she was thinking or how she felt, before scooping them up.

They were cold in her palm before her skin warmed them. She closed her fingers around them and tightened her fist, feeling the sharp bite of metal teeth. Then she put them back in the drawer, carefully this time, almost reverently.

St. Bridget's, she thought. Deconsecrated. The beautiful old church. What would happen to it then? Winsome shook her head.

Who would buy it?

Would Wellsford still want it? For what purpose?

Winsome thought furiously about it.

The vicarage would also be sold. Winsome wrinkled her nose. She was less sentimental about the old vicarage. It was too large for a single woman.

But it might have other uses, might it not?

Winsome huffed out a breath. Things were changing. All around her things had been changing for the last year.

She could be part of it, couldn't she? Still? Even after her mistakes?

After all, in the process of making those mistakes, she'd learnt a great deal.

Or of course, she could dig her heels in, concentrate on the fact that things were changing, falling apart, and they would continue to do so around her. And she could simply wander about picking through the rubble feeling sorry for herself.

The answer was clear and obvious, once it was put like that. Winsome blinked at the email still on the page, then bent over, unplugged the laptop, and walked with it back into the kitchen. She set it down on the table and put the kettle on.

While the water heated, Winsome closed her emails, and opened up the parish website Krista had helped her set up. She stared at it for a long moment, then blinked and hurried back to her study, snatched up a pad of paper and a pen.

Cup of tea steaming gently beside her, Winsome bent her head over the paper, rapidly writing notes.

Change the name of the website – could she do that? There was no point building a completely new one, was there? She would have to remove the parish links from the site as well. Winsome sighed over this one. Then made a note to add a page about services in Banwell. Perhaps, for those who wanted to, they could arrange driving down there together. Maybe a minibus, one day. She put a question mark against that.

It would take money and where would they get that?

It was a question that could wait until further down the

track, she decided. Right now, she'd have to get Krista to help her with the website.

Perhaps one of the first things she could set up for the village was some computer classes. God knew she could do with them, Winsome thought.

She made a note on the pad about it. Computer classes. Someone (who?) to teach them.

Winsome frowned, deep in thought. Perhaps she could provide free wi-fi as well. She blinked. The vicarage's reception rooms were big, and they weren't being used. Perhaps she could rearrange those and get some computers, and it could be a place to come and learn, or just for folks to socialise.

Another note on her pad.

But where would she get computers from?

That would take some looking up. Winsome made yet another note to herself.

Maybe the whole ground floor of the vicarage could be given over to the community. They never had found anywhere very suitable for the parent and kiddies coffee mornings.

Winsome bowed her head. Computer classes were all well and good. And coffee mornings. And getting the charity shop back up and running, of course, as well as everything else they'd been doing...

But she wanted to do more than that, didn't she?

She wanted to tend to the village's spiritual life.

That was why she'd taken the position in the first place. She'd realised that just looking after her own spiritual life wasn't enough. She needed to serve a community.

How could she do that now, when she'd disgraced herself so badly?

Winsome sat back on the kitchen chair and took a long, slow breath.

'Tell me, God,' she said. 'Is this the right path? Can I do this – should I do this?'

A flood of feeling washed through her, making her sway slightly and grip the table. It was as though every atom of her body had lit up and begun sizzling with joy and anticipation.

She shook her head.

Perhaps it was the right path, then. What she was considering.

Winsome gulped, blew out a breath and got up. Her legs were slightly unsteady. She'd make a cup of tea, she decided, and then she'd log back into the soul midwifery course and see what she was due to do next. Because if she was going out with Morghan on Thursday to see a client, then there was no reason not to continue with the course, was there?

And she needed work to do. Real work. A job. A job she could love, doing work that was meaningful and necessary.

Enough hiding, Winsome thought. It was time to step back into her life.

And perhaps the life of Wellsford.

Or at least peep out at it.

She thought suddenly of the messages that had been left on her answering machine and went back to her study to listen to them again, head bent in humility as she heard three of her ex-parishioners asking her to visit them.

Support them.

There were tears in Winsome's eyes as she called each of them back and made a time to go see them. When she was done, she felt drained, exhausted.

But clean as well. Clear.

Determined.

She'd rebuild, she decided. One hard, heavy brick at a time.

16

THERE WERE MANY WAYS TO ENTER THE FAIR LANDS, THE realm of the Queen, and Morghan suspected she knew only a few of them. She took the steps carefully, unable to stop herself from looking across at the expansive view, over the desert that always reminded her of somewhere such as Egypt, the dust yellow, the faraway buildings squat and square, made of the same stone as the sand and dust. She'd never been there, or at least, not in this lifetime.

She shifted her gaze to the glittering blue sea at her right and her chest tightened at the sight of its sparkling beauty. But her path didn't take her to either city or the sea, and she turned away from both, stepping along the way that was little more than a track that rabbits might make. There were many paths like this in the Otherworld, she knew. They twisted and turned and appeared and disappeared. Once, when she was much younger, she'd thought about making a map of the place, of the trails she knew, the landmarks.

But somehow, she'd never gotten around to it – and what did it matter, really? What use would it be? For those who travelled there, the way opened itself. There was no need of a map.

An old man waited for her, standing in front of the great boulder that hid the entrance to the tunnels. Morghan bowed her head.

'Father,' she greeted him while Hawk came to land on her shoulder, and he nodded his head, a genial smile on his face before he turned and ducked into the darkness of the tunnel.

The floor was sandy under Morghan's feet and there was room enough for her to walk upright. The old man conjured a sphere of light to guide them, and they followed as it bobbed along deeper into the Other-realms, Snake slithering ahead into the darkness, and Wolf by Morghan's side, as ever.

The old Druid led them deeper into the tunnels, threading through one entrance after another until they came to a river that Morghan recognised. This time, however, she did not have to spin a bridge to cross, as there was already one there, and she stepped onto the curving arch of it and across the dark water, in which small figures swam and played, their laughter and gasps lazy on the slow current.

The Druid led her without speaking, his face creased and at ease. They had met before, several times, and once Morghan had asked him who he was, but his reply had only been that he was as she had greeted him – her father. He had not elaborated upon that, and she had left it as it was, content in the sweet mystery of it.

They entered the Fair Lands, and the cave roof widened out to glorious sky, and Morghan breathed in the scents of flower and fruit and grass, for in these lands it was perpetual summer. She could understand why Clarice was so fond of coming here.

The Queen approached and Morghan bent from the waist in a respectful bow.

'Morghan, Lady of the Forest,' the Queen said, acknowledging the greeting. 'Come and sit with me for a moment. It has been some time since we've seen each other.'

'It has, indeed, Your Majesty,' Morghan replied, following to a bench under a fragrant bower and sinking down beside the Queen, feeling suddenly awkward and gawky next to the Fae woman's fine beauty.

'Tell me what brings you here?' A smile quirked at the Queen's lips, as though she already knew but was prepared to humour Morghan.

'It had been too long between visits, my Lady Queen,' Morghan replied. 'And I seek your wisdom, for your guidance is always welcome as I strive to follow this path.'

The Queen looked shrewdly at Morghan and laughed. 'Clarice asked you to come, didn't she?'

Morghan smiled. 'She did.'

'Ah, that does not surprise me.' The Queen reached out and touched a softly blooming rose. 'She takes her banishment hard?'

'She does,' Morghan confirmed.

'And wishes to know why?'

'Yes.'

The Queen turned and looked directly at Morghan, her

fine, ageless features serious. 'Do you know why, Lady of the Forest?'

Morghan considered the question. 'I can only speculate,' she said at last.

'And I'm sure you'd be correct,' the Queen said generously. She sat back and contemplated her garden. 'I value your daughter's presence in my court,' she said after a long moment. 'She is well loved here, and as well you know –' The Queen gave Morghan a sly, sideways glance. 'As well you know, we do on occasion value human company among us.'

Morghan thought immediately of Mariah, but pressed her lips closed over asking after her.

The Queen continued. 'But Clarice is gifted to be able to come and go from here. It is not something that everyone is able to do, or indeed comfortable doing.'

She paused and Morghan nodded.

The Queen smoothed her hand over her silvery skirt. 'But balance is important, and Clarice lacks it. She comes here because she does not want to be in your world, and yet she must find her way there. She is human.' A sigh. 'She has much to offer, if she will not hide from it.'

Morghan sat still, digesting what the Queen had said.

'It's true,' she said quietly. 'She is unsettled in our world. I have set her a task that I hope will remedy that.'

'I have made the ban until Midwinter's,' the Queen said. 'But I shall make it for longer, if necessary.'

'I understand,' Morghan said, bowing her head in acquiescence.

The Queen stood and turned to look up the hill from where they sat. 'Good,' she said. 'That is settled, then.' She glanced back at Morghan. 'And now, there is the matter of yourself.'

'Myself?' Morghan asked.

'Indeed,' the Queen answered with a slight smile. She pointed up the hill. 'Go up there,' she said. 'And do not return to me until you have something of value to offer. I have given you gifts, and now you must do what is needed of you.'

Morghan rose from her seat, looked up the hill, seeing nothing particular up there, and nodded. She bowed again, lower this time.

'My Lady,' she said. 'As you wish.'

'As I insist,' the Queen corrected her, before turning away and disappearing through the bower.

Morghan stood for a moment, bemused, her gaze upon the hill, and then she set her feet upon the path and climbed the hillside. Hawk launched from her shoulder and took to the air.

At the top of the hill stood an ancient stone circle, and Morghan entered it to stand in the middle looking about. There was nothing else there and she frowned, trying to place what was wanted of her.

Snake looked at her, then arranged himself in the grass as though settling in to wait, and he kept his gaze steadily upon her. Morghan looked up and saw that Hawk circled around and around on the air currents above her, a dark shadow against the blue of the sky.

Wolf sat down beside one of the stones and waited.

Morghan tamped down the frustration that threatened, and breathed in the clear, fresh air instead. The answer would come to her, she thought, if she just stood here and let it. The air was sweet with honeysuckle in her lungs. The stones stood in their circle around her like ancient dancers.

Hawk called out, a faraway cry. Snake licked the air with his tongue, then settled to watch her again. Wolf gazed at her, alert, still.

Morghan stood in the middle of the circle.

And then, as she breathed in, something inside her clicked into place and she stretched her arms upwards, transforming herself into a tree, digging her roots deep into the rich soil, seeing them pushing down and further down to drink from the rich darkness underneath the hill, while her branches reached out into a glorious green crown, heavy and ripe with glossy leaves and plump fruit.

She stood there, a tree, and watched people appear and pluck her pears from her branches, enjoying the shade of her limbs as they ate, the sweet juice running down their chins. She swayed in the breeze and watched as a stone church was built to her right, and a schoolhouse to her left. She looked at them, taking the long, slow breaths of a tree, and understanding grew.

Something moved towards her in a blur of dark fur and muzzle and Wolf stood up against her trunk, his forelegs planted against her. He gave a small, sharp jump, and then Wolf was inside Morghan, part of her wood and sap, and she let go, turned from tree back to woman, and for a moment, Wolf was still inside her, curled around her heart, and then he stood once more in front of her, and she bent down, plunging her hands into his thick fur, and stared around at the hilltop, at the ring of standing stones.

·   ·   ·

'You're distracted,' Ambrose chided her, laying aside the architect's plans for the medical centre and straightening to gaze at Morghan. 'I can feel your thoughts a thousand miles away.'

Morghan drummed her fingers on Ambrose's heavy desk for a moment, then drew away, walking over to the fire and crouching to put on another fragrant log. The old house was cool even into summer.

'Tell me what's on your mind.' Ambrose looked at Morghan, her stillness as she knelt in front of the fire. Her energy, like static, crackled in the room louder to his spirit than the burning logs.

'We are on the right path,' Morghan said, gaining her feet and standing in the room, hands on her hips now, head still bent, her brow furrowed.

'I'm pleased to hear it,' Ambrose said. 'So why the frown, then.'

Morghan shook her head. 'I cannot think but that we have to do more. Reach further.' She blew out a breath between pursed lips. 'But I have little idea about how to go forward with that.' She closed her eyes for a moment, remembering her audience that morning with the Queen of the Fae. 'You know that the Queen has banned Clarice from her realm until after the winter solstice?'

Ambrose nodded, feeling sympathy for his niece. She was not taking the banishment well, and he had seen her more than once walking aimlessly about in the woods. 'Do you know why yet?' he asked.

'She didn't tell Clarice.' Morghan looked contemplatively around the room. 'But it was as I expected when I went to visit her in the Fair Lands this morning.

'And what was that?' Ambrose asked, his voice gentle while he watched Morghan closely. The last months had seen much change for her, since her vision had widened, since the Queen had replaced her hand of flesh and blood and bone with one of gold. Ambrose knew Morghan still pondered over the meaning of it, and the task she was sure came with it, and he had been able to contribute frustratingly little in the way of illumination.

And he had been preoccupied himself, the last weeks. Winsome was avoiding him, and he was at a loss as to what he should do about that, or even if there was anything he could do. He could not force his attentions upon her, but only hope that one day, she would come to him, even if just to talk, even if just to say it was impossible between them.

'That she must find her place here in this world, instead of avoiding it.' Morghan put her hands on her hips, thinking. She changed the subject. 'Erin has begun travelling,' she said and walked over to Ambrose's shelves and plucked up a silk bag. 'May I?' she asked.

Ambrose didn't know where this was going. 'Certainly,' he answered.

Morghan gave a brief nod and brought the bag to the desk, tugging it open and upending it so that the runes inside spilled over the plans for the medical centre. Her long fingers sifted through the stones, drawing aside the three Erin had told her she'd been given.

Morghan cleared her throat. 'She met the Old Woman,' she said. 'And was given these.'

Ambrose gazed down at the three runes on the table. 'Any particular order?' he asked.

'Does it matter?' Morghan smiled. 'She didn't say.'

'And what do you infer from them?' Ambrose asked, lifting his eyes to watch Morghan.

'I find them a message to myself, and to all of us.'

Ambrose did not respond straight away. Instead, he let Morghan's words sink in.

'How so?' he asked at last.

Turning, Morghan flung herself down on the armchair by the fire. 'Erin asked me what the duties of the Lady of the Grove were,' she said.

Ambrose was still, waiting. This was not, he sensed, a conversation he could direct, or hurry along. Morghan would say what was on her mind in her own time and in her own way.

'I told her I no longer know,' Morghan said.

'What?' Abruptly, Ambrose shook his head. 'What do you mean? It is the same as it has always been, is it not? To keep and celebrate the ancient knowledge?'

Morghan nodded. 'Yes,' she said. 'We keep the knowledge.'

'But?'

'I cannot help but think, to what purpose?' she asked. She waved a hand at the room, at the world beyond it. 'When things are in this amount of disarray? When people are lost and frightened? We keep the Way so that a few select people can live the truth and be comforted, connected?'

Ambrose considered her thoughtfully. 'What else has happened?' he asked at last.

Morghan laughed. 'It has always been impossible to keep anything from you.'

'Why would you want to?' Ambrose asked, one brow raised to underscore the question.

With a grin, Morghan held up a hand. 'Two things,' she said. 'Today, the Queen sent me up the hill in her land and told me to *not return until I had something of value to offer.*' She paused. 'That's a direct quote, by the way.'

Ambrose frowned. 'What did you do?'

Morghan sighed and spread her hands on the arms of the chair, looking at the golden fingers on her right hand. 'I did what she told me to do, of course. I went up the hill and there's an ancient stone circle there, and I stood in the middle of it wondering what she meant.'

'And?'

'And eventually it struck me, what was needed, and I became a tree.' She looked pointedly at Ambrose. 'A pear tree, and my branches were heavy with fruit, and as I stood there, people came and plucked the fruit from my limbs and ate it, and to one side of me, a church was built, and to the other, a school.'

Ambrose sank down on the chair opposite Morghan, linking his hands between his knees as he frowned in thought.

'Molly Wainwright called me yesterday,' he said at last.

'Molly Wainwright?' Morghan asked. 'Isn't she the journalist?'

'She is, yes,' Ambrose said. 'And she had a curious proposition.'

Morghan's restless hands stilled on the arms of the chair. 'She did?'

Ambrose looked up, considering her. 'She asked if she might come live in the village for a while and write a book.'

'A book?' Morghan's brows flew up in surprise. Whatever she'd been expecting Ambrose to say, it certainly hadn't been this. 'What about?' she asked.

'Ah,' Ambrose replied, straightening. 'This is where it gets very interesting indeed. She wishes to write a history of Wilde Grove, and by extension, Wellsford.'

Morghan considered this for a long moment. 'How deeply does she wish to go?' she asked. 'How deeply does she know there is to go?'

Ambrose thought about it. He had liked the woman. Molly Wainwright had been smart, articulate. And deeply curious about the world, he thought.

'It could be the opportunity we need,' he said. 'If your travelling to the Fair Lands is to be taken seriously.'

'Which of course, it is,' Morghan interjected. One did not lightly ignore the Queen's lessons.

She considered it. 'Interesting,' she said. 'When was she hoping to come here and begin this project?'

'She suggested next month,' Ambrose answered. 'So we have time to decide if it is the right course of action.'

Morghan nodded. 'A church and a school,' she mused out loud. 'The church reflects keeping the Ancient Way, I am sure, but the school – that is where it gets interesting. And problematic. Does it symbolise the teaching we are already doing, with Erin and Stephan, and the other members of the Grove, or is it a directive to take that further? And if so, then how would we do that?'

'A book would have the possibility of reaching many people,' Ambrose said.

'Yes,' Morghan agreed, nodding slowly. 'It would.' She tapped her fingers against the armrest. 'We need to give this matter more thought.' She blinked. 'And talk to Ms. Wainwright.' Morghan paused.

'What else are you thinking?' Ambrose asked, knowing Morghan too well not to recognise from the expression on her face that her mind was busy making connections, testing plans.

Morghan gazed at the fire, barely seeing the leaping, crackling flames. 'We need to make contact with the other Groves,' she said. 'All that you feel have potential – ancient, and newer.'

'Potential?' Ambrose asked.

She nodded. 'We can learn from many of them,' she said. 'And they from us.' A pause. 'I have seen that several have training courses that anyone may apply for, held online and in person.'

'You're thinking of doing the same thing?' Ambrose was surprised. This was genuinely a new area for them.

'I don't know,' Morghan answered. 'But I would like to get together with them and talk about it.' She shifted in her chair and sighed. 'I am casting around for that pin cushion, Ambrose. The Queen has thrown it down and I am looking for the direction in which it has gone.'

Morghan sighed. 'Life requires such courage, Ambrose,' she said. 'And a position such as Lady of the Grove requires a keen sight.' She nodded. 'I have the feeling that these changing times are asking more of us. Our spirit kin – in this case the Queen and Elen of the Ways – have made this point particularly. It is another great Time of Turning, and this time, it must be in the right direction. Back toward the truth.'

Ambrose nodded in agreement. He saw the veracity of

what Morghan said and felt the urgency of it also. 'What was the second thing?' he asked.

For a moment, Morghan looked at him, nonplussed, then laughed. 'I'd forgotten I'd said that,' she told him. 'But you're quite right.' She looked down at her hands. 'I've been thinking about why Grainne's house is still in my space,' she said.

Ambrose looked keenly at her. 'And what conclusion have you come to?'

Morghan shook her head. 'The house is a potent symbol,' she said, glancing up at Ambrose, who nodded in agreement. 'And because I know I've done the work, personally, to come to terms with all that happened between Grainne and I, and the man who was her father in this lifetime, I've had to think upon it more broadly.'

She paused.

'That is good,' Ambrose said. 'I've had much the same thoughts myself.'

'And I spoke to Catrin the other day,' Morghan said.

Ambrose's brows rose in surprise. 'You did?'

Morghan's smile was brief but full of humour. 'I did.' The smile faded. 'The woman is as confronting as ever.'

'You realise you and she are much the same?' Ambrose asked.

'Please,' Morghan said. 'Don't you start.' She laughed. 'But Catrin challenged me – she said that she fought with magic on her lips and a sword in her hand, and then asked what will I fight with?'

Ambrose leant back in his chair and considered this. 'That's quite a thing to say.'

'Yes, and I didn't entirely welcome it.' Morghan sighed.

'But what if she has a point? Is this not the time to stand up and step forward?'

'What are you suggesting, Morghan?' Ambrose asked.

'I have no idea,' Morghan said, spreading her hands in a gesture of helplessness. 'I am not equipped to do more than pass my knowledge on to one or two such as Erin and Winsome.'

'Hmm.' Ambrose considered it. 'Or we have simply not thought of a way to do more,' he said.

MORGHAN STOOD OUT ON AMBROSE'S FRONT LAWN, AND stared at the trees, her mind alight with questions, possibilities. Where to start?

She shook her head. It was necessary to see more clearly than this. Right now, everything was a great swirl around her, and she closed her eyes, seeking her breath, seeking calmness, to slow the flow of the deep underground river that was her mind.

What was it that she had told Erin?

To stand within the strong centre of her connection with spirit and be guided.

'Goddess help me,' she whispered.

'Goddess guide me.'

17

ERIN KISSED STEPHAN GOODBYE AND LEANT AGAINST THE
door, mug of tea warming her hands as she watched him let
himself out the gate, turning to grin at her before giving her
a last wave and setting out on the road back to the village.
She closed her eyes, knowing she was still smiling like an
idiot, but not caring. Burdock sniffed about the bushes and
trees, scooted around the gaggle of three or four ravens
having their early-morning confab on the hedge, and Erin
sucked in a breath of morning air. It was damp and fresh,
with a hint of grass and sunlight and it filled her to the brim
with happiness.

Another brilliant morning. And the night before hadn't
been too bad either, she thought. She and Stephan had
spent it bent over her laptop, scrolling through all the
different naturopathy courses available, trying to decide
which one would be the best. He was going to have do a
bunch of health science courses since he'd not done
anything like it in school, but that didn't matter. Erin smiled

again. He'd been so enthusiastic and excited. It had made her beam with happiness.

Maybe spending more time with Stephan wasn't so bad at all. He was coming back for dinner, and she was already looking forward to it.

'Ah, Burdock,' she said, reaching to stroke the dog as he brushed past her. 'Isn't it a wonderful day?'

She turned and went back into the cottage, checking the time on Teresa's kitchen clock. She wasn't starting work for another hour and a half, so there was time, wasn't there?

Erin stood in the kitchen considering. Then set her cup down and took a breath. 'There's time,' she said, and felt a frisson of nervous excitement thread through her.

Outside in the garden, she shivered slightly. The mornings were cool, and it was early. She and Stephan had been up with the rising sun and out to greet it together before coming in for breakfast, making tea and toast, dodging around each other in the small kitchen like they were dancing, and giggling together like a couple of co-conspirators as Burdock methodically crunched his way through his biscuits, one ear cocked towards their goings-on.

Erin drew in a deep breath, forcing herself to calm as she let it out and breathed in again.

'Relax,' she murmured. 'You can do this.'

Part of her wanted to burst out into effervescent laughter, or go spinning off to dance ecstatically around the garden. She was in love, filled to the brim with it.

'Relax,' she told herself, more sternly this time. 'Calm down for goodness' sakes.'

It was hard to be calm when she felt almost delirious with happiness, but she had to do it. She remembered

Morghan a couple days ago, telling them how to see Winsome's spirit dog.

There. That was right. One breath, in, hold, out. Nice and slow. A relaxing, a spreading.

She could see Fox, and she smiled in delight at her. Fox's ears twitched, and the white tip of her tail gleamed in the early morning light.

Erin stepped forth out of one garden and into another. Her visionary garden. She breathed again, holding the relaxed state, holding herself open, all her senses relaxed and open. She breathed and smelt every scent on the air.

What had Morghan said to her during their last conversation?

That the spirits would lead her teaching for the next part of her training.

The words made Erin shiver. She thought of the old woman sitting on her stool on the island in the lake. Would it be her again? She with her runes and their mysterious message.

Erin didn't know, and because there was nothing else to do but to forge onwards with this adventure, she took a breath and called out.

'I am Erin,' she said, and to her ears her voice rang and trilled like a bell. 'I am Erin of the Grove and I call my kin to me.'

She swallowed, standing in the centre of her garden, which was no longer completely overgrown but benefiting from being well-tended over the last weeks.

Another breath, and the words came to her.

'I call my kin to me, in the name of peace and life.' She smiled and spread her arms, warmth and joy flowing through her. 'I call my kin so that I may listen to your wisdom and learn the ways I have forgotten. I call in peace so that I may hear your voices, and those of the gods, so that I may stand in this place and sing the wheel to turning.'

She swayed slightly where she stood, her head fuzzy and dizzy with a sensation that was a glowing and a gleaming. Another breath.

'In peace may my voice be heard,' she said. 'In peace may I follow the voices of my kin.' She breathed out, head swimming, eyes closed now, the sunlight golden upon her lids.

'May there be peace in the east,' she said. 'May there be peace in the south. May there be peace in the west. May there be peace in the north.'

The directions swung on their wheel around her.

Erin cleared her throat. 'I call my kin of the south,' she said, and she touched her heart as she did. 'The fire of my heart, my passion for the world.' A pause. 'I call the spirit of Dragon, who guards the treasure of my own bright gold, my eternal being, whose purpose never tarnishes. I call and greet you.'

The dragon swirled behind her closed eyes, tooth and nail and fire. She bowed her head.

Then continued.

'I call my kin of the west, great whale of the depths, whose song is ageless, whose memory is longest, bless me with your wisdom.'

Erin lifted her hands towards the sky then spread them wide once more, her body alive and thrumming, spirit singing, calling.

'I call my kin of the north, spirits of the earth upon

which I stand to sing my song of the turning wheel. Bless me with your nurturing wisdom, great Bear Mother.'

Her voice fell to a whisper, a caress.

'I call my kin of the east, spirits of air whose breath fills me, and whose breath I return in offering. Hawk, Raven, Seagull, sharp-visioned, far-seeing, I call and greet you.' She tipped her head again to the sky and the sun was hot and bright against her closed eyes.

'Keep this space with me,' she whispered. 'Guide me in your ways that are my own ways also, so that I may learn the harmony of the world, the turning of the wheel, the singing of our spirits.'

She let her arms float down and bowed her head. 'North, south, east, and west,' she said. 'Above, below, and inwards. World upon world upon world.'

Erin opened her eyes and found herself staring into Macha's face.

'Wha...?' she asked.

Macha smiled, her green-brown eyes bright amidst the swirls of her tattoos.

Erin licked her lips.

'You called, did you not?' Macha asked.

Erin looked at her, nodded.

'Who were you expecting?' Macha asked, her smile widening in amusement.

'Fox, perhaps,' Erin said. 'Or the old woman.' She dragged her gaze away from Macha and looked around. 'Where are we?'

She turned and looked behind them, saw in the distance, her garden gate, and felt the lightening of relief.

'We are ready to follow the paths of the Wildwood,'

Macha said. 'And you will meet many here along the way, such as the Old Woman, but it will be myself who will lead you on your quest to remember – and Fox, of course.' She looked down beside Erin, where Fox stood, snout sharp and whiskers quivering.

Erin, nonplussed, didn't know what to say. She followed Macha's gaze and found Fox there, who looked back at her, baring her teeth in what could only be a grin.

'Okay,' Erin said. 'What do we do first?'

'We begin,' Macha said, and turned, striding away.

Erin, startled, scurried after her. 'We begin doing what?'

Macha looked over her shoulder. 'Fewer questions,' she said. 'More attention.'

Erin widened her eyes at the rebuke but pressed her lips closed over all the questions that tumbled around in her brain. She drew breath instead and focussed her attention on the scenery.

She didn't recognise any of it. Wherever she was, it certainly wasn't the same place Fox had taken her the last time. No calm, lovely lake. No conical island in the middle.

And speaking of Fox, she was walking beside Erin, her beautiful orange fur rippling as she trotted along. Erin was very glad for her.

Otherwise, they walked through woods, much like the ones back in Wellsford. Only, Erin didn't recognise the path, and there was something else too, something perhaps about the air, that was different.

It was a different place entirely, she concluded.

But where were they going and what were they doing?

Macha didn't seem in a hurry to answer Erin's questions, simply giving a shake of the head whenever Erin asked anything – or even opened her mouth to ask. So Erin tucked her head down and followed, feeling simultaneously exhilarated and apprehensive to be blindly following Macha, not knowing what was ahead.

They walked for what might have been hours, or only minutes. Erin stepped along behind Macha and relaxed, keeping her breathing steady, herself firmly in spirit. She felt as though she were in a vivid dream and looked down at her skirts, shaking her head. It was so real, she thought.

But it had been the same way when she'd visited Kria, had it not?

And when she'd gone with Winsome after Morghan.

She took a deep breath.

It was real.

'We are here,' Macha said suddenly, and Erin, roused from her thoughts, looked up blinking. They had stepped out of the woods and the sunlight was a soft haze in the air.

'Where are we?' Erin asked, staring about herself. 'Where's here?'

They stood on a high bank, overlooking a great spread of land, and in the distance, a sight that made Erin squint in perplexity.

'What is that place?' she asked.

Macha, leaning casually against her staff, turned her gaze to Erin. 'That place is your task,' she said.

Erin looked at her, alarmed. 'My task?' She shook her head and looked out again over the land. 'But what is it? It looks like a...maze or something.'

That was exactly what it looked like. A great stone maze. Dug down into the ground and at least the size of a football field.

Her mouth was dry. She cleared her throat. 'What am I supposed to do?' she asked.

Macha's answer was firm. 'Go there.'

Erin shook her head. 'Go there?' she said. 'But how? It must be miles away.' It would take her all day to walk that far. And no matter that time was different here in the Otherworld, she couldn't rely on that.

'I've got to go to work,' she said.

'This is your task,' Macha told her, implacable.

'I don't understand it.'

Macha waved a hand at the faraway maze. 'You must find your way there and do what needs to be done when you are there. See what needs to be seen. Understand what needs to be understood.'

But Erin didn't even understand these directions and she shook her head. 'Will you come with me?' she asked.

'No.' Macha shook her head. 'I am here as guide only. These are tasks I have already done, in my own time.' She smiled and the spirals drawn on her cheeks rippled. 'This is your initiation, Erin. Your remembering.'

Erin peered over the edge of the cliff. It was a very long way down. 'It seems impossible,' she said. 'How do I get down there?' She twisted her neck to look down to the left, then the right. 'There's no way down.' The cliff seemed to stretch on forever.

But Macha was silent, the task set.

Erin glanced over at her, but the woman stared back, brows raised, face smooth. Erin shook her head. 'I'll have to come back,' she said. 'I don't have time to walk all that way.' She chewed her bottom lip for a moment. 'I have to go to work.'

Macha stared at her for a long moment, and Erin felt her cheeks flare with heat under the inscrutable gaze.

'As you wish, then,' Macha said at last. 'Remember this place, however. We will be back.' She repeated her earlier words. 'This is your task.' She paused. 'Your first task.'

'Oh, great,' Erin groaned.

And suddenly Macha was grasping her arm, fingers hard against her skin.

'Stiffen your spine,' she hissed before letting go.

Erin looked at her, rubbing the soft flesh of her upper arm where Macha's fingers had dug in.

Macha stared at her. 'It irks me to hear you whine and moan. Where is your spirit? Your sense of adventure? We have done great things and are capable of much more – but you must take it seriously.'

'I take it seriously!'

'You've a long way to go,' Macha said on a sigh.

Erin turned around to look back the way they'd come. 'That's because I have only begun,' she said coldly. 'Now take me back. I've other responsibilities to see to.'

Macha startled Erin by laughing. 'It is true,' she said. 'You have only just begun, and I would do well to remember this.'

The unexpected pronouncement made Erin gape at Macha.

'What?' she said.

Picking up her staff, Macha strode back into the trees, unerringly finding the path they'd taken. 'Impatience always was my downfall,' she said, laughing again.

Erin shook her head, even as she fell in behind the priestess from another time, another lifetime. 'I don't understand you,' she said. 'I might be whiny – a little bit – but you...' She frowned, trying to find the right words. 'You're...a mystery to me,' she said finally.

'I am a part of you that is yet a mystery to yourself,' Macha said, then glanced back over her shoulder. 'But you are learning, and well. I will give you that.'

'Gee,' Erin said. 'Thanks.'

Macha stopped walking and for a moment Erin thought she would reach out and shake her again, but instead Macha only sighed.

'What?' Erin asked.

Another sigh. 'A priestess does not speak that way,' Macha said, then turned for the path again.

Erin, pressing her lips together and frowning, walked silently behind her.

18

ERIN FOLLOWED BURDOCK INTO THE BEDROOM. 'GOOD morning, Wayne,' she said, and watched as Burdock tried his hardest to lick Wayne's cheeks in his own greeting.

'Call your dog off, will ya!' Wayne said, but he was laughing, tussling with Burdock.

This had become their daily habit.

'I have no control over the dog,' Erin said primly. 'Are you ready for our big day?'

'Is it warm out?' Wayne asked, patting Burdock's head where he'd rested it peacefully on Wayne's knee. 'I'm too damned thin for anything but the Bahamas these days.'

His voice was gruff, belying the fact that he was thrilled about the prospect of getting outside.

'The sun is out,' Erin said, then wrinkled her nose dubiously. 'It's not the Bahamas though, by a long shot.'

Wayne glanced at her. 'Sun out will do,' he said and patted the dog again. He wanted to reach out and grasp Erin's hand, and give her fingers a squeeze.

He'd never imagined he'd be here, feeling this way.

Feeling...okay. Not brilliant, but not so...burdened.

He looked quickly down at Burdock, glad for the distraction of the dog as hot tears suddenly threatened to squeeze out from behind his lids.

Really, he was ridiculously emotional these days. He cleared his throat.

'I think you'll be fine as long as you wear your warm jacket,' Erin said, going to the wardrobe and plucking it from the coat hanger. She'd bought it for him herself, and it was snug, lined for warmth. She took it over to where Wayne Moffat sat on his bed.

'Do you want a hand shaving before we head out to the wide world?'

Wayne lifted a hand and felt the stubble on his cheeks. 'No,' he decided. 'I want that coffee and cake you've been promising me.'

Erin laughed. 'Coffee and cake coming up. Pop this on, though, because we'll have to sit outside.'

Wayne snorted, standing up and taking the jacket, threading his arms into the sleeves. 'Rules around everything, these days.'

'Ah,' Erin replied. 'But it's paying off.'

'You get jabbed too, then?'

'I did,' Erin said. 'Almost everyone in Wellsford has had the vaccination now, so we'll be safe enough today – but we're still going to sit outside and get some of that vitamin D shining on you.'

. . .

BURDOCK LED THE WAY DOWN THE STREET TO THE COPPER Kettle, his thin tail whipping from side to side as he cleared the footpath for his people behind him.

Wayne lifted his face to the sun. 'This feels better than almost anything,' he said, soaking in the warmth. He had been pretty sure he wouldn't be around for another summer, and yet, here he was. Walking down the street to have a cup of coffee and a piece of cake with a pretty girl hanging on his arm. He glanced at Erin.

A girl who might have been, in a parallel world, perhaps, his daughter. Stepdaughter, but still.

He swallowed down the sudden lump in his throat.

'When's the pub opening, then?' he asked.

Erin squeezed his arm. 'You know I'm not going to let you go drinking there,' she said.

'I could have a lemonade,' Wayne said innocently. Truth was, he had no desire to drink anymore. It had left him completely, the urge to drown his sorrows, and he couldn't say he was sad to see the back of it.

Not sad at all.

'Isn't your boyfriend going to sing with his band for the opening celebrations?' Wayne asked, knowing full well the lad was. He just liked hearing Erin chatter away to him. She was a great girl.

An incredible girl, really. To have come to terms with, well, what he'd done.

Some days – most days – he could hardly fathom it.

And yet, here they were, her arm tucked under his, even if it was mostly to steady him as he walked down the short path to the shops.

The Copper Kettle had a lovely little courtyard, and tables set out there, a nice distance away from each other, Wayne thought. Less chance of hearing other people's yapping, and them hearing his.

There was even a dog bowl in the corner, from which Burdock took great noisy gulps, before coming to sit at Erin's side. He knew how to behave at The Copper Kettle, and that if he did, there was usually a treat that came just for him, along with the order of human food.

'Hello Erin,' Lucy said, an apron tied around her waist and a pencil stuck in her messy bun of hair. 'Lovely day to be out, isn't it?' She looked at Wayne and her smile widened. 'You must be Mr. Moffat,' she said. 'Erin said she was bringing you here for some of our cake just as soon as she could.'

Wayne coloured and hoped his whiskers would cover the blush. 'Our Erin's a charmer,' he said. 'And she says your cake is the best she's ever eaten.'

Erin laughed. 'Which means we'll have two nice thick slices please, Lucy. And coffee.' She lifted her eyebrows at Wayne. 'What sort of coffee would you like?'

'Oh. Ah, just a flat white would be lovely,' he said.

'And I'll have my usual,' Erin added.

They sat for a moment after Lucy had bustled away to wrestle with the espresso machine, and soaked up the still, clear light.

'I've something to show you, Wayne,' Erin said suddenly, reaching for her bag and digging around in it.

Wayne sat forward eagerly. The sunlight on his head, the smell of coffee, the great shaggy dog by his side – and

Erin, looking for something to show him, of all people – he couldn't believe his luck. What had he done to deserve this?

He coughed and shoved the thought away. He hadn't done anything, but by god, he was trying to make amends.

'What is it?' he asked, and his voice was rough with feeling again.

'These!' Erin pronounced, producing the fan of cards from Krista, and spreading them out on the table. 'What do you think?'

Wayne's eyes widened. 'These are your pictures,' he said. Then shook his head. 'Didn't I say you were talented?'

Erin looked over the spray of cards with an assessing eye. Yes, she decided. They were lovely. 'I'm kind of proud of them,' she said, then shook her head. 'Seeing them like this, made into something someone can take home with them, put on the mantel or whatever, or post to a friend...' She trailed off, then smiled. 'It's a good feeling. It's different than having them just in my sketchbook, you know? They're somehow more real, now.'

Wayne sifted through them with clumsy hands. He stopped at the one with Fox twitching her tail in front of a wrought-iron gate, and smiled. 'She looks like you, this little vixen,' he said.

'She's my kin, that's why,' Erin answered.

Wayne nodded. Erin had told him a bit of the things she was doing. Her imaginary garden. She wanted him to try it, he'd thought. And the fox who was some sort of spirit companion. He thought it was all a bit odd and strange, to be honest, but was also alarmed to find that there was a growing part of him that accepted it as...real.

Especially after what he'd been through. That Morghan

woman retrieving the bit of him that had been stuck in that basement. He shivered, despite the sun and his thick jacket.

Maybe there was something to it, for all that.

Erin certainly thought so. He looked over at her clear, fine face, the something around her eyes that reminded him of her mother.

'Are these ones for sale?' he asked. He didn't have much, but he could buy one of these cards from Erin.

But Erin shook her head and laughed. 'These are just samples,' she said.

Wayne cleared his throat. 'Can I have one?' he asked. 'I'll buy one from you?'

'Of course you can have one,' Erin said, and reached over to touch his hand that was knotted into a fist on the table. 'Any one you like, and no paying for it. There are going to be a lot more of these.' She looked with satisfaction at the spread of cards. 'You can have more than one, if you like?'

But Wayne shook his head. 'One will do fine, love,' he said. He nodded towards the one with the Fox. 'She looks like she's just waiting for you to follow her through the gate and on to a grand adventure.'

'She is,' Erin said, remembering the journey they'd gone on just that morning. And her task.

'I'll have that one, then, if I may,' Wayne said. 'She reminds me of you.' He blinked. 'Makes me think I wouldn't mind an animal kin of my own.' He gave a gruff laugh to make sure Erin knew he wasn't being serious.

'But you do have an animal kin of your own,' Erin said. 'Morghan tells me everyone does.'

Lucy arrived with their order, and a treat for Burdock.

She set the cake and coffee down on the table, slipped a grateful Burdock his beefy stick, and looked with pleasure at Erin and Wayne. 'Anything else you need, just give me a yell,' she said.

'Thanks, Lucy,' Erin answered.

But Lucy had spotted the cards and gazed at them in delight. 'Are these what I think they are, Erin?' she asked. 'Oh, but they're wonderful.'

'They're going to be for sale in Haven for Books,' Erin said.

'She's a talented artist,' Wayne said, feeling pride swelling up inside his chest. He puffed it out.

'That she is,' Lucy breathed. 'These are beautiful. Have you ever thought of illustrating oracle cards, or even a tarot deck, Erin?'

'Oracle cards?' Erin asked, brows lifted in surprise. 'I've never even used oracle cards or the tarot.' She shook her head.

'You'd make gorgeous illustrations for some,' Lucy said, straightening. 'I'd use them every day, with pictures like those.'

'Wow,' Erin said. 'I'd never thought about it.'

'You should,' Lucy told her. 'Right, duty calls – enjoy your morning tea.'

Erin stared after Lucy then turned to Wayne and shook her head.

'She's right,' Wayne said. 'I don't know what oracle cards are, but I reckon you'll illustrate anything beautifully.'

Erin laughed suddenly, thinking of her mother deciding that she should one day do children's picture books. Well, this was the farthest thing from that Erin reckoned you could get.

'Maybe I will,' Erin said, looking over her greeting cards and sighing. 'I'll pop over to Haven later and look at the decks that Krista has.' She shook her head. 'I don't know why I've never thought to use anything like that.'

'What are they then, these cards?' Wayne asked.

'The tarot at least, is a really old system of telling the future,' Erin said. Then she shook her head. 'Probably not telling the future, really, but talking to yourself and spirit.' She blew out a breath and picked up her coffee cup. 'Like runes, I expect.'

Wayne didn't ask what runes were but picked up his fork to take a bite of cake. He didn't really care what Erin talked about. He was happy just to be outside enjoying the sun and her company.

'So how was your morning?' he asked. 'How's that boyfriend of yours?' He tipped her a wink and smiled slyly. 'I bet you're enjoying seeing a bit more of each other.'

Erin let herself smile. 'Just a bit,' she said. Then her face clouded.

'What's the matter?' Wayne asked. 'You're not having a tiff with him already, are you?'

'Oh, good grief no,' Erin said. 'Everything's great with Stephan. More than great, actually.' She looked down at her cake, brows drawn together. 'Wayne, what's the best way to get down a cliff, do you think?'

Wayne's eyes widened. 'A cliff? What do you mean?' He looked around as though a cliff might suddenly have materialised, but of course one hadn't. There was only the courtyard, a trellis with some sort of scented, flowering vine twining its way all over it, and the village green behind them. Burdock lifted his head from where he'd stretched out on the grass in the sun, looked at him for a moment, then flopped back down to sleep.

'Well,' Erin said, swallowing a mouthful of chocolate cake. 'Imagine that you were standing on top of a cliff, which, by the way, stretches out for miles, and you had to get down. Only it's really, really high.'

'Why would I want to imagine that?' Wayne asked.

Erin considered for a moment. 'So, it's like a task, right? A puzzle.'

A puzzle all right, Wayne thought. 'Well, you'd need special equipment,' he said. 'Like climbers have, wouldn't you?'

'But what if you don't have any of that?' Erin asked, sipping at her coffee and sighing.

'Then you'd have to go around, wouldn't you? A cliff can't go on forever, can it? Somewhere along the way, it's got to turn into something else.'

Erin nodded. She'd had that thought too. 'I agree. But I think I need a quicker way.' She gave a hollow laugh. It wasn't as though she could jump or fly down, was it?

'You need yourself a pair of wings, then,' Wayne said. 'A hang glider, or something.'

'A pair of wings.' Erin beamed a sudden, dazzling smile at Wayne. 'You're brilliant,' she said. 'A pair of wings.' She took another bite of cake, chewed, swallowed, and nodded again. 'That is exactly what I need.'

Wayne looked dubiously at her. 'You're not really serious, are you?' He flashed on all the things that could go wrong jumping off a cliff, even with a hang glider.

'Not literally, no,' Erin said. 'I mean, I need to, but the cliff is in the Otherworld.'

That made Wayne pause for a moment. He wasn't sure he believed in this Otherworld of Erin's, but he wasn't sure he didn't, either. It would have been a tricky position, but he was just happy to go along with whatever Erin believed, so that they could talk together.

'So,' he said, and mushed some chocolate cake crumbs with his fork. 'You have to find your way down a cliff? To do what?'

Erin sighed, not at the question, but because she had no idea of the answer. 'I don't know, exactly,' she said. 'There's this big cliff, which I have to find a way down from, and then a long walk, and way in the distance, there's what looks like a maze.'

'A maze?' Wayne squinted at her. 'I don't get it.'

That made Erin laugh. 'You and me both.' She shook her head. 'I thought I'd be learning stuff, when I finally followed Fox into the Wildwood, you know?' She picked up her cup. 'But it's all just puzzle after puzzle.' Her face fell suddenly.

Wayne, attuned finely to her moods, spotted it instantly. 'What is it?' he asked.

Another shake of the head, but Erin answered. 'I got given some sort of warning, or message, last time I journeyed,' she said. 'Only, I don't know what it's about.'

'A warning?'

She frowned into her coffee. 'I'm not sure, but it talked about coming to a standstill, probably – possibly? – because of something, and having to get through it.'

Wayne snorted. 'Sounds like everyday life to me,' he said.

'Your life and mine,' Erin laughed. She tipped her coffee cup towards him. 'Here's to us, and the whole great mess of things.'

Wayne toasted her back, and grinned, the sun warm on his back.

19

Erin wasn't sure how she ought to go about doing what she was considering. She looked down at Burdock and gave him a pat. He was warm from lying in the sun and leant against her, solid and comforting.

'I always wanted a dog,' Erin said, toying with his ears while he put up with it good-naturedly. 'And now I have the biggest, most wonderful dog in the world.'

Burdock pressed more heavily against her, liking the tone of her voice. She was saying sweet things to him, he knew. He licked her hand.

I love you too, he told her.

'And now,' Erin said, sitting out in her garden after work, the air sweet and low and warm, and fragrant with herbs. 'Now, I have you, and Fox as well.' She looked over at the wall surrounding the garden, where two ravens were bustling about, feathers fluffed up with self-importance.

'And possibly a bird of some sort,' Erin mused.

A bird. She drew in a deep breath, remembering the first

time Morghan had taken her on the trek around the hills to where they could see the ocean. And how they'd grounded and centred themselves, then called their feathered kin to their sides.

A seagull had come to her. First, there had been a raven, but then Erin had blinked, and the seagull had come instead.

Kria's seagull.

Erin swallowed at the memory of Kria and reached into her pocket to pull out the small bag she carried around with her all the time now. Her fingers plucked at the drawstring, and she tipped the bag up to empty out the six small stones.

Diamonds, she thought, holding them up to the sun.

Not real diamonds, of course, but clear chips of quartz crystal to remind her of the Goddess's gift.

They glittered and sparkled in the lowering sun.

This is how brightly I can shine, Erin thought, watching how the stones glinted and reflected the sun.

'Me,' she said. 'The bright, essential, immortal me.'

It was hard, she thought, putting the crystals back in their bag and returning it to her pocket, to reconcile that image of herself with sitting here in a body that she had to feed, toilet, walk around. Her lips curved in a sudden smile.

But it could dance, this body of hers.

It could reach for the sky, shimmy in the sea, dance upon the earth.

It could laugh, make love, do a hundred things. It could shine too. Body and spirit entwined.

Erin sighed.

Should she go back to the hill overlooking the faraway sea to try what she had in mind? Or should she go back out the gate from her garden and into the Otherworld and try it there and then at the cliff?

Erin considered Macha's watchful, knowing gaze. She patted Burdock again.

'The hillside,' she said. 'That way you can come with me, and I can have a practice go. Right?'

'Go where?' Stephan asked, coming up to where she sat and stretching the kinks out of his body. He'd been up on old man McKenzie's place with Martin and Ambrose, talking about their rewilding plans. They wanted to extend the woods, right along the back of Martin and Charlie's place, and out to most of the McKenzie farm.

He settled down happily beside Erin, wrapped an arm around her, and with his other, gave Burdock a good scratching.

'Where are we going?' he repeated.

Erin laughed and rested her head on his shoulder. 'I didn't hear you come in,' she said.

'You were miles away and I am light on my feet.' Stephan sought her lips and kissed her, thinking she was never not going to taste sweeter than berries to him.

Erin told him about her travelling, and her idea for getting down the cliffside.

'Wayne thought of it, really, or at least, he gave me the idea for it.'

Stephan nodded. 'It's a good one,' he agreed. 'The right one, I'd say. Makes perfect sense.'

'What do you think the maze is about?'

That question made Stephan rub his chin as he thought. He shrugged. 'Haven't a clue,' he said. 'Have you asked Morghan about it?'

Erin shook her head. 'I haven't seen her today.' She pushed her hair back from her face. 'Besides, she probably wouldn't tell me, even if she knew.'

'She'd know.'

Erin nodded, thinking Stephan was likely right. 'She still wouldn't tell me. She'd say it was my task to find my way there and decipher what it is about, and what I need to do.'

'Yeah,' Stephan agreed. 'You're right. It's not a task – an initiation – if someone gives you all the answers.' He yawned. 'Are you going up there now?'

Erin squinted at the sky, where the sun was drawing down close to the treeline. 'It's too late, I think. It's an hour's walk just to get there and I don't fancy coming back down in the dark.'

'Moon will be out,' Stephan answered.

'Are you offering to come too?'

But Stephan yawned again. 'If you're set on going tonight, then definitely.'

'I'm not.' She shook her head. 'I think it's a day off sort of thing.' She nudged Stephan. 'For both of us. You're tired.'

Stephan did not disagree.

THEY WENT TOGETHER, A COUPLE DAYS LATER WHEN NEITHER had to be at work, and Burdock led the way, tail waving like a stick, his grinning face turning every now and then to urge them on as the sun rose over the hills.

'I am the fittest I've ever been,' Erin said, coming to a stop on a grassy bank overlooking the far sea. 'All this walking and climbing and going everywhere by foot.'

Stephan slung an arm around her. 'It's good for you. Bet you don't even miss your car.'

'Don't go that far,' Erin laughed. 'Walking to work in the dead of winter was not always a fun thing, and I don't want to repeat it next year.'

'We'll have a car by then,' Stephan said, the words falling casually from his mouth, without thought.

Erin looked at him. 'We?'

He shrugged. 'You, me, we, whichever suits,' he said, then changed the subject, not willing to push. 'It's gorgeous up here,' he smiled.

Erin gave him another look, then let it go and breathed in the early morning, drawing it deep into her lungs as she looked out over the sea, at the bank of clouds on the horizon like a thick, white wall. 'Will the weather hold, do you think?'

'Long enough,' Stephan answered. He swung the rucksack off his back, unzipped it and got out Burdock's bowl, found a good spot for it, and filled it with water. 'There you go, chum,' he said, and backed away in a hurry when Burdock stuck his nose in the water to take a great gulping, messy drink from it.

'Right, buddy,' he said. 'That's you settled.' Stephan looked over at Erin. 'How do you want to start, then?'

For a moment, Erin shrank back, feeling her skin pull tight with embarrassment at attempting the shapeshifting in Stephan's presence, but she shook it off. She was being silly – didn't she do things with Morghan watching her? Didn't she and Stephan, every morning that they'd spent together, go into the garden and greet the day and the world, and do their daily devotions together?

She swallowed. Took a breath, gathered her courage. 'Are you going to try this with me?' she asked. 'Or just watch?'

'I'm going to try it with you,' Stephan said. 'I've never flown as a bird before.'

Erin nodded. 'Do you think a bird will come to you?'

'Yeah,' he answered. 'Why not? I bet we all have birds as kin.'

'I'm still not quite sure if mine is Raven or Seagull,' Erin confessed. She straightened her shoulders. 'So it will be interesting to find out.'

Stephan grinned at her. 'It's going to be great,' he said. 'Let's get to it.'

'All right,' Erin answered. 'We start simply, I think, with grounding and centring.' She cast back, trying to remember what she and Morghan had done after that. Hadn't they reached for the sun? She pursed her lips. Did they need to do that this time, too?

'Heck,' she muttered. 'Why not?'

She found a good place to stand, the hill at her back, the sea spreading out in front of her, the clouds crowding the horizon. Stephan came and stood next to her, close enough that she could feel him, but just out of touching distance, so that they would have space to move.

Erin cleared her throat. 'We are here,' she said. 'At this place where sea meets land and sky.' She swallowed, let herself glance over at Stephan, but he wasn't looking at her. Rather, he stood relaxed, face to the sky, eyes closed, chest rising slowly and evenly. She could feel him relaxing, breathing the world in, spreading his spirit.

He wouldn't laugh at her for speaking, for saying the words as they came to her.

'We are here,' she said, 'at this time when day grows upon the land. This is the liminal time, and this is the liminal space, and here we can pierce the veil.' She licked her lips.

'We are here to exercise our gift of true sight,' she said. 'And to call our kin to us. Both furred and feathered.'

They stood in the clearing on the side of the hill, shaking the tension out of hands and arms, loosening their shoulders. They slowed their breathing until it was deep and unhurried, inhaling and holding the scent of soil under their feet, the breath of salt upon the air, the warming sunlight. They let their breath out in the same, considered measure, and cleared themselves of clogging and discordant energy, grounding themselves upon the ancient, humming, hillside, feeling it under their feet, the ancient wisdom of the earth.

'We are here, where we are,' Erin said, stretching her arms towards the sky, as Stephan did the same, following her lead. 'We connect to the world through our hearts.'

Stephan glanced over at her, a smile on his lips to echo the one in his eyes.

She smiled back at him.

'We connect to the world through our hearts,' she repeated. 'We thread ourselves deep down into the earth, digging into the dirt under our feet and deep into the world of stone and soil.'

Erin breathed out, feeling herself reach down into the depths under her feet. 'We seek the sacred fire and heart of the earth,' she said, almost whispering. 'We touch it with our thread and a spark ignites us.' Her eyes were closed, but she was deep in the world. 'It does not singe or burn, but illuminates,' she said, 'And we draw this spark up the thread of ourselves and into our heart. We are connected to the world upon which we walk.'

She licked her lips, breathing in, feeling the fire brighten inside herself. 'Into our hearts,' she continued, 'and then upwards, through the top of our heads.'

Her mind filled with fire and light and she glowed. Erin reached her arms up to the sky.

'We send this spark from deep in the heart of the earth, through ourselves, and upwards to the sun, where the flame of the sun is there to meet it, twin sparks now, joined together, and we draw them back down into our hearts, where they fill us with light, tethered between the heart of the planet and the heart of the sun, and we are the spark that walks between the two.'

Stephan breathed in light. He breathed it out. Light poured from behind his eyes, from the pores in his skin, radiating outwards from his heart. He was the bridge between earth and sky, he was the connection. His mind ceased thought and became brilliant, pure, clean, and his heart pounded with the glory of the light. He took a breath.

'The spark of the earth sinks back down our threads and into the burning heart of the world,' Erin said, her breath made of light. 'The spark of the sun returns up our threads to the flaming heart of the sky.'

She breathed again, slowly, deeply, filling her chest. 'We bring our threads back to ourselves,' she said. 'And we are here, where we began, standing where we are, between sun and earth.'

Stephan reached across until his fingers touched hers, their skin almost sizzling. She smiled at him, seeing how he glowed still.

'This is where we are,' she repeated. 'This is the way we sing our connection with the world.'

Her voice hitched a moment, as she considered how to do what came next.

'Breathe,' Stephan murmured, his voice a gentle reminder.

She nodded slowly, deepening her breath once more, letting a wellspring of joy flood through her body until it brought a broad smile to her face.

'Come to us, our friends,' she called, her voice the sound of a wing beating upon a breeze.

But it was not her voice that beat upon the wind, but wings, and she opened her mouth again. 'Come to us, our friends,' she called. 'Come to us on the wind, come to us with the beating of heart and wing.'

Her eyes were closed, but she could see perfectly well, and her lips curved in recognition at the raven that swept down from the sky to fill her inner vision. She reached for him, admiring his dark feathers, bright eyes, his outstretched wings.

Raven caught her up in his strong, clawed feet, and hoisted her into the air with him and the wind streamed through her hair, through her feathers as she beat her wings, lifting into the sky over the hill, heeling over first one way to swoop and dive, then the other, flying in great loops over the hill.

Erin laughed, opening her beak, and spread her feathered fingers wide, feeling the whoosh of wind lift and toss her, and flapped her wings, bones light and strong under her fringe of feathers. She swooped and opened her mouth, her whoop of delight a loud cawing.

And then there was a glitter of jewelled feathers, humming wings like a bee's and Erin's sharp raven sight took in the vision of Stephan dressed in the shining, gleaming feathers of a hummingbird.

Stephan fluttered and twirled, sending his small, light, agile body spinning about Erin's black feathers in a dance that made both shiver and laugh with delight.

They danced together in the sky over the hill, the sea dancing to shore behind them, the sun rising to the side, and on the grass beneath them, Burdock watched them, his doggy brows furrowed at their fun.

And beside him, drenching his senses with the smell of their magic, Fox and Hare watched also.

20

Stephan put a hand on Erin's wrist, bringing her steps to a halt.

'What is it?' Erin asked, but he shook his head.

'We'll startle her,' Stephan said, gesturing with his chin at the stone circle and catching Burdock by his collar.

Erin, who had been busy watching where she was putting her feet, and thinking over and over of flying, the wind in her feathers, looping and soaring while Stephan danced about her, dressed in the bright plumage of a hummingbird, more beautiful than rubies, looked across the clearing at the stones.

Clarice was dancing between them, and Erin remembered suddenly the first time she'd been in ritual with the Grove, and how Clarice had danced with Stephan, a bright white star twirling around and around and around until Erin had been dizzy.

'What do we do?' Erin whispered, unwilling to admit to the fact that she was a little afraid of Clarice.

Clarice who could be tart of tongue, and who kept to herself, stalking the woods with her owl, and who was a member of the Fae Queen's court.

'Nothing,' Stephan said. 'I just didn't want us to walk right into her.' He stepped out of the trees into the clearing. 'Hey, Clarice,' he called, announcing their presence.

Clarice stopped dancing, dropping her hands and coming to a standstill. Burdock rushed over to her, his tail wagging furiously as he pressed himself against her legs.

Erin blinked at her. Clarice wore sunglasses, loose trousers green as the grass that had swirled around her legs, and a tee shirt as milky white as her skin and hair. 'You dance so beautifully,' she breathed.

Stephan walked over to the circle, put his hands on one of the stones as though saying hello for a moment, then leant against it and grinned at Clarice. 'You know Krista is looking for someone to lead the sacred dance classes she wants to run, don't you?' he asked. 'Now that things are going to be opening up.'

Clarice lifted her eyes from Burdock and narrowed them at Stephan. 'You know I can't do that,' she said.

'Why?' Erin breathed. 'You dance so wonderfully. I wish I was half as coordinated as you.'

But Clarice shook her head. 'What are you two doing up here anyway?'

Stephan glanced back at Erin. 'Flying,' he said.

'Flying?'

'Oh, have you tried it?' Erin asked, coming up and leaning against Stephan, gazing up at him with a smile on her face for a moment. 'It's amazing.'

'Flying?' Clarice repeated.

'As your kin,' Erin said. 'Morghan taught me to do it a couple months ago, but this was only the second time I've tried it.' She took a breath and shook her head. 'I felt so light and free,' she said.

Clarice frowned. She'd never tried to fly. And while Sigil was her kin, she was also flesh and feather. 'What sort of bird were you?' she asked.

'Raven came for me,' Erin answered, then smiled again at Stephan, curling her arm around his back. 'And Stephan here was the most brightly-coloured hummingbird.'

'A hummingbird?' Clarice laughed.

'I'm sure hummingbird has many lessons to teach us,' Erin said, grinning at Stephan. She turned to look at Clarice. 'We're going down to Haven now, to see if we can find out any information about Hummingbird.'

'Yeah, and we thought we'd sit outside and have whatever is on the menu for lunch at The Copper Kettle,' Stephan said. 'Neither of us have to work today.' He looked at Clarice. 'Come with us,' he said.

She shook her head, long white hair rippling against her shoulders. 'No,' she said. 'I'd rather not.' Clarice bared her teeth in a smile. 'Besides, I wouldn't want to cramp the love-bird's style.'

Erin laughed and let her arm drop from around Stephan's waist. Burdock came and sat beside her. 'Do come,' she said, sure suddenly that Clarice was lonely, although she didn't know how or why she felt that. 'Come and have some lunch with us - I'd really like that.' She glanced back at Stephan. 'So would Stephan.'

Clarice looked at him.

'You bet,' Stephan said.

Clarice looked down at her feet. They were bare in the grass. She didn't want to go into the village, did she?

But Morghan had asked her to pick up a book for her, hadn't she? From Haven. Clarice cleared her throat.

'All right,' she said.

'Yeah?' Stephan couldn't keep the surprise out of his voice and Clarice glared a moment at him until he shrugged and held up his hands in surrender. 'That's great, I mean,' he said.

'Yes,' Erin said. 'And even if you don't take Krista's dance class - maybe we could talk about giving me some private lessons?'

She hadn't known she wanted to be able to dance the way that Clarice could until right now, but it was suddenly true.

Clarice walked over to the pile of her clothes and jammed her feet into socks and boots, then pulled a long-sleeved shirt over the pale skin on her arms where the blue tattoos wound in spirals the same colour as her veins.

'I can teach you,' she found herself saying to Erin. She shook her head. 'I've got a lot of spare time at the moment.'

Erin lit up. 'You would?' she said. 'You and Stephan were magnificent doing the Bear dance.' She shook her head. 'I'll never forget it. I'd never seen anything like it.'

'Dance is a good way to connect with spirit,' Clarice said. 'And just to make yourself feel better too.' Which is why she was out at the circle right now. Dancing made her feel better, especially when she could feel depression sliding up behind her like a dark shadow. It was hard keeping it at bay, without being able to cross over to the Fair Lands.

But maybe teaching Erin to dance would be okay. It

might help, give her something to do. And Erin was okay. A bit clueless sometimes, but then she was only starting out, really. And kind of thrown in the deep end. She didn't have the luxury of being brought up on the Path. Clarice looked at her through the curtain of her hair and watched Erin as she was smiling at Stephan, sharing some private feeling. A strong feeling – Clarice could almost see it between them.

She cleared her throat and the two lovebirds jumped away from each other and turned red faces towards her.

'Shall we go, then?' she said, then frowned. 'I don't have my bag – we'll have to stop in at the house.'

'No problem,' Stephan said easily, leading them off down the path towards Hawthorn House.

Erin sidled up closer to Clarice, who smelled pleasantly of sunscreen. 'I'm glad you're coming,' she said, her voice low. 'We've never really spent any time together, but you're such a part of the Grove, I want to.'

Clarice gazed at Erin, her clear hazel eyes, then looked away and shrugged. 'I'm not part of the Grove like you are,' she said. Because it was true. Not that she wanted to be the next Lady of the Grove. Morghan had asked her if she did, and she most decidedly did not.

'No,' Erin said. 'You've been part of it most of your life, and I've only just arrived.' She sighed. 'I haven't been to the Fair Lands yet. What's it like?' She blinked in the dappled light of the trees. 'I mean, is it like in the stories – as beautiful as that?'

Clarice stared down at her feet. It still hurt, almost a physical pain in her side, right under her heart, that she had been banned from the Queen's realm. She nodded. 'It's as beautiful as the stories tell you,' she said.

'Must be amazing, to go back and forth from there, and to be able to see the Fae as a matter of course.' Erin looked around as though she would be able to see one appearing beside them.

'I don't know if it's amazing,' Clarice said, drawn into the conversation despite herself. 'I've always been able to do it.' She glanced ahead, past Stephan into the trees. 'And it's not like they're hanging around here all the time. There are certain places where you find them.' She stopped talking, lifted her shoulders in a tight shrug. 'It's complicated,' she said.

Erin nodded, barked a little laugh. 'Everything is complicated,' she said. 'Everything is...*more*...than I ever thought.'

'I bet,' Clarice said, finding herself curious despite herself. 'Did you have any inkling, or talents, or anything before you came here?'

Erin didn't answer straight away. She wrapped her arms around herself and kept walking. Finally, she cleared her throat and answered. 'I had dreams that came true,' she said. 'And...and sometimes I got...lost.'

Clarice looked at her, realising suddenly that she'd probably put her foot in it with her question. She stopped walking. 'Listen,' she said. 'I'm sorry. I didn't mean to pry.' Maybe she wasn't the only one who had trouble fitting into the world.

Except Erin fitted now, didn't she?

And Clarice had been banished from the one place she felt comfortable.

Erin was shaking her head. 'No,' she said. 'It's all right. It was just hard, you know?' She started walking again and watched as the trees thinned and Hawthorn House appeared on its green stretch of lawn.

Clarice looked towards the house and nodded. 'Yeah,' she said. 'I know how it can be.' She sighed. 'Look, maybe I'll give this a miss, all right?'

'Oh,' Erin said, her face falling. 'No, please come – we'd love it if you did, wouldn't we, Stephan?'

'Of course,' Stephan said. 'And Krista said something about a book that's come in for Morghan. You could pick it up for her.'

The mention of Krista's name made Clarice turn her head away, ignoring Stephan's deliberately innocent look.

'Fine,' she said. 'Wait here, and I'll grab my bag.'

CLARICE TRAILED THROUGH THE DOORWAY OF HAVEN FOR Books behind Erin and Stephan, her dark sunglasses on and a hat pulled low over her head. She'd knotted her hair into a bun and with her head down thought she could probably pass for someone normal. Her heart thumped uncomfortably against her ribs, and she pressed a hand there as though she could still it, thinking how ridiculous it was that she was having this reaction.

She wanted to be back in the woods. Where it was dark and peaceful, and she wanted to go back to the Fair Lands. There, she didn't have to wear sunglasses to protect her eyes from the light, and she barely looked different from many of the Fae, some of whom were dark, and others as fair as herself. She blended right in.

'Clarice,' Krista said, swinging herself off the stool where she'd been perched, bent over the binding for a new journal, and staring at the slender woman who had just stepped into her shop. Her mouth went dry.

'We dragged her along with us,' Erin said, then saw what else was laid out on the wide table at the rear of the shop. 'Oh my Goddess,' she said. 'Oh wow. Stephan, look.'

Krista cleared her throat to say something, but shook her head wordlessly instead.

Clarice blinked slowly in the room, glad for once for her sunglasses, trying to look anywhere that wasn't at Krista.

'These are amazing,' Stephan breathed, looking at the prints of Erin's paintings. 'Are these going up for sale?' he asked.

Krista stared at Clarice a moment longer, then found her voice and turned towards the others at the table. 'Yes,' she said. 'I was getting so many requests from people, both in the shop and online, wanting full-size prints for their walls, that I decided to try it out. What do you think?'

She made herself look at the prints on the table, at Erin bent excitedly over them. She could smell Clarice, the sunscreen she always wore. It smelled good.

'Clarice,' Erin said, beaming. 'Come look! Krista has worked miracles – the colour is so good.'

Clarice took a breath and sidled up to the table, going around to the side opposite Krista. She blinked at the pictures.

'They're amazing,' she said, genuinely impressed.

Erin lifted her head and grinned at her. 'I don't think you've seen any of my art before, have you?'

Clarice shook her head. Had a sudden, wild idea. 'Could you paint Sigil for me?' she asked. 'In return for the dance lessons?'

'Dance lessons?' Krista asked, feeling like she was talking through glass.

Clarice subsided into silence, a lump in her throat.

'Yeah,' Stephan said, picking out a picture of a long white hare gazing at the moon. 'I want this one for myself,' he said, then looked at Krista. 'We've almost got Clarice to agree to leading your dance classes.'

'My dance classes?' Krista asked.

'I haven't agreed,' Clarice said.

Krista looked at Clarice, blinked slowly. 'You'd be brilliant,' she said.

It was true. Clarice was a beautiful ritual dancer. Krista nodded. 'You really would be.'

Clarice stared intently at Erin's artwork. 'People want dance classes?' she asked.

'That was the plan originally, wasn't it, Krista?' Stephan asked, putting his arm around Erin and reaching down to pat Burdock on his head. 'With the place next door?'

Krista nodded again. 'I was hoping to do community classes, with things like art classes, and dance.'

'Hey, look at that,' Stephan said with a laugh. 'Erin can teach art, and Clarice can teach dance.' He smiled. 'Perfect.'

'I've never taught anything before,' Erin said, nonplussed, nudging Stephan with her elbow. 'How do I know I could do that?'

'It's just for people here in the village,' Krista explained, feeling her excitement grow again at the old plans she'd had before the lockdowns. 'Come, look at the space with me – see what you all think.' She pushed away from the table and walked across the bookshop to a door at the far side, reached into the pocket of her jeans for her keys, and unlocked it.

'I'm not sure what this shop used to be,' she said, but it's a lovely big space, and once we get the windows cleaned and so on, it should have some good natural light as well.'

'It was a haberdashery when I moved here,' Clarice said, surprising herself by speaking up. She looked around the space. 'It sold fabric and notions, and sewing stuff. I don't remember when it closed down.'

'You know,' Krista said. 'That's what we're missing here – some sort of craft store.'

'There's only a few hundred people in Wellsford,' Clarice said. 'How would it make any money?' She wasn't sure how Haven made any money.

'Same way Haven does, I imagine,' Krista said, already dreaming. 'Online sales.'

'There's an art and craft shop in Banwell,' Erin said, almost apologetically. 'It's where I buy my supplies. Clarice is right, there aren't enough people here to open up a whole new shop.'

Krista rolled her shoulders. 'Perhaps you're right,' she said. 'But you know – we could have a craft section and an art supply section in Haven.' She thought about it a moment. 'That would work.' Then she grinned and shrugged. 'I just really want people to get inspired and do stuff, you know? Because doing something, anything really – even knitting a hat or a sock – well, it keeps the faith in the world and despair at bay.' She gestured at the shop space. 'I was going to make a lending library here,' she said. 'But if you two will do art and dance classes, that's even better.'

'I never said I would!' Erin giggled.

'Me neither,' Clarice said, more darkly.

Krista's mind was racing. 'Maybe there's somewhere else in the village we can hold classes, or put the library.' She pursed her lips.

Her gaze drifted over to Clarice, whose pale skin almost glowed in the dim room. Clarice would be an amazing teacher, if Krista could get her to agree.

'I'm going to figure it out,' she said.

Clarice looked away, stared out the window at the street. She was sure Krista would do just that.

What she wasn't sure about, was if she would actually say no to teaching the classes.

21

CLARICE TOUCHED HER FINGERS LIGHTLY TO THE SMALL PIN cushion under the pillow and sighed, closing her eyes, willing sleep to come. The fire chattered away in the grate, and she squeezed her eyes shut, turning her mind away from Krista, from dance lessons, from everything that made her feel anxious, her muscles tense, her body ache.

Outside the one-room cottage, Sigil hooted, spread her wings, and flew over the gardens of Hawthorn House to where Clarice lay sinking into sleep. She circled the cottage once, twice, then made for the woods, her bright eyes searching the ground for prey.

And Clarice deepened finally into her dreams. She twitched slightly beneath the covers and behind her eyelids, her eyes rolled back and forth.

There was the path between the birches. The birches were in the photograph, but they were also inside her and she stepped down the path she'd made leading between them and onwards, strewn with petals and moss.

She stepped between the trees, reaching out a hand to touch their papery white bark in a brief greeting.

Then she was in a car, driving down a road on an island. A hurricane raged outside, the sky roiling with charcoal-black clouds, and she looked out the window towards the shore where the waves threw themselves upon the shore, reaching for the inland roads, then withdrawing with a roar to gather themselves for another attempt.

A tsunami was coming. Clarice could feel it out there in the ocean, the swell of the wave growing larger with every mile of sea it crossed. Soon, maybe only in minutes, it would draw all the water from the coast, sucking it back, heaving it up into its own bulk, and then it would be upon them.

She pushed her foot down on the accelerator, willing the car to go faster through the buffeting wind. Her fingers were white where she gripped the steering wheel, and somewhere deep inside her sleeping mind, she was aware that she couldn't drive.

Home in her dream, however, was not far away and she pulled the small car into the driveway and got out, making a dash for the house, pulling the front door open and stepping inside, looking for safety.

She hurried through the house, each room bare and white-walled, empty. Perhaps one of the rooms at the back of the house would give shelter, but when she opened the door to look, she saw that there were too many windows.

All that glass was not safe. Clarice stared outside for a moment, looking at the rain that fell horizontally in the wind. She moved on to the next room, then the next.

They were the same.

Bare, too many windows.

No shelter.

Closing the door on the last room, she retreated down the hallway, a mirror on the wall catching her reflection. She paused a moment to look at herself.

But she must find a place of safety from the storm outside, from the oncoming wave. And so she moved on, opened another door.

This room was not bare. It opened out into a beautifully panelled suite of rooms at the heart of the house. Clarice, dreaming, stared at the elaborate furniture and decorations. It was warm in these rooms, a hearty fire blazing in the grate, sending sumptuous shadows flickering over the warm walls.

She walked deeper into the space, wandering through the rooms, and stopped at the entrance to a grand drawing room. A woman sat in there, waiting, her hands folded on her lap. She was wealthy, this woman, Clarice knew immediately. Her clothes were expensive, her hair beautifully cut. Clarice looked at her, a slight frown on her face, and then walked to another door, twisted the knob, and pushed it open.

It was a lunchroom, the sort Clarice imagined existed in office buildings. Plain, functional.

But it was not the room she looked at, hand suddenly pressing against her heart, shock making her blanch.

Her mother sat at the table.

Clarice turned her head, afraid to look at Grainne.

This was not part of the dream, she thought, glancing back at her mother, who looked calmly at her, a slight smile touching her lips.

She looked the same as she had the last time Clarice saw

her, before Grainne had left on the trip from which she hadn't come back.

Except she was here, Clarice thought. Come to meet her in her dream.

Grainne smiled at her, gestured to the other seat at the table.

'Just for a moment,' she said, in the same voice Clarice had known so well.

Swallowing, Clarice sat. She was shaking inside her dream body. Quivering.

Grainne leant across the table and took Clarice's hand in her own. Clarice looked down at their fingers linked together. Her mother's hand was warm.

'How...' Clarice said. 'How are you here?'

But Grainne smiled. 'You needed me,' she said.

Clarice blinked.

Grainne squeezed Clarice's hand. 'It is time for you to get to work,' she said, then nodded towards the door. 'The woman in there has been waiting.'

Clarice looked back at the door, frowning. Dimly, she realised that in this dream, she did some sort of divination, and the woman waited for a reading.

'She needs the truth from you,' Grainne said. 'You must give her a genuine reading. This you can do - it is natural for you, if you let it be so.'

Clarice looked at her mother, then shrugged, wrapped up in the dream again. 'Pass me her teacup,' she said, and took it from her mother's hand.

She cupped it in her palms and focussed, let herself relax and open, took a long, slow breath.

The door opened behind her mother and a young

woman walked in, holding a stack of letters. Clarice stared at her, at the otherworldly looks that marked her as one of the Fae, and she forgot everything else. The dream dissolved around her.

CLARICE SAT UP IN THE BED, BLINKING AT THE FIRST LIGHT OF the day peering in between the curtains at the window. She put a hand to her forehead, holding it there, then swung her feet out from the blankets and set them upon the floor.

Had she really dreamt of her mother?

She shook her head. No. It hadn't been quite like that.

She had dreamt, and her mother had met her inside her dream.

Clarice remembered the woman in the drawing room waiting for a reading. She remembered her mother's words.

The truth. A genuine reading.

Grainne had done more than meet her in a dream – she'd orchestrated the dream.

Or some such thing.

The flagstones were cool under the rug and Clarice reached for her slippers, then bent to tend the fire. It had burnt down during the night, and she brushed away silver ash to fan the embers back to life.

The journal was on the desk still, and Clarice sat down, bent over it, and wrote out her dream, shaking her head as she did so.

Her mother.

Grainne had come to speak to her.

Clarice put the pen down and took a deep breath, trying to compose herself. She'd been willing to go along with

Morghan's suggestion to try dreaming with purpose, but never, not for a moment, had she expected to meet her mother in her dreams.

It had felt so real, seeing her there. Clarice shivered with the memory of the shock she'd felt, coming upon Grainne waiting there for her.

She touched her fingers to the words she'd written on the page and shook her head over the dream. It was important – she didn't need anyone to tell her that.

But it was also a puzzle. She had to work out what it meant.

What did it mean? The storm, the tsunami, the rich woman waiting for a reading.

Clarice winced, shame washing over her at the thought of how she'd seen the Fae woman and let herself be distracted, losing her grip on the dream.

That was probably a message too, she thought, and sighed.

Her runes were in their cloth bag and Clarice reached for them. She didn't know about doing readings for anyone else, but she could do one about the dream. They were, right now, the only resource she had. Dipping her hand into the bag, she let the cool stones flow through her fingers until one, then another, and another, felt right. She set them out on the desk and looked at them, putting the bag down and touching her hand to her thumping heart. Her lips twisted in dismay. It was a hard spread of runes. She reached for the book she used to discern their meanings, so that she could be clear on what they were saying.

'Isaz,' she said. This wasn't her favourite rune, and one of the reasons she didn't use them often. It came up too many times. She could almost recite the meaning by memory.

'The winter landscape freezes.' Clarice shivered, then thought of her mother's hand warm around her own and drew breath, felt better, smiled a little. Her mother had come to visit her.

She wasn't gone. Clarice wasn't alone.

'The wind howls across the ice,' she continued. 'Know too, that if you are frozen, unable to act, that after the winter freeze comes the thaw, and new life is born from the time of cold and stillness.'

Clarice wrinkled her nose. So far, she thought, she hadn't got to the thaw part of things. She dipped her head. Not if she were being truthful, she knew. If she were being honest, then the Queen was right. Morghan was right. Every-damned-body was right. She didn't live in balance. She hid in the Fair Lands and avoided everything she could back here at home.

Home. She hadn't left home. She hadn't gone to university or gotten a job. She'd taken advantage of being Morghan's stepdaughter and kept living at Hawthorn House, helping with the Grove rituals here and there, but mostly wandering the woods, ducking through the veil to the Otherworld, and the Queen's realms. Where there was no responsibility but enjoyment.

Clarice blew out a breath. Turned to the next rune. *Tiwaz*. Another old friend. The trouble with runes and other such things – dreams now included – was that they required one to look at themselves, coolly, clearly, honestly.

And that could get uncomfortable.

Clarice thought of the touch of her mother's hand again and turned to the page of the book with *Tiwaz's* meaning.

Victory and honour comes when one grows into the life demanded by spirit, not heedless of the difficulties and trials along the way, but upright and full of the conviction that comes when one unfurls in balance with the universe.

Perhaps, Clarice thought, she should just be looking at the dream, not pairing it with a rune reading.

But there was that avoidance thing again that she was so good at.

She swallowed. Unfurling in balance with the universe didn't sound so bad. Was a pretty good payoff, she supposed.

The last rune of the three was another difficult one. *Naudhiz.* Grimacing, Clarice turned back to the book.

Need creates only desperation and despair. It plants itself on stony ground and brings forth only unfulfilled desire. There is a flow to the world into which you must enter instead. The flow of your own spirit, for the soul's dream is to seek connection and growth and to blossom in its fertile ground.

Need, Clarice thought. What had she always thought she needed? Safety, security. They weren't bad things, were they?

She remembered the dream. Driving through the hurricane, seeking safety in her house, only to find all the rooms had too many windows. Windows that would shatter with the high winds, that would let the tsunami wave in. She closed her eyes. Shook her head.

Who did she know who could help her with this dream? To understand its symbols, her mother's message?

Morghan, of course. Or Ambrose. Clarice picked up her pen and wrote the runes into the book under her dream.

There was someone else who was an expert in symbolism, Clarice thought, although her heart beat faster at the idea.

Krista. She knew more about symbolism than Morghan did. Maybe more than Ambrose.

Clarice shook her head. She couldn't go to Krista.

Could she?

Did Krista stand along the path of unfulfilled desire?

Or the path that led to growth?

22

'MORGHAN?' WINSOME ASKED, KNITTING HER FINGERS together in a complex knot. 'Can I ask you something?'

'Of course,' Morghan said, putting her seatbelt on and looking at Winsome sitting beside her. 'Anything.'

'Hmm.' Winsome looked at Morghan's clear face for a long moment, the grey, direct gaze, the mouth that rested in the slightest of smiles. She dropped her eyes and shook her head.

'What is it?' Morghan asked, pausing before starting the car.

Winsome shook her head. 'It's nothing really,' she said.

Morghan got the car going, pulled out onto the road, and turned towards Banwell.

'Have you ever had a recurring dream?' Winsome asked, tucking her chin down as they drove down Wellsford's main road. Someone waved at them, but she couldn't bring herself to return the greeting.

'Of course,' Morghan said. 'I'm sure everyone does at

some stage.' She glanced over at Winsome in the passenger's seat next to her. 'What are you dreaming?'

But Winsome asked another question instead. 'Do they mean anything, do you think?'

'They mean something is bothering you, that needs to be looked at.' Morghan's hands rested lightly on the steering wheel. The day was overcast, clouds the colour of old bruises washing across the sky. It would be raining by the time they returned. The air was heavy with the promise of it.

Winsome nodded. It was the answer she'd expected, of course. She disentangled her hands and spread them over her knees. She was wearing a pair of dark trousers and a neat blouse. Also black. She still remembered her first outing with Morghan to do this job – the night they'd discovered Wayne Moffat in his basement of despair.

She kept her hands on her knees, resisting the urge to touch her neck, where there was no vicar's collar. She took a deep breath instead.

Morghan waited for Winsome to speak. She could feel the anxiety coming in waves from her, and also her efforts to calm herself. Letting her own energy loose for a moment, Morghan sent it swirling out to touch Winsome's aura, calming it.

Winsome sighed, relaxed. 'It's the same dream I told you about last week,' she said. 'The one where I'm scrabbling through the rubble of the vicarage. It still has some walls intact, but most the rooms are damaged, great piles of bricks and stone and rubbish everywhere.' She pressed her palms against her legs. 'I'm searching through it, thinking about how to set everything right.'

'Didn't you say you had a child with you?' Morghan asked. 'Young children often represent new lives, plans, or endeavours – which is perfectly appropriate in your case.'

Winsome nodded. 'A couple of them, I think. One on my hip, just a wee thing, and another following me about, a little older.' She looked over at Morghan. 'Why am I still having it, do you think?' She glanced out the window. They were out of the village now, and that was a relief. 'I mean,' she continued. 'I mean, I'm doing something, aren't I? I'm going to do this with you. I even logged back on to the Soul Midwifery course and started that up again.'

Morghan nodded. 'That's good,' she said. 'You were enjoying it.'

'I even made this absurd list of all the things I could do going forward.'

Morghan's eyebrows rose. 'Why absurd?'

Winsome gave a tight shrug. 'Well, you know. I can't assume that anyone will be interested in doing anything with me, after what happened.'

Morghan glanced away from the road at Winsome. Saw the tightness about her eyes. 'Have you called them back?' she asked. 'The people who were wanting you to come talk to them?'

'Yes.' Winsome turned towards the front again, watching the road. 'I'm going to visit two of them tomorrow.'

Morghan let the silence spin out for a minute, then asked another question. 'What was on it?'

'On what?' Winsome blinked, frowned.

'On your list of things you could do going forward.'

'Oh, that.' Winsome laughed a little. 'Well, computer classes, for a start. The Lord knows I could use those myself.' She remembered what else she'd written down. 'A prayer group. And I thought perhaps I could teach meditation, or something.'

'Meditation?' Morghan glanced over at Winsome and smiled.

'Yes, well, you know, those exercises I pinched from you and did the little video about – they were popular. I'd like to do more of that. Even in person, if it's possible.' Winsome paused. 'The church is being deconsecrated next month.' Her throat was suddenly dry. 'And the vicarage is mine for a year, and then it's going to be sold.'

Morghan was quiet.

'The vicarage is quite large,' Winsome continued, determined to plough past the bit where the church was also likely to be sold. 'I thought I could rearrange some of the furniture and hold the classes in there.'

'I think that's a brilliant idea,' Morghan replied.

'If people will come.'

Morghan nodded. 'I fear there's only one way to find that out.'

'Yes,' Winsome sighed. 'And then perhaps I can stop having that bloody dream.'

They were almost there. 'It's been a traumatic time for you,' Morghan said. 'The dream shows that, shows where you've been stuck for a while now.' She nodded. 'Keep going with your plans and see what happens to the dream.' Now, Morghan smiled. 'And if I can help in any way, please do let me know.'

. . .

WINSOME GAZED AROUND THE BEDROOM. IT HAD CHANGED, just like that, as soon as she and Morghan had opened the space around them, just as they'd done in Wayne's hospital room. She shivered and glanced over at Morghan. Hopefully this time they wouldn't have to slip off to any dark, dank, scary place to retrieve any lost soul shards, but she wasn't sure.

The room was draped in spiderwebs. Sooty ones. Or at least, that's what it looked like to Winsome.

She didn't want to look at the woman in the bed. Eileen. Winsome took a deep, steadying breath, glanced at Morghan who had made herself comfortable next to Eileen and had taken her hand, as though nothing were wrong, nothing was unusual, as though the elderly woman in the bed wasn't covered in a black husk or shell, through which one rheumy blue eye peered suspiciously. Morghan's Hawk stood on the back of her chair, feathers smooth and unruffled, eyes sharp, fixed on the woman they'd come here to see. Winsome reached a tentative hand down to touch the warm fur on Cù's back.

She had to breathe through her shock at the sight of Eileen. Winsome took a deep breath, let it out, and straightened. Here, she told herself, was a soul who had lost her way. The woman in the bed deserved her loving care, and that was that. Winsome moved from where she stood at the door and went to sit on the other side of the bed, bending closer to listen to Morghan's murmuring voice.

'Tell me how you came to be like this,' Morghan asked the dying woman.

The one clear eye looked from Morghan to Winsome

and back again. The black husk moved, broke apart at the lips.

Winsome folded her hands on the bed and breathed.

'Bitterness,' Eileen said and quivered. 'It grew and grew after my husband left me, until I was black inside with it, and mean alongside it.' Her eye looked toward the door. 'They'll all be glad when I'm gone.'

Winsome glanced over at the closed door to the bedroom, thinking of Eileen's son and daughter downstairs, their pale, stressed faces.

'They love you well enough to call us in to help you pass,' Morghan said, still holding the woman's hand.

The blackened lips pressed together, then parted and a sigh escaped.

'When he left me, I was angry. Left on my own with two kids. And afraid,' she said. 'I was afraid of how I was going to take care of them. I had nothing, you see. He took it all. House and car, he took those.' She shook her head again. 'How was I supposed to look after them? I had nowhere to live. No job.' Her hand clenched in Morghan's. 'I couldn't bear being afraid like that, so I made myself be angry instead.'

There was a long moment of silence. Winsome could hear her heart thudding inside her chest.

'Being angry turned me hard. And mean.'

Another long pause. 'I've done things I'm not proud of. Yelling at them, the kids. Taking it out on them.

'I was happy once.' The eye blinked slowly. 'I wasn't always like this.'

'You don't have to stay this way,' Morghan said.

Winsome nodded. Reached tentatively for the woman's hand. Found it and pressed it between her palms.

'When was such a time?' Morghan asked, her voice smooth and calm. 'Tell me about a time when you were happy.'

'When I was young and pretty and thought the world was mine for the taking,' the woman said. 'When I had my home and my garden, and there was food in the cupboards.'

Morghan nodded. 'Do you remember how that felt?' she asked. 'How it lit you up inside?'

The blue eye swivelled towards her and stared.

There was a smile on Morghan's lips, as though she knew the feeling well. 'Can you remember it now?' she asked. 'Remember how that excitement felt? How warm it was inside you, Eileen?'

'It was a lie, though, wasn't it?' Eileen said. 'All of it lost in the span of five minutes when he came home and said he was divorcing me and moving his cheap tart in.'

Winsome glanced over at Morghan.

But Morghan was shaking her head. 'The happiness you felt before that wasn't a lie,' she said. 'The pleasure in your home, your babies, your garden – that wasn't a lie.' She didn't let go of Eileen's hand. 'I want you to remember that feeling now.'

Eileen shook her head. 'Can't remember what it felt like.'

'Yes,' Winsome said. 'You can. It's inside you somewhere, that memory, that feeling. Your body will remember it.'

Now, Eileen coughed a laugh from behind her black mask. 'This body is dying,' she said. 'It can't remember anything.'

Winsome drew back, abashed.

Morghan looked over the bed and gave her a reassuring smile. 'Tell me about your garden, Eileen,' she said. 'Did you like gardening?'

Grudgingly, Eileen nodded. 'Always did, since I was a nipper, helping my Nan in hers. She used to let me dig the veggie patch for her.'

'What did you grow there?' Morghan asked.

'Sugar snap peas,' Eileen answered promptly. 'They were my favourite, see? You didn't have to do anything but snap the pea pod from the plant and eat it there and then.' The black mask on her face contorted.

Winsome realised the woman was smiling.

'I don't think many made it to the dinner table,' Eileen said. 'I ate them all out there in the garden.' Her one good eye blinked. 'Golden days, they were. Golden days.'

'What else did you grow there?' Morghan asked.

'Nan,' Eileen said. 'Nan gave me a little patch of ground to plant flowers in. All to myself.' Another ghastly smile. 'I spent hours poring over her seed catalogues.'

'What did you choose?' Winsome asked, leaning forward, trying desperately to imagine this woman as a happy, innocent child choosing flowers for her garden.

'Sunflowers along the fence,' Eileen said, her voice turning wistful as she remembered. 'They grew too, real beauties they were.' She blinked. 'And sweetpeas, I loved those. All colours, I had.'

'That must have made you feel so good,' Morghan said. 'Planting and tending such beautiful flowers.'

Eileen nodded.

'Can you feel that same happiness now?' Morghan asked. 'Hold it inside you like you're holding your breath.'

The blue eye closed.

'What about when your babies were born?' Morghan asked. 'What was it like to hold them in your arms?'

Eileen opened her eye and gazed back at her memories. Her hand twitched in Morghan's.

'They smelled so good,' she said. 'After their baths, their skin so soft. I'd hold them against my chest, and just breathe in their scent. Small, sweet darlings, they both were.'

'Can you remember how they smelled?' Morghan asked. 'Remember and hold that feeling inside you, let it expand in there until you glow with it.'

Eileen could remember. Like it was yesterday, she thought, closing her eyes, and breathing it in. Baby shampoo – she'd always used the one that promised it wouldn't hurt their eyes if she was clumsy with the water and splashed their faces while washing them. And a little bit of powder afterwards, to make their skin like silk. Shampoo, powder, and milk. That's how her babies had smelled, and she'd thought it the best scent in the world.

Morghan put down Eileen's hand and lifted a piece of husk away from the dreaming face. Eileen's lips were smiling.

'What about when the children were bigger, Eileen. Did you let them help in the garden too?' Morghan knew the family had been intact until the children were in their early teens. It was part of the history she'd taken down before ever coming upstairs to sit with Eileen.

'Oh yes. They each had their own little part of dirt to dig about in.' Eileen licked her lips. 'Good for kiddies to be outside, not like they are now, always inside playing their video games.'

'What did you grow then?' Winsome asked, not wanting Eileen to get side-tracked.

'I grew roses, then,' Eileen said. 'They were my love. All different types and colours.'

'I love roses too,' Winsome said. 'Especially the scented ones.'

Eileen nodded and her eyes drifted closed again as she sighed. Morghan looked across at Winsome and nodded and Winsome drew in a deep breath.

The rest of the dark mask came easily from Eileen's face and Winsome stared down at it in her hands for a moment, not knowing what to do with it. Cù reached up and took the piece in his mouth, turned, and carried it away from the bed, then let it drop to the floor. Winsome patted him in thanks when he came back to her side.

Morghan and Eileen continued their murmuring talk, and gradually, piece by piece, Winsome was able to remove the black, crusted shell from Eileen, noticing as she did so, that the room was lightening also, the dark cobwebs falling from the ceiling, from the corners where they'd draped thick and shadowy. They drifted down in great swaths from the ceiling and melted away upon hitting the floor.

Eileen talked away. About all the things that had lit up her heart.

Winsome took up the facecloth from the bowl of warm water and began to bathe her, smoothing the cloth over her skin, as gentle as a mother with a new baby. She dried her, and with Morghan helping, they got Eileen changed into a clean nightdress, and brushed her hair until she lay back in the bed, relaxed, her aura weak but glowing.

'You've turned my room into a garden,' Eileen said.

Winsome frowned, then turned to look at the bedroom. And gasped at what she saw.

It was a garden. Roses grew in the corners, vines laden with heavy blooms across the walls where the webs had been. The carpet blossomed with sweetpeas in every colour. Winsome shook her head and looked at Morghan with wide eyes.

But Morghan was looking down at Eileen again. She touched her hand to Eileen's shoulder.

'Your children are downstairs,' she said. 'Would you like to spend some time with them?'

For a moment, Eileen looked frightened and worked her mouth without a sound. Then she flattened her hands on the blankets and took a wavering breath.

'Yes,' she said. 'I need to explain. Tell them I'm sorry.'

Winsome blinked back tears.

23

Krista looked up in surprise as the bell above the door jangled and Clarice sidled in.

'Clarice,' she said, and gripped the counter as though to keep her balance. Clarice always did make her feel like she was losing her balance. But the woman was as slippery as a fish, as skittish as a cat, and the obvious attraction between them didn't stand a chance.

Clarice nodded and walked through the shop to the counter behind which Krista stood, dark eyes focussed on her. She plastered a smile on her face. Cleared her throat.

Felt like an idiot.

'I was supposed to pick up a book for Morghan while I was here the other day,' she said, and thrust her hands in her pockets for something to do with them.

'Oh,' Krista said. 'Right.' She shook her head slightly. 'Of course.' She blinked, smiled automatically. 'It's right here.' She ducked down and opened the cupboard under the counter and checked the bagged books.

'Got it,' she said, putting it on the counter and sliding it across to Clarice.

'Great,' Clarice said, picking it up and tucking it under her arm. 'Thanks.'

They stared at each other for a moment.

'Have you given any more thought to...'

'Do you have any...'

They spoke at the same time.

Krista grinned suddenly. 'Sorry,' she said, drawing breath and forcing herself to relax. 'You go first.'

But Clarice looked at the floor and shook her head. 'No. What were you going to say?'

'Oh. I was going to ask if you'd given any more thought to leading some dance classes?' Krista leant on the high counter and let herself drink in the sight of Clarice, long and thin, her eyes hidden behind dark sunglasses.

Krista wondered if Clarice knew she had an expressive and mobile mouth, lips that twitched while she thought.

But Clarice shook her head. 'I haven't,' she said. 'Given it any thought.'

Krista looked down at her hands for a moment. 'That's too bad,' she said, straightening. 'You'd be brilliant, though I expect you're too busy, with you know – your service to the Queen.'

Clarice snorted, took Morghan's book in her hands, looked at the paper bag it was in, then put it back on the counter. 'The Queen has decided I must stay here in this world until after midwinter.' She pursed her lips, shrugged, tucked her hands back in her pockets. 'So no, I'm not too busy, not with that, anyway.' She glanced over at Krista.

Krista's eyes were wide. 'Why?' she asked.

Clarice shook her head slowly. Licked her lips. 'Ah, something about needing balance.' She winced, turned, and looked around the shop. Anywhere rather than at Krista. 'I spend too much time there and not enough here, she thinks.' Another shrug. 'Whatever, I'm stuck here for a while.'

'Gosh,' Krista said. Then smiled slyly. 'So you might have time, after all?'

Clarice looked at her, at Krista's wide, infectious smile, and found herself laughing. It was a good sound. 'Maybe,' she said. 'I mean, yeah, I do have time – but I'm not sure.' She huffed a breath. 'I've never done anything like that before.'

'You dance at the rituals,' Krista pointed out.

'Yeah, but that's different. That's sacred dancing.'

Krista tapped her nails on the counter. 'That's what I want you to teach,' she said. 'Movement as a way to flex the spirit.' She raised her brows. 'You'd be great at it – you do it as part of your practice.'

But Clarice frowned. 'You think people will be interested?'

'Yeah,' Krista laughed. 'I do. We'll have to find the right phrasing for the flyers or whatever, but I think we'd get 10-20 people at least.'

'That's a lot to stand in front of.' Clarice said.

'You do it at rituals.'

Clarice shook her head. 'That's different. It's sacred, like I said.' She paused, mouth dry. 'And I know all of you.'

'I'm sure you know practically everyone in the village as well,' Krista said, stretching. 'But I'm not going to badger you into it – just think about it, okay? It's something you could really share with people who need it and will appreciate it. Doesn't have to be anything fancy, or long, or involved, just getting people to move. Their body and their energy.'

Clarice nodded. 'All right,' she said. 'I'll think about it.'

'Great!' Krista looked at Clarice, reached over and put a hand on the book. 'Is there anything else you need?'

The question repeated in Clarice's mind. What did she need? What did she really, deeply need?

What did her soul need?

'Yes,' she answered. 'Do you have any books on dreams?' The corners of her mouth turned down in a grimace. 'As in, how to work out what they might mean.'

Krista looked at her in surprise. 'I do,' she said. She moved out from behind the counter and led Clarice over to the shelves where she kept what she thought of as the witchy books. It was quite a large section, and she was always being surprised at how many people from the village slid surreptitiously over it to peruse the books and tarot cards.

She scanned the shelves. Plucked one book down, then another. 'Here,' she said. 'These are good ones.' Then she grinned. 'Well, I only stock books I think are good ones, so there we go.'

Clarice took the books and glanced at their covers. 'Can I sit and look at them for a minute?' she asked, then looked around the shop. There were three other customers browsing the displays.

'Of course,' Krista answered. 'Make yourself comfortable in any of the chairs.' She looked at Clarice. 'Would you like a coffee, or a cup of tea?'

Clarice was still looking around the shop. 'Can I sit in the back room?' she asked awkwardly. She took a breath and shook her head. 'No, don't worry about that. And I'm fine, thanks for the offer.'

Krista reached out and touched Clarice's sleeve. 'Come and make yourself at home in the other room,' she said. 'I'll be nipping in and out, and I'm going to boil the kettle, so it's no bother.' She paused. 'And I know a bit about dreams, if you need some help.'

Clarice stared at her, mouth pursing while she thought furiously. Hadn't she come here for Krista's help? Was she actually going to turn it down now she had it on offer?

And why? Why would she do that?

Hadn't she been avoiding Krista for long enough?

'Yes,' she said. 'I'd like that, and I'd like your help.'

Krista was startled by the answer, even though she'd made the offer in the hopes of it. She stood still for a moment, then smiled widely. 'Good,' she said. 'Great. Go through, and I'll bring us a drink in a minute.' She scanned the room. 'Everyone here seems happy enough for the moment.'

Clarice nodded, walked through the shop, picking up Morghan's book off the counter and made her way to the doorway leading to the shop's spacious back room, where Krista did most of her work.

'Clarice?'

She stopped and turned at the unfamiliar voice.

'Oh, it is you,' the older woman said. 'It's so nice to see you, dear. Aren't you glad we can get out and about again?'

Clarice searched her brain for the woman's name, then

nodded and cleared her throat. 'Hello Mrs. Bain,' she said. 'It is, yes.'

Mrs. Bain nodded enthusiastically. 'Call me Irma, for heaven's sakes. Nothing like actually coming into Haven to look for books, is there?' She smiled. 'I'll let you get on - I just wanted to say hello.'

Clarice sidled away, bemused.

'Mrs. Bain just said hello to me,' she said to Krista in a low voice, gesturing back into the shop.

Krista looked at Clarice for a long moment. 'Why wouldn't she?' she asked, then leant away to look through the doorway, smiling. 'Irma's lovely, and she adores a good cosy mystery. Particularly the ones with cat sleuths in them.'

Clarice stared at her. 'There's such a thing?'

'Sure there is,' Krista laughed. 'Irma runs the local book group, and I'll bet she's super pleased they'll be able to meet up again soon.'

'There's a book group?'

'Yup. Do you want to join?'

'Are you part of it?'

Krista put Clarice's mug of tea in front of her. 'Of course I am,' she said. 'It would be poor form for the local book-seller not to be, don't you think?' She smiled widely. 'Although I think they just want the discounts I can get them.' She laughed.

Clarice shook her head. 'There's so much going on here,' she said.

'Yeah,' Krista agreed. 'And more to come, I think. Wells-ford is small, but mighty.'

Putting the books down, Clarice rubbed at her arms,

then sat, took a breath, and removed her sunglasses. She blinked over at Krista.

'I'm sorry,' she said abruptly.

Krista stared at her face, taking in the white eyebrows, lashes, Clarice's pale, beautiful eyes. There was a lump in her throat.

'Why?' she asked.

Clarice shook her head. 'For being a coward,' she said. 'For running away from you.' She closed her eyes for a moment. This wasn't what she'd planned to do, thought she would ever say. She cleared her throat. 'From us. What could have been us, anyway.'

Krista regarded her steadily, even though the rush of blood between her ears made her feel slightly woozy. 'It's okay,' she said after a moment. 'Not everything works out.' She paused again. 'You had your reasons.'

'Yeah,' Clarice said. 'I suppose so.'

'Your mother had not long died.' Krista looked down at the table, drew her cup of coffee nearer. 'And there was, you know, the thing with the Fae.'

That had been the real reason, Clarice thought. Living more fully there, than in this world. The world where Krista lived.

'Maybe,' she said, surprising herself. 'Still. I'm sorry.'

'It was a few years ago,' Krista said. 'It's okay.'

Clarice looked down at the books on the table, not really focussing on them. Her cheeks burned. 'Are you seeing anyone?' she asked.

Krista shook her head. 'No,' she said. Then added, 'I haven't been looking.'

'Right. Okay.'

'What about you?'

Clarice shook her head.

Krista sat back, looking at Clarice. Her hair was loose today, falling over her shoulder in a gauzy white curtain.

The silence stretched out between them.

'Okay,' Krista said finally. 'What do you want to find out about dreaming?'

Clarice jumped on the change of subject with relief. Still, her voice was halting as she told Krista what Morghan had asked her to do, and the dream she'd finally had.

Krista gave a low whistle. 'That's some dream,' she said. 'Your mother was really there?'

'She was,' Clarice replied. 'It was so jolting – I just walked into a room in the dream and there was Grainne, sitting there looking just as she had the last time I'd seen her.' Clarice shook her head. 'I'm convinced it was really her. Her spirit.'

'Oh, I agree,' Krista said, nodding in fascination. 'Even though for the most part, each person in our dream is likely to be symbolic of an aspect of ourselves, I absolutely believe that dreaming is one of the easier ways for our beloved dead to contact us.'

Clarice glanced over at her, then sipped her tea and gave a grimacing smile. 'But what about the rest of it?' she asked. 'What is the dream trying to tell me – what did Grainne mean?'

Now Krista shook her head. 'Your dream is so full of symbolism it's like, where do you want to start?' She paused. 'Do you have a notebook to write stuff down in?' She looked around the room. 'I've some spare, I'm sure.'

'Morghan gave me one,' Clarice said, reaching down to pull it out of her bag and putting it on the table.

Krista looked at it and nodded. 'Now I know what she wanted it for,' she said.

'This is one of yours?' Clarice smoothed a hand over the cover.

'Yeah.'

'It's beautiful.' She lifted her eyes to Krista's and held her gaze for a long moment.

'All right,' she said finally, feeling the quickening beat of her heart under her ribs. 'So, where do I begin with the dream?'

Krista took a quick breath, glanced out the door to check on her customers, then nodded. 'I love your dream,' she said. 'And if it were my own, I would look at it in three parts.'

Clarice nodded.

'Firstly, there's the fact that in the dream, the weather is dangerous, and you're driving in it, right?'

'Yes. I don't drive, though, in waking life,' Clarice said. 'I never got my license.'

Krista nodded. 'When I dream of driving, I usually end up looking at it in terms of trying to control my course,' she said. 'And if I was driving through a hurricane, and anticipating a tsunami, I would think of that as feeling at the mercy of the world, of seeking security from the storms life makes us weather.'

Clarice winced, then attempted a grin. 'I see what you did there,' she said. 'Storms we weather.'

Krista shrugged and smiled. 'Dreams often use our own

metaphorical language.' She shook her head. 'It's really so interesting.'

'Okay,' Clarice said, sighing. 'So, I'm trying to navigate a course through all this bad weather, and I'm afraid it's going to get worse – there's a tsunami coming. I go home, because that's where shelter is, right?'

'Usually,' Krista said. 'But your dream is showing you that your home isn't somewhere you feel safe.'

Clarice shook her head. 'I don't understand. Morghan was going on about the house as a symbol for the state of your life...' She raised her eyebrows, thinking about it. 'Oh,' she said. 'I see.'

Krista let her consider it.

'So,' Clarice said slowly, then shook her head and sat back frowning. 'This is complicated, isn't it?' She reached for her cup and took another sip of the tea. 'All right, then. The dream is telling me that I find the world a stormy place, and I have a crap, empty house to shelter in, that has too many windows to keep me safe – and which means too many people can look in and see me.'

'Water as a symbol is often about the emotions, as well,' Krista added.

Clarice couldn't help it. She rolled her eyes. 'Of course it is.' She thought for a moment then nodded. 'Okay, that all seems pretty obvious to me – I know what I'm like and I'm not going to pretend I don't.' She risked a glance at Krista. 'I know my shortcomings.'

She put the cup down. 'What about the bit with the rich woman and the gorgeous rooms at the heart of the house? And my mother telling me I have to give this woman a true and honest reading?'

'Yeah,' Krista agreed. 'That bit's interesting, don't you think?'

'I liked those rooms,' Clarice mused. 'They were beautiful, well-furnished, clean and tidy.' She took another sip of tea. 'And where Grainne was sitting was like a break room in an office, you know?'

'Indicating, don't you think, that there's behind the scenes work to do?'

'I guess so. Grainne certainly was telling me I had to get to work.'

'Giving a true reading to the woman waiting in the heart of your house.'

Clarice smoothed a hand over the cover of her journal again and sighed. 'That's me, isn't it? Or could be me?' She frowned. 'Only that house – that's me, the state of my life. Morghan said she was sure I would have good, strong foundations, but the dream says...' Clarice trailed off.

'That you have a good, rich, knowing heart, and you can put this to service, if you're willing to put the work in.' Krista paused, then risked the rest. 'Which would probably make you feel confident enough to furnish the rest of your house and calm the weather outside as well.

Clarice shook her head, gave an unsteady laugh.

'Well then,' she said. 'That's all right then, isn't it?'

24

THE CLIFF STILL SEEMED TO STRETCH ON FOREVER, BUT THIS
time Erin took a breath and nodded to herself.

'You have found the way forward?' Macha asked.

Erin rubbed her nervous hands against her skirt, then
straightened and nodded. 'I believe so,' she said, glancing at
Fox, who looked over at her, ears twitching. She thought for
a moment that Fox smiled, but then she blinked, and Fox
had turned her head, looking out over the vast view.

'And you don't have to hurry back to go to work, this
time?'

Erin let herself grin at Macha. 'No,' she said. 'I have the
day off.'

And nothing to do this day but figure this out. To find
her way down from the impossible cliff that stretched out to
her right and to her left into the distance. She took a step
back from the edge, the sheer drop making her worry about
losing her footing.

'Good,' Macha said. 'Proceed, then.'

Erin glanced at her. 'Will you come?'

'No.'

'Not even over there to the maze?'

But Macha shook her head again. 'I will stay here, and you will go.' She looked at Erin and sensed that the girl needed something more. 'You must trust your intuition,' she said. 'You have all the knowledge and answers here, inside you.' She touched a fist to her centre, under her ribs. 'Quiet your mind and let your knowing lead.'

Erin swallowed but said nothing. She nodded. This was possible. It was only a task – and a task that Macha had completed. And others. Morghan, Ravenna, all perhaps who came this way to do the work she was training to.

'This is my initiation?' she asked, and her voice sounded thin upon the breeze.

'Yes,' Macha answered. 'But only the beginning. You will know when you have reached the end of it.'

Erin didn't think that sounded terribly reassuring. She glanced over at Macha, but the woman's face was impassive, relaxed. There were no more clues to be found there.

For a moment, Erin thought of the runestones the old woman had given her and clenched her skirts in anxious fists, then forced herself to breathe and relax.

If she was going to do this, she had to trust what Macha said, what the runes said too, for that matter, that all problems had to be dealt with in spirit.

And that the spirit was bright enough to cast aside all shadow.

Erin had the meanings from her book memorised.

'It's time,' Macha said, but for once, her voice was low, almost gentle.

Erin nodded. Took a deep breath, blew it out through her open mouth, and stepped carefully forward until she was near the edge of the cliff again.

She could see for miles. So much sky between where she stood and where she needed to go.

She breathed again, but slower this time, drawing herself up into her own strength, then letting herself expand outwards into the air around her.

She spread her arms out wide.

Raven was a black shadow against the sky, a smudge that could have been cloud or soot, but Erin, still breathing deeply and rhythmically, knew it was him as soon as she saw the darkness of his feathers.

She called to him.

He swooped over her, plucking her up with his strong claws and lifting her from the cliff top and out over the edge so that she swung under him in the sky.

And then she was him, sharing his feathers, seeing through his eyes, both looking together at the vast distance they had to fly, and she was grinning, their wings scything through the air, taking them onwards, effortlessly.

She laughed, and they flew, and Raven opened his mouth and cried out, and it was Erin's mouth too, and they crossed the distance in minutes.

Raven let her drop onto the grass and swooped around to land on her shoulder. She reached up and stroked his warm feathers, black and oily with iridescence.

'That was wonderful,' she breathed, then stilled. 'Thank you,' she said. 'Thank you for coming, for helping.'

She wouldn't have been able to do it without him.

He lowered his head for a moment, as though accepting

her gratitude, then launched himself from her, turning back the way they'd come.

Erin watched him go, shading her eyes and wondering why he was leaving her.

The cliff looked like a giant wave from this distance, made from soil instead of water. She wondered if Macha stood there still, watching her.

Raven winged his way to it, and Erin watched him, wanting him to turn around and come back to her. She'd liked his weight on her shoulder, the feeling that she wasn't alone.

She was alone, wasn't she? The sudden question had her turning and peering about her, unsure if she would be more at ease if she were alone, or if it would be better that someone was about.

But she was alone, and below her was the maze.

The breeze blew a strand of hair across her face and Erin absently pushed it back.

What was this place?

A wide stone stairway led down to the maze, and she inched forward, then went gingerly down the first step.

It was odd, she couldn't help but think, to dig a maze down into the ground like this. What was it for? Would she be able to find her way through it?

And what would she find if she did?

There was a sudden flurry of movement behind her, and she spun around, astonished to see Fox grinning at her, Raven perched comfortably on her back, black eyes glinting.

'You're here,' she said to Fox. 'You went to get her,' she said to Raven.

So, she wouldn't have to do this alone. The knowledge made her want to weep with relief.

Raven sprang from Fox's back and walked over the grass towards where Erin stood. He gazed down the steps.

But Fox trotted down them without a second glance and disappeared into the shadows at the bottom.

'Okay then,' Erin breathed. 'I guess we're doing this.' She nodded to herself and climbed down the stairs, trying to bear in mind Macha's admonition to let her intuition guide her.

Where was her intuition, though? She touched the middle of her chest, much like Macha had, and nodded. That was where she had to stay centred. Out of her head and in the centre of her breath.

Easier said than done – but hadn't she managed it when she'd been with Kria at the end?

Erin nodded. She'd done what had felt right then, letting herself go with the flow of it, of what something inside her had said was true.

'The singing,' she murmured, stepping down into the depths of the maze and finding herself standing on a sand-stone path, a wall towering up beside her, and Fox waiting.

'Are you going to lead the way?' Erin asked Fox, hoping very much that Fox would.

Fox's white-tipped tail waved in the dimness.

Erin took a steadying breath and looked to the left, then the right.

Fox sat down.

Which way, Erin asked herself.

She put her hand out and touched the stone. Felt the dryness of it, rough under her fingers.

'This way,' she said and nodded to her left. 'Let's go this way.'

She glanced upwards and saw Raven against the sky, wings spread in a great dark fan. The sight of him there helped.

She wasn't alone. Raven was there. Fox was right beside her.

And she had her intuition. Her inner knowing. If she could bring herself to listen, to trust it.

She followed the wall to the left, trailing her fingers along the stone as she walked, Fox quietly at her side.

And when there was a gap in the wall, she slipped through it, stood again on the path for a quiet moment, not letting herself talk, even inside her head, and instead listening to the beat of her heart, and the small knowing that made her turn left again.

She walked farther this time, and then slipped through another gap in the wall, chose a direction, and kept going. Deeper into the maze.

The shadows between the walls grew cooler.

Raven flew overhead.

Erin slipped through the next gap then stopped abruptly. In the wall opposite, a statue stood in a niche. Erin pressed the heel of her hand to her thumping heart. For a moment there, she'd thought it was a real person.

But it was stone.

She is stone, Erin corrected herself. For it was indeed a woman, life-sized, standing there, palms cupped together, staring down at them from her dais in the niche in the wall.

Erin bent over the statue's hands, wanting to see what they held, but they were empty.

She glanced at Fox, but Fox had her inscrutable face on and refused to say anything about the statue. Erin reached out and touched the stone folds of the woman's garment, then rested her fingers briefly on the stone woman's cupped hands.

And then turned to walk onwards.

Fox did not follow, and when Erin looked for her as she made to slip through another archway, she was not there.

'Fox?' Erin called, looking back the way she'd come.

Fox sat beside the niche where the statue was. She stared unblinkingly at Erin.

'Why aren't you coming?' Erin asked, but she said if softly, so only she could hear. Shaking her head, she retraced her steps and looked from her Fox to the statue.

There was something Fox expected her to do. That much was obvious, but what was it? Erin blinked at the stone woman, bent over her cupped hands.

Except, she wasn't really bent over them, was she? Erin looked at her more carefully, taking in the curls of long hair that flowed down the woman's back, the simple stone shift she wore, belted at the waist. Her hands were cupped, that much was true, but she wasn't bent over them. Not really. Her head was bent, that was true, but her hands were raised, as if in offering.

Erin swallowed and looked at Fox.

Then she looked down at herself, noticing properly for the first time what she wore. A long dress, much like the ones she had inherited from her grandmother. That was why she hadn't paid attention. It was familiar.

But it was belted with leather, and from the belt hung a pouch. Erin shook her head over it, not entirely sure it had been there before. Did things just appear in this world when she needed them?

She would have to pay more careful attention.

Her fingers fumbled with the buckled pouch and drew it finally open.

Inside was a mess of moss and seeds. Erin frowned, dipped her fingers into the pouch and stirred them around. Nipped up a small square of paper and drew it out. Her eyes widened when she saw that it was one of her own drawings – a miniature portrait of herself and Fox and Raven.

She held it between thumb and forefinger and looked at the statue of the woman. Who was she making her offering to? Or was the offering to herself?

Erin didn't know, and she shook her head, feeling confusion descend on her like a damp cloud.

Fox opened her mouth and yapped a series of high-pitched barks, then snapped her jaws shut and looked at Erin.

'You know,' Erin hissed at her. 'I bet some spirit kin actually talk. You could try that – it would certainly make things easier.'

Now Fox grinned at her but didn't say a word.

Erin straightened and sighed. Her intuition, that was what she needed to use, obviously, she thought, recalling Macha's words. Was this the right offering?

It had been in her pouch, hadn't it?

Erin bent her head and tried not to think. She breathed instead, quietly, steadily, and waited to know, to feel her knowing.

Yes. Her body vibrated slightly with the knowing. Yes,

she thought, lifting her head. It was the right offering to make.

But her hand trembled slightly as she dropped the tiny portrait into the stone woman's raised hands.

Fox yapped again, and Erin looked at her, then back at the woman set in stone before her. She cleared her throat, scrabbled around in her pouch again, and grasped a stalk of lavender. She set it on top of the picture and felt immediately that it had been right.

Should she say something as well? Erin cleared her throat again, glanced at Fox, who stared back at her, then she took a breath.

'I am Erin,' she said. 'Erin of Wilde Grove, and I come this way with my kin, Fox and Raven.' She paused for a moment, took another breath, and let the words flow. 'We come to seek the mystery of this maze and I ask your blessing upon us, and that our offering, given with reverence and gratitude, be accepted.'

She lifted her eyes, but the statue had not moved, and the picture and flower lay still in the stone woman's cupped hands. Nevertheless, Erin felt as though she'd done what she'd needed to, and she nodded, going with the feeling, with the quiet voice inside her that was her intuition.

'My thanks,' she whispered, and turned once more back to follow the path deeper into the maze.

This time Fox followed, mouth open in a toothy, sharp-nosed grin.

The next niches in the wall were smaller, little more than shelves hollowed out of the stone. Two of them, side by side and Erin stopped, looked, and shook her head.

'They're like the sun and moon,' she said to Fox, who made no reply but looked at the crystal spheres as well.

Erin licked her lips. Why were they there? She reached out her hand and picked up the yellow crystal ball. It warmed at her touch, and without thinking, she opened her pouch and dropped it in.

The other crystal ball was milky, made from quartz, Erin thought, and she held it to the sky for a moment, looking into its depths, before she tucked it away in her pouch next to the sun stone.

'Sun and moon,' she said, feeling the rightness of it flow through her. And then she continued on her way.

Abruptly, she was through the maze, and she stopped in surprise, staring at the grassy lawn in front of her. Fox slipped past her and trotted across the expanse of grass towards the one tree that grew there.

'Where are we?' Erin asked, but Fox only swished her tail and kept going.

'All right, then,' Erin replied, and stepped out onto the lawn.

A shadow passed overhead, and Erin looked upwards, then shaded her eyes to watch Raven fly in a circling loop overhead. His presence made her nod, the tension in her neck and shoulders easing.

Head down again, she followed Fox across the grass, gazing all about her. The space was large, but she could see the walls at either side, where the maze had been dug down into the ground. Why, she had no idea, and couldn't think of a reason for it, but it did mean that all she could see was what was directly around her, and the sky above her.

It reminded her a little of her walled garden at home,

where right now, her body sat by the well, and in the potting shed, Stephan would be tinkering about with his plants. The thought comforted her.

Fox bared her teeth in a grin for Erin again, but Erin didn't notice. She fell to her knees instead and planted her hands on the grass.

'It's a well,' she breathed, and looked at the circle of water, so deep the surface was almost black except for the hint of sky reflected in it. Erin flattened herself to the ground, afraid suddenly of an impulse to slither forwards into the well, to dive deep down, down, down.

She shook her head. She'd done that with the well at Hawthorn House, and it had been an amazing sensation, to go so deep that she fell out of the world and floated in a great, pregnant nothingness, looking back at it, but she wasn't keen to repeat the exercise.

What did the well mean, though? She shook her head at the obsidian beauty of the water, and reached out a tentative hand, dipping her fingers in and sending tiny ripples out across the surface.

The water was warm, and she pulled her hand from it, staring at her fingers as though they might be stained by the water. But they were her fingers and the water dripped down them clear and warm.

Erin sat up, set her gaze to the rest of the space.

An oak tree grew next to the well, in full leaf, its trunk thick and strong. She looked up at its branches and grinned suddenly, surprised to see Raven looking back at her, his feathers smooth and as inky as the well.

There was nothing else. Only the well, the tree, and the

grass. It was flat, a great rectangular area, and a complete mystery.

Erin got slowly to her feet.

On the other side of the rectangle of grass was another stone wall, but this one had a large wooden gate in it, and something about it drew her attention, a tickling in her chest, a tightness behind her ribs, a thumping of her heart.

She walked around the well, giving the hypnotic darkness of it a wide berth, eyes fixed on the gate.

The wood was carved with swirls and spirals and knotted designs and Erin ran her fingers over them, tracing the intricate carvings before closing her hands around the end post and tugging. It swung open and with it came a breath of fetid wind, that immediately brought to Erin's mind one of Morghan's warnings.

Some places, Morghan had said, are not to be crossed into lightly. In some places, you must be silent, and not wake what lives there.

Erin shivered.

25

'No,' Stephan yelled. 'You can't touch her!'

But it was too late, and Erin jolted back from her travelling, eyes rolling in their sockets like marbles for a moment, before she blinked, disoriented, trying to focus.

Her lips were stiff, tongue dry.

'Wha?' she said, swaying where she sat, not knowing where she was.

She'd been at the gate, hadn't she? There had been a wind on her face, a wind that blew through her hair, carrying a stench with it.

A stench of what?

She tipped to the side and strong hands caught her.

Of shadows. That's what the wind had carried with it. The stench of lost and frightened shadows.

Erin opened her mouth again. 'Wha?'

The world blurred around her, spun in a sickening circle and she couldn't get it to stay still. She swayed with it.

Someone held her upright.

There were voices. Stephan's.

Someone else's.

She squeezed her eyes shut, realising dimly that she was back. Sitting in her own garden.

But she'd come back before she was ready. Jerked home. She lifted a hand, pressed it to her face, tried to hold herself still.

'What's wrong with her?'

A face came close, peered into hers, eyes wide and so close Erin could see the pores on the face's skin. She reared backwards, away from the monstrous face so close to hers.

'I told you not to touch her!'

'Is she drunk?'

Erin heard the question and tried to sit upright. She groped for the arms around her, found them and clung on. 'Stephan?' she asked, her tongue twice the size it ought to have been. She found some saliva in her mouth and tried again. 'Stephan?'

The arms tightened around her, and she smelt the familiar scent of Stephan's shirt next to her face. She leant against it, breathing in the smell of him. Soil and sweat. She smiled.

'You smell good,' she said, the words slurring in her mouth. She took her hand from her face and pressed it against the tight muscles of Stephan's stomach.

'You feel good,' she said, and slid her hand down a few inches.

Stephan plucked her hand away and shifted to kneel beside Erin, tucking his palms either side of her face and holding her so that she could see him.

'Erin,' he said softly. 'I'm going to carry you inside to the sofa, all right?'

Erin looked into his serious eyes. 'I love you,' she said.

Stephan winced, then smiled. 'Come with me,' he said, then scooped her up into his arms and carried her inside. Laid her on the sofa where she couldn't fall and hurt herself. She'd been brought back too quickly. He shook his head, concern turning to a quick, bright flare of anger.

'I told you not to touch her,' he said, and stalked into the kitchen, snatching up the kettle from the cooker. The water was hot enough for tea. 'Get the biscuit tin out of the cupboard,' he barked. 'She needs to eat something.' He shook his head. 'She was far away.'

'She should be in the hospital. Something's wrong with her.'

Stephan shook his head. 'She'll be fine,' he said, tight-lipped. 'You just can't touch someone when they're in trance like that.' He poured hot water into the teapot. He'd already thrown a heap of his tea in there.

'Trance? What is going on here?'

Erin staggered into the kitchen. 'Mum?'

Stephan and Veronica spun around, and Veronica lunged forward, gathering up Erin in a tight hug.

'Oh sweetheart, you gave me such a start!'

Erin struggled out of the embrace and blinked at the woman in her home, not sure she wasn't seeing things. Her hand groped for the stair banister, found it, and used it to hold herself upright as she stared in foggy disbelief.

'Mum?' She bent forward, squinting. It helped. A little. Except it really did seem to be her mother standing there in her kitchen. In Ash Cottage. In Wellsford.

Erin looked over at Stephan.

'Stephan?' she asked.

He came to her and looped an arm around her. 'It's all right,' he said. 'You just came back too abruptly.' He shot a venomous glance at Erin's mother. 'Come back and sit down before you fall down. I'm making some tea.'

Erin shook her head, pointed at a kitchen chair, swayed her way towards it with Stephan's arm still around her, then sank down gratefully. Stephan went to straighten, and she snatched up a handful of his shirt, dragged him back down.

'Am I seeing things?' she whispered.

Stephan shook his head. 'Your mother's here. She just turned up.' He glanced at Veronica. 'Out of the blue. I told her not to touch you, but she didn't listen.'

Veronica cleared her throat. 'Would someone kindly tell me just what is going on here?' she pointed a finger at Stephan. 'You,' she said. 'Leave us. I want to talk to my daughter, and she obviously needs help.' She gave a frosty pause. 'Professional help.'

Which was dismaying, really, Veronica thought, because it certainly wasn't what she'd come here for. She'd wanted help and support from her daughter; she was in no mood really to have to be dishing it out.

But still. Veronica puffed out her chest.

Stephan stared at her, then shook his head, slowly, emphatically. 'No,' he said. 'I'm not leaving.'

'I want to speak to my daughter,' Veronica repeated. 'Alone.'

'So you said,' Stephan replied. 'But she needs some things first. Something to eat and drink.' He patted Erin's shoulder and scooted past Veronica into the kitchen, determined not to be derailed. Erin had come back hard and fast. There'd be a price to pay for it.

'Mum?' Erin's voice wavered. 'What are you doing here?'

Stephan brought the teapot and a cup over to the table for Erin, poured some of the steeped tea into the cup and passed it to her. 'Drink,' he said firmly.

'Perhaps a cup for your guest?' Veronica asked tartly, deciding she didn't like this young man, despite his curls and big baby blues. What was he doing here with her daughter?

Stephan shook his head.

Veronica's eyes widened. 'You are being very rude,' she said.

'Mum,' Erin said. 'Sit down.'

Veronica turned her gaze on Erin, who really was far too pale.

'Please?' Erin said. 'You just came at an awkward time, that's all.' She sent Stephan a pleading glance. 'Stephan will make you a cup of tea.'

'Some of yours will be fine,' Veronica said, sniffing. 'You don't need to go to any trouble.'

Erin frowned, flattened a palm on the table and drew in a deep breath. She was still woozy, but the tea was already helping. She shook her head. 'Not this brew, Mum,' she said. 'It's an herbal blend especially for...' She wound down to silence, realising there was no way she could get her mother to understand.

'Why are you here?' she repeated instead.

Veronica sat. She cast a suspicious glance at the young man who did indeed seem to be putting the kettle on for another pot of tea.

'You've not introduced us,' she said stiffly to Erin, looking at her daughter again. 'And you haven't explained what is wrong – what you were doing out there, and why you're swaying in your seat like you're drunk now.'

Erin stared at her mother for a long moment, a frown digging a line between her brows. There was something wrong with her mother, she realised. She didn't know what it was, but it was coming off her mother in waves. She shook her head.

'What's wrong?' she asked. Her eyes widened. 'Has something happened to Dad? Why are you here? Is Dad sick? Is he in the hospital?'

Something had happened. She could feel it. Actually, she suddenly realised, bewildered, she could see it.

'Your aura,' she said, shocked.

Veronica scowled. 'My what?' she looked down at herself as though she had something spilled down her front.

'Your aura,' Erin said, and this time her voice was low, horrified, fascinated. She shook her head carefully. 'It's... churning around you.'

'I'm upset,' Veronica said, the words finally bursting out of her. 'I don't know what's going on with you, but I came with some terrible news.'

Erin blanched. 'Is everyone okay?' she asked.

Stephan came over with a fresh pot of tea, and a cup for Veronica. He slid them unobtrusively onto the table, pushed a plate of biscuits towards Erin, then retreated behind her chair.

Neither woman seemed to notice him.

'Everyone is fine,' Veronica said, the words coming out of her mouth clipped and dismissive.

Erin closed her eyes. 'That's all right, then,' she said. And nodded and picked up her cup, took a sip of the tea. The room still swayed and drooped alarmingly around her, as though she'd had far too much to drink, but she felt a little clearer.

Stephan picked up a biscuit and pressed it into her hand. She took it and bit into the shortbread without thinking. Then shook her head again.

'So why are you here?' she asked.

Veronica didn't want to say while the boy with the curls was hovering over her daughter like a protective mother hen. She pressed her lips together. 'Where's your dog?' she asked instead.

Erin's eyes widened.

'You've seen sense and found it another home, haven't you?' Veronica shook her head. She was slowly regaining her composure. Erin seemed all right. Not one of her episodes, then. She still looked a bit befuddled, but perhaps she'd been at the wine over lunch or something.

'Burdock?' Erin looked around the kitchen.

'He must be still in the potting shed,' Stephan said. 'I'll go get him.'

Veronica watched Stephan disappear out into the garden and got up to close the door behind him.

'Good,' she said. 'We can have five minutes alone, can't we?' she asked. 'If you're feeling all right now?'

Erin nodded dumbly, and when Stephan poked his head through the door a moment later, she shook her head at him, and he backed out again, closing the door once more. Erin took another bite of the shortbread, knowing Stephan would want her to eat the whole thing. She washed it down with the tea.

'You must be wondering why I'm here,' Veronica said, sitting straighter and tugging on her fitted jacket so that it wasn't bunched up under the arms.

Erin stared at her. 'Why are you here, Mum?' she asked. 'I haven't seen or heard anything from you in weeks, and suddenly you're in my kitchen telling my boyfriend to make you a cup of tea?'

Veronica narrowed her eyes. 'That is your boyfriend?' Her mouth twisted in distaste. 'He has dirt under his fingernails and needs a good haircut.'

'He's a gardener, and the salon has been closed. Why are you here?'

Veronica stared at her daughter. 'I thought you'd be pleased to see me.'

'I might be if you tell me why you're here!'

Veronica picked up her handbag and groped around inside it for a tissue. She swiped it under her eyes, then sat and stared at her daughter.

'I've left your father,' she said.

26

'WHAT?'

The word came out as little more than a squeak.

Veronica shifted in her seat, dabbed at her eyes again.

'But,' Erin said, shaking her head. 'You and Dad,' she said, groping for understanding. 'The Double V's.'

'Bah,' Veronica spat. 'I don't ever want to hear that stupid name again.'

Erin stared at her mother, then looked around the kitchen to make sure she was really in her small house where she should be and hadn't slipped into some alternate dimension.

'I don't understand,' she said.

'What's there to understand?' Veronica said, picking up the teapot and pouring herself a cup of tea, the spout clanking against the cup's rim. She set the pot down and sagged suddenly against the table. 'I've left him, that's all,' she said, and now she was looking through a haze of tears.

'But why?' Erin shook her head. 'I thought you two were fine.'

'Well, we're not fine,' Veronica said. 'Your father and his personal assistant are fine. I am quite rotten.'

Erin looked at her mother, stunned. 'He's having an affair?'

Veronica waved a hand in the air before going back to dab at her eyes again. 'Well, it's not the first time, but this time he kept seeing her, even in lockdown.' She dropped her hands to the table and glared at Erin. 'He could have brought the virus home,' she said, wild with renewed fury. 'He could have gotten me sick, put everything we have in jeopardy.'

Stunned, Erin pressed a hand against her forehead and stared out at Veronica from under it. 'What?' she said, and she shook her head.

'You heard me,' Veronica said, deflating again. She picked up her cup and took a determined sip, made herself brighten. 'So I thought I'd come and stay with you a night or two and then we can go to the London flat.'

Erin dropped the piece of shortbread she'd been holding in her other hand. 'Stay with me?' she asked, her voice faint.

'Yes.' Veronica cast a glance up at the ceiling. 'I assume there are at least two bedrooms in this poky little place?'

Erin shook her head slowly from side to side. Her mind was a blank screen with only static playing over it. She made herself focus.

'But I'm a member of a cult, remember,' she said. 'Isn't that what you think?'

. . .

OUTSIDE, STEPHAN AND BURDOCK STARED IN DISMAY AT THE flashy Audi sitting in the driveway to Ash Cottage. They didn't need to get close to it to see the back seat was piled high with suitcases.

Stephan turned and stared at the kitchen window. The sun was lowering in the sky, and the window was in shadow already. He couldn't see Erin behind the glass, sitting at the table. His hand sought out the softer fur on Burdock's head and he stroked the dog absently.

'So,' he said in a low voice. 'We weren't expecting this, were we, boy?'

VERONICA SET HER CUP DELICATELY BACK DOWN ON ITS saucer. 'Well,' she said. 'I'm prepared to be open-minded to your strenuous assertions that this isn't a cult after all.' She coughed slightly. 'You went to great lengths to tell me so, every time we spoke.'

Erin shook her head. 'You can't stay here,' she said.

'Why not?' Veronica looked around the kitchen and through into the sitting room. 'It's small, but there's room enough for two, for a couple nights anyway.'

Erin squeezed her eyes shut in incomprehension. 'Dad has been having an affair?'

Veronica's tone was annoyed at having to repeat herself. 'Didn't I just say so?'

Erin opened her eyes and stared at her mother. She looked just the same as always, hair carefully styled, clothes immaculate. Her feet in high heels even though she'd driven all this way. Erin knew there'd be a pair of flats on the floor in front of the passenger's seat in her mother's car.

She would have swapped them for the heels as soon as she'd arrived.

'With his personal assistant?'

'Yes,' Veronica's tone was acerbic. 'That's what they call secretaries these days.'

'And this isn't the first time he's done this?'

Veronica shook her head. 'No, but this time he's gone too far. It's impacted me and my home.'

'Because he kept seeing her during the lockdown?'

'He could have made me sick! I haven't worked this hard to have everything put at risk because your father can't go two months without his bit on the side.'

Erin looked down at the crumbs on the table. 'I have a headache,' she said.

'Drinking in the afternoon always gave you a headache,' Veronica said, sitting back comfortably. The news had been delivered, and she was staying. It was done. Now she could afford to be generous with her daughter. She reached for her handbag again. 'I've some painkillers if you need them.'

'I haven't been drinking,' Erin said, planting an elbow on the table and resting her head on it, her thoughts whirling.

Veronica shook her head and leant forward. 'So it was one of your episodes, then,' she said. 'You told me you hadn't had any since you moved here.'

'I haven't,' Erin replied. 'It wasn't one.'

'Then what was going on? That boy had to carry you inside, for heaven's sakes.'

Erin rubbed her face with both hands and groaned. 'Mum,' she said. 'I can't even begin to tell you what I was doing.'

That made Veronica reach over the table and pick up

Erin's cup. She brought it to her nose and sniffed. 'What is this?' she asked.

'It's tea,' Erin said. 'Stephan made it.' She swallowed down the impulse to groan out loud again. 'It's to ground you after you've been...' She trailed off.

There was no way to explain to her mother what she'd been doing.

Her mother of all people.

Here was a giant spanner in the works. And things had been going along so well.

'After you've been what, exactly?' Veronica asked. She put the cup to her lips and tasted it. The tea was slightly sweet. 'And how does your gardener get to make you tea?'

'He's not my gardener.' Erin peered at her mother through splayed fingers. 'He's my boyfriend.'

'And your gardener.'

Erin rolled her eyes. 'Of course he's not my gardener – how am I supposed to afford a gardener, for crying out loud! I work part time at a care home, for goodness' sakes.'

'I'm her boyfriend,' Stephan said, coming back into the kitchen with a wary Burdock.

Veronica's lip curled. 'I see you still have the dog. I wouldn't have thought you'd keep it.'

Burdock sniffed the air then skirted around the strange woman at the table and pressed himself against Erin.

'Of course I still have Burdock,' Erin said. 'And yes, Stephan is my boyfriend, and he's a gardener and an herbalist, and he made the tea you're drinking too.'

She was tired suddenly. Deathly tired. Exhausted. One moment, she'd been in the Otherworld, following the path of her initiation, and the next, she was jerked back into a world that couldn't possibly be real. What on earth was she going to do with her mother around? And going back to the flat with her? She couldn't even think about that.

'I'm dreaming, aren't I?' she asked. 'This can't be happening.'

Her mother stared at her. 'You're not dreaming. I'm here, I'm staying. I need some support and you're my daughter so I'm staying with you.'

Erin looked past Veronica to where Stephan stood in the kitchen, uncomfortable, his hands shoved deep in his pockets. She met his eyes and found no help there. Neither of them had expected this.

'*Isaz*,' she murmured. 'The winter freeze.'

Stephan looked back at her, taking in the shadows under her eyes even while the afternoon sun set her hair alight.

'*Thurisaz*,' he said back to her, reminding her.

She straightened, dropped her hands from her face, and smiled a little.

Veronica looked suspiciously back and forth between them. 'What are you saying? What language is that?' she asked. Maybe her daughter was caught up in some sort of cult, after all. One with their own language.

Maybe she'd stay a little longer, sort out exactly what was going on here. She'd be able to see through a cult for what it was in three seconds flat.

27

WINSOME WIPED HER HANDS AGAINST HER JEANS, THEN before she could stop herself, she reached up to her collar – or lack of collar.

'Come on,' she told herself. 'You've got to move on. A silly bit of fabric missing doesn't make any difference.' She closed her eyes. The white collar might not make a difference, but not being a vicar anymore did.

The door opened and Cynthia Ruskin beamed at her. 'Winsome!' she said. 'Isn't this wonderful – you actually being able to come to the house again?'

Winsome was speechless for a moment in the face of such a welcome. She hadn't been sure what to expect when she'd called Cynthia back and made a time to come see her. Winsome cleared her throat.

'It's wonderful,' she agreed, and stepped inside the house when Cynthia backed up to let her in. 'It makes such a difference knowing we're allowed to see each other again.' She pressed her palms to her thighs and risked a quick glance over at Cynthia, to see if the smile was still on her face, that it hadn't slid right off the moment the door was closed.

But it was still there. Although Winsome's glance caught Cynthia in mid-eyeroll.

'Having said that...' Cynthia began.

Winsome's heart pounded. Here it came, she thought. The recriminations. The blame. She glanced down at Cù, who had followed her down the street from the vicarage for all the world like a real dog determined not to be left at home alone. But Cù was staring past both women and not paying her any attention.

'We have to sit out in the garden anyway,' Cynthia said. 'Since there's more than six of us.' She shook her head. 'Thank God the weather is holding. It's a blessing to see the sun again, even if it will likely be raining again by evening.'

She stopped chattering and looked more closely at Winsome.

'Vicar,' she said. 'Are you all right?'

Winsome reared back, eyes round, stricken. 'I'm not the vicar anymore.'

Cynthia smiled sympathetically. 'Sorry, Winsome,' she said. 'Force of habit.' She puckered her eyebrows in a frown. 'But are you all right?'

Her hands were sweaty again, so Winsome pressed them harder against her legs. 'I, erm...' She blinked in the cool dimness of the hallway. 'I erm, guess I'm not sure what's happening here?'

Winsome grimaced at how her voice sounded – all thready and insipid and unsure. She cleared her throat. 'You wanted to...have a chat?'

Understanding dawned on Cynthia's face and she reached out and gave Winsome a sudden hug. 'I don't know if we're strictly allowed to do this, yet,' she said over Winsome's shoulder. 'But that's just too bad.'

Winsome made a whimpering noise, and Cynthia let her go and went back to beaming at her instead. 'I was so glad when you called me back and said you would come, Winsome.'

Winsome nodded dumbly.

'We've been desperately looking forward to when we could meet up, all of us.' Cynthia blinked, then hurried on. 'Not that all of us are here today. Just a few. But it's a start, isn't it?'

'What's a start?' Winsome felt hopelessly lost. As though she'd opened a novel to a page in the middle and had no idea what the story was.

'Come on,' Cynthia said. 'Why don't you come and say hello to the others and then we can get this little meeting rolling, don't you think?'

The word *meeting* set alarm bells off in Winsome's head, and she looked longingly at the front door, imagining dashing back out it and onto the street, running home to the vicarage and diving back under the covers of her bed.

But Cù stood in front of the door, and the look on his face said very clearly that opening it and leaving was not on her to-do list.

She swallowed down the lump in her throat and followed Cynthia's retreating back instead.

Cynthia ushered her outside and Winsome stood for a moment blinking in the afternoon sunlight on the cobbled courtyard, stunned at the women waiting for her.

'Winsome,' Rosalie said, getting up from her chair and coming over to hug her.

'Hello Rosalie,' Winsome squeaked into the softness of the older woman.

The others greeted her too, coming up one after another to wrap their arms gently around her.

When Fiona Davis, the last one of the group, let her go, there were tears in Winsome's eyes. She shook her head.

'I didn't expect this,' she said, and her voice was rough with feeling.

Cynthia patted her on the shoulder. 'Sit down, Winsome,' she said.

Winsome did as she was bidden, blindly. 'I thought you'd all be terribly angry with me. I'm terribly angry with myself.'

It was Rosalie who answered. 'If our Minnie were present to hear you say that,' she said. 'The girl would have a fit.'

Winsome found a bleary smile. 'How is Minnie?'

'Not happy about having to go back to school,' Rosalie said fondly. 'She's making noises about leaving to work at Haven full time, but Krista won't have it.' She sighed happily. 'And Natasha has found work – did you know?'

Winsome shook her head. Of course she didn't. Really, she'd been hiding away from everyone but Morghan with her comforting, mostly silent walks. 'What's she doing?'

'She's got a position as bartender at The Green Man, and is over the moon about it, and looking forward to it opening.' Rosalie patted her lap. 'That will leave me looking after Tiny and little Robin, but I don't mind – you pull together don't you, when that's what you need to do?'

Winsome nodded, the lump back in her throat. She cleared it and found her voice, making herself look around at the circle of women, meeting each gaze in turn. It hurt to do so, but she made herself.

'I want to apologise,' she said, and held up a hand at Emily Bright who had opened her mouth to interrupt. 'No,' Winsome said. 'I need to.' She took a breath and made herself say the words. If she didn't say them, then they would just be in between herself and these women, floating there, tainting everything. She flashed on her dream, scrabbling around in the ruins.

'It was my actions,' Winsome said. 'My personal actions, that got St. Bridget's closed. And I'm sorry. I took away from Wellsford – from each of you – something valuable, something that can't be replaced.'

Around the circle of women, heads were shaken. It was Melody Roper who spoke up. 'I'm not going to say it wasn't a shock, Winsome,' she said, 'but I think I'm speaking for everyone here when I say that what's done is done, and now isn't the time to just be sitting on our backsides moaning.'

Now everyone nodded. Winsome stared at them.

'You're being very generous,' she said.

'Isn't that the only way things are going to work?' Cynthia asked in a low voice. 'If we're each generous with each other? You spent every Sunday in that church reminding us of that.'

Winsome bowed her head, looked at her knotted hands in her lap. There were high spots of colour in her cheeks and tears threatened to spill from under her lids.

'Now,' Cynthia spoke again, more briskly, and Winsome looked up and across the circle at her. 'What we wanted you here for, is so that we can decide on some sort of plan of action. Because things can be replaced.'

The statement made Winsome frown. 'Some sort of plan of action?' she asked helplessly.

Emily replied. 'That's right,' she said. 'We may not be able to use the church building just now, but we still have needs that require care.'

Winsome looked blankly at her. 'Needs?'

'Spiritual needs,' Emily said.

'But I'm not a vicar anymore,' Winsome answered.

'Does that have to matter?' Fiona asked.

Winsome spluttered at the question. 'How can it not matter?'

Cynthia held up her hands. 'Winsome,' she said. 'Here's what we've been discussing amongst ourselves and why we've invited you here today.'

Winsome turned wide, unseeing eyes on her. She felt shivery, as though a fever was coming over her.

'There's a lot that's been happening in Wellsford,' Cynthia said, and the rest of the ladies in the circle nodded, letting Cynthia Ruskin speak for them all. Cynthia held up a hand and ticked the points off as she spoke. 'The new way we're pooling together with the grocery subscription. The community garden, so that everyone has access to fresh fruit and veg. The care home, so that our oldest folk can stay close.' She blinked.

'The new doctor's office,' Sharon Johnston said. 'I hear plans for that are being drawn up.' She shook her head. 'I can't believe our little village is going to end up so well off.'

Everyone was silent for a moment, thinking about that.

'And then there are our own efforts,' Rosalie said. 'The

little charity shop. The Men's Shed. Our coffee mornings and play groups.'

Winsome looked at her.

'These are all things we need to keep going, Winsome,' Rosalie explained. 'These are all things we are determined to keep going.' She wrinkled her nose. 'As and when we can, of course, considering the health risks and all of it.'

Winsome opened her mouth, thought for a moment, couldn't come up with anything to say, and closed her mouth again.

Emily Bright leant forward. 'We also want to start up a prayer and meditation group,' she said. 'And we want particularly for you to lead that.'

'I was so pleased to see that you'd begun writing on your blog again,' Melody said. 'And please,' she said, 'for the love of God, perhaps you could teach us some more of your exercises?'

Everyone nodded.

Winsome stared at them, then away at the flower beds that lined the fence around Cynthia's back garden. She shook her head.

'I'm...overwhelmed,' Winsome said at last. 'This is the last thing I expected, really.'

'I suppose we ought to have asked, if you're planning to stay on here in Wellsford?' Rosalie said, her soft face wrinkling with concern.

'That's right,' Cynthia said. 'It's all very well us wanting a lot of things from you – but what do you want? What are your plans?'

'I can't imagine Wellsford without you,' Linda Wattle broke in to say. 'You helped me settle back in.'

'That's right,' Sharon said. 'Without you and the woman from Haven, I wouldn't know how I'd be surviving.'

Winsome looked at her. 'Anyone could have done that for you, Sharon,' she said.

But Sharon shook her head. 'There you're wrong, though, Winsome. You took it upon yourself to make sure we were okay, and to do something about it when you found out we were floundering.' She rubbed bony knuckles against her chin. 'I know others here now would help, if it came to it now that they know me, but you did it as a matter of course.'

'It was my job,' Winsome said.

'It could still be your job,' Sharon said, and glanced around at the rest of the group. 'Who else is going to do it all – everything that you used to? Them down in Banwell, they're not going to come all the way up here to check on any of us. It's up to us.'

'Have you organised another job, Winsome?' Cynthia asked. 'I did some research and in situations like this, the Church usually pays for another year after a vicar has been retired?'

Winsome pressed a hand to her forehead. 'Erm,' she said. 'That's right. I've a year's salary, as a sort of severance package, and the vicarage for that time too.'

Sharon sat back in triumph. 'So you could carry on, then,' she said.

'And we can work on how to continue paying you when the year comes to an end,' Melody continued. 'We're thinking perhaps the proceeds from the charity shop, and whatever else we can come up with.'

Winsome shook her head. 'This is too much,' she said. 'My head's spinning.'

Cynthia stood up and clapped her hands. 'Coffee break time,' she said. 'I did some baking as well, so we've fresh ginger cake, one of Simon Wishall's recipes; did you know he's putting together a book of his recipes?' She smiled widely. 'I'm one of his testers. Great fun!'

Winsome watched in bemused silence as the women bustled about, pouring coffee and tea, passing around slices of cake, laughing and joking with each other. She glanced at Cù, sitting at her side, tongue hanging out as if for all the world he was enjoying the gathering as much as everyone else.

'So,' Cynthia said after everyone was sitting down again, mugs at their elbows, plates on laps. 'Mmm, this cake is so good, even if I do say so myself.'

'I'll be getting his book for sure,' Rosalie said. 'I've been doing a bit more baking, what with kiddies in the house.' She mopped up some crumbs. 'Mind you, with Natasha working soon, she says she'll be looking for a place of their own.'

'There are several houses empty,' Fiona said. 'What with those who have moved elsewhere to be with their families.'

'And there's Mariah's house,' Melody said. 'Does anyone know what's going to happen with that?'

'She still hasn't been found, then?' Emily asked. 'What do you think happened to her?'

'Fairies got her,' Cynthia said.

'Cynthia!' Emily said, swallowing a gasp along with her last bite of the cake.

But Cynthia just shrugged. 'Well, we know there's more

that goes on in these hills than we can see, don't we? And the stories of the fairies go back before memory.'

Suddenly, all eyes turned to Winsome. 'You know Morghan better than any of us,' Melody said. 'Was it the fairies?'

'Oh,' Winsome said. 'Erm.' She blinked, at a loss for what to say. 'What does Morghan have to do with it?'

Rosalie laughed. 'Most of us have lived here our whole lives, Winsome,' she said. 'And you don't live next door to Wilde Grove without noticing a few odd goings-on.'

'Maybe,' Winsome managed, because it was undeniably true. 'But fairies?' Winsome remembered the man Morghan had summoned, dark-haired and beautiful. Otherworldly. 'You think it was fairies?'

'My grandmother used to say she'd danced with them once,' Linda said. 'I was only a little tot when she told me the story, and by the time I moved away I'd gotten around to not believing it.' She sat for a moment, musing, then shrugged. 'But Rosalie's right. Living in these hills, you see and hear things.'

'She danced with them?' Winsome asked, astonished.

'Yeah. Said it was the best night of her life.' Linda's eyes narrowed. 'You know, now that I think about it, and the way my Mum told her to hush whenever she mentioned it, I wonder if 'dancing' was a bit of a...what is it?'

'A euphemism,' Cynthia said.

'Yeah. That,' Linda said. 'A euphemism for a bit of the old you-know.' The smile on her face widened. 'Granny said they told her she could stay with them almost forever if she wanted to.' Linda shook her head. 'She didn't – obviously –

but I think there was a little bit of her that was sorely tempted.'

'Who would want Mariah, though?' Sharon asked. 'I don't want to be uncharitable, but the woman was not a nice person.'

Winsome followed the conversation, her head reeling.

'You know,' Rosalie said, leaning forward. 'There was a bit of a story about Mariah, when she was young, not even in her twenties, I'd say.' Her eyes turned faraway as she tried to remember.

'It was just gossip, so you'll have to forgive me bringing it up. But it was whispered around the village that she'd sneaked up to the stone circle one midsummer's or the like, and danced with the Fae.' Rosalie blinked herself back to the present. 'Her Ma didn't let her out of the house for a month after that, and when she did see the light of day again, Mariah was changed.'

Everyone was quiet for a long moment after that, and then Cynthia turned to Winsome once more.

'Will you think about it, then?' she asked. 'Leading us in prayer and, well, study, I suppose. Once or twice a week?'

'And we could go through your exercises together, and maybe you could teach us some more of that sort of thing,' Emily said. 'They've been so useful, with all the worry of these last months. I've bookmarked your little videos so I can go back to them every day.'

Rosalie nodded. 'I've practically worn your pamphlet to shreds.'

Everyone looked at Winsome, waiting for an answer.

28

Prayer and deepening into their spiritual lives.

Healthy habits in the changing world.

Community support.

Well, Winsome thought. A lot could be done with that sort of brief. She sat back in her chair at the vicarage kitchen table and looked thoughtfully at the ceiling. And hadn't she already decided? To do exactly this?

Still. She hadn't expected it all to just fall into her lap.

That made Winsome think of something, and she frowned into space for a moment, then got up and went upstairs to her bedroom, and plucked up the book Stephan had given her the day Cù had led her down to see him and Erin. She'd popped it there that evening, but hadn't opened it, her breath catching whenever she looked at it. Runes. Some sort of divination tool, she'd thought, unable to overcome the hesitancy her faith had instilled in her over such things.

Now, she took it downstairs with her, and slid out the

piece of paper on which Stephan had drawn the strange symbols.

At the table, she sat back down and flipped through the book, pausing to read part of the introduction, her brows raised as she realised the symbols were a great deal more than just something for fortune telling. At last, she looked up the three symbols Stephan had copied down for her.

Tiwaz. Winsome cleared her throat, read through the meaning for the rune, then read it again, out loud.

'Victory and honour comes when one grows into the life demanded by spirit, not heedless of the difficulties and trials along the way, but upright and full of the conviction that comes when one unfurls in balance with the universe.'

Well, she thought. If that wasn't a message she needed to hear. She shifted in her seat, uncomfortable with the truth that she'd unwittingly discovered.

'Into the life demanded by spirit,' she repeated. Then blinked and flipped through the pages seeking out the next symbol.

'*Thuriasaz,*' she read, and cleared her throat again. 'The threats of the world seem to loom over you, and their shadow looks vast and dark. Know however, that all problems must be dealt with in spirit before you can act in the world, and the spirit is bright enough to cast aside all shadow.'

Winsome sat back, feeling winded. How could such simple things like these seem to sum up her life as it stood right at that moment? She shook her head and cast her eyes over the words again. What did it mean, that all problems must be dealt with in spirit before you can act in the world? She tapped her fingers against the piece of paper with

Stephan's symbols on it, then shook her head and found the last of the three.

'*Isaz*. The winter landscape freezes. The wind howls across the ice. Know too, that if you are frozen, unable to act, that after the winter freeze comes the thaw, and new life is born from the time of cold and stillness.'

Winsome put the book down and reached up to touch her cheeks, startled to find that they were wet with silent tears. She sniffed and looked at the page in the book again. This was where she was, she thought. In the winter freeze.

Coming out of the winter freeze, she corrected herself, and that was better. She blinked at the words again.

'And new life is born from the time of cold and stillness.'

That's what she was doing, wasn't it? She was growing a new life. A new life that spirit was demanding of her. Was God demanding it of her? Were they the same thing?

Did that matter? The world was so big. She drew in a deep breath and looked around the room and at her laptop and notepads on the table as though she were seeing them for the first time.

It was time, Winsome decided, for that new life, for the one that is hard won after the freeze of winter, after picking through the rubble.

One thing was bothering her though. Sitting up, she picked up her cup of tea and sipped slowly at it, letting herself relax, picking at the knots of what was dancing around on the edge of her awareness.

The thought that something was missing. Something big. Something she needed to make right, especially now that such graciousness had been given to her by the women of her old parish.

Winsome closed her eyes and saw again Morghan's gaze as she stood on the wooden cart, the noose around her neck.

She saw how that gaze had not wavered. Not wavered an inch as she stood there, waiting to hang in Blythe's place.

And there was Erin, Winsome suddenly thought. Erin, who went to work every day and cared for the man who had been there when her birth mother had died. Who had been partly responsible for that death.

And there was Eileen, who had let herself be poisoned by her own fear and anger. Winsome closed her eyes at the memory of the dark shell that had formed around the poor woman.

She put down her cup, closed the screen of her laptop, and picked up her keys, shoved her feet back into her shoes and was out the door before she'd even finished shrugging on her light jacket.

Cù, when she looked for him, was already on the foot-path waiting.

No one came to the door when she knocked, and Winsome raised an eyebrow to Cù, who glanced at her, then narrowed his eyes at the curtained window beside the door.

Winsome nodded. She'd seen the slight twitch of fabric as well. She knocked again.

'Julia,' she shouted. 'I'm not going away, so you may as well open the door.'

She waited.

It took Julia another three or four minutes to come to the door and Winsome couldn't help the smile at the woman's intransigence. She hid the smile quickly.

'What do you want?' Julia asked. The door was open the bare amount necessary for her to look through.

'I'd like to come in, if I may,' Winsome said, keeping her voice low, gentle. Julia was pale, with dark hollows under her eyes.

Winsome held up the small box in her hands. 'I brought cake,' she said.

Julia blinked.

'Two slices of The Copper Kettle's chocolate fudge cake. Your favourite, if I remember rightly.'

It was Winsome's favourite as well, and she hadn't had any since...since before her personal world had fallen apart. It seemed appropriate somehow to eat it again with Julia.

If she could get Julia to let her in.

'What do you want? Why are you bringing me cake?'

Julia shuffled back a step and the door creaked closed.

Winsome stuck her foot in the doorway, then winced as the heavy door jammed against it. It's what they always did in books and movies, she thought irrelevantly. They never showed it hurting, though.

'What are you doing?' Julia tugged against the door, then kicked Winsome's foot to dislodge it.

That hurt too. Winsome should have worn her hiking boots.

'Please, Julia, let me come in,' she said. 'Just for five minutes.'

The door opened slightly wider. 'Get your foot out of my door,' Julia said.

Winsome removed it.

'Please, Julia,' she said. 'I just want to check in with you. Make sure you're okay.'

The door didn't open any wider, but it didn't close either. Julia's eyes were suspicious.

'Why do you care?' she asked.

That was a good question, Winsome thought. Julia had every right to ask it. She cleared her throat, grasping the box with the cake in front of her.

'Because you've suffered a loss, Julia,' Winsome said, keeping her voice low and calm, kind. Julia looked about as ready to startle and bolt as a young deer. 'No one should have to deal with the aftermath of a loss on their own.'

The door cracked open half an inch more. 'You've lost your position,' Julia said.

Winsome hung her head, examining her feet for a moment before nodding and raising her face to look Julia in the eye. 'I have, yes. And it's been difficult, I won't lie.' She frowned. 'It's been dreadful, actually. I couldn't have imagined it.' Winsome drew breath. 'But you've lost what you valued as well.' She paused and gripped the bakery box tighter. 'And Mariah. You've lost your aunt too.'

Julia's eyes narrowed. 'I don't know what happened to my aunt,' she said. 'The police questioned me and cleared me from the investigation.'

Winsome knew that, of course, but she was surprised by the way Julia said it so quickly. She remembered Cynthia and the other woman saying the fairies had got to Mariah and wondered what, if anything, Julia had seen.

'Of course,' she said. 'I don't think you had anything to do with your aunt's disappearance. I only came to see how you are, make amends. If you want to talk about your aunt, that's up to you.'

'I don't,' Julia said.

Winsome nodded, waited, glanced at Cù, who seemed to be watching Julia with fascination.

The door opened at last. 'Fine,' Julia said. 'Come in then.' She turned away. 'But the dog has to stay outside. I don't like dogs.'

Winsome almost dropped the box that held the two slices of Simon's chocolate cake. 'You can see Cù?' she asked, her voice hoarse with shock.

Julia looked back at her and frowned. 'Why wouldn't I be able to see your dog?' she said. 'He's right there.'

A minute's silence stretched out while Winsome groped about for a reply. She looked down at Cù, but all he did was stare up at her with his grin on his face and his eyes shining.

Julia turned away again, and this time Winsome scrabbled to follow her, closing the door on the smiling spirit dog.

'I'm surprised you got yourself a dog, Winsome,' Julia was saying. 'When you'll have to be moving.'

'Ah, he just sort of turned up,' Winsome said.

'Taking in strays,' Julia said, wrinkling her nose. 'I hope you gave him a bath.'

Winsome tried to imagine getting Cù into the bathtub at the vicarage and shook her head. 'He's perfectly clean,' she said.

Julia led her through the house to the kitchen at the rear and cleared the table quickly of last night's tea dishes. She dumped them swiftly into the sink and reached for the electric kettle, filling it up and switching it on.

'Tea?' she asked. 'Coffee?'

'Tea would be lovely,' Winsome said.

Julia jerked her head in what Winsome supposed to be a

nod and told her to sit down. Winsome sat and focused finally on her surroundings.

The kitchen was a mess. Dirty dishes, and the floor could have done with a good mopping. Winsome looked over at Julia's stiff back and felt a pang of sympathy. Despite everything.

'How have you been, Julia?' she asked gently. 'It's been a rough few months, hasn't it?'

But Julia just shook her head. She didn't know why Winsome was there, inside her house, sitting in her kitchen, her face creased with concern, and what looked like kindness.

Except it couldn't be kindness, could it?

After everything she and Mariah had done.

She took two mugs down from the cupboard, rinsed the dust from them, and took them over to the table, setting them down in an abrupt clatter.

Winsome watched her go back to stand over the kettle, looking at it while it heated, her back towards the room. She tried again.

'Have you been getting out regularly, Julia?' she asked. 'It's important not to stay cooped up inside all the time, I think.' Even though she herself was guilty of it, choosing to walk in the woods rather than show her face in the village.

'People in the village don't like me anymore,' Julia said, her voice strangled.

Winsome nodded. This didn't surprise her, and Cynthia had said that the couple of Mariah's friends had come slinking around to admitting that Mariah and Julia had gone too far, as though they hadn't helped.

Or as though they realised they'd been wrong.

But Julia hadn't finished and Winsome listened again.

'And I can't go in the woods,' Julia said with a shudder. 'There are things in the woods.'

'Things?'

Julia turned, her pale tongue darting out to wet her cracked lips. She nodded. 'Things,' she repeated. 'People.'

'People?'

This was not at all how Winsome had imagined her conversation going with Julia. It seemed she would have to change tack a little. And there was little point pretending that nothing had happened to Mariah that night, that Winsome didn't know.

'You were with Mariah when they took her, weren't you, Julia?' Winsome said, keeping her voice as soothing as possible. 'That must have been distressing.'

Julia stared at her, tears suddenly streaming down her cheeks. She didn't notice them.

Winsome nodded. 'You saw them, didn't you – the Fae?'

Julia shuddered, shook her head, closed her eyes. 'It wasn't real.'

The kettle wailed, clicked itself off.

'It wasn't real,' Julia repeated. 'They weren't real. I was high, that's all. I don't know what you're talking about.'

High, Winsome wondered? Then nodded to herself. Petrol fumes.

'I don't think so,' she said. 'I've seen them too.'

Now Julia shook her head more violently. 'I don't know what you're talking about,' she repeated. 'They're not real. You're deluded.'

Cù wandered into the kitchen and sat down on the dirty floor, staring at Julia.

'How did he get inside?' she asked. 'Didn't you close the door? I told you he had to stay outside.'

'I closed the door,' Winsome said gently.

Julia shook her head, lank hair slapping her cheeks.

'He's not a real dog,' Winsome said. 'He's a spirit guide.'

Julia clamped her hands over her ears and stared wildly at Winsome.

'No,' she said.

Winsome got up and walked over to her, placing her hands softly over Julia's and drawing them away. She held onto Julia's cold fingers and gave them a squeeze. 'Sit yourself down,' she said. 'I'll make us that tea.'

29

ERIN CREPT DOWN THE STAIRS, BURDOCK AT HER HEELS. SHE winced with every creaking step, desperate not to wake her mother, who had finally gone to sleep in the spare room the night before.

She still couldn't believe her mother was there, in Wellsford, staying at Ash Cottage. How had that come about?

There was a light on downstairs and Erin frowned. Had she forgotten to turn it off before she went to bed?

'Good morning, Erin,' Veronica said. 'You needn't creep about. I've been up for hours.'

Erin straightened and gaped at her mother. 'Hours?' she said. Her mother never used to get up until well after the sun had risen, unless she had an early hair appointment, of course.

'I couldn't sleep.' Veronica said, getting up from the table.

Erin came down the rest of the stairs and stood at the

bottom, watching her mother move over to put the kettle back on the boil.

'Tea?' Veronica asked.

'You got the fire going?' Erin said.

Veronica turned and looked at her daughter. 'I wasn't born yesterday, you know. I can stir some embers to life and throw on some kindling.'

Burdock went and stood by the front door, not pleased the strange woman with the hard voice was still in the house. He liked things just the way they had been. And where was Stephan, he wondered? The bad lady had chased him away.

Erin gaped at her mother, then covered her mouth with her hand. 'I just never imagined...' she said.

'What? That I'm capable of looking after things?'

Erin shrugged awkwardly. 'I thought you'd be grumbling about the kitchen,' she said.

'Yes,' Veronica answered. 'But grumbling wouldn't get me a cup of tea, now, would it?' She picked up the teapot and swished out the leaves under the running tap. 'Besides, my grandparents used to live in a place like this, did I ever tell you?' She looked around the kitchen, one corner of her mouth turned down at the memory.

'No,' Erin said, shocked. 'You never told me that.' She did a quick inventory of her relatives. 'I can't imagine Grandmother in anything like this.' She was the one who was spending the lockdowns in a hotel on the French Riveria.

'Not your grandmother, and not your father's side of the family.' Veronica spooned fresh tea leaves into the pot. 'My grandparents, I said.'

Erin let Burdock out the front door, watched for a moment as he galloped off over the lawn, disturbing the early morning birds from catching their worms, then closed the door.

'Have you ever told me about your grandparents?' Erin said, a frown pressing between her brows. She scooted around her mother and got Burdock's biscuits from the cupboard.

'I shouldn't think so,' Veronica said. 'They died when I was eight.'

'And they lived in a cottage like this?'

'Worse than this,' Veronica said, wrinkling her nose. 'There was no indoor toilet.'

Erin's eyes widened. 'What?'

'It was perfectly common. The outhouse was literally an outside house, at the bottom of the garden.' Veronica plucked up the kettle just as it started to whine. She splashed hot water into the pot. 'My grandmother had a coal range and a copper for boiling clothes in to wash. All very primitive.'

Erin, standing over Burdock's bowl, gaped at her mother. 'But I thought your family was, well, rich.'

Veronica shook her head. 'No,' she said. 'They weren't. Not my grandparents, and certainly not my mother.' She paused, her lips tightening. 'I never knew my father.'

'How did I not know this?' Erin asked. 'Why did you never tell me?'

Veronica sniffed and carried the teapot to the table, along with a fresh cup for her daughter. 'Why would I?' she asked, sitting back down.

'Why wouldn't you?' Erin said, putting the dog biscuits

back in the cupboard and going to the door to let Burdock back in. He smelt of rain and ran straight to his bowl, happy to find it blessedly full.

Erin shut the door and stood behind one of the chairs at the table, gripping its back with both hands.

But Veronica just shrugged. 'I left all that behind,' she said. 'Why would I give it any thought?'

'What?' Erin said, frowning. 'I don't understand.' She shook her head. 'What do you mean you left it all behind? It's your history – your family.'

'Was,' Veronica shrugged. 'I wanted better for myself, and I got it.'

It was true, Erin realised. Her mother had never talked about her family except to say they were gone. And Erin had been too preoccupied with her own adopted status to wonder why her mother was never interested in talking about her own past.

'So,' Veronica said. 'I can find my way about a wood-fired cooker, and I'm very glad the loo is inside. I'm pretending I'm on some sort of rustic retreat.'

'You're visiting your daughter in her home,' Erin said.

'Not the home I chose for her,' Veronica retorted.

There was silence in the kitchen then, except for the ticking of the fire and Burdock crunching through his biscuits. And faintly, the sound of drizzling rain. Erin glanced out the window.

She needed to go out into the garden, greet the day with her usual devotions.

'What are you doing standing there?' Veronica demanded. 'Sit down for crying out loud. Your tea's going cold.'

Erin hesitated a moment, then sat. How could she go out into the garden and say her prayers there, while her mother looked on at her through the window, wondering what on earth she was up to?

The thought was dismaying. Erin sat down, not knowing what else to do. She wrapped her hands around the mug her mother slid over to her.

'The tea is surprisingly good,' Veronica said grudgingly. 'I guess your gardener knows what he's doing after all.'

'He's not my gardener,' Erin said. 'Stephan is my boyfriend, as you know perfectly well.' She'd missed him last night, in the bed beside her. And that was a worry too. It was the first night they'd spent apart since the first night they'd spent together, and she was already wishing he hadn't gone back to his flat over Haven For Books.

Although, sleeping with him when her mother was in the next room sounded so much like an awkward idea.

Veronica watched her daughter sitting frozen at the table like a deer in the headlights. The girl's colour was good though, she thought. And despite the odd choice in clothing – Erin wore a colourful Arran knit jumper over a long skirt – she looked fit and healthy, as though the country air had been good for her.

'We should get your car back for you,' she said, and reached for her phone to add it to her list.

'What?'

'Your car,' Veronica repeated. 'How on earth have you managed here in the middle of nowhere without it?'

Erin stared at her mother. 'You took it off me,' she said. 'How do you think I've been managing?' She shook her head. 'Remember having it towed from here? Remember stopping my allowance without any warning?'

But Veronica just sniffed. 'Of course we can get your allowance back as well,' she said, and smiled grimly. 'Your father isn't in a position to negotiate right now. I say we use that to our advantage.'

Erin sat up, pushing away her tea. 'I don't want my allowance back,' she said. 'I've been doing just fine without it.' She thought of the cards Krista had printed up from her artwork, and the prints to frame for the wall. 'I have a job, and I'm starting to sell some of my artwork.'

'Don't be silly,' Veronica said, her laugh making Burdock prick up his ears from where he'd gone to sit warily at Erin's side. 'You can't want to keep working at a care home when you don't need to, and it's lovely that you're selling some of your pictures, dear, but let's be reasonable here, once we get back to London, you'll need your allowance.'

'What do you mean once we get back to London?'

'You're not going to make me stay there on my own, are you?' Veronica arranged her features in a wounded expression. 'This is a difficult time for me. I need your support.'

'I don't want to go back to the city,' Erin said stiffly. 'I'm busy here.' She shook her head. 'I'm needed here.'

Veronica looked at her, taking her time, carefully and consideringly. 'Who needs you here?' she asked after a minute.

But Erin shook her head. 'You wouldn't understand,' she said.

'Ah,' Veronica answered. 'The cult that's not a cult, am I right? You can't go because of your involvement in this Wilde Grove whatever.'

'It's not a cult.'

'What is it, then?'

Erin looked down at her tea, then took a sip to give herself time to figure out how to answer her mother's question. She cleared her throat.

'It's a...a spiritual group,' she said, then groaned inwardly. That made it sound exactly like a cult.

'That sounds exactly like a cult,' Veronica said, one eyebrow arched.

Erin shook her head. 'It's hard to explain,' she said. 'I guess it's a group of Druids and witches who are deeply involved in seeing the world as it actually is.'

Veronica looked at her. 'As it actually is,' she repeated. 'I can tell you how it actually is.' She bent across the table, eyes narrowed.

Erin could smell the tea on her breath.

'It's a hard world out there, Erin,' Veronica said. 'If you don't climb and claw your way out of the gutter, then there are plenty who are happy to stand on you while they do it instead. And plenty who will throw you back down there, if you let them.' She sat up and picked up her cup. 'That's the real world, Erin, and I worked hard to make it as far up as I got, and none of your spiritual mumbo jumbo is going to make anything any different.'

30

Winsome squared her shoulders and took a deep
breath. 'So,' she said to Cù. 'Here goes nothing. Maybe.'

The spirit dog looked at her, then dropped his jaw into a
grin and let his tongue loll.

'You're no help,' Winsome muttered, but the dog just
hung his tongue out further. Winsome shook her head and
looked away, at the front door.

Just a short walk up the path, knock on the door, and try
her best. That was what she had to do. All she had to do.

Maybe this time, she wouldn't have to jam her foot in
the door to get let in.

Julia opened the door, saw Winsome there, and immediately shook her head. 'No,' she said. 'No way.'

'Please?' Winsome said.

'No.' Julia shook her head, but she opened the door
wider, so that Winsome could enter. She stalked back down
the hallway to the kitchen and sat down at the table. The
remains of a pie sat cooling on a plate.

'That looks good,' Winsome said, sitting down opposite her. 'Did you make it?'

Julia shook her head. She'd bought them on special in Banwell. A pack of four. But she didn't think she liked pies anymore.

They reminded her of Mariah.

'What do you want?' she asked Winsome, keeping her eyes carefully averted from the dog that sat itself casually beside Winsome as though all was right with the world, and it wasn't some sort of unnatural abomination.

Winsome took a breath, trying to ignore the scent of the congealing pie and planted a smile on her face instead that she hoped was determined rather than wheedling. She glanced at Cù, but he was relaxed, his light brown eyes looking at Julia with what could only be called a great deal of interest.

She was right to be here, Winsome thought. She was following her impulse, her intuition, if she liked, and Cù certainly seemed to be going along with it.

'Well,' she said. 'I know we had our...differences of opinion when you were churchwarden...'

'And you the vicar,' Julia said. 'Which you aren't anymore.'

Winsome looked down at her lap and stamped down on the question she was asking herself.

Why are you doing this?

She took another breath. 'Yes, when I was vicar and you the churchwarden, that's right. When that was the case, you were very good at organising things.' Winsome wound down, then determinedly started back up again. She was here for a good reason, she thought, looking at Cù again, and not failing to notice exactly how Julia kept her gaze averted from him.

Julia's narrowed eyes looked at Winsome instead.

'Well,' Winsome said. 'I would like you to help me with organising some things now.'

'What sort of things?'

Winsome nodded. That was good. That was better than a straight no. 'I want to – and some of our old parishioners, as well – we want to...set up some initiatives.'

Julia's eyes narrowed even further. 'What sort of initiatives?'

'Such as a prayer and meditation group,' Winsome said, shifting slightly in her chair and wondering for roughly the hundredth time why she was trying to get Julia's help. 'Such as an exercise class, and perhaps also some computer classes, and the like.' She gave a quick smile. 'We haven't decided on everything, yet.'

Julia's head sank down and she looked at her hands, barely able to believe that Winsome was sitting here at her table asking her to help organise things with her. After what had happened, what Mariah had done...

And her. What she had done.

Julia squeezed her eyes shut for a moment.

'I thought I'd have to move from here,' she said, looking under her lashes at Winsome. 'That's what I've been working myself up to doing.'

'Moving?' Winsome asked, wondering why she was surprised to hear Julia say it. 'From Wellsford?'

Julia nodded. 'After what Mariah did.' She took a slow breath. 'After what Mariah and I did.'

They sat at opposite sides of the table, simply looking at

each other. Then Winsome reached over and put her hand on top of Julia's.

'It's all right,' she said, feeling how cold Julia's hand was. 'You didn't go through with it. We can make mistakes, realise we were wrong, and get up again, start over.'

Julia drew her hand away, set it in her lap, looked out the window. Trees edged her small lawn. Because of course they did. This was Wellsford. The trees owned the village.

So did what walked between them.

'I saw them,' she said, the words dropping like small hard stones from her mouth.

Winsome looked sharply at her, then glanced at Cù, who was sitting now with his ears perked, listening.

'Saw who?' she asked.

Julia shuddered. 'Them,' she said, admitting what she'd refused to during their last conversation. 'The Fae.' She looked down at her hands, twisted her fingers into tight knots.

Outside, a thrush let loose a string of syllables.

Julia closed her eyes, shuddered, then looked across the table at Winsome. 'You've seen them, haven't you?'

Winsome's mouth was dry. 'Yes,' she said. 'I have.'

Julia nodded. 'They were beautiful,' she said, and closed her eyes again, seeing them in her memory. The way they shone. She licked her lips. 'One of them walked right by me,' she said. 'It even smiled at me.' She looked out the window. 'And heaven help me, the sight of it brought me to tears.' She shook her head. Then looked at Winsome.

'They took my aunt, didn't they?'

'Yes.' Winsome didn't know what else to say.

Julia nodded and looked down at her hands again. She

sighed. 'I knew they were there to stop us. Her.' She twisted her fingers. 'Are they hurting her?'

'I don't think so,' Winsome replied. 'She had met them before, your aunt. When she was young.' Winsome paused. 'If the stories about the village are to be believed.'

Julia stared at the remains of her lunch, cooling on the plate in front of her. She didn't think she'd ever eat a pie again. Not a savoury one.

'How can things so beautiful be an abomination?' she asked, her voice strangled around the words.

Winsome shook her head. 'They are not an abomination,' she said. 'They're simply another species of being.'

'What?' Julia asked, spitting out a laugh. 'Like owls, or lions, or something?'

Winsome shrugged. 'Maybe,' she said. 'It's a big world.'

'Bigger than I want it to be,' Julia muttered. She sighed, pulled her hands apart and got up from the table, picked up her plate and slid the uneaten pie into the rubbish. The dish clattered in the sink, and she ran hot water over it, scrubbed it clean.

'Why are you here?' she asked on another sigh, coming back to stand by the table, avoiding the ghost dog, and staring at Winsome. 'What do you really want?'

Winsome looked up at her. 'I want you to be okay,' she said.

Julia laughed out loud. 'Is that a possibility?' She shook her head. 'Doesn't feel like one.'

Winsome stood up, and Cù scooted out of her way, for all the world like a real dog. She grasped Julia's hands and held them tightly. 'It's a possibility, Julia,' she said.

'Why do you care?' Julia stared down at their linked hands but didn't pull away. 'We tried to ruin you.'

'I thought you had, for a while,' Winsome said. 'But nothing you did changed anything essential about me. I see that now.'

Julia pulled her hands away, went and stood against the kitchen bench, and folded her arms across her breasts.

'You're part of this village, Julia,' Winsome said. 'And so I care what happens to you. I can't do everything in this world that I want to, but I can come here and offer my help in whatever way I can. I can care about those close to me. I can try to make a difference right where I am.' She paused, took a breath. 'Let us help each other, Julia. Let us shift past this and learn from it.'

Julia looked away. 'I don't want to move,' she said. 'I like my house. I liked my job, too. Now I don't have that and I'm living off savings that are steadily dwindling.' She rubbed at sudden goosebumps on her arms. 'I don't know what we were thinking,' she said softly. Her forehead wrinkled. 'I wanted what you had,' she said. 'I liked running things, being the one everyone looked at and turned to, especially when Alfred Robinson died.'

Winsome nodded, letting her talk.

Cù sat down again, listening.

'It made me feel important,' Julia said, her mouth turning down. 'I didn't have anything else. There was just the church, and my aunt, and Mariah was nasty. I never wanted to admit it to myself, but she was nasty.'

'She carried a great burden,' Winsome said.

'What burden?' Julia asked, scoffing. 'She was just a sour old woman, who enjoyed needling me.' She shook her head.

'And I let her poison me because something inside me was just the same.'

Winsome picked up the electric kettle and filled it under the tap. 'I think we need some tea,' she said, and set it to boil. She plucked up two cups from the draining rack and looked for the teapot.

'Your aunt met the Fae, for the first time or not, I don't know, when she was about eighteen years old,' Winsome said.

Julia stared at her. 'How do you know that?'

'It was mentioned as an old village story.'

'You've been gossiping about me?' Julia took a step back, outraged.

'No,' Winsome said mildly, finding the teapot and looking for the tea. She was used to fossicking around in other people's kitchens now, while having the difficult conversations. A hot cup of tea always did wonders.

'It was Mariah I was told about,' Winsome said. 'Not you.'

Julia looked at her.

'Have you heard the story?' Winsome asked, opening the cupboards.

Julia shook her head. 'No,' she said, and got out the teabags.

Winsome took them from her with a smile. 'Like I was saying – and none of this is verified, of course, just an old bit of village history.' She paused. 'Have you always lived here, Julia?'

'No.'

'Ah,' Winsome nodded. 'So, it goes like this – your aunt

went sneaking up to the stone circle one solstice, to watch the ritual there.'

Julia's eyes widened and she slapped a hand over her gasp. 'She wouldn't,' she said, her words muffled behind her fingers.

'She was only eighteen, remember,' Winsome said, switching off the kettle just as it began to boil. She poured the water in the pot, over the teabags.

'And so, apparently, she was spotted there, spying,' Winsome said. She put the cups on the table, folded up the newspapers and magazines strewn across the surface and looked for somewhere to put them.

Julia took them from her, stood holding them.

'It was some of the Fae who saw her there.'

Julia's breath whooshed out. 'What happened?' she asked, shuddering to think of it.

'They danced together,' Winsome said. 'Which everyone seems to think means a lot more than just dancing, if you understand.'

Julia paled.

'But that isn't actually the part of the story that makes me feel bad,' Winsome said, carrying the pot to the table and sitting down.

'It isn't?'

Winsome shook her head. 'No, it's that afterwards, when Mariah's mother found out what she had done, she locked her in the house for a month.' Winsome paused, looked down at the cups. 'I think whatever went on in that house over those weeks changed your aunt irrevocably.'

Julia was silent, her fingers white against the papers.

'Mariah also carried the burden of her family history,

and her own past life – being the one that charged another Lady of the Grove with witchcraft, resulting in a hanging.'

Julia sat down, still hugging the papers to her chest. 'She always said, they'd got one once, and she'd make it happen again.' She blinked. 'I don't believe in past lives, and nor should you. It isn't Christian.'

'I didn't believe in lots of things I do now, since coming here,' Winsome said. 'Like spirits, for example.'

Julia glanced at Cù, then looked quickly away. 'He's not real,' she said.

'Then how come you can see him?'

'I can't,' Julia said, wishing it was true. 'I'm imagining it.'

'Like you imagined seeing the Fae in the woods that night.'

Julia stared at Winsome, tears streaming suddenly down her face.

'Shh,' Winsome said. 'I felt the same way when I realised.' She smiled, and got up, went around the table and pulled Julia into her arms.

'It's going to be all right,' she said.

'Everything's going to be all right.'

31

ERIN GLANCED OUT AT THE WINDOWS OF ASH COTTAGE, THEN hunched her shoulders and looked away over the garden. 'Stephan,' she hissed. 'What am I going to do?'

Stephan straightened and wiped an arm over his forehead. 'I don't know,' he said. 'How long is she staying?' He wanted to tell Erin he was missing spending his time with her, but she could probably feel that, and really, it wouldn't be a good thing to make her feel bad. Her mother was already doing a good job of that. 'It's only a few weeks until Midsummer.'

'That's just it!' Erin said, then lowered her voice, even though there was no way Veronica could overhear them from the glasshouse. 'I've no idea. She's showing no signs of budging unless I go stay at the flat in the city with her.'

'What?'

'I know. I don't want to, of course I don't.' Erin sighed and leant against the potting bench. 'Stephan, she's making it impossible for me to do any of my practices. She's been here three days, and I haven't got outside once in that time to do my daily devotions, let alone anything else.'

Stephan stepped over to Erin and wrapped his arms around her. 'I'm sorry,' he said.

'Me too,' Erin said, her voice full of misery. 'I don't know what to do. She won't go back home.'

'Have you spoken to your dad?' Stephan asked.

Erin shook her head. 'What would I say to him? Hey Dad, how's banging your secretary going, because Mum's pretty upset about it and she's cramping my style?' Erin bumped her forehead against Stephan's shoulder and groaned.

'Yeah,' Stephan said. 'When you put it that way.'

'I just don't know what I'm supposed to do,' Erin said.

Stephan cast around for an answer. 'Remember the runes?' he said after a moment. 'They kind of talked about this, right?'

Erin just groaned again. 'Sure,' she said. 'But the problem is, I can't get any time to do the work in spirit, you know?' She shook her head. 'There's no privacy. Mum is up in the morning at the crack of dawn, so she's there before I go to work, and she's there when I get home, and this is practically the first moment I've had away from her.' Erin lifted her hands and tugged on her hair in frustration. 'And she's so weird,' she said.

'Weird?'

'Awful. You know her mother brought her up on her own? They were poor.' Erin rolled her eyes. 'I never knew that. I always thought Mum's family was well-off. That's how she always acted. And now I find out that was a complete lie.'

'Yeah?'

'Mum hated being poor when she was a kid, so she set out to marry someone with money. I mean, planned it all. She told me yesterday how she took secretarial courses at school and wrangled a job in a good company, and then set out to bag the boss's son.' Erin's eyes widened. 'It was so calculated. So cold.'

'And it worked,' Stephan said.

'Yep. So, of course she can't understand what I'm doing. It's like a million miles away from what she thinks is important.'

Stephan tucked his chin down, deep in thought. 'I think we have to reframe this,' he said.

'Reframe it?' Erin asked. 'How? And why?'

'Because I think this needs to be an opportunity. It already is, if you think about it.'

Erin groaned. 'I've done nothing but think about it, so how's it an opportunity?'

Stephan shrugged. 'Well, you're already learning more about what makes your mother the way she is. How she ticks, you know.'

Erin pulled a face. 'True, but I'm not exactly liking what I'm learning about her, you realise?'

'Should you be judging her?' Stephan asked. 'Should we really be judging her?'

Erin opened her mouth to answer, then snapped it shut. She just looked at Stephan instead.

Stephan shook his head and relaxed back against the potting bench. He looked at the scatter of pots and seedlings over its surface.

'I've spent hours standing at this bench,' he said.

Erin frowned.

'I came here when I was sixteen and bugged Teresa to teach me what she knew,' Stephan said. 'I didn't know what I was getting myself into, not really.' He wrinkled his nose, thinking about that. 'Or maybe I did, a deep part of me, at least. I mean, everyone knew what she was – the local witch. She didn't make a secret of it. She didn't shout it from the rooftops, but this is a small village. Everyone knew.'

Erin folded her arms, waiting to hear what Stephan was trying to tell her. She thought about her mother, about the way she'd plotted and planned, clawed her way up the social ladder. She rubbed her arms. It made her feel dirty – the sheer calculation of it. Had there ever been any love?

'Anyway,' Stephan said. 'She taught me a lot more than how to make smoke blends and teas and pretty nasturtium salads.' He looked at Erin. 'Are you listening?'

She straightened. 'Yeah,' she said. 'I am. Truly.'

Stephan smiled at her. 'Okay. So, I was about to say that one thing she taught me which was really hard to learn, actually, was that everyone you meet is just the same as yourself.'

Erin blinked. 'What?'

Stephan repeated it. 'Everyone you meet is just the same as yourself.'

'No,' Erin said and shook her head. 'I don't know what you mean.'

'Everyone you meet has a spirit and a body and a deep inner life of which you know absolutely nothing.'

Erin looked at him. 'What do you mean by a deep inner life?'

Stephan shrugged. 'Think about it for a moment,' he

said. 'Everyone has their fears, and their needs, and their desires, and most of the time we never recognise that. We all think about the world, and our place in it, and the way we think about it is influenced by so many things – our upbringing, where we lived, what happened to us as kids, the health or otherwise of our spirit, our body, so many things.' Stephan paused, blushing slightly, then shrugged. 'People generally have reasons for acting the way they do, is all I'm really saying. And most of the time we know nothing about those reasons, or how it feels inside to be them.' He cleared his throat. 'Teresa told me that when you meet someone, you have to give them space to have an inner life, just like you have one.'

Erin was slowly shaking her head. 'I've never thought of my mother as anything but shallow,' she said.

'Except that can't be true, can it?' Stephan asked, picking up a folded envelope of seeds and checking the label on it. 'She might have what we see as a shallow view of the world, but she still has an inner life underneath that.'

'You mean dreams and fears and so on?'

'Yep,' Stephan said turning to Erin and drawing her into his arms. 'You said she grew up poor?'

Erin closed her eyes against Stephan's neck and breathed the scent of him in. 'I never knew until now,' she said.

'Maybe that explains some of the reason she's so set on financial security.'

Erin nodded. She'd not thought of it like that, but it made sense. Veronica's fixation on having a nice home, all the trappings of wealth, her insistence that Erin make choices that wouldn't leave her vulnerable.

'It's sad,' she said. She snaked her arms around Stephan's neck and pressed her lips to his. They were warm, comforting. 'You're wonderful,' she said. 'You know that, right?'

Stephan smiled into her eyes. 'I'm just me,' he said. 'Just like anyone else. I'm lucky though,' he said, picking Erin up and swinging her around to sit on the potting bench. 'Having you. You make me wonderful. You make everything magical.'

Erin tucked herself around him, pulling him closer so that she could feel the lean strength of him, so that she could taste his clean, citrussy scent.

Veronica cleared her throat behind them, in the doorway to the potting shed. 'Excuse me,' she said, eyebrows arched, eyes narrowed. 'I'm not interrupting anything, am I?'

Stephan jumped away, startled, saw Erin's mother at the door, and flushed a deep scarlet.

'Mum!' Erin squeaked.

'We're out of bread, and several other things,' Veronica said, letting herself examine her daughter's boyfriend frankly. The boy, much the same age as Erin, she guessed, was red-faced and Veronica felt a quick flash of approval. At least he had the decency to be embarrassed at her walking in. She'd done that once with Jeremy, catching him with his hand up Erin's top, and Jeremy, whom otherwise she liked very much – he was very well-connected – had simply smiled slyly and knowingly at her, not at all alarmed.

She found she preferred this one's flustered response.

'It's Stephan, isn't it?' she said, knowing it was.

Stephan nodded, relieved the shock had doused him

like a bucket of cold water. He cleared his throat. 'Yes,' he answered. 'We met the other day.'

'My daughter's boyfriend,' Veronica said, ignoring Erin's slit-eyed gaze. 'You're a gardener?'

Stephan grinned. 'Yep,' he said. 'Erin lets me pretend Ash Cottage's gardens are my own.' He spread an arm at the mess of seeds, seedling trays, and cuttings.

Veronica sniffed. 'How much do you earn?' she asked.

Erin's eyes widened. 'Mum!' she said, shocked. 'You can't ask that.'

Veronica turned to look at her daughter and raised an eyebrow. 'I certainly can if he is serious about you. I would like to know how he plans to support you.' She drew herself upright. 'Or even if he can.'

'God, Mum.' Erin shook her head. 'Not everything is about money.'

'It is if you don't have any,' Veronica retorted.

That was something of the truth, Erin realised, remembering her panic when her car had been repossessed, her income cut off. No money, and life suddenly became extremely hard, options limited.

'It's okay, Erin,' Stephan said, and looked at Veronica. 'I also run the community gardens, which is a paid position now, because we use it to distribute fresh vegetables to the whole village, as well as encouraging whoever wants to, to come and learn how to grow them themselves.' He smiled at Erin's mother. 'I'm also going to be studying herbalism, and have plans to open my own practice, when I'm qualified.' He grinned at the thought, unable to help himself. He couldn't wait to dig into the course he'd finally picked. Pun definitely intended, he thought happily to himself.

'I also make and sell locally and online a range of tea blends, and smoke bundles.'

Veronica frowned. 'Smoke bundles?'

'Yeah,' Stephan answered, knowing Erin was staring at him. He glanced at her and shrugged. She frowned. 'They're for clearing stale and unfriendly energy from a room, and also to create a clean, protective ritual space, among other things.'

'You're one of these woo woo people too, aren't you?' Veronica said, wondering why she was even bothering to be surprised.

'I'm a member of the Grove, yes,' Stephan said, then pretended to brighten. 'Have you been to Haven yet, Mrs. Faith?'

'What's Haven?' Veronica asked. It sounded like a cult centre, and just when she was on the brink of allowing herself to think that Erin might not be involved in a cult after all.

'It's a bookshop,' Erin hurried to say.

Stephan nodded enthusiastically. 'Krista, who runs the shop, has made some of Erin's artwork into prints and cards. They're selling them. You need to go have a look – Erin's art is wonderful.'

Veronica turned to her daughter. 'You're selling your art?' she asked.

Erin swallowed down the lump in her throat and resisted the urge to glare at Stephan. 'Yes,' she said. 'I told you I was. I've got some of the proofs for the cards inside, if you want to see them.'

'Hmm.' Veronica thought about it. 'I think we should visit this Haven,' she said. 'You can show me them there.'

She nodded. 'We need to stock up on a few things anyway. Is there somewhere we can buy food here?'

Stephan nodded. 'There's a local shop,' he said. 'You should go to The Copper Kettle as well; Simon makes the best cake.'

Erin turned and looked at him, wanting to know what he was doing, but Stephan just smiled back at her and shrugged.

Simon did make the best cake.

'Yes,' Veronica agreed. 'It's been ages since I've been able to go anywhere.' She looked at Erin. 'Time you showed me around, don't you think?'

32

'Is there a hairdresser in this place?' Veronica asked, parking on the side of the road in the middle of Wellsford.

'A hairdresser?' Erin asked. She shook her head. 'No, I don't think so.'

'Shame,' Veronica said. 'That young man of yours could do with a haircut. He looks like something out of an old painting, with all those curls.' She touched her own hair. 'I don't suppose they'd be open yet, anyway, if there was one, or I might think about getting my own touched up.'

'Your hair still looks lovely, Mum,' Erin said.

That made Veronica smile and she leant forward a little to look at herself in the rear vision mirror. 'My hair always was my best feature.' She smiled wider. 'And my secret weapon.'

Erin looked dubiously at her mother. 'I don't think I want to know.'

Veronica giggled. 'Let's just say that long hair trailed over sensitive skin is very pleasing.'

'Mum!'

Veronica shook her head. 'Don't tell me you're at all innocent,' she said. 'I saw how you were wrapped around that young man.'

Erin kept her mouth shut and Veronica sighed. 'Well,' she said. 'My glory days were long ago, so never mind.'

Shaking her head, Erin got out of the car and looked over the roof at her mother. 'You're still beautiful,' she said. 'I'm sorry Dad isn't giving you your due.'

Veronica tossed her head. 'Don't be,' she said. 'We haven't been close for years. The unforgivable thing this time was putting me in physical danger, not carrying on with whatever her name is.'

'I don't know how you have managed to live like that, Mum,' Erin said as they stepped up onto the footpath and walked along to Haven.

'I wasn't after the whole fairy-tale, darling,' Veronica said with a jaded laugh. 'Just the castle was enough.'

Erin shook her head. She didn't know what to say. Instead, she cast a surreptitious glance at her mother, and remembered what Stephan had said.

Everyone had a deep inner world.

She just didn't know that her mother's was in good shape.

'HI LUCY,' ERIN SAID, 'I'D LIKE YOU TO MEET MY MOTHER, Veronica.'

Lucy's eyes widened and she turned to the well-turned-out woman next to Erin and smiled. 'Pleased to meet you – what a treat. Erin is such a lovely person; you must be very proud of her.' She resisted the urge to wink at Erin.

Veronica let herself preen for a moment. 'Thank you,' she said. 'I've just been looking at some of her artwork in the bookshop. It's very nice.'

'Oh yes,' Lucy said, sliding her hands in her apron pocket to stop herself from reaching out and touching Erin's mother, just to...see. 'She's extremely talented.'

'I can see that,' Veronica said. 'I hadn't really realised.'

'Oh? Well, we're all very excited about her work.'

Veronica frowned. 'Are you one of them, too?' she asked.

'Mum!' Erin hissed.

'One of who?' Lucy asked, genuinely disconcerted for a moment. Then she tipped her head back and laughed. 'Right. Yes, we – my husband and I – belong to the Grove. I think that's what you're asking?'

Veronica gave a tight nod.

'Can we have two cappuccinos, please, Lucy?' Erin said. She glanced at her mother. 'And some chocolate blueberry cake? Has Simon made any today?'

'Sure has,' Lucy said. 'I'll go get that for you right now.' She looked at Veronica. 'It was nice to meet you,' she said, then scooted away back inside.

Erin gazed at her mother. 'What is it, Mum?' she asked at last.

Veronica shook her head. 'It's not like I imagined it,' she said.

'What isn't?'

Veronica waved a hand. 'Here. The cult.'

'It's not a cult, that's why.'

'No, or if it is, it's nothing like what I expected.' Veronica leant over the table slightly, towards her daughter. 'So, if it isn't,' Veronica said, her face crumpling into confusion, 'then why did your birth mother tell us it was?'

Erin reached out and put a hand over Veronica's. 'Mum,' she said. 'I think you know the answer to that.'

Veronica looked away. 'We were desperate to have a family,' she said. 'I was desperate to have a family.' She glanced back at Erin, then looked away again, blinking as though the sun was in her eyes. 'I wanted a child, but it was such a process! And especially if you were looking for a new-born.'

'Which you were?' Erin placed her hands in her lap and blew out a slow breath.

'Yes. I wanted a child I could believe was my own.' Veronica shifted in her seat, then put on an automatic smile as Lucy brought them their coffee and cake.

Lucy paused before turning back to the kitchen, tasting the atmosphere at the table. She looked at Erin. 'All right?' she asked.

'Yes, thank you,' Erin said, plastering on a smile. 'It looks delicious.' She knew Lucy wasn't asking about the food. 'Everything's fine,' she added.

Lucy nodded and went back inside.

'You were saying?' Erin asked.

Veronica stared at the food, not really seeing it. 'Not too many young babies were available for adoption,' she said. 'Fewer than you'd think, anyway. And it really was up to the mothers, who they'd go to.'

'Which is why Rebecca came to you,' Erin said, drawing her cup closer. 'And why the talk got around to money.' She ducked her head down to take a sip of the coffee, so that she wouldn't have to look at Veronica.

'Yes.' Veronica cleared her throat. 'She probably hadn't needed to tell us about growing up here, and how desperate she was to put it behind her and start over.'

'You mean you would have paid anyway,' Erin said flatly.

'Well, she was considering several others, you know. And she was very pretty; the baby was going to be beautiful.' Veronica picked up the paper napkin and dabbed at her mouth, though she hadn't touched the coffee or the food. 'She did make this place sound like a nightmare, though.'

'It's not,' Erin said. 'Not for me, anyway, although maybe it was for her, in some ways.' She picked up her fork and stared at it. 'I've come to see that people can experience the same thing in different ways.'

'Yes. Well, whatever, she hated it here.' Veronica looked around. 'It is very small.' She blinked rapidly for a moment. 'It reminds me of where my grandparents lived when I was a child.'

'Where did you grow up?' Erin asked. 'I don't know if you've ever said, now that I consider it.'

'I don't like to think about it,' Veronica admitted, finally taking a sip of her coffee. 'This is good,' she said, surprised.

'Wait until you try the cake,' Erin said, and she discovered that she'd relaxed slightly. Even though it felt unreal to be sitting outside The Copper Kettle with her mother.

Talking truthfully to each other.

Veronica tried the cake, nodded with her mouth full. 'Yes,' she said, swallowing. 'Delicious.' She smiled across the table. 'My mother was seventeen when she had me,' she said.

Erin put her cup down. 'Seventeen?'

'Yes, and she was lucky my grandparents didn't disown her, that they tried to help her, even when she moved out. It might have been the sixties, but it was early sixties, and it wasn't the done thing to have a baby when you weren't married.' Veronica put her fork down. 'I don't know why I'm telling you this,' she said. 'It's all in the past, and it wasn't a bed of roses when it was happening.'

But Erin shook her head. 'It's important,' she said. 'I want to know.'

Veronica grimaced. 'I don't see why it's important, Erin. It's tawdry, and we could be thinking about much more pleasant things.'

Erin lifted a brow and Veronica sighed, then brightened. 'Let's talk about going back to the flat,' Veronica said.

'We're not properly out of lockdown yet,' Erin reminded her mother, desperate not to be dragged back to the city. 'We're not supposed to be shifting around the country – you shouldn't even have come here, not really.'

Veronica shook her head. 'I couldn't stay there,' she said. 'And I wanted to see you. Make sure you're all right.' She picked up her cup. 'It was your father's idea to stop your allowance and take your car.'

'I'm pretty sure you went right along with it,' Erin said, not wanting to be reminded. 'Besides,' she said. 'It turned out to be the best thing you could have done.' Erin paused, rerunning that statement through her mind. 'Well,' she said. 'Stopping my allowance was. It would have been nice to keep the car.'

'How have you been getting around?' Veronica asked.

'Walking.'

Veronica shook her head. That was impossible. 'No,' she said. 'Truly? What about when you want to go further afield than this place?' She glanced around the courtyard and the small, quiet village beyond it. 'There's nothing here.'

'I haven't left Wellsford for ages,' Erin said, looking at the rest of the cake on her plate, her appetite gone. 'There's no need to, and I've been really busy.'

'Working,' Veronica said, curling her lip in distaste. 'In the care home.'

'Yes,' Erin said. 'And I've come to really enjoy it.' She drew breath. 'It's been good for me.'

Veronica waved a dismissive hand. 'You won't have to work when we get back to the city.'

'I don't want to go back to the city.'

'You're right,' Veronica said, having an idea. 'We should tell your father he has to live in the flat.' She smiled. 'And then we can have the house.'

Erin pushed away her plate and looked at her mother. 'I don't want to go back there, either. I have a life here.' She shook her head. 'A job, a boyfriend. Friends.' She winced slightly. 'And there's the Grove.'

Veronica narrowed her eyes at her daughter. 'What about it? If it's not a cult, then you can leave, isn't that right?'

'No,' Erin said. 'I mean yes, of course I can leave, because it's not a cult, but I don't want to leave. I'm being trained to take over the Grove.'

'What?' For a moment, Veronica thought there must be a mosquito or something flying around, because there was a sudden high-pitched buzzing in her ears. What had Erin just said? 'I don't understand.'

Erin picked up her cake fork and twisted it in her hands. 'It's complicated,' she said.

'Find a way to simplify it,' Veronica suggested, her voice frosty. So this was a cult, after all. And her daughter was a lot more caught up in it than she'd expected.

'I don't know if I can,' Erin said, not meeting her mother's eyes. 'There's Morghan Wilde, I guess, who is Lady of the Grove...'

'Lady of the Grove?' Veronica said, appalled. 'What sort of title is that?'

Erin gave a tight shrug. 'That's what they've always been called.'

'Since when?' Veronica laughed. 'How long has this cult been going?'

'It's not a cult,' Erin hissed, ducking her head when the two older ladies at a table on the other side of the courtyard turned and looked at her, cups paused in mid-air.

She blew out a breath. 'It's not a cult, and the Grove has been around for thousands of years.'

'Thousands of years?' Veronica shook her head. 'This is worse than I thought – and just when I was starting to think it was nothing.'

'It's not a cult,' Erin repeated, more quietly this time, relieved that the other women had turned back to their lunch. 'It's...'

Almost impossible to describe to someone like her mother, Erin thought.

Veronica looked at her daughter, feeling profoundly sorry for her. Erin had always been a dreamer, never quite had her feet on the ground, and she'd had...problems. She shook her head. 'Tell me about being groomed to take over,' she said, her voice icy with a cold, growing fury.

Erin shook her head, quickly. 'You make it sound like something it's completely not,' she said. 'I'm not being groomed.' She cleared her throat. 'I'm being trained.'

'Trained?' Veronica's eyebrows shot upwards. 'How? In what?' And the last question, which suddenly burned neon-bright in her mind. 'By whom?'

'Morghan's training me,' Erin answered in a bare whisper. She looked over at the other table, and the two women there were staring at her again. She dropped her gaze to her plate.

'Morghan,' Veronica said, unable to help her voice rising. 'This is the Lady of the Grove?' She was also unable to stop her sneer at the grandiose title.

Erin nodded miserably.

Veronica looked intently at her daughter. 'Why you?' she asked, already knowing the reason. Erin was young, inexperienced, pliable. Just the right person to get herself caught up in something like this.

'I want to meet this Morghan person,' Veronica said, pushing her chair away from the table and standing up. 'Now,' she said.

'And we'll be driving, not walking, you can count on that.'

33

'I'M NOT SURE ABOUT THIS,' JULIA SAID, TRAILING FURTHER
and further behind Winsome. She clutched her handbag
with whitened knuckles.

Winsome turned and waited for her to catch up. 'I told
them you were coming,' she reminded Julia. 'They were all
okay with it.' She touched Julia briefly on the elbow. 'This is
what it means to be a community,' she said.

'They hate me,' Julia muttered. 'There's no way they
don't.'

Winsome was philosophical on this. 'If they can accept
me back into the fold, so to speak, after all I did, then they
can do the same with you.'

Julia shook her head and would have turned right
around and scurried back to her house if Winsome's spooky
dog hadn't been blocking the way behind her. It felt as
though he were about to nip at her heels any moment and
she shuffled reluctantly forward.

'I don't know how my life has come to this,' she said.

'Oh goodness,' Winsome laughed. 'I don't know how many times I've said exactly the same thing.'

Julia scowled at the footpath. 'It wasn't supposed to go like this,' she said. 'Nothing was supposed to turn out this way.' She blinked, ashamed to find she was on the verge of tears. 'Do you know what I wanted to be when I was a girl?'

Winsome turned around again and looked at Julia. 'No,' she said. 'I've no idea.'

Julia shook her head. 'It was a silly dream, really.'

'I think we all have dreams like that, when we're young,' Winsome answered. 'But we oughtn't really to make fun of them.'

'Everyone laughed at mine,' Julia said, her lips turning even further down. She glanced at Winsome. 'What did you want to be?'

'A nun,' Winsome shrugged. 'I was horribly disappointed when my mother told me only Catholics can become nuns and that we weren't Catholic.'

'But that's not true,' Julia said.

'Yes, but I didn't know that at the time, and nor, obviously, did my mother.' Winsome shook her head. 'The dream shaped me anyway, as it turned out.' She smiled at Julia, letting herself look briefly at the woman's colours. They were better than they had been, a few days ago, but still a far cry from looking healthy.

At least though, Winsome thought, they weren't the acid wash of envy and jealousy anymore.

'Tell me what you wanted to be, Julia,' she said.

'I read a book,' Julia said. 'When I was a girl.' She glanced back at the dog, who stood there grinning mockingly at her. 'I wanted to be a healer,' she said.

'A healer?' Winsome asked. 'What sort of healer?'

Julia's shoulders hunched in tighter. 'I don't know exactly now. The book was about someone who could heal others by putting their hands on them.'

Winsome gazed at Julia for a long moment. 'That's not what I expected you to say.'

Julia lifted her head. 'What did you expect?'

'I'm not sure,' Winsome answered. 'Possibly something like you wanted to be a ballerina?'

Julia snorted a laugh. 'I was large as a child and had two left feet.'

'Oh,' Winsome said brightly. 'Like I am now!' She smiled wistfully for a moment. 'I love to dance, though. Usually where no one can see me.'

'Isn't that a thing, now?' Julia said. 'Dance like no one's watching, or some such rubbish?'

'How did the person in the book become a healer?' Winsome asked, knowing she was changing the subject.

Eyes shadowed, Julia gazed at her. She could feel the spirit dog at her back, like it had weight, real presence. 'I don't remember,' she said. 'But when I told my mother, she laughed and said no daughter of hers was going to have anything to do with religion or faith healing or any such thing.' Julia gazed up the path to Cynthia's cottage, where they were expected. 'She said she'd had enough of that growing up with her mother. And if I wanted anything like that, I should have been her sister's child, not hers.'

Julia looked down at her hands. 'And then she died, and I was sent to live with Mariah, so I guess that came true.'

Winsome looked at her, thought about it. 'How old were you when you came to live with Mariah?'

'Thirteen,' Julia said. 'I hated her. Right from the start. I hated her even as I got more and more like her.'

Julia let her hands fall from their grip on her shoulder bag. 'And now it's too late,' she said. 'It's all too late for me. I shouldn't be here. I should go home.'

'It's not too late,' Winsome said. 'Don't go, Julia – it's never too late for anyone.'

But Julia shook her head. 'I've done such awful things,' she said. 'I've thought such stupid things – conspiracy rubbish and all sorts. I don't know how I could have done that.'

'But it's a good thing that you feel this way now,' Winsome said. 'It's good to realise that you were on the wrong track.'

Julia snorted. 'I'm almost fifty, Winsome,' she said. 'I'm not that silly little girl who read a book one day and wanted to do miracles.'

'No,' Winsome said, wanting to take Julia's arm and tuck it in hers. 'You're a grown woman who gets to make new and different choices every single day. Just like me. So, we're here now, let's go in and see what some of those choices are that we might like to try today.'

But Julia shook her head. 'No,' she said. 'I don't think I can.' She turned around and the dog stared at her, but she wasn't going to let it stop her this time.

She skirted around it, and took off down the street, coat flapping.

'WELL,' CYNTHIA SAID. 'YOU TRIED.'

Winsome sighed. 'I'll keep trying,' she said.

'How do you know it's worth it?' Cynthia asked, as they both stood on the footpath watching Julia's retreating form.

'Isn't everyone worth it?' Winsome asked. 'You and the others in there didn't give up on me.'

'Yes,' Cynthia said. 'But you're talking about Julia.' She shrugged. 'She was always a very efficient organiser, but no one really liked her.'

'No,' Winsome agreed. 'I never really liked her either, but I also never tried to understand her.'

'And now you want to? After all she did?' Cynthia shook her head. 'Don't get me wrong,' she said. 'We were all shocked but willing to go along with it, when you said you were bringing her with you.' She sighed. 'But maybe she doesn't want to be helped?'

'Who doesn't want to be helped, Cynthia?' Winsome asked. 'Really, when it comes down to it – who doesn't want someone to try to understand them, accept them, help them? Julia is going through a very difficult time, and she is so terribly lonely. And all those years with Mariah have had their toll on her.' Winsome turned and smiled at Cynthia. 'I don't think she's beyond reaching, that's all.'

Cynthia nodded. 'Okay,' she said. 'Perhaps you're right.' She turned for the house. 'Goodness knows, the damage that family has always carried has to stop somewhere.'

JULIA REACHED HER COTTAGE AND FLUNG HERSELF AT THE door with a heaved sigh of pleasure, then turned suddenly, the hard doorknob pressing between her shoulder blades, and swept the path and front garden for any sign of Winsome's ghost dog.

Her shoulders dropped in relief. The ghastly animal was nowhere to be seen. Which, Julia thought, was exactly how it could stay. She stood up and did another visual search of the garden, just to make sure.

It wasn't there.

She gave a small yelp – her roses! – she'd been neglecting them, and it showed. Dropping her bag on the step, Julia hurried over to the garden beds that rimmed the small path of green lawn and stood there shaking her head.

When was the last time she'd been out here to take care of them?

They were in a miserable state. She should have cut them back weeks ago. More than that. She reached out and touched tentative fingers to a shrivelled rosehip. How could she have let this happen?

The plant quivered under her touch. They should have been pruned back in March, once the frosts were over. Julia shook her head.

'Black spot,' she whispered. 'Powdery mildew, rose rust, grey mould, sooty mould, cankers.' She listed all the calamities that could have happened while she was busy following Mariah around in her craziness. 'Rose mosaic, rose wilt, rose rosette disease.' She started on the pests, tears dribbling down her cheeks. 'Greenfly, spider-mites, red spider mite, thrips, rose sawflies, caterpillars, eelworms.'

Julia wiped the tears away with the heel of her hand and looked around the garden in dismay.

A cat crept out from under one of the bushes and sauntered over to her, sitting down to look at her with large golden-green eyes.

'Where did you come from?' Julia asked it.

The cat blinked, lifted a ginger paw, and began to clean itself. Julia stared at it for a moment, then looked back at her plants, a dull heaviness settling into her body.

There was a greenish haze around one of her rose bushes – her favourite, in fact, a usually splendid burnt orange hybrid tea rose with the perfect name *Simply The Best*. Right now, it was simply past its best, but Julia went over to it, squinting. What was the haze around it? She waved her hand through the greenish air. Some sort of bug infestation?

She couldn't see any bugs.

There was some new growth, despite the lack of pruning, and Julia bent down, bringing her face closer to the glossy green leaves, trying to work out what she was seeing. She waved her hand through the green haze again, and it moved as though it was some odd sort of mist, but it didn't go away. She stood back again.

'What's wrong with you?' she said, blinking. 'What have I done to you, my poor plant?'

The green haze got momentarily darker, and Julia rubbed her eyes, then looked around at the rest of her garden.

All the rose bushes were surrounded by the same sort of haze. Julia took a step back, squeezed her eyes shut, then inched them open again, peering through her lashes at the plants.

All of them. They all had the same sort of haze around them. Some were lighter, some darker. One plant seemed to have black spots in its haze and Julia stumbled backwards.

'No,' she said. 'This isn't happening.' And she turned back for her front door, her hand reaching for her bag, to dig out her keys. She shook her head. 'No,' she repeated. 'This isn't happening.'

Her hands shook so much it took three goes to get the key in the lock. The cat nipped inside when she finally pushed the door open.

She stared at it as it walked down her hallway, tail in the air, then through the closed door to the kitchen.

34

'Mum,' Erin said. 'Please – we can't just go storming up here like this.'

Veronica unbuckled her seat belt. 'It's not storming when you drive up and park, Erin,' she said grimly. 'And even if it were storming, then we would be completely within our rights, because this situation is obviously way out of control.'

Erin shook her head, getting out of the car and looking at Veronica across the roof. 'No,' she said. 'You just don't understand, that's all.'

'Well, of course you'd say that,' Veronica retorted, straightening her clothes and shutting the car door. She rather wished Vincent was there with her. He'd know what to say. She pushed her shoulders back. He wasn't there, he was cavorting about the place with some other woman. Therefore, she could only rely on herself.

Erin tried one more time. 'Please, Veronica,' she said. 'It's really not what you think.'

Veronica stopped still and looked at her only daughter. 'Veronica?' she said. 'Now you're calling me by my first name?' She blinked. 'What will it be next? Deciding I'm not your mother at all? Disowning me and your father and your brother? Isn't that what these cults do? You'll soon be believing we treated you terribly all your life.'

Erin shook her head. 'Mum,' she said. 'Of course not.' And a bit of her own temper flared. 'And didn't you effectively disown me a few months ago?'

'We did not disown you,' Veronica hissed. 'We cut off your allowance so you couldn't give it away to this cult and to get you to come home!'

Erin groaned, pressing her hands to her head. Every time she'd thought her mother was coming around, something happened, and they were back to this again. 'It's not a cult, for crying out loud.'

'Good,' Veronica said. 'Then your Lady of the Grove can explain to me exactly what it is.'

Erin trailed behind Veronica as she went up to Hawthorn House and pounded on the door. She wanted to melt away in embarrassment, and she desperately did not want Morghan to be at home.

The door opened and Mrs. Parker looked out, saw Erin, and smiled. 'Erin,' she said. 'How lovely to see you.' She turned towards Veronica and gave her an enquiring look.

'Hello Mrs. Parker,' Erin said miserably. 'This is my mother.'

Understanding dawned in Mrs. Parker's eyes and she nodded. 'I'm so pleased to meet you,' she said. 'Would you like to come in?'

Veronica glanced uncertainly at Erin. 'Is this the Lady of the Grove?' she asked.

Mrs. Parker laughed and patted her chest. 'Goodness me, no,' she said. 'I'm the housekeeper.'

'The housekeeper?' Veronica blinked, then frowned. 'How many people live here?' This was a very strange set up for a cult, she was deciding. Everyone living in their own houses.

She reminded herself that this Morghan woman owned Ash Cottage.

'Oh,' Mrs. Parker said. 'Well, there's myself and my husband, and Morghan, and her daughter Clarice.'

It was very odd, Veronica decided. 'I'd like to speak to this Morghan,' she said, putting on her best I-will-not-be-intimidated voice.

'Please, come in,' Mrs. Parker said, giving Erin a warm smile and thinking that the poor girl looked like she'd rather be anywhere doing anything than here at the door with her mother. 'Morghan is outside around the back at the moment, but she won't be long, I'm sure.'

'We can come again some other time, if she's busy,' Erin said, jumping into the conversation with a growing hope of heading things off.

'We cannot come back,' Veronica said. 'Around the back, did you say?'

'Yes,' Mrs. Parker said. 'But she's busy right now.'

It didn't matter. Veronica stepped away from the door, swept her gaze over the house, then took off around the outside of the building.

'Mum!' Erin called, then shot an anguished look at Mrs.

Parker. 'I'm sorry,' she said. 'I'm really sorry – she won't listen to me.'

Mrs. Parker nodded. It was an afternoon for it, apparently. 'You'd best go after her, dear,' she said. 'Morghan will be quite besieged.'

Erin's eyes widened. Besieged? That didn't sound good. She took off after her mother.

She almost ran right into her.

'Mum?'

Veronica cleared her throat. It appeared she would be interrupting a bit of a scene. She smoothed her skirt down. Well, there was nothing for that, now, was there?

She strode forward over the soft grass, saw the well, stopped for a moment, disconcerted by the strange deep colours of it, then skirted around it and hurried onto the terrace.

Where, Erin saw with a sinking heart, Morghan was already dealing with Julia Thorpe. Of all people.

JULIA SHOOK HER HEAD VIOLENTLY. 'NO, YOU HAVE TO MAKE IT go away.'

Morghan stood on the terrace outside the house, wishing she could find a way to stop Julia tearing at her own hair. 'Julia,' she said, trying again. 'It's all right.'

'I don't want it though. I don't want any of it – and it's all because of them! I didn't mean to see them that night.'

Morghan looked pained. 'It's true,' she said. 'Sometimes a shock like that can break you open enough to start seeing auras.'

Veronica narrowed her eyes. 'What's going on here?' she demanded, stepping up onto the terrace.

Julia dropped her hands and stared at the newcomer. 'Who are you?'

Erin sidled up. 'I'm sorry to interrupt,' she said, looking at Morghan. 'This is my mother.'

'Veronica Faith.' Her mother shifted on her feet, the grey-haired woman's sudden gaze making her uncomfortable. She straightened, reminding herself that none of these brainwashing ways would work on her. She hadn't got this far in life to be sucked in at the last moment by some awful cult that made you believe you were god knows what.

'Mrs. Faith,' Morghan said, a smile touching her lips. 'It's a surprise to meet you finally.'

Veronica squinted. 'Finally?' she said.

'Erin has been here in Wellsford for some months now,' Morghan said. 'I'm glad of the opportunity to meet you.'

'Morghan and I were talking,' Julia said, tears springing mortifyingly to her eyes once more. 'We weren't finished.'

'I'm so sorry,' Erin said. 'We shouldn't have barged in like this.'

'It couldn't wait,' Veronica said, ignoring her daughter.

'What couldn't?' Julia asked. 'I'm having a crisis here!'

'It's all right,' Julia,' Morghan said.

'It's not though,' Julia wailed. 'You said it won't go away.'

'I said it probably won't go away. But do you really want it to? You said you see your plant's auras – how useful will that be?' She tipped her head to the side and smiled at Julia. 'I know how you love your roses – they're probably the most beautiful roses in the village. Now it will be even easier to take care of them because you can see them more clearly. Their spirits can talk to you.'

Erin wanted to groan at the sight of her mother's mouth falling open.

This was even worse than she'd thought it would be. What were they talking about? Julia could see auras around her roses?

'Is that even possible?' she asked, her curiosity overcoming her despair at the situation. It wasn't like it could get much worse, now, was it?

Morghan turned her attention to Erin and her smile widened. 'It certainly is. After all, plants have consciousness as well, don't forget.'

Veronica's frown deepened. 'What?' she said. 'Don't be ridiculous. Next you'll be saying that the carrots I have for dinner scream as I'm eating them.'

Morghan's eyes gleamed. 'I don't know,' she said. 'Do you eat them raw?'

Erin shook her head at her mother. 'Morghan is joking, Mum,' she said. But she was filing away the information about plant auras for Stephan. Or maybe he already saw them. It wouldn't surprise her in the slightest.

'That is a stupid joke,' Veronica said. 'And not in the least bit funny.' She looked over at Julia, standing wild-eyed and dishevelled. Veronica curled her lip. 'And what are you telling this poor woman?' she asked. 'There's no such thing as auras and all that other New Age stupidity.' She shook her head and made a moue of distaste. 'There's only what you can see and touch.'

Veronica put her hands on her hips.

'But Julia here can see the auras around her roses,' Morghan said.

'No, she can't,' Veronica countered.

Morghan raised an eyebrow. 'She can't?'

Erin suppressed a groan and wished she could just grab her mother by the elbow and drag her away.

This was not going well.

She hadn't thought it would.

But it really wasn't.

Julia straightened and glared at the newcomer. The woman was obviously rich with her fancy clothes and high-lighted hair. And hadn't Julia heard that Erin came from money – and gave it all up to live in Wellsford. Which she'd always thought an idiotic thing to do – what was that about gift horses and not looking them in the mouth?

But if this was her mother, then no wonder the girl wanted to get away.

'But I can,' Julia said. 'I just did.'

'Rubbish,' Veronica spat. 'You're clearly not thinking or seeing straight.' She wrinkled her nose at Julia. 'Maybe you ate something that disagreed with you.'

'Mrs. Faith,' Morghan said, breaking into the conversation. 'I'm afraid you're being very rude to tell Julia here that she is imagining something when she says she is not. You may not understand what she is going through, but that does not give you permission to dismiss it out of hand.' She looked past Veronica's stunned face and smiled at Erin.

'Erin, would you be so good as to walk Julia home? She's had a shock.'

'But...' Erin glanced at her mother, then looked back at Morghan.

'Your mother and I will have a nice chat,' Morghan said.

'Yes,' Veronica said. 'We certainly will.' She looked pointedly at her daughter. 'And then we will be going back and packing our suitcases. There is no way we are staying on here.' She narrowed her eyes at Morghan. 'Not after this.'

Erin shook her head. 'I'm not leaving. I'm not going anywhere.'

Morghan remained placid. She turned to Julia. 'I'm sorry for the interruption, Julia,' she said. 'Erin will see you home, and put the kettle on, perhaps. I know these things are a shock – I'll be happy to speak to you about it again. Or you can always seek out Winsome.' Morghan blinked. 'She has some experience with these things, as I'm sure you know.'

'I don't need anyone to see me home,' Julia said, but she felt suddenly very tired and pushed her hair back from her face, shaking her head.

Erin walked across to her, wishing this day were over already, even though it wasn't two thirds done. 'Come on,' she said. 'Let's go put that kettle on. You look about ready to drop.'

'I DON'T WANT TO GO THROUGH THE WOODS,' JULIA SAID, balking at the thought of what she might see in there.

'You don't?' Erin asked, glancing behind them to see that Morghan was ushering her mother into the house. She blew out a breath. 'How did you get here, then?'

'By the road, of course.' Julia shuddered at the sight of the trees. 'There are things in there,' she said, her voice a hoarse whisper.

'Things?'

'People,' Julia said, then elaborated. 'Shining people.'

Erin's eyes widened. 'Wow,' she said. 'You really are seeing things.'

'I'm not lying,' Julia snapped.

Erin shook her head. 'No, that's not what I meant – I'm sorry. I meant that you're really seeing a lot. No wonder you're a bit worn out from it all.' She glanced at the path that wended through the woods down to the village. 'It's much quicker,' she said. 'And I've never seen the Fae in there. Not when I've just been walking around.'

Julia still balked at the thought of stepping under the leafy arms of the trees, into their secret dimness. 'I didn't believe in such things,' she said.

Erin shrugged. 'Most people don't, though, do they? I didn't, before I came here.' She sighed. 'I mean, I wanted to – I wanted to live in a world that had that sort of mystery to it, but I'd never seen anything. Not really. Not that wasn't a dream.'

'I would happily go back to not having seen anything.' Julia folded her arms around herself. She wanted to be home already, maybe with her gardening books out, making plans to help her roses.

If there was anything at all she could do for them.

'Oh, come on then,' she said, suddenly impatient. The girl said she never saw anything in the daylight, and she'd know. Erin would be up and down these tracks every day.

Julia stepped onto the path, kept her eyes on her feet, just in case.

'So, that's your mother, then,' she said after a few minutes. The woods were hushed, the quiet broken only with occasional birdsong. There was no wind, and Julia decided that conversation would help her to think of something else. Anything else, but what might walk in these woods alongside them.

'Yeah,' Erin agreed, glum. 'She turned up unexpectedly.'

'I heard she thinks Wilde Grove is a cult,' Julia said.

Erin lifted her head. 'You heard that?'

Julia shrugged. 'It's a small village. Everyone hears everything, really.'

'I suppose so,' Erin said. 'If you listen to gossip, that is.'

'My aunt ate gossip for breakfast,' Julia said. She stopped suddenly and lifted her tired face to the canopy of tree branches above her. 'They came for her right here,' she said.

Erin looked around. 'They?' She cleared her throat, remembering Morghan talking to the dark-haired faerie man.

Julia glanced at her. 'Don't pretend you don't know what I'm talking about,' she said.

'Okay,' Erin said. 'You saw them?'

'They were beautiful,' Julia said, and rubbed her eyes. She really did feel exhausted. Like she'd been cracked open, scooped out, rolled around in magic dust, then put back together.

'Beautiful?' Erin repeated.

'Yes.' Julia started walking again. 'They stepped out of the night like they were made from the light of the moon and stars.'

Erin stayed silent, running Julia's description through her mind. It did sound beautiful.

'One of them walked right by me,' Julia said, blinking at

the memory. 'I was grovelling on the ground, terrified, but I couldn't look away.'

'What did they do?' Erin asked.

Julia shook her head. 'He, or she – I couldn't tell – walked right by me, looked down at me scrabbling in the dirt, and smiled.' She sniffed, alarmed to see she was crying again. 'That smile, though.' She wiped her eyes. 'Their face. They shine, like moonlight, cold and beautiful. Julia shook her head again. 'They're not human,' she said. 'Not even a little bit human.'

Erin thought of the Fae she'd seen come to dance with them at the circle, during their rituals.

'They might have hearts,' Julia said. 'But they're not like ours.'

'They're just another species, Julia,' Erin said. 'We can't expect them to be human.' She reached out and touched a tree with light fingers. 'They live different lives, they see different things.' She paused. 'They know different things. Maybe more than us. I don't think they've forgotten things the way we have.'

Julia looked at her. 'What have we forgotten?'

'How to see the auras of plants,' Erin said, feeling certain she was right. 'How to flex our spirits. How to see the real world.'

'If the real world has them in it, I'm sure I don't want to see it.'

'But it does,' Erin said. 'Have them in it.' She thought about Macha, and Raven, and Stephan's Hummingbird. 'It has a great deal in it that we've forgotten to see.'

'Maybe there was a reason we forgot,' Julia said, her jaw

set stubbornly. 'Maybe we needed to forget. So we could live properly.'

'Do you think so?'

Julia wondered. Did she think so? 'It frightens me,' she admitted. 'I don't want to see my roses hurting because I neglected them.'

'Is that what you're seeing?' Erin was fascinated. 'You should talk to Stephan about it. He's not a rose expert, or not as far as I know, but he'd be really interested.'

Julia hunched her shoulders to her ears and shook her head.

'I don't want to see everything in the world I hurt,' she said.

They walked the rest of the way in silence.

35

BURDOCK WATCHED ERIN PACE ACROSS THE KITCHEN, ARMS crossed, a serious frown bunched between her eyes. He'd tried going to her and getting her to stop and pat him, but her scritches had been half-hearted and brief.

Erin pulled out her phone and checked the time again. What was her mother doing? What were she and Morghan talking about?

It was nerve-wracking not knowing.

Perhaps she should have walked back up there after seeing Julia home, but she'd thought it was probably better not to. Morghan had sent her away with Julia for a reason and hadn't suggested she come back afterwards. Erin sighed. Having her mother around all the time was exhausting. She pulled her phone from her pocket again, woke it up and stared at the screen, at the photo of her and Stephan she'd used as a wallpaper.

They were smiling, arms looped around each other.

Erin scrolled through her contacts list, hit call. Chewed on her thumb nail waiting for the call to go through.

'Dad?'

She listened to her father's voice for a moment, trying to sort out the feelings that flooded through her at hearing it. Then she gave herself a little shake.

Now wasn't the time.

'Mum's staying with me,' she said. 'What have you been doing?'

She stared down at the floor while her father put forward his excuses. She shook her head. Took the phone away from her ear and hit end. It had been stupid to call her father – had she really thought he should come get her mother?

No, she decided, putting her phone down on the table and going outside, Burdock at her heels. That wasn't the answer.

But what was?

She should have gone back to Hawthorn House, helped Morghan talk some sense into Veronica. If that were possible.

Honestly though, she'd thought her mother would be pretty quick to storm out of there.

Stephan was working, and the garden seemed empty without him. He hadn't stayed overnight with her since her mother had turned up, and Erin missed him. More than she'd expected.

Nor had she been doing any of her daily practice since Veronica had come to stay. And that couldn't go on, or she might as well pack up her things and go.

Which couldn't happen. This was where she belonged.

Erin walked over to the well and lifted the heavy lid. She dipped a finger into the cold water and touched her forehead.

'Bless me, holy water, with your clarity,' she said, and drew in a long, slow breath. She lowered her hand again, splaying her fingers over the surface of the well, looking down into the deep, dark water, and thought about the well in the maze.

She dipped her hand under the surface, swirling it about, feeling the cold sink right to her bones.

The water in the well at the maze had been warm. Body temperature, at least. It had been like dipping her fingers into silk.

Why was a well there, she wondered. Why was the maze there?

She decided she might as well have asked why she had two eyes, a nose, and a mouth. Perhaps it was just the way it was. There was another world, or part of the world, and in it was a high cliff that spread as far as she could see in both directions, and from which the only way to get down, was to fly on the wings of a bird.

Her lips twitched in a smile as she remembered Raven going back for Fox.

And across a far meadow, was a maze, dug down into the ground. Why, she didn't know. Did she need to know?

Erin drew in another deep, slow breath, missing her work, missing her practice. She wanted to go back to the maze, find her way through it, look deeply into the well there – perhaps it was some sort of scrying mirror. Perhaps she did need to let herself fall into it, see where that took her.

And she needed to retrace her steps to the gate.

The gate she'd reached just before being dragged suddenly back to the waking world.

She took another deep breath.

Erin stepped down from the raised well and positioned herself on the path in the centre of her garden. It had been Teresa's garden, but it was hers now.

She swept her arms around in a wide circle, then stretched them up to the sky, wondering how she'd managed to let this fall by the wayside, even for a few days. She breathed in the afternoon air, tasting the yellow sunlight, the scent of the plants Stephan was growing all around her, the freshness of the air. She let her breath out slowly, lowering her arms, then moving them out to the side, embracing the air, the world, the mystery of it all.

Julia's faerie people of star and moonlight.

The auras around her roses.

The cat that had been waiting for them in Julia's kitchen, sitting on a chair, eyes round and knowing, for all the world like a cat of flesh and blood.

Her own travelling.

Macha who stood at her right shoulder, waiting for her to walk the path.

Fox, her dainty pointed snout, whiskers quivering with the jokes only she knew.

Raven, with his broad, strong wings, feathers the colour of dusk and night and storm and dream.

She breathed it all in. All the wonder and mystery of the world.

And then she exhaled, offering her breath back to the world with an outward gesture.

Her breath and her heart. Her love and her service.

'Air,' she murmured. 'Breath of life.'

Now, she reached upwards again, towards the sun, feeling for its faraway fire with her fingertips, seeing the red haze of it behind her closed eyes.

'Fire,' she whispered, head full of blazing light. 'Spark of life.'

Now, she floated in the air as though it was water. She thought of the well, of her tumble down the well, of floating in that pregnant darkness.

'Water,' she sighed. 'Womb of life.'

And then, she was back on the ground, her feet secure on the earth. She lifted onto her toes, sank onto her heels, then spread her arms over her head and around and down, feeling them as branches bursting with buds as her toes dug roots into the soil.

'Earth,' Erin breathed. 'Root of life.'

She reached back to the sky, then down to the earth, bending to touch the ground beneath her before straightening and drawing her tingling hands to her chest, to her heart.

'Above,' she said, and her voice was clear on the still air. 'Below.'

She opened her eyes, saw the world glowing, saw the filaments of the web connecting everything, blinked, let it fade.

'I am part of the wheel,' she said. 'And this is my singing.'

. . .

ERIN WAS IN THE KITCHEN, FOLLOWING ONE OF STEPHAN'S bread recipes, when Veronica opened the front door and came in, setting her keys and bag on the table.

Burdock lifted his head from where he was snoozing on his bed, looked at her, then lay back down again, wondering when Stephan was going to come back.

Erin put a damp tea towel over the bowl of dough so that it could rise, and looked at her mother, standing there in the kitchen.

'Well?' she said, unable to help herself. 'Do you know it's not a cult, now?'

Veronica's gaze wandered around the room, unwilling to settle on her daughter. She picked up her bag. 'I'm tired,' she said.

Erin's brows rose in surprise.

'I'm going to go and have a nap,' Veronica said. 'I'll be down for dinner, if that's what you're making.'

Erin nodded dumbly.

Veronica looked at her for a moment. 'Good, then,' she said finally, and turned to the stairs.

Erin looked after her mother, her body taut with unanswered questions. What had Morghan said to her? Veronica never had afternoon naps. She glanced at Burdock, whose dark eyes were quizzical, watching her. She shrugged, and he thumped his tail.

'I don't know either,' she whispered, and Burdock got up, stretched, and came over to her. Erin stroked his back absently, wondering what to do. Should she go and see Morghan? Ask her what had happened?

No, she decided. That was silly. She gave a sigh, and

Burdock yawned, and she grinned at him affectionately. 'Silly pup,' she murmured.

Well, she decided. If her mother was going to have a nap, and dinner was all under control, she had some more free time. Wasn't that what she'd been wanting?

Erin crossed the sitting room and went into her little ritual room with its altar and desk. She wondered what her mother had made of this space, and decided she wasn't sure she wanted to know.

The tarot deck she'd bought from Haven was on the desk, unopened. Lucy's suggestion about tarot cards had made her curious, and she'd gone to Haven after work one afternoon to look at them. Krista, it turned out, stocked quite a few different decks, and she hadn't had a clue which to pick. In the end, she'd picked one that had a dear-headed figure on the front.

'She makes me think of Elen of the Ways,' Krista had told her. 'I'm not surprised this one calls to you. It's the same one Morghan uses – she says it looks straight out of her travelling to the Wildwood.'

And it was called the Wildwood Tarot, so Erin figured that made sense.

She broke open the packaging and lifted the cards out of the box, feeling her heart tripping along inside her chest. They were beautiful. She flipped through the cards, feeling as though she'd stepped back into time, into a time when Macha and Ravenna lived and walked the paths of Wilde Grove.

How had Krista told her to use them? A good way to start. Erin held the deck and shuffled them, closing her eyes, letting herself breathe and feel and expand. Then, eyes still closed, she thumbed through the cards, picking out one that felt right, then another, and a third. She put them on her desk, then opened her eyes.

The first was the King of Arrows – Kingfisher, and she smiled a little, wondering what Kingfisher had to tell her. But it was the next two cards that really drew her eye. Card o, The Wanderer. She shook her head a little - The Wanderer, that sounded just like herself. She knew she was going somewhere, but that was about it. The rest was just a journey fuelled by faith.

The last card of the trio was number ten. The Wheel. Erin put a finger on the card. There was the wheel. She shook her head slightly. What was the likelihood of getting this card, when the wheel was such a part of her life? She glanced at the deck. There were a lot of cards.

They came with a book, and that was a good thing, because Erin had no idea what the cards were telling her. She only knew they looked right.

She began with the King of Arrows, finding it in the book. Arrows, apparently, were associated with air, with creativity, communication, ambition, and all things of the mind. Erin turned to the King of Arrows and read the card's meaning with growing astonishment.

The Kingfisher was the symbol of ancient knowledge and wisdom.

Which was exactly what she was learning, following the Ancient Way.

She read more.

Representing a person, the King of Arrows was a moral leader, whose *highly principled discernment sees to the heart of things.*

That was Morghan, Erin thought. It certainly sounded like her. She looked at the card, then went back to the book.

As an aspect or process: Finding a way through chaos by calm clarity.

Well. That fit too. Erin was more than willing to describe the current situation with her mother as chaos. *Discerning the truth of a situation. Finding an impartial standpoint.*

The book added a list of questions for the King of Arrows.

What must you focus upon clearly?

Who can give you good advice?

What wise words will help the situation?

What is your duty to society?

That was interesting, Erin thought, that the card asked what her duty to society was. Not her duty to her family, or in this case, her mother, but to society.

They might not be quite the same, she thought, wincing.

The next card, The Wanderer, was the first card of *The Path Through The Forest.* She liked that. That was exactly what she was doing – taking the path through the forest. The Ancient Path.

She read what the book had to say about the card closely, astonished.

At this moment the burdens of the past are set aside - either for the Wanderer to pick up and take along, or to leave behind if the weight is too great. The Wheel of the Year is beginning its great cycle, bringing a new range of possibilities and challenges. The Wanderer is ready to make the leap into the unknown - all that is required is faith.

That was what she was doing, Erin thought. Leaping

into the unknown. She'd been doing that since she'd arrived in Wellsford.

And as for faith - she'd taken a giant leap of faith deciding to stay, join the Grove. She smiled slightly. And wasn't even her name Faith? Erin Lovelace Faith.

But the book wasn't finished.

You have come to a junction or turning point in your life... *Your spirit must move on and the desire to leap into the unknown beckons. This may mean leaving behind or giving up some baggage or burden that you have carried with you from the past.*

Erin put the book down and looked out the door at the stairs leading to the rooms above where her mother had gone to lie down.

She thought she'd already put aside the baggage she carried from her past, but perhaps that was an ongoing project. Perhaps there was more to do.

Her mind drifted to her travelling, to the gate at the end of the maze. What lay behind it?

Erin shivered suddenly, picked the book up again and turned to the page for card number ten, The Wheel.

The Wheel has turned; change is at hand. In all nature there is a time and tide. The cyclic laws of birth, death, and rebirth are ever revolving and, without change, all things stagnate. How you deal with this change is the issue here. Within the tangled and tightly woven fabric of chance you have the power to make a difference. By your own actions you can change your life.

She could change her life. Erin put the book down and contemplated the cards spread out in front of her. Wasn't she already changing her life? Hadn't she been doing that all along?

She had. Everything had changed since deciding to join the Grove, since setting out upon the Ancient Path.

Except, she'd stopped everything since her mother had turned up, hadn't she? She'd not done her morning devotions, or her evening ones, or anything in between. This was the first time she'd even come into this room, let alone cleaned her altar, made an offering.

She hadn't even done any drawing.

It was to be expected, though, she told herself. Her mother's arrival had been a shock, and she was around all the time. There was no privacy from her.

And her mother needed her, didn't she? Didn't she have a responsibility to her mother? Erin's eyes wandered to the card with the Kingfisher on it. What had it said to her?

What is your duty to society?

Usually, Erin would have answered that her duty to society, if she had one at all, was the same as her duty to her family, but now she was no longer sure. They seemed such different things.

She wished Stephan were there to talk to. She wished she could speak to Morghan, who to her would always be the discerning, moral leader, who saw to the heart of things.

But Morghan had been disturbed enough already.

And Stephan was out with Martin and Charlie, making plans for the rewilding of Rafferty's farm. He wouldn't be back until dusk, and even then, he'd be going back to the flat above Haven.

Well, Erin thought. Her first go with the Tarot had been interesting.

'What are you doing?'

Erin spun around, stared wide-eyed at her mother.

36

'YOU GAVE ME A FRIGHT,' ERIN SAID, SCOOPING UP HER CARDS and placing them face down on the deck.

'What are those?' Veronica asked, coming into the little room and looking around, blinking.

Erin cleared her throat. 'Tarot cards. I was using them for the first time.'

Veronica looked at her daughter. 'What's this?' she asked, pointing at the altar.

'It's my altar,' Erin said.

But Veronica shook her head. 'What's an altar? What's it for?' She picked up one of the photographs and gazed at it.

'That's Becca,' Erin said, shifting uncomfortably in her chair. She took a breath. 'And my altar is sort of a visual representation of the Wheel.'

'The Wheel?' Veronica picked up the next photo, of an older woman, this time.

'Yeah,' Erin answered. 'The Wheel's the seasons, and the directions, and a way of seeing the world.' She tapered off, knowing the explanation was lame, but not knowing how to explain it any better. Especially to her mother. 'That's Teresa,' she said. 'My grandmother.'

Veronica put the photos back. Why are they the only ones you have?' she asked.

'I've got plenty more of Teresa, not so many of Becca,' Erin said. She'd had to get the picture of her mother from Charlie.

But Veronica shook her head. 'That's not what I mean,' she said. 'Why only those two?' She turned and looked at Erin. 'I'm your mother – why aren't I there?'

Erin stared at Veronica, aghast. 'Ah,' she said. 'Because, ah, I guess because I've been doing a lot of work healing things between me and my birth family.'

Veronica looked back down at the photographs, then spoke around a sudden lump in her throat.

'Healing?' she asked.

Erin got up. She didn't want Veronica looking at her altar anymore. 'You don't really want to talk about this, do you?' she asked. 'Let's go have a cup of tea. I need to finish making the bread.'

But Veronica stood where she was. The nap hadn't done her any good. She felt fragile, as though she were made now of glass. She even felt as though, if she looked down, she would be able to see through her very skin, to everything that was underneath.

She could hear her heart beating.

'What sort of healing?' she asked again.

Erin stood awkwardly in the doorway. 'You don't want to know, Mum,' she said. 'You don't believe in any of this stuff.'

'How do you know what I believe and don't believe?' Veronica asked.

'By the way you've acted my whole life?' Erin said, shaking her head.

'You've been so angry at me the last months,' Veronica said. 'Maybe years.'

'What's wrong with you?' Erin said. 'You're acting weird.' She stared at Veronica. 'What did Morghan say to you?'

Veronica shook her head. That wasn't a conversation she wanted to replay out loud. Not yet anyway. She'd lain on the bed upstairs, staring at the ceiling, unable to stop thinking about it.

'Tell me, Mum,' Erin demanded. 'Tell me what she said to you.'

'It wasn't anything to do with you,' Veronica said, then sniffed, realising she was mortifyingly close to tears. She licked her lips. 'Maybe a cup of tea would be nice.'

Erin stared dubiously at her mother for a moment, then really looked at her. 'Are you all right?' she asked.

Veronica swallowed the tears back and sniffed. 'I don't believe any of this,' she said.

'Any of what?' Erin asked the question cautiously. Something was going on with her mother. What had Morghan said to her?

'Any of this,' Veronica repeated. She shook herself a little, looked at Erin. 'I think it's time we left.'

'What?'

'Go back to the flat. I don't think I can stay here any longer.'

'I'm not leaving Wellsford, Mum,' Erin said. 'I've told you that – I can't. This is where I belong.'

Veronica nodded. That was what Morghan had said to her. That Erin belonged exactly where she was.

'I don't belong here,' Veronica said.

Erin shook her head. 'Of course not.' She turned and spoke back over her shoulder. 'I'll make that tea.'

'Do you have anything stronger?' Veronica asked. 'And why of course not?' She followed Erin to the kitchen, then lowered herself gingerly, like an invalid, into a chair at the table. She still felt as though made of glass. As though she'd had a big shock.

'Something stronger?' Erin asked, then shook her head. 'Just coffee.'

'You don't have anything else?' Veronica wanted a glass of something nice and alcoholic. That would be very good.

'No,' Erin said, understanding dawning. 'There's nowhere in Wellsford to buy wine or beer or anything yet, and I haven't been anywhere else.'

'Herbal tea,' Veronica said on a sigh. The caffeine would only make her more jittery.

She watched Erin filling the kettle and putting it on to heat. She watched her move gracefully about her small kitchen, reaching for this, picking up that, spooning tea leaves into a pot. Erin was completely at home in this cottage, in this village. Veronica looked down at her hands, at all the rings on her fingers. The diamonds caught the light and gleamed fire back at her.

'So,' she said. 'Tell me about this healing work you've done, or whatever it is.'

Erin looked over at her. 'Why do you want to know?' she asked.

'I'm interested,' Veronica said. 'Am I not allowed to be interested?'

Erin brought the teapot and cups over to the table. 'I don't know,' she said, putting them down and looking at her mother. 'Don't you still think this place is a cult? What did you and Morghan talk about? What did she say to you? You were gone for ages.'

And then you went straight upstairs and had a nap when you came back, Erin thought.

Veronica drew one of the cups closer. 'It doesn't matter what Morghan said, or what we talked about.'

Erin frowned. 'Are you sure? You've been acting a bit odd since you got home.'

'Of course I'm sure,' Veronica snapped. 'What's wrong with me asking questions about what you've been doing?' She shook her head. 'I'm still your mother, even though my photo isn't on your altar.'

Erin opened her mouth on a quick retort, then closed it and took a breath instead. Fighting with Veronica wouldn't achieve anything, even if she didn't know what she needed to achieve. She thought of the tarot cards she'd pulled. Was she the only person in the room they might relate to? Maybe her mother was the Wanderer as well.

It was an unsettling thought.

'What is it?' Veronica said, scowling. 'Now you're staring at me like I've grown a third eye.'

Erin shook her head. 'Sorry,' she said, dropping down onto a chair. She picked up the teapot and poured for them both.

'I was furious with Becca,' she said. 'My birth mother.'

She glanced over at Veronica, who was pale, but attentive. 'Are you sure you're all right?'

Veronica nodded. 'You were furious with me too.'

'It's true,' Erin said. 'I guess I kinda still am, as well.' She avoided Veronica's gaze. 'It's hard, getting it all sorted. It's been a big process, coming to terms with it all.'

'Why do you need to?' Veronica asked. 'Can't you just get on, and leave it behind? It's in the past, after all – and you never even met Becca.'

'Really, Mum? It's that easy?' Erin shook her head. 'Not for me. And the past, as you call it, has a way of casting a long shadow over the present.'

Veronica didn't answer. She was thinking about that one. About what sort of shadow the past had drawn over her life. She would have said it hadn't. It didn't.

But then she'd met Morghan Wilde, who had reached out and touched her, and shown her something she didn't want to see.

'Anyway,' Erin was saying. 'I had this wound inside me, you know? Because I never felt like I fitted in at home.'

'At least you had a home,' Veronica burst out. 'You were safe and warm and wanted for nothing.' She straightened, glaring at her daughter. 'I made it that way for you. I gave you that. I made sure of it.' She shook her head. 'If I had left you with Becca,' – she spat the name out – 'then you would have had nothing. She wouldn't have taken care of you. I recognised her type. She couldn't wait to get back to her parties and her drugs, and her strings of boyfriends. She didn't even know who your father was.' Veronica bent her head and pressed her hands around the cup until it burned her palms. 'I made sure you didn't have to grow up that way,' she said, teeth gritted. 'I did that. I rescued you.'

Erin stared at her mother in shock.

'Where did that come from?' she asked.

Veronica just shook her head. 'You had it so easy,' she said. 'I made sure of it. I made sure we would have it easy, that you would never have to go through anything like I did.'

Erin spoke slowly. 'What did you go through?'

But Veronica pushed back her chair and got up from the table. Her heart was thumping against her ribs, and there was the pulse of blood between her ears as well, as though suddenly she'd become some sort of tidal creature inside her glass shell.

'Where are you going?' Erin asked, standing up. 'Sit back down and talk to me, please? Mum?'

Veronica shook her head. 'I'm going home,' she said. 'There's something there I need to get.'

'What?' Erin was confused.

'I'll be back in the morning,' Veronica said.

'In the morning?' Erin reached for Veronica, grabbing hold of her sleeve. 'What's going on, Mum?'

'You'll see,' Veronica said. 'I'll show you and you'll see.'

'Show me what?'

Veronica tugged her arm away and went up the stairs. She'd get her bag from her room and drive back to the house. Get what she needed, have a sleep, then come back in the morning.

This was the right thing to do.

Erin needed to see. She needed to see what Veronica had done for her. Why she'd done everything she had.

She'd see, and then she'd understand.

She was back in minutes.

Erin watched her mother go to the door, keys in hand, and shook her head in consternation. 'You can't just go, Mum,' she said. 'You're not feeling yourself.'

Veronica turned at the door and smiled at her daughter. 'I'll be fine,' she said.

Erin stared at her. Should she go with her? Make sure she was all right? 'Do you need me to go with you?' she asked. 'I can drive if you need me to?'

But Veronica shook her head, feeling suddenly crystal-clear. 'No,' she said. 'You stay here. I'll be perfectly all right. I need the time alone, I think.'

'But you're coming back?' Suddenly, it seemed important that her mother came back.

Veronica smiled. 'First thing in the morning.' She looked down at her feet. 'I have to come back, to show you.'

'Show me what?' Erin asked.

But her mother was already out the door, closing it behind herself.

37

ERIN WAS UP AT THE FIRST STIRRING OF THE SUN, THROWING off the blankets and shivering in the early dawn air. Burdock lifted his head and looked at her, his shaggy eyebrows pulled together in a frown.

This was early, he thought, even for them.

'Come on, boy,' Erin said. 'Things to do, people to see.'

Burdock stood up, yawned, stretched, watched while Erin pulled on her clothes, then padded out of the room behind her, waiting while she visited the bathroom, then leading her down the stairs to the front door.

Erin plucked up her cloak, let Burdock out and followed him, much to his delight. They were going somewhere, early in the morning when all the smells were fresh and bright, ready for him to sniff. It didn't even matter that they weren't stopping for breakfast first, because it was still early and his tummy wasn't telling him it was time to eat.

They headed straight for the woods.

Erin breathed in clear, bright air. Even though it was still cool, and rained a lot, she could taste June's early summer in the air. It was different, she thought, to every other season. She looked around her, at the dim trees in the faint dawn light, and heard the rustling of creatures either getting up or heading back to their nests and burrows.

A raven cried out somewhere and Erin lifted her head, looking around for it. Was it one of the ravens that roosted around Ash Cottage, or was it Raven, her Otherworld kin? Her fingers tightened on her cloak, and she tugged it closer around her.

It cawed again, a harsh, triumphant sound and Erin stopped walking, peering around the trees for the bird.

Burdock pressed against her thigh, and she stroked him, happy at his warm solidity.

'Come on, Burdock,' she whispered. 'The sun's getting higher.'

They followed the path, its twists and turns memorised, until Erin found the track she wanted, the one that led to the stream where it was Morghan's habit to greet the dawn.

'Clarice?' Erin said, realising the figure at the stream's edge wasn't Morghan at all.

Clarice glanced at Erin, eyes wide with surprise. 'Erin,' she said. 'I wasn't expecting you.'

'Where's Morghan?' Erin asked.

A shadow crossed Clarice's expression, and Erin shook her head. 'Sorry, Clarice,' she said. 'I just needed to speak to her, you know?'

Clarice dipped her chin in acknowledgment. 'She was called away to see one of her dying.'

'Oh.' Erin's heart dropped. Morghan could be gone all day, if that was the case. And Erin only had a little while before she needed to get back to the cottage and wait for her mother.

Clarice looked at her for a moment. 'Shall we greet the day?' she asked. 'And then maybe I can help you.' She shrugged and gave a diffident smile.

Erin nodded. Clarice wouldn't be able to help her – not unless she knew what Morghan and Veronica had spoken about the day before – but she was here now and seeing Clarice had reminded her of other things.

But for the moment, Erin simply slipped her boots off, gave Burdock a smile and a pat, and then drew breath, letting it out slowly, letting herself relax, become part of everything, letting all her worries float away. The ground was cold under her feet, but she let it be, settling into it, forging connection with the earth.

Clarice reached out a hand and Erin took it with a graceful smile. It felt like time was stopped, that they were timeless, and she knew it was because she'd done this so often before, in this body, and in others, and that she went on, the world went on, and she loved it.

Erin lifted her face to the sky, where the light was growing stronger, unveiling the world. She closed her eyes for a moment, then took another breath and stepped into the water beside Clarice.

The stream gripped her by the ankles, cold as though it was the same water from her well, from deep in the earth, and she breathed into the shock of it, breathed deeply, greeting the stream, reaching out with her spirit to touch that of the water, and her lips curved in a smile at its familiar response, at its gurgling, laughing song.

Clarice spoke beside Erin, words Erin was familiar with from being with Morghan.

'Spirit of this stream, we greet you in honour and pleasure,' Clarice said, relaxing into the ritual and letting her spirit reach for that of the water.

Erin picked up the prayer. 'We move in and out of the worlds together and it is a joy to be with you on this day.' As though speaking it could make it so, she felt uplifted, her heart filling with a slow, sweet welling of joy.

'Spirit of water,' Clarice said, drawing in a breath. 'We touch you with our own spirits and find that we know each other.'

'We bring you our gratitude,' Erin said, and bent over, touching the water with her fingers, listening for its song, for the stories the water could tell any who listened about its journey from deep within the earth, through this way and out to the ocean.

'Carry our song with you,' Clarice said. 'Carry our song of spirit and flesh, our gratitude for you, our awe of you, because without you, we would not live the lives we do.'

'Carry our blessings with you on your travels,' Erin said. 'Take our love of the world with you, and the promise of our service to it.' She spread her blessing on the water with her fingertips, then straightened and reached her hands to the sky, breathing the world in, the scent of green upon the trees, the sparkling water's clear tang, the rich scent of soil.

Clarice dug her toes into the stream bed, anchoring herself as though she had grown there, as much a part of the natural world as the trees behind her. She dug herself deep, anchored in the world and reached for the stars, for the rising sun, for the light that illuminated the world, and her heart.

'We hold ourselves in honour to you, earth, sky, water,' Erin said. 'We walk in balance between you, world to world to world.' She closed her eyes.

'By sky and root, through all worlds,' Clarice said. The words came from deep inside her, and she saw herself in amongst the elements, connected, part of the web.

Walking in balance.

Learning to walk in balance.

She took a long, grateful breath and opened her eyes to gaze over at the other side of the stream, where a shining figure watched them, another joining them. Clarice's eyes teared over and she bowed her head, speaking in a voice thick with emotion. 'My greetings to you, my friends,' she said. 'May you be honoured and blessed this day.'

Erin blinked, glanced at Clarice, then across the stream where she was looking. She pressed an involuntary hand to her chest at the sight of the Fae come to greet the day with them. They were marvellously Otherworldly, the dawning sun touching them like halos. No wonder, she thought, that Julia's world had come apart at a glimpse of them. Erin bowed to them.

She and Clarice watched them for a moment longer, until they turned smiling and walked away from the stream, leaving only the dazzle of the sun on the water. Stepping from the stream, Erin looked at Clarice.

'Are you all right?' she asked.

Clarice thought about it. A week earlier, her answer would have been no, she wasn't all right. But somehow, dreaming as she had, and meeting Grainne there, had changed things.

More than a little.

She still longed for her Fae friends, for her visits to the Fair Lands, but she was also determined to follow her dreams and find a way to bring their wisdom and their lessons into her life.

The thought of which made her almost quiver in trepidation.

Except there were those rooms at the heart of herself. And there was her mother, telling her she needed to be truthful and do the work necessary.

'Yes,' Clarice said. 'And no.'

Alarmed, Erin reached for Clarice's hand, caught it, and held on to her fingers. 'But why?' she asked. 'What's wrong?'

'I miss them, that's all,' Clarice said. 'I can't help that.'

'Miss who?' Erin gazed around. 'Them?' she asked after a moment. 'The Fae?' She knew Clarice spent a lot of time with them. 'Why do you need to miss them?'

Clarice slipped her hand from Erin's and bent to retrieve her boots. 'The Queen has said I can't go back there.'

Erin gasped. She hadn't heard about this. Clarice hadn't said anything when they'd gone into town together. 'What?' she asked. 'Not at all?'

'Until the solstice.' Clarice said. She tugged one boot on. 'Winter solstice.'

'But we're only coming up to Midsummer.' Erin shook her head. 'I don't understand.'

'Nor did I to begin with,' Clarice said. She shoved her other foot in its boot and tied the laces before standing up and letting herself see the way Erin was looking at her.

'So there is a reason, right?' Erin said, shell-shocked on Clarice's behalf. 'What did the Queen tell you?'

Clarice gave a humourless smile. 'Nothing,' she said. 'As Queen, she doesn't have to give reasons for anything she does.'

'But she must have one?'

'Yes. I made Morghan go and ask her,' Clarice admitted, patting Burdock so that she had something to do with her hands, somewhere to look. 'She said the Queen wished me to have more balance in my life.' She straightened and glanced back at the opposite bank. 'And she's right, of course. I'm coming to see that. I need to find a way to walk in balance between the worlds. In this one.' She shrugged. 'I'm learning to,' she said.

She looked at Erin and changed the subject. 'Do you still want some dance lessons?' She gave a wincing smile. 'I'm thinking I'll go along with Krista's dance class plans, but do you want private ones?'

Erin's eyes widened. 'You're really going to lead the classes? That's terrific.' Her face crumpled a moment then she laughed. 'Great, now I've no excuse not to do the art classes.'

'It might be fun, right?' Clarice asked, then shook her head. 'I'm trying to convince myself of that, anyway.'

'I think I'll find it a challenge,' Erin said, then held her hands up in defeat. 'But aren't most of the best things? If there's been anything I've learnt the last months, it's that stepping out of your comfort zone usually ends up being a good thing.' She laughed. 'It'll be the same for this, too, right?'

Clarice shook her head. 'No,' she said. 'I'm pretty sure it

will just be terrifying.' She sighed. 'At least the first fifty or so times.'

That had Erin laughing again. 'Yeah, you're probably right, but it sounds like we're going to do it anyway.' She nodded. 'I definitely want the dance lessons. I've got stuff going on at the moment with my mother, but what about in a day or two? We're going to be having the summer solstice ritual soon enough, and I'd love to get some in before that.'

'Anytime will work for me,' Clarice said, and stopped herself from adding that it wasn't as though she didn't have anything else going on. That wasn't the right attitude to take, she reminded herself.

'Yeah,' Erin said. 'Okay. Where shall we do it?'

'At the circle,' Clarice said. 'I'm still getting used to going into town.'

'Why's that?'

Clarice shrugged, stepping onto the path away from the stream. 'I had a rough time when I was younger, with people – especially the kids at school – staring and jeering because I'm different. It made me...retreat, I guess,' she said.

Erin nodded. 'I bet it would,' she said. 'But everyone here knows you, surely?'

Clarice hunched up her shoulders then made an effort to relax them. 'Mostly, I suppose. But it's a process, right? I still feel like I don't fit in.'

'It sure is a process,' Erin said, and shook her head, falling in beside Clarice. 'I know what that's like. Except it was my family I never fit in with.' She frowned, thinking about her mother's strange behaviour. She would have liked to ask Morghan about it, but that wasn't going to happen now. She looked curiously at Clarice. 'What was your mother like?'

Clarice huffed a reluctant laugh. 'I loved her so much,' she said. 'She was wildly creative, crazy full of magic, but always restless.' She paused. 'Coming here was good for her, though. For us.' She blinked. 'Things were a bit hard before that, I think.'

Erin shook her head. 'Life is so complicated, isn't it?' she said, her voice low. 'Something weird's going on with my mother. She's left my dad, which isn't great, but I don't know. She's said a few things about her life that I never even knew – didn't have the faintest idea about.'

'People are complicated,' Clarice said. 'I think the world's pretty straightforward, or at least it should be. It's us who mess it all up.' She sighed, thinking about the state of things. 'Over and over and over.'

Erin nodded. 'I wish there was something we could do.'

'I never wanted to be part of it,' Clarice admitted. 'I preferred it when I could just take off, leave, stay with the Fae.'

'Most of us don't have that as an option.'

'Yeah, well nor do I anymore,' Clarice said.

Erin nodded and reached down to lay her hand on Burdock's back as he walked beside them. 'We should do something, though, don't you think?'

Clarice glanced sideways at her. 'You sound like you have something in mind.'

'I don't know.' Erin was thinking about her art. About all the other things she'd learnt over the last months. 'Shouldn't everyone be learning the things we have? That the world is bigger than they realise? That what they do and how they think is important?'

'I don't know how you tell them that,' Clarice said, lifting her face to the warming light that shifted on the breeze between the trees. She listened to the birds, awake now, serenading the rising sun. 'There are already piles of books written on the subject.'

'True,' Erin sighed. 'I don't have the answer.'

'There might not be one,' Clarice said.

Erin looked across at her, dismayed to hear Clarice say such a thing. 'Tell me you don't believe that,' she said.

Clarice winced. 'No,' she said. 'Probably not. Do you want to come and dance now?' she asked. Dancing was what was helping her to work through things. She had discovered that she could dance her dreams, and it was really helping her to embody them.

'I wish I could,' Erin sighed. 'But my mother ran off last night back home to get something she wants to show me.' Her hand slid from Burdock, and she rubbed her temple. 'Something that will *show me*.'

'Show you what?'

Erin shook her head. 'I don't know.'

38

Winsome got out of Morghan's car, leant down to look in the door and smiled. 'That was...amazing,' she said. 'Thank you for making me come along with you.'

Morghan laughed. 'You're very welcome.'

Winsome closed the door and waved the car off, then stood on the footpath a moment longer, gazing across the road at Mariah's old house. It was dusty and dispirited and Winsome wondered what Julia's plan for it was. From the looks of it, the small lawn allowed to grow long, the garden tangled and unkempt already, Julia didn't want to go near it.

Winsome couldn't really blame her for that one. The place would need a good cleansing and scrubbing. She remembered the day Ambrose had come down to clear the vicarage with his smoke and prayers and then she was trembling, her hands clenched around the straps of her bag.

Ambrose.

She'd been avoiding him. It was shameful, really. She ought to be ashamed of how she'd been treating him. She'd backed out of having dinner with him, hadn't gone near him, and never explained herself either.

'I'm a coward,' she said. And sighed.

The day was warm and still, the sky overcast. Winsome looked up at the clouds, then down her driveway at her car.

Was she really thinking about going to see him?

She realised she was. Just to apologise.

Her throat was dry, but suddenly she was determined. Heart thumping, she turned and walked down the path to the house, then skirted around the side and walked across the lawn, keeping her eyes averted from the locked, lonely church.

Except something flickered at the edge of her vision, and she blinked, stopped, and turned to look. Perhaps it was Cù, she thought.

But it was not Cù.

The woman, her skin dark and swirled with strange designs, turned and regarded Winsome with eyes the colour of winter oceans.

Winsome swayed where she stood, and would have fallen to her knees, if she hadn't thrust out a hand to steady herself against the house.

She was dreaming. It was the woman from her travelling. From the day she'd followed Morghan deep into the cave and deeper into the Otherworld.

The woman who had told her a story about the wind.

Winsome backed up against the cool stone and pressed herself there. She closed her eyes, opened them, and the woman was still there. Shimmering, wavering in and out like a dream, but there.

Undeniably there.

A white sow stared at Winsome from beside the woman.

A hawk sat impassive upon the woman's shoulder.

The only thing missing was the man who had been her companion.

Winsome's voice was a squeak. 'What do you want?'

But the wild woman didn't answer. She stood instead amongst the graves of Wellsford's dead and looked at Winsome.

They held each other's gaze for what felt to Winsome like an eternity, and then the woman blinked, smiled, and faded out of the world.

Winsome dropped to her knees and covered her face with her hands, shaking her head. 'I didn't see that,' she said. 'I didn't just see that.'

How could that ancient, inhuman woman appear here, in Winsome's world?

Winsome took her hands away from her face and pressed her palms against the grass.

All she'd lacked, Winsome thought, had been her antlered companion.

What had been the story she'd told?

Winsome licked her lips.

Once upon a time – had that been how it started? Once upon a time there was a woman stumbling through the forest, blinded by her tears, her mind reeling with all her problems.

Once upon a time there was a woman who was chased by the wind as she ran toward the cliff from which she would hurl herself to escape all her problems.

Once upon a time there was a woman, caught by the

wind as she fell, and the wind whispered to her soul that she would never die.

Winsome shook her head, got unsteadily to her feet, and risked a glance over at the church.

A blackbird hopped between the graves, searching for its lunch.

There was no strange woman, or white sow, or speckle-feathered hawk.

She dusted off her knees and looked around for Cù.

He was at the entrance to the path into Wilde Grove, tongue hanging out, waiting for her.

Winsome shook her head, then remembered the story again. The woman, fleeing the noise inside her head, the worries, the fears, the thoughts that went round and round and round without cease.

Was that still her, she wondered? Head full of unnecessary noise?

Perhaps it was.

She nodded at Cù. 'I'm coming,' she said, her voice hoarse.

Cù grinned at her and turned, trotting away into the woods.

AMBROSE WAS OUTSIDE BLACKTHORN HOUSE AND WINSOME stopped on the edge of the property to watch him. He stood in a small patch of sunlight, eyes closed, fair hair shining, and was doing a series of fluid exercises that Winsome guessed was Tai Chi, or something similar. She pressed her lips together to stop herself admiring the graceful way he moved, the serene expression on his face, everything about him.

Ambrose opened his eyes and stopped moving. He stood and looked at her.

'Winsome,' he said at last. 'I thought I felt you there – but then I decided it was just wishful thinking.'

She edged closer across the lawn. Cleared her throat. 'Wishful thinking?'

He nodded. 'I've wished many times to see you.'

Winsome ducked her chin down, her cheeks heating. 'I've been avoiding you,' she said, lifting her gaze to look at him. 'I'm sorry.' Her fingers knotted together. 'Everything got very confusing for a while there.'

His face relaxed into a smile. 'I understand,' he said, then shook his head slightly. 'It's been an eventful time.'

Winsome took another step closer. 'A lot has changed, for me,' she said.

'I'm so sorry,' Ambrose told her, letting his gaze linger on her. How greedy he'd felt for a glimpse of her. She looked thinner, as though she'd been through a trial. Which she had been, of course. 'I'm sorry about the church,' he said. 'I wish things hadn't gone that way for you. I know it was important to you.'

Winsome nodded.

'I've just been with Morghan,' she said. 'We went to see a woman, to help her plan how she wanted to die.' She winced a smile. 'It's humbling work.'

Ambrose nodded back at her. 'It's good work,' he said.

Winsome cleared her throat. 'How are you?' she asked. 'What have you been doing?'

Ambrose looked at her across the stretch of grass. 'I'm

good,' he said. 'Been busy, really. I'm thinking of writing a book.' He widened his eyes, surprised to find he really was.

Winsome broke out into a smile. 'You'd be good at that,' she said. 'What will it be about?'

'Well, it would be a collaboration with a journalist,' he said. 'She wants to write about the history of Wilde Grove and Wellsford.'

'Then she couldn't have found a better person to help her,' Winsome said. 'You'll be wonderful.'

Ambrose shrugged. 'It seems the right time for such a thing,' he said. 'Would you like a cup of tea?'

'Yes please,' Winsome said. 'I'd like that very much.'

Ambrose nodded. 'Inside, or out here?'

Winsome looked around. Saw the garden bench she'd sat on with him last time she'd come here. 'It's very mild out,' she said. 'Perhaps here?'

Ambrose nodded again, looked at Winsome, then turned and went inside to put the kettle on.

Winsome looked around at the house, at the trees that crowded about, at Cù, who stood grinning at her as though this were all a grand joke. She rolled her eyes at him, then picked up her courage and followed Ambrose inside.

He heard her steps in the hallway and turned to the door to see her there in his kitchen.

'Are you all right?' he asked.

'Yes, thank you,' Winsome said. She looked around. 'Your house is very neat,' she said.

'That's so I can find things.' Ambrose switched the electric kettle on and reached for clean cups. 'Sit down if you like,' he said.

She sat down at the table under the window. The room

was cosy, and surprisingly bright, considering all the trees. 'How long have you lived here?' she asked.

Ambrose had to stop to think about it. 'Forever, it feels like,' he said with a smile. 'But in reality, only about twenty years, I'd say.'

'That long?' Winsome didn't know why she was surprised. Perhaps because she'd moved around a fair bit, had trouble finding where she belonged.

She belonged here, in Wellsford.

'I've moved around quite a lot,' she said. 'Over the years.'

Ambrose set the cups on the table and sank down in the chair opposite her, waiting for the water to boil. 'Was that the way you liked it?' he asked. 'Some people seem born wanderers.'

Wanderers. Winsome liked the word. But she shook her head. 'I don't think so,' she said. 'I think I was looking for where I belonged.'

'I was lucky,' Ambrose said. 'I found that place. Many don't.' He looked across the table at Winsome. 'Will you be staying in Wellsford?'

Winsome took a deep breath. Nodded. 'I didn't know for a while,' she said. 'I felt guilty about the church. And I didn't know who I was if I couldn't be part of the clergy.'

Ambrose's green eyes looked steadily at her, and she lowered her gaze, stared at the table.

'But I don't want to go anywhere else,' she said at last. 'I want to stay in Wellsford. Things are happening here I want to be a part of.' She met his eyes again, risked a smile. 'I think I belong here.'

Ambrose reached across the table and touched her hand. 'I'm glad,' he said. 'I'm glad to hear that.'

Winsome nodded and turned her hand over so that she held his.

The kettle boiled, switched off.

Ambrose stayed where he was. Winsome's hand felt marvellous in his. He didn't want to let it go.

'The kettle's boiled,' Winsome said.

Ambrose nodded. 'I know.'

'Is this real?' Winsome asked.

Ambrose squeezed her fingers. 'I believe so.'

'I'm sorry I never came for that dinner,' Winsome whispered.

'It doesn't matter,' Ambrose said. 'You're here now.'

It was Winsome's turn to nod, to speak around the lump in her throat. 'I'm free the day after tomorrow. For dinner. If the invitation still stands.'

'It does.'

She smiled. 'It's a date, then.' Ambrose was still holding her hand, and she didn't want him to let go.

'A date?' Ambrose tightened his grip on her fingers.

'Yes. Is that what you want?'

'Since the first minute I saw you.'

There were no arguing voices in her head, Winsome realised. No voice questioning her choices, no voice berating her for doing this or not doing that. No voice asking her if she was sure, if she was certain, if she knew what she was doing.

It was all blessedly quiet in there, as though a strong wind had blown through and swept them all away.

'Do you know why I suggested the day after tomorrow?'

Ambrose raised his eyebrows. 'Because you're busy tomorrow?'

Winsome shook her head. 'So I can savour this,' she said. 'The anticipation.' She laughed. 'I feel suddenly like a giddy schoolgirl.'

Ambrose gave a wide smile. 'Anticipation is nice. And it will give me time to decide what to cook. What do you like?'

'I'm not much of a cook,' Winsome said, grimacing. 'I'm learning to bake, though. It's a lockdown trend, I hear.' She looked shyly at him. 'And I don't mind what you make. I don't have any dietary restrictions, probably to my detriment.'

Ambrose laughed. 'Anything it is, then.'

There was a pause. 'You still haven't made the tea,' Winsome said.

'No,' Ambrose replied. 'I should though, shouldn't I?'

'Maybe,' Winsome said. 'Maybe in another moment.' His fingers in hers were strong, fine. A scholar's hand, she thought. Her gaze drifted over his arms, shoulders, and she flushed. He wasn't just someone who sat around. She swallowed, drew her gaze safely back to his face. Groped around for something to say.

'Is it usual to see...erm...people from the Otherworld in this one?' she asked. It was the first thing she thought of.

Ambrose sat straighter, gaze sharpening. 'Has that happened to you?'

Winsome nodded. 'Yes, just before I came here.' She glanced at the door. 'And Cù, my spirit dog, he practically led me here.'

'Cù?' Ambrose asked. 'Your spirit dog?'

'Morghan hasn't told you about Cù?' Winsome asked.

Ambrose shook his head. 'Morghan doesn't tell me that which isn't her place to.'

'Oh.' Winsome thought about that for a moment, then nodded. That would be right, she decided. A smile spread over her face. 'Well, Morghan took me...travelling...' The word was foreign in her mouth, at least with that meaning. 'And when I asked her about her spirit kin...' Spirit kin. Another term she had to get used to. She blew out a breath.

'Well,' she continued, still holding Ambrose's hand. 'When I asked her about them, she said I had kin also, and I could call them to me.'

'So you did.'

Winsome nodded. 'And a dog that looks a lot like Erin's wolfhound has walked with me ever since.' She smiled, almost fondly. 'I call him Cù. Morghan said that was Welsh for Dog.' She shrugged. 'It suits him.'

Ambrose slid his hand out of Winsome's and pushed his hair back. 'Wait,' he said. 'When you say walks with you – do you mean in this world too?'

'Yes. Ever since that day. He never leaves.'

Ambrose looked at her with astonished green eyes. 'He's here now?'

Winsome broke out in a big smile. 'He was outside lazing under a tree, last I saw him – as though he'd done his job bringing me here, and was giving us some space.'

'That's incredible.' Ambrose stood up. 'Will you show him to me?' His eyes were bright with excitement.

Winsome lifted her brows. 'Of course,' she said. 'Will you be able to see him?'

'I've no idea, but I'd certainly like to try.'

Ambrose's excitement was infectious. Winsome grinned and led him back out to the lawn, and there, sure enough, was Cù, head up, looking at them.

'He's there, under that tree,' Winsome said. 'He's looking right at us.'

And grinning like usual, as though it were all a great joke.

Ambrose slowed his breathing, taking deep lungfuls of air, and he slipped sideways slightly, adjusting his vision so that the world of spirit came into view, like an overlay to his normal world.

And there was Winsome's dog, just as she'd described him. Ambrose reached for Winsome's hand.

'Winsome,' he said. 'You most certainly belong here.'

39

ERIN RUSHED OUTSIDE AS SOON AS SHE HEARD THE CAR PULL
in off the lane.

'Mum,' she said, opening the driver's door. 'I've been so
worried – you said you'd be back in the morning.'

'I texted you,' Veronica said, getting out of the car and
blinking with relief that the long drive was over.

'Yeah, but that was two hours ago.' Erin looked at her
mother in sudden dismay. 'You look really tired.'

'I am.' Veronica yawned as if to prove it. 'I didn't get
much sleep.' She opened the rear door and pulled out a
cake tin. 'I was talking to your father.' He'd wanted to know
why she was back in the middle of the night, tearing things
out of the cupboards in her dressing room, looking for
the box.

Erin stilled. 'Was everything okay?' she asked cautiously.

'Well, he's stopped seeing his floozy.'

'He has?'

Veronica allowed herself a smile, but she didn't feel like

talking about Vincent right that moment. He could wait. She looked down at the big square tin in her arms. Did she still feel like doing this?

When she'd gone careening out of Erin's little house the night before, she'd been determined to show her the truth. The reasons why she'd done what she had.

But now it was the next day, the sun was up after a long night, and she was exhausted. Did it even matter anymore?

But then she thought about Erin's table, her altar, with the photographs on it of her birth mother and grandmother and her lips tightened.

The past, her daughter had said, had a way of casting a long shadow over the present.

She shivered. And that woman, Morghan, the way she'd leant over and touched her suddenly, and said things in a voice that wasn't hers, words that weren't hers.

Veronica cleared her throat.

Morghan had spoken to her in her grandmother's voice.

'Mum?' Erin said, interrupting her thoughts. 'Are you all right? Come inside.'

Veronica nodded. Let Erin lead her into the cottage with all the plants and the scent of burning herbs and incense. 'I could do with a cup of coffee,' she said.

'Of course,' Erin said. 'Sit down, and I'll make you one right now.' She looked at the cake tin, curiosity burning inside her to know what was in it. But Veronica looked exhausted, and whatever it was in there could wait. 'I'll make you something to eat, as well.'

Veronica put the tin on the table and watched Erin move about the kitchen, her long dress swaying about her ankles, her hair in a braid down the middle of her back.

'Your hair's grown,' she said.

Erin glanced at her. 'I haven't bothered with getting it cut since I came here,' she said, and shrugged.

'I guess it goes with the new look,' Veronica said. 'The long dresses like it's the Middle Ages again.'

Erin brought over the cup of coffee to her mother, then went back to make her a sandwich. The bread she'd made the evening before had turned out okay. Not too bad for a first effort.

'I like the dresses,' she said. 'One of the women living here in the village makes them. And I mean, she really makes them. Spins the wool, weaves the fabric, dyes it, everything. I think it's amazing. She even makes her own linen from plants she grows.'

'It sounds like a lot of work,' Veronica said.

'I'm sure it is,' Erin answered. 'But it's better than fast fashion, mass-made with cheap, exploited labour.'

'And the jumper you're wearing? I suppose someone terribly clever made that too, in their spare time? Right off the sheep?'

Erin sliced tomato grown from seed by Stephan and the other gardeners in the new glasshouse. She smiled. 'Right off the sheep,' she agreed.

'Well, it certainly is a rustic look.'

'It's warm, breathable, sustainable,' Erin said. 'And beautiful.'

'If it's your taste to look like someone several centuries behind the times,' Veronica grouched.

Erin laughed, sliced the sandwich in half. She wondered what Veronica would think if she saw someone like Macha. Maybe she ought to get tattoos like Macha's.

Then Veronica would really have something to be shocked about.

'What's the egg for?' Veronica asked when Erin brought her lunch to the table and sat down.

Erin looked down at the crystal egg on its string around her neck. She wrapped her fingers around it, and it warmed against her skin.

'It was my grandmother's,' she said. 'Teresa's.'

Grandmother. Veronica took a gulping mouthful of the coffee. She wasn't ready to think about her own grandmother again.

Even though that was all she'd thought about on the long drive there and back to her house.

Morghan's lips moving, her grandmother's voice coming out.

My darling Vera, she'd said. *I'm so sorry we had to leave you.*

Veronica blinked, shook her head slightly, hoping to dislodge the memory. The sound of her grandmother's voice.

She'd loved her grandparents.

'What's it about, though?' she asked Erin, her voice harsh. 'Why an egg?'

Erin looked down at the crystal. She'd asked Morghan what it meant. One of the first things she'd asked, probably, but by no means the last.

Turned out, the egg was an ancient symbol, and meant a heap of different things.

'It symbolises the soul,' she said, giving the meaning the Grove used.

'The soul?' Veronica shook her head. All such rubbish.

My darling Vera. We didn't want to leave you.

All such rubbish. Wasn't it?

'The bread's good,' she said grudgingly. 'Is this the loaf you made?'

Erin smiled. 'Sure is. My first real go at it. I've only helped Stephan before this.'

'Stephan makes bread?' Veronica asked. 'The gardener?'

'He's not just a gardener, Mum,' Erin said, then shook her head. 'As we've talked about before.' She shrugged. 'Teresa taught him to cook when he was a teenager.'

Veronica raised one eyebrow. 'Teresa taught him?'

'He lived with her for a while.' Erin rubbed a finger over a groove in the table, hoping Stephan wouldn't mind her talking about him. A little bit. 'His parents kicked him out when he was sixteen.'

Veronica was surprised. 'So not everyone in this village is a complete angel then.'

Erin stared at her mother. 'I guess not,' she said, then shook her head. 'Why are you being like this?'

'Like what?' Veronica's appetite vanished.

'So negative about everything? You've poured scorn over the clothes I wear, over my boyfriend, over everyone who lives in this village. What's wrong with you?'

Veronica stared at her.

Oh my Vera, what's become of you?

'Nothing,' croaked Veronica. 'Nothing's wrong with me.' She shook her head, waved a hand in the air. 'There's something wrong with this place,' she said. 'It's not me.'

'You mean Wellsford, or Wilde Grove?' Erin asked. 'Or just me and my home?'

'All of it,' Veronica said. 'Grocery subscriptions, community gardens, spinning wool, making linen, knitting things. Making bread. Drying herbs. Making teas.' She shook her head. 'It's all so...' She couldn't think of a suitable word.

'Right?' Erin asked. 'Real? Sustainable? Caring? All those things we're supposed to be?' She put her hands on the table, fingers curled into fists. 'What would you rather? Oh, that's right.' She nodded. 'I remember. You wanted me to be an Influencer – someone who showed off their horribly conspicuous consumption, as though having money and buying and spending and consuming, consuming, consuming until the world ends was the perfect thing to do. Like that guy – what was his name? Nero, playing his violin while Rome burned. Or some such thing.' She wound down, spoke more quietly, aware that Burdock had lifted his head, was looking at her from across the room. 'I can't be that person. I won't be. It's not healthy for us, and it's not healthy for our planet, and we've fucked that up enough already.' She took a breath. 'I want to live in a community where people care, Mum. Where they care about each other and for each other.'

Veronica looked at her. 'I cared,' she said, her voice strangled. 'I cared enough to give you everything you needed.'

Oh my Vera, what's become of you?

She shook her head, ignoring her grandmother's voice.

'I cared enough to give you everything I never had,' she said, and grabbed the tin, shoving it across the table at her daughter. 'There,' she said. 'It's all in there, what little there is.' She dipped her head at the metal box. 'Open it. Look at it. Look at what I saved you from.' She prodded a finger at her own chest. 'I saved you from it. I did.'

Erin looked carefully at her mother, aware that there was something going on, but not sure what it was. She reached a hand across the table and put it on top of Veronica's.

'You're crying, Mum,' she said softly. 'Are you okay?'

Veronica tugged her hand away, folded her arms over her breasts, shook her head. 'Look in the damned box,' she said.

Erin nodded slowly and lifted the lid off the tin. It was a cake tin, an old one, the metal rim around the lid rusted with age. The picture on the front was faded, the words *Darby Maid Rich Fruit Cake* written on it, next to a picture of the cake in question.

'How old is this tin?' she asked, grimacing as she pried off the lid.

'Probably from the '50's,' Veronica answered dully. 'It was my grandmother's. She brought it around one day, with a Christmas cake in it that she'd made for us.'

'Us?'

Veronica shrugged. She was tired again, all the fight gone out of her. Now she just wanted this over with.

Oh my darling Vera.

'Me and my mother.'

The lid popped off and Erin set it down, staring into the box with a feeling of shock. 'How come you've never shown me any of this?' she asked.

'I've never shown it to anyone,' Veronica said.

Erin looked at her. 'Not even Dad?'

Veronica looked away. 'No, though he knew some of it, of course. He was there.' Her lip curled. 'He met my mother. Once.'

'Only once?' Erin shook her head, realising she knew none of this. 'Why only once?' She looked down at the pile of old photographs and memorabilia. She picked up a small, threadbare teddy bear and looked at her mother.

Veronica's throat was thick. 'My grandfather won me that,' she said. 'He took me and my grandmother to the attractions at Hastings Pier. It was the best day of my life.'

Erin's eyes widened. She put the small, scruffy bear reverently on the table and picked up a photograph. It was of a small child, hair a snarled and tangled halo, eyes too wide. 'Is this you?' she asked, showing it to her mother. She turned it over and squinted at the writing on the back. 'It says Vera.' She looked over at her mother, a frown on her face.

'My name was Vera, before I changed it.'

'Vera?' Erin shook her head. 'What? When did you change it?'

'When I was sixteen. As soon as I could.'

'But why?' Erin was stunned.

Veronica snorted. 'Do I look like a Vera to you? I needed something with a bit more style.' Her lips twitched into a grimace. 'It was part of the plan.'

'The plan?'

'To leave all that behind.' Veronica shrugged.

Erin looked down at the small heap of photos. She put the one of the little, unkempt child down and picked up another. 'Who's this?'

Veronica glanced at it. 'My mother.'

Erin cleared her throat. 'She looks...'

'Like a neglectful slut?'

'Ah, okay.'

A shrug. 'That's what she was.'

Erin stared at the photograph, then at her mother. 'She was neglectful?'

Another shrug. Veronica stared at one of Erin's pot plants. Some delicate, leafy thing.

'She neglected you?' Erin asked.

'When you're partying with every guy you meet, there's not much time to worry about whether your kid has had a proper meal, or a bath, or a bedtime story.'

'Oh.' Erin looked back at the photo of her mother as a small child, then sifted through the pictures in the tin. There was her mother as a baby, held snugged in the arms of an older woman. Erin showed it to her mother. 'Who is this?'

Veronica looked at it, pressing her lips together. She took the photograph off Erin and gazed at the long-gone face.

'That was my grandmother,' she said. 'Her name was Edna. Everyone called her Jean though. Jean was her middle name.'

'Did you live with her?'

Veronica shook her head. 'No,' she said. 'But I wanted to.'

Erin was silent a moment. 'Because of your mother?'

'Yes,' Veronica said bitterly. 'Because she spent what little money there was on going out and having herself a good time. While I was at home on my own, usually, and hungry and frightened.' Veronica put the photograph down.

'You don't know what it's like,' she said. 'What it's like to be dirty and hungry and the laughingstock of everyone at school because your clothes are never washed, and you stink of piss and grime. What it's like to have even your teachers hate you because you're always coming to school with headlice, and you never had any breakfast in the morning, so you're always disruptive, unable to concentrate.'

Erin looked at her mother, at the fastidious way she was dressed, her carefully done hair. 'But...' she said.

Veronica shook her head. 'No buts, Erin. I'm glad you don't know any of this, don't you see?' She leant forward, her eyes locked on her daughter's. 'I took care of you so that you would never have to know. So that your birth mother, Becca...' She spat the name. 'So that Becca would never leave you at home while she went out and got smashed and didn't come back until lunchtime the next day.' Veronica barked a laugh. 'Not that it mattered if it were lunch time because there was never any bloody lunch.' She sat back and looked at the plant again. 'Yes, I paid extra to that dirty slut to get you. She said she was clean during the pregnancy, and her tests said she was too, but I knew her type – she would go straight back to it once you were born. She wouldn't be able to help herself. And all her talk of black magic and cults just made me surer that she was going to be a danger to any child she had.'

Erin was cold with shock. She hadn't known what to expect when her mother had taken off the night before to go and get whatever, but she'd never had any idea it would be this.

'Couldn't you have lived with your grandparents?' she asked tentatively.

'They wanted me to. They tried to get my mother to let them have me, but she wouldn't hear of it.' Veronica looked down at her hands. Her nail polish needed redoing. What she wouldn't give for a manicure. She tucked her hands away.

Oh my Vera, what's become of you?

She'd survived, that's what she'd done. Not just survived but made sure she'd never go hungry again. Never wear old or torn clothes. Never stand and stare at people better off than her and wish she could disappear. Veronica squeezed her eyes shut. Swallowed.

'I stayed with them sometimes, for holidays,' she said, and pulled the cake tin towards herself, digging through the snaps. She found what she was looking for and held it out to Erin. 'See.' It was the Easter her grandad had won the teddy bear for her. She'd never been so happy.

Erin took the picture and looked at her mother beaming at the camera, hugging a small teddy bear. She was wearing a pretty dress that was obviously new, and sweet knee-high white socks.

'These are your grandparents with you?' she asked.

Veronica nodded. 'That was the last time I saw them, that visit.'

Erin gazed at her mother. 'Why?'

'Car accident,' Veronica said. 'A stupid bloody car accident.'

Erin got up and went around the table to her mother. She leant down and put her arms around her. 'I'm so sorry, Mum,' she said. 'I never knew. Why didn't you ever tell me?'

Veronica didn't know whether to push Erin away or hold onto her.

'I didn't want to think about it,' she said, her words muffled. 'I worked hard to put it all behind me.'

Erin straightened, sat back down, and stared at her mother. There were high, bright spots on Veronica's cheeks.

It was like Stephan had said, Erin thought.

Everyone had a story. A deep, inner life that nobody else really knew about.

40

'Julia,' Winsome said in surprise, walking across the grass to her kitchen door. 'What are you doing here?'

Julia turned from trying to peer in through the glass and looked bleakly at Winsome. 'I went to see Morghan,' she said.

'You did?' Winsome thought, not for the first time recently, that she may have inadvertently stepped into some sort of parallel universe.

'I can't stop seeing things,' Julia said, and wrung her hands. She could see Winsome's damned spirit dog right now. It was staring at her, tongue lolling out, grinning. She turned her face from it and looked at Winsome instead.

'What sort of things?' Winsome asked slowly, unlocking the door and opening it for them. 'You can see more than my spirit dog?'

'Things I ought not to be able to see,' Julia retorted. 'And it's all Mariah's fault.'

Winsome thought of Mariah's empty house, the garden overgrown, the grass too long. 'It is?'

'Of course it is,' Julia snapped, standing in the kitchen, trying not to look at Winsome staring at her, because she could see an odd, hazy colour around the woman. For a moment, she seriously considered yanking open the kitchen drawer, snatching up a fork, and sticking it in her eyes.

Winsome's gaze widened. 'Julia,' she said slowly. 'What were you just thinking?'

'That I ought to stab myself in the eyes.' She blinked. 'Didn't Jesus say *and if thine eye offend thee, pluck it out and cast it from thee?*'

Winsome frowned. 'Erm, in Matthew, yes.' She set her bag and jacket down carefully on a chair. 'But Julia, that is not meant literally. Jesus is just saying that anything that causes you to sin should be avoided, cast away.'

'I am seeing unholy things,' Julia said, squeezing her eyes shut.

'I don't think so,' Winsome said. 'You are not seeing anything unholy; I promise you.'

Julia snapped her eyes open and glared at Winsome. 'You are surrounded by a sort of haze,' she said.

'You can see my colours?' Winsome asked. This was a turnout for the books.

'You know about these hazes?' Julia asked, then shook her head. 'Of course you do. You are a pagan priest now.'

'Julia,' Winsome said gently. 'Sit down, please. I'll make you a good strong cup of tea, and we can talk about this sensibly.'

'There's no sense to be made of it,' Julia said, shaking her head. But she let herself sit down and drooped over the table, all the fight going out of her. 'Nothing has gone like it was supposed to.'

'Perhaps not,' Winsome answered. 'Perhaps not the way you had planned it – but on the other hand, perhaps it is going exactly as God wishes it to.'

Julia raised her head and stared at Winsome. 'God would not want me to be able to see spirits and whatever else.' Her mouth turned downwards. 'Colours, as you say.'

'God would not?' Winsome asked, looking at her unexpected visitor. 'These things are real, Julia – you can see them. I can see them. As can others. Not everyone, I grant you, but enough for us to be able to say they likely are real.'

Julia shook her head. 'I can see the poor health of my roses,' she whispered.

Winsome sat down. 'The poor health of your roses?' she asked.

'I neglected them,' Julia said. 'I didn't do any of the things they needed. I was too busy.' She blinked, clasped her hands together. 'With Mariah, and what we did to you.' Her throat jumped as she swallowed. 'It was like being on a crusade,' she went on, voice hoarse. 'I liked the purpose of it, the sense of things having meaning, of being on the righteous side of it all.' She looked briefly at Winsome, then down at her hands again. 'And I wanted you to go away. I wanted to take the services again, like I had after Robinson died. I organised everything then.'

The words tumbled from her mouth as though she had no control over them. Why was she saying all this? To Winsome Clarke of all people. The enemy.

Except she wasn't really an enemy, was she? When everyone else refused to have anything to do with her, forgot probably – and gladly – that she even existed, who had knocked on her door and refused to go away?

Winsome Clarke. The person with the most reason to hate her.

'Everything is a terrible mess,' Julia said. 'I've made a terrible mess of everything.'

'Messes can be cleaned up, Julia,' Winsome said. 'Just like your roses can be taken care of.' She looked at Julia carefully, then stood up.

'Come with me,' she said.

'What?'

Winsome nodded. 'Just for a minute. There's something I want to show you.'

Julia shook her head. 'Where do you want to take me?'

'Just upstairs for a moment. Please, Julia?'

Julia stood up, reluctant. 'Just for a minute, then,' she said.

'Good, thank you,' Winsome said, and led her out of the room and up the stairs. She opened her bedroom door.

'What is this?' Julia said. 'Why are you taking me to your bedroom?' She narrowed her eyes. 'You've been spending too much time with Morghan Wilde, haven't you? Her ways have rubbed off on you?' She twisted the word *ways* with her insinuation.

Winsome rolled her eyes. 'Sexuality is not contagious, Julia. You're being ridiculous, and more than a little offensive.' She led the way into the bedroom, glad it was neat and tidy, the window open to air it out.

'Here,' she said. 'Come and stand right here.'

Julia sidled suspiciously into the room, glancing around.

The bed was made and there was a Bible on the bedside table. It didn't look dusty, either.

'What do you want me to do?' she asked, coming slowly to stand where Winsome indicated.

Winsome put her hands on Julia's shoulders and turned her to look in the full-length mirror.

'Look at yourself,' she said.

Julia shook her head. Looked at the floor instead. 'I don't want to.'

'I think you should,' Winsome said, looking in the mirror at their reflections and letting herself relax, letting her vision expand. She could do it easily now.

Her colours flared around her, pearlescent, glowing. She smiled, knowing her aura was deeper, richer than usual, because of Ambrose. Because of how she felt about Ambrose.

'Why is yours so bright, and mine isn't?' Julia asked, interrupting Winsome's reverie.

'Because I am relaxed and used to this by now,' Winsome answered.

'Mine looks sick.' It was ragged around the edges and curled tight about her. Julia frowned at it. 'Why is it like that?'

Winsome let her look.

'And those darker spots – what are they?' Julia wished she wasn't looking, but she couldn't make herself draw her eyes away. She shook her head. 'How do I make it better?'

'That's a good question,' Winsome said. She smiled. 'Mine used to be all tight and close like yours.'

Julia glanced at her.

'Then I learnt a few things, and I let go of a lot of fear.'

She giggled. 'And I practiced the exercises I did in that video. I practiced them a lot. And I became calmer, and my spirit strengthened.'

Julia shook her head. 'Mine's an ugly colour. Why is it so ugly?'

'It's not so bad,' Winsome said. 'It's only because you're unhappy.'

'I don't know how to be anything but unhappy,' Julia whispered. 'I've always been unhappy.'

Winsome nodded, took Julia by the hand. 'Come on,' she said. 'Let's go and look at those roses of yours.'

'What?' Julia took a last, perplexed look in the mirror and let Winsome lead her from the room. Her head was spinning.

That was what she looked like? That tight, ugly thing?

WINSOME STOOD IN THE GARDEN AND BREATHED DEEPLY. 'AH, Julia,' she said. 'They smell so wonderfully.'

Julia looked around. 'I chose a lot of them for their scent,' she said. 'I love a fragrant garden.'

'It's beautiful,' Winsome said. 'You've put a lot of work into this. I never knew.'

Julia gave a tight shrug. 'It's my baby, I suppose,' she said. The spirit cat was sitting on her steps, ears twitching, for all the world like a real feline. Julia looked away, back at her plants.

'Can you see what they need?' Winsome asked.

Julia could. And not just because she knew how to look after roses. She nodded. 'I can see their haze,' she said, and reached out a hand toward the closest, an Eden Rose climbing up a trellis in front of the cottage. She touched her fingers to the haze around it and blinked.

'My fingers tingle,' she said. 'Sort of like static electricity.'

'Trees sing,' Winsome said. 'I wonder if roses do?'

That was absurd, Julia thought. But then, so was being able to feel the plant even though her hand wasn't close to touching it. So was being able to see this hazy cloud around it. She leant slightly forward, listening.

She thought she heard something. Or felt something. It wasn't real hearing – not like hearing the phone ring, or someone speaking right beside you. It was hearing through her skin, rather than with her ears.

But yes, she thought she could hear something.

'I don't understand this,' she murmured. 'I don't understand any of this.' She turned to Winsome and shook her head. 'Why is this happening to me?'

'I don't know,' Winsome said.

'It was because I saw *them*,' Julia said, answering her own question. 'The Fae.' She touched her hands to her temple. 'It cracked me right open. Like I was an egg.'

Winsome thought of the crystal egg Morghan and Erin wore around their necks.

'Perhaps,' she said. 'Probably.' She looked around the garden. 'How are we going to help your plants?' she asked.

Julia blinked, gazed at her roses. Cleared her throat. 'Oh. I can prune them, just lightly, but it's too late in the day to do it,' she said. 'I'll need to give them a good watering tomorrow in the morning, so that they don't get heat-stressed during the pruning.' She hugged herself and thought about it. 'I'll need to prepare my pruners as well –

they'll have to be dipped in a bleach solution before and after doing each bush – so that I don't spread any diseases from one rose to another.'

'Do they have any diseases?' Winsome asked.

Julia gazed around at the ones in that part of the garden. Then shook her head in relief. 'I don't think so. They're just a bit parched.' She winced in embarrassment. 'And a lot overgrown.'

Winsome grinned at her. 'You can tell that just by looking?'

She could, Julia thought in sudden amazement. 'I can,' she said.

'That's pretty fab,' Winsome said. 'All right, then. What else do they need?'

Julia gazed around at them. She was getting used to seeing the odd haze around them, she realised. 'Nothing for now,' she said. 'I'll have to wait for tomorrow to water them.' She'd get up early to do it, she decided. Up with the sun, get a head start. And after she'd watered them, she could make sure she had everything else ready.

Did she have any bleach? If she didn't, she'd have to get some. She didn't need much. One part bleach to ten parts water.

Julia nodded. 'Let's go and look at the plants in the back garden,' she said.

'You have more?' Winsome asked.

Julia gave a diffident shrug. 'I like gardening,' she said.

'Lovely,' Winsome said. 'Let's go take a peek, then.'

Julia nodded but didn't make any move.

'Are you all right?' Winsome asked.

'Why are you doing this?' Julia wanted to know.

Winsome smiled and spread her arms. 'Gardening makes you happy, Julia,' she said.

Julia looked around. It did, she realised. It did make her happy. She looked over at Winsome, a frown still tucked between her eyes.

'Is that enough?' she asked.

'It's a very good start,' Winsome replied.

41

Erin crept to the bathroom as the day's first light touched Ash Cottage's windows. She did her business as quietly as possible, then stopped outside the door to the spare bedroom, where her mother was, hopefully still asleep. She leant close to the door and turned an ear towards it to listen.

It was quiet. She couldn't hear anything.

But the door was closed, so with a bit of luck that meant Veronica was still sleeping.

Erin shut her eyes for a moment, took a quiet breath, then slunk down the stairs to where Burdock waited to be let out. She stepped outside after him and stood under the entranceway to her cottage, rubbing her arms and looking out at the dawning day. It was cool, and she lifted her face to the air. Living around so many trees meant the air was soft, full of moisture, a balm for her tired and gritty eyes.

Everything felt tired and gritty, if she was honest. And raw.

She felt raw, inside and out. As though she'd scraped up against something hard.

Which she had, she supposed. Veronica's childhood. That had been hard. Rough enough to take a layer of skin off.

No wonder her mother had done everything she had.

Erin pressed the heels of her hands against her eyes. No more tears, she told herself. She'd shed plenty of them the day before.

And she'd spent most of the night dreaming about looking for a child, trying to take it to safety.

If it hurt her this much just to hear about – what had it been like to live through?

Burdock came trotting back around the side of the house and squeezed past Erin to go stand in front of his bowl. It was breakfast time, and he was always careful to remind her of that now.

Erin patted him on the way past to get his biscuit tin. 'I only forgot the once, boy,' she said.

He looked at her with luminous brown eyes. Once had been plenty, as far as he was concerned. He eyed the great tin with his food in it and wished, not for the first time, that he could get his own meals.

Of course, he forgot about that straight away when Erin filled his bowl. It didn't matter that he didn't have thumbs or know his way around fiddly tins, because his person loved him, and she made sure every morning that he got his breakfast.

She'd only forgotten once, and that had been a long time ago, now.

Burdock picked up one of the biscuits and crunched it up.

Erin went through the utility room and outside into the garden, breathing deeply of the morning air. She went to the well and pried up the lid, shivering at the sight of the deep, cold water. But still, she dipped her finger in, touched it to her forehead.

'Blessed water,' she murmured. 'May I flow as you do.'

She straightened and looked around, trying to pick the prayers to begin the day.

But none seemed right. Erin felt too raw. She needed something that would be as a balm to her.

'Ah, my Lady,' she said. 'You have shown me the brilliance of your face and form and given me the gift of the treasure that is knowing my own soul.'

Erin lifted her face to the sky, closing her eyes, summoning to her memory the sight of the Goddess. She trembled slightly.

'Let now me feel your sure strength, the calm beating of your heart. Let me stand with you, inside your light, let me follow you, along the path. Let me be comforted, guided, healed.'

She took a breath. 'Let me sing the beauty of the world with you.'

Erin stretched her hands towards the sky, feeling the cool caress of air upon them.

'May there be peace in the east,' she said. 'May there be peace in the south. May there be peace in the west. May there be peace in the north.'

The wheel swung around on her chanting song. She

could feel it, in the sky above her, in the ground beneath her, inside her, filling her.

She was the wheel; she was the song. She opened her eyes and looked tenderly upon the world. 'In peace may my voice be heard,' she said. 'In peace may I follow the voices of my Goddess, of my Kin.'

From somewhere over the garden wall, from within the trees, a slow, lilting tune lifted on a breeze towards her.

She danced, slowly, deliberately, her spirit shining.

And then, there was Raven, and Raven picked her up and carried her inside himself, spreading his dusky feathers over her skin, until they reached the maze.

And Erin stood upon the stone steps, and saw that Fox was already there, her sharp muzzle lifted to taste the air, whiskers quivering, before she turned and trotted away between the tall walls of the maze.

Erin raised her arm for Raven who landed lightly upon it, turning his head to look at their path with his bright, black eyes.

The stone woman looked down at them from her niche in the wall, her sightless eyes blind stone, and yet...not. Erin dipped a hand into the crane bag around her waist and brought out an offering, bowing her head as she placed it in the woman's upturned hands. She touched the cool stone fingers and whispered.

'I thank you for guarding the way,' she said. 'I give you this offering in blessing and gratitude.' The acorns fit snugly in her palms.

The sun and moon stones were back upon their shelves, and Erin stopped a moment to regard them with unblinking eyes. She had forgotten about these, she realised. With everything that had been going on, she had forgotten.

But she would remember, she told herself as she picked them up and slipped them in her bag. She would remember to find waking world versions of these. This time.

Fox's plumed tail disappeared around another corner. Erin followed.

Soon, she was stepping on the lawn, crossing it towards the oak tree and well.

'My greetings, Lady Oak,' she said, reaching the tree, and touching her bark with her fingers.

She turned and regarded the well, a frown knitting itself between her brows. The water in this well was warm, she remembered.

But what was its purpose? Why was it there? Erin lifted her head and looked at the far walls of the maze. Why, she could well have asked, was any of this there?

What did it all mean?

She had no more idea than she'd had the first time she'd come.

But perhaps that was all right. Perhaps it was a mystery she did not need to unravel at this moment.

Raven dug his toes into the flesh of her arm, then lifted himself into the air with a powerful beat of his wings. A moment later, he was flying, circling overhead, a black gleam against the blue sky.

But where was Fox?

She was not resting under the oak. Nor was she looking at her reflection in the dark water of the well.

Erin saw her, over at the gate.

Her heart tripped over its beats as she walked towards Fox and the heavy gate in the wall.

This was as far as she'd come the last time. Before being woken and brought, dizzyingly suddenly, back to the waking.

What was her body doing there now, she wondered, and reached out with part of her mind to touch it there.

She was in her garden still. Dancing.

Erin came back to the maze. To the gate. She took a breath, threaded her fingers through the hand hole in it, and tugged it open.

This could not be, she thought.

What was this place?

The light here was not the yellow of the sun, the blue of the sky. It was grey, greasy, and Erin's heart thumped in her chest. She pressed a hand against her breast as though to still it.

She wanted to be quiet here.

This was a place where she needed to be quiet.

Fox did not trot ahead, and Raven swooped back down to perch silently upon her shoulder.

Fox walked close by her legs.

The green grass was gone. Under their feet, it was the cracked tarmac of a road. Litter lay clumped in the gutters. A plastic cup, Coke written in faded script on its side. A glass bottle, broken, the shards wickedly sharp.

Erin turned around to look back at the gateway, at the grass and tree beyond it, but it was gone.

There was only the street upon which she stood, another branching off it. There were only the buildings lining the streets. Broken down, boarded up, and yet...

And yet, she thought there were people within them.

'Mean streets,' she murmured. 'These are the mean streets of a city of shadows.' Her mouth was dry.

What sort of people were here? Why was she here?

'Lady, be with me,' she whispered, one hand reaching into her pocket to feel for the diamonds that were her gift from Elen of the Ways. 'Lady, guide and protect me.'

They slunk along the street, crossing the pitted road to keep to the shadows, Erin ducking her head each time they passed a window that had not been boarded up, as though if she did not look through the grimy glass, then no one would stare out at her either.

'Where are we going?' she whispered, but Fox just glanced up at her, a wide-eyed expression on her face, as though surprised Erin did not know.

Erin frowned. She had no idea. But there had to be a reason she was here, had to be something to it. She looked around, at the litter, the weeds growing in the cracks in the road, at the dark windows of the buildings, some of which may once have been shops and flats and apartment buildings, but which were now not fit for anything to live there, but, she thought, rats.

And yet, every now and then she was sure she caught movement behind the gaping doorways, through the cracks in the boarded windows. Every now and then she was sure she heard a distant shout, running footsteps.

'What is this place?'

City of Shadows, she thought, and knew the name had resonance. Knew it intuitively to be right. Her intuition. That was what she had to trust.

There was an alleyway beside her, full of rusted shopping carts, bags leaking rubbish. Something moved in the shadows and Erin shrank back.

Her intuition, she decided, was telling her to get the hell out of there.

'That's it,' she said, talking to Fox and Raven. 'I need to know more about this place before I go any further.' She blinked. 'And why we're here.'

Which meant, since there obviously wasn't going to be an information centre anywhere nearby, with a friendly soul behind the counter who would give her a handful of maps and shiny tourist brochures – which meant turning back.

Going home.

Talking to Morghan. Maybe even Macha.

She retraced her steps, heaving a sigh of relief that this time the gate was there, where it ought to be, in the high stone wall, and she fell through it, grabbing the gate and slamming it shut behind them. She looked at Fox, Raven's feathers brushing against her cheeks.

'We are not going back in there without knowing more,' she said. 'And I don't care what you have to say about it.'

Fox didn't appear to have anything to say. She wrinkled her lips, pulling them back in what might have been a grin, then trotted out onto the grass.

Erin followed, relieved to be in the fresh air again.

SHE WAS STILL DANCING WHEN SHE CAME BACK TO HERSELF, IN her garden at Ash Cottage, on the border between Wellsford and Wilde Grove.

On the border of a great many more places than that, Erin thought, drawing in a breath full of summer air and fragrant herbs. The scent made her wish Stephan was there. She wanted to be near him, to look over and see him, reach out and touch him.

She would invite him over for dinner, she decided, going inside. Right now, though, she needed something to eat and drink.

It would help bring her back properly. Ground her.

'You dance beautifully,' Veronica said, startling Erin. 'I was watching outside the window.' Veronica flushed slightly. 'I didn't want to disturb you.'

Erin leant over and kissed her mother on the cheek, the gesture surprising them both. 'Thank you for not inter-rupting me,' Erin said.

Her mother's eyes narrowed slightly. 'Were you doing some of your funny stuff again?'

Erin went over to the cooker and touched the side of the kettle. It was hot.

'There's coffee in the cafetiere,' Veronica said. 'Still fresh.'

'Thank you,' Erin said, and pushed her hair out of her face, then poured herself a big mug full. She took a sip. 'That's better,' she said, leaning against the kitchen bench and closing her eyes. 'I'll make some toast in a minute.'

'I've already got some in,' Veronica replied, and checked the toaster to make sure the homemade bread wasn't stuck in there. She glanced over at her daughter. 'So,' she said. 'Why were you dancing at seven o'clock in the morning?'

Erin opened her eyes and gazed at her mother, then shrugged. 'I was travelling,' she said.

'Travelling?'

'Most people call it journeying, I suppose,' Erin said,

and took another sip of the coffee. It was good. 'Shamanic journeying, to the Otherworld.'

'What?' Veronica shook her head. 'Is this some of the weird cult things you do?'

'It's not a cult,' Erin said. 'It's a spiritual practice.'

Veronica opened her mouth to argue with Erin, then thought better and took the toast out in silence. Thinking about Morghan, and the things she'd said.

Or rather, the things Veronica's grandmother had said.

From Morghan Wilde's mouth.

'What good does it do?' she asked. 'This spiritual practice?'

Erin gaped at her mother, then accepted the plate of toast and followed her to the table. 'What do you mean, what good does it do?'

Veronica turned her mind away from the things she'd heard coming out of Morghan's mouth.

Oh my Vera, what's become of you?

'Religion, as far as I've ever seen, makes bigots and hypocrites out of people.' She shrugged tight shoulders. 'And spiritual practice? That's a bit wibbly wobbly New Age, isn't it?'

'It's a bit necessary, is what it is,' Erin said, and took a bite of the toast, determined not to let her mother irritate her. Veronica was asking questions – that was a good thing, wasn't it? Erin put her toast down and looked across at her mother.

'What?' Veronica asked, feeling suddenly self-conscious. She touched her hair. She wasn't dressed, and she hadn't put a brush through her hair, either.

Usually, she didn't come downstairs until she was washed and dried and primped and painted.

'You should try a few things,' Erin said. 'Some basic stuff, you know.'

'Like what?' Veronica asked, looking at Erin like she'd grown two heads. 'I don't think so.' She sniffed a laugh. 'I tried meditation once.'

'You did?' Erin's eyes widened.

'I fell asleep. It's not for me.'

Erin laughed. 'Winsome has some really basic exercises to relax and ease stress levels a bit. Those might be good to have a go at.' She glanced upstairs where her laptop was. 'They're online so I can show you.'

'Who is this Winsome?' Veronica asked. 'Have I met her?'

'She's the Wellsford vicar,' Erin answered, swallowing the last bite of her toast and checking the time. She had to get to work, and she needed to see Morghan. She wished it didn't have to be in that order.

But Veronica was looking at her in consternation. 'The vicar? What sort of place is this?'

'Well, retired vicar, now,' Erin said. 'The church here is being decommissioned, or whatever they call it.' She frowned. 'But I'm pretty sure Winsome is staying on, and I'm also pretty sure she still has her website up.' She got up from the table and made for the stairs. 'Wait a minute and I'll show you.'

The website was still available, although Erin looked at it for a long moment before she figured out what was different.

'Ha,' she said, putting her laptop on the table in front of

her mother. 'Winsome's updated it.' It was no longer a parish website, but more of a community one. 'Gosh,' Erin said, scanning the page. 'She's been really busy – look, she's going to hold classes in the old vicarage.' Erin turned the screen towards Veronica. 'Try the exercises,' she said. 'They're there somewhere. I have to get to work.'

'Work?'

Erin bent down and kissed her mother's cheek again. 'Yup,' she said. 'It's how I pay for stuff,' she said.

'The care home,' Veronica answered, curling her lip. 'I can't believe you work there.'

'It's been good for me,' Erin said simply. She meant it. Working there had been good for her.

Now she just needed to figure out what this spooky City of Shadows was all about.

Erin shivered, then went upstairs to change.

42

Veronica watched Erin fly out the door with her great hairy dog to walk to work. Which reminded her that she needed to get Vincent to return their daughter's car.

It was a ridiculous thing to have tried in the first place. What had they been thinking?

She shook her head, dug her phone out of her dressing gown pocket and sent Vincent a text message. Her phone flashed a minute later, and she pursed her lips at the screen. He'd organise the car right away and when was she coming home?

She didn't have an answer to that. The phone went back into her pocket.

It was quiet in the cottage, the only sound the gentle ticking of the fire in the cooker. Veronica blinked at it, then looked out the window to the garden at the back of the house. Where Erin had been dancing.

It had been a strange sight, coming downstairs in the morning to see her daughter outside, dancing silently to music that must have been playing only in her head. Eyes closed, as if in a trance.

Veronica pursed her lips. Turned to the computer on the table.

She clicked on a new tab and typed in *shamanic journeying.*

Then shook her head over the search results and picked one that looked like it might give her a general overview. What was it, she wondered? What was it for?

Did it let dead people speak through you?

Veronica shuddered, waited for the page to load. The connection was slow, and she didn't know how Erin could stand it.

The page loaded and she scanned what was written there. *Interconnectedness. The expression of humanity's connection with earth and spirit. Healing.*

So, a lot of New Age flim-flam, then. She'd been right.

Veronica clicked away from the page, tried one of the videos.

Four and a half minutes in, the woman speaking started talking about a conversation she'd had with a goddess – Isis – and Veronica hit pause. Conversations with goddesses? This person was obviously delusional.

Is that what Erin had been doing?

Veronica clicked on a different video. *The oldest form of spiritual practice on every continent of the world.*

She sat down. Well, she thought. Not that New Age, then.

All life is viewed as sacred.

Which would, Veronica was forced to admit, make the

world a little bit of a better place. She could have done with her mother viewing her like that.

Veronica pressed her lips together at the thought. That one was too painful. The past, which she'd worked so hard to leave behind, felt as though it had pressed right up against her, rubbing her raw.

Oh my Vera, what's become of you?

She scowled. Nothing had become of her, except that she was rich and safe, and wasn't that a good thing?

Even if she never went back to Vincent now, she would still have enough money to be safe. To afford nice things. Somewhere to live.

Why had her grandmother asked what had become of her?

Veronica shook her head. It hadn't been her grandmother. It couldn't have been. Her grandparents were dead. Dead people didn't speak through the mouths of living people they'd never met before. Or even through the mouths of people they had met. It was all a load of rubbish.

Except it had been her grandmother, calling her by the name Vera. Veronica looked around the room, as though her grandmother might speak again, from the ceiling this time, from thin air.

She shook her head. This reminded her of the time she and Ginny Finlayson had gone to a sound healer. It had been Ginny's mad idea, of course, but it was supposed to be relaxing at the very least.

Veronica snorted. She hadn't thought about this for years.

She'd expected it to be a cross between a massage and meditation. Which she thought she'd just grit her teeth through. Meditation was for people who liked mung beans and yoga. Veronica didn't even know what mung beans were, but they certainly didn't sound tasty.

It had been relaxing – to begin with. A massage table, and at first, she hadn't minded the sound of the tuning forks. It had been pleasant.

But then, when the woman waving them around had started zooming them in and out from Veronica's body – her left side – and asking her if she'd had problems with her mother not meeting her needs, Veronica decided she wasn't in the right place and called a halt to all proceedings. She'd sat in the reception, waiting for Ginny, reading about probiotic yoghurt or some such thing, and wishing she'd never come.

She drifted away from her friendship with Ginny afterwards and that had been all right with her.

Veronica watched another few minutes of the video.

Shamans actively engage with the spiritual realms for the benefit of themselves and their community.

She shut the page down. Which left her looking at the website Erin had opened for her. The vicar's website. Apparently. Veronica's fingers hovered above the mousepad, ready to close it as well.

But she was already reading it. Then she was scrolling down the page, and there was another video, showing a smiling, slightly plump woman in her forties with pretty hair.

Veronica sighed and clicked play. Really, she ought to go have a shower, get dressed, get in her car, and drive home. Sort something out with Vincent.

The vicar woman had a nice smile.

Veronica took a deep breath when the woman told her to.

She held it, let it slowly out. Found herself sitting straighter in the chair.

She watched the video all the way through.

Then shut the computer down. Really, she needed to go home. Decide whether she was going to leave Vincent or not.

He said he didn't want her to. Veronica hugged herself. She didn't want things to be the same if she went back. No more other women.

No more...she didn't know what else. But maybe – maybe something.

When she went upstairs, however, she didn't pack her things. She just had a shower and got dressed, then got into her car.

There was no sign of Erin on the way into the village. Veronica guessed she was too late to catch her walking to work. She slowed though, as she drove past the old house with the sign outside that told her it was the Wellsford Care Home. That was where her daughter worked, she told herself. Taking care of old folk. It didn't look such a bad place. Pretty garden. The windows were open to let the fresh air in.

Veronica wondered what sort of place she would end up in when she was old. Who would look after her?

She'd never thought about growing old, and what would happen. It was still some time away. Not as far away as it had used to be, though. She was almost sixty. Vincent was three years younger. Veronica had lied about her age to him, hadn't told him until after they were married, that she was actually the older one.

She parked in front of The Copper Kettle. She'd meant to go straight to the big house where Morghan Wilde lived, and knock on the door there, demand some answers, but she decided she wanted another coffee. Maybe a piece of the cake she'd had last time.

She wasn't ready to talk to Morghan again, yet. What if that whispery voice spoke through the woman again? What if her grandmother spoke to her again?

Veronica sat down at one of the tables in the pretty little courtyard outside. A little brown and white spaniel sniffed its way over to her and looked up at her with dark, luminous eyes.

She backed away, her chair barking against the paving stones. 'Get away!'

'Are you okay?' Winsome, paper bag full of Simon's bliss balls, stopped on her way out and looked over at the well-dressed woman cowering away from a small dog. She stepped over and shooed the spaniel away.

'Go on, Poppy,' she said. 'Get back home.'

The spaniel lifted her soft ears, then wagged her tail and turned away, heading back home.

'Don't mind Poppy,' Winsome said. 'She lives next door, and sometimes makes an unauthorised visit over here to see if any hoovering might be needed. She's absolutely harmless.'

Veronica shook her head, feeling pale. She clenched her hands into fists to stop them from shaking. 'I'm not too keen on dogs,' she said.

Winsome tried not to wince at the fact that Cù had gone and sat himself right beside the woman.

'Did you have a bad experience once?' she asked. 'That does tend to put you off, I find.'

Veronica shook her head. 'My grandparents had one like that spaniel,' she said.

'Like Poppy? She's a good girl.'

Veronica dragged her gaze away from where Poppy had padded away and looked finally at the woman talking to her.

'You're the vicar,' she said.

Winsome wrinkled her nose. 'Was, I'm afraid. Now I'm just plain old Winsome.' She looked more closely at the woman, ignoring Cù sitting almost on the poor thing's lap. 'I don't think I've seen you here before.'

'This is a very odd place,' Veronica said, tucking her hands under her arms.

The poor woman looked like she'd seen a ghost. Winsome was more than familiar with the look, having seen it in the mirror a lot when she'd first moved to Wellsford. Until she stopped looking in the mirror, of course, for fear of who else she might see in the reflection.

'May I sit down?' she asked. It didn't look like Cù had any intention of going back to the vicarage with her anyway.

'I was just watching your video,' Veronica said.

'Oh!' Winsome's brows shot up. 'You were?' She coloured slightly, still unused to the thought that she'd made it in the first place – and was planning more. 'Did it help at all?'

'I didn't do it,' Veronica said. 'I didn't follow along.' She blinked. 'I was just looking.'

'Ah, well, I've heard that it's helped quite a few folks relax in these stressful times.' She took the continuing conversation as an invitation to sit and pulled out a chair. 'Do you live in Banwell?' she asked. There wasn't supposed to be much travelling going on, and Winsome was fairly sure she knew almost everyone in Wellsford, at least by sight, more often by name.

Lucy came out and stopped at the table. 'Mrs. Faith,' she said. 'How pleasant to see you again – still staying with Erin, then?'

Mrs. Faith, Winsome thought, with understanding dawning. 'You're Erin's mother,' she said, face creasing into a wide smile. 'How lovely.'

It also explained why the woman was looking a bit spooked.

'Veronica,' Veronica said, eyes widening in horror at the realisation that for the first time in forty years, she'd almost called herself *Vera*.

Really, she thought. She needed to go home. This place was stirring up things best left alone.

'Are you all right?' Lucy asked.

'You look a bit peaky,' Winsome said.

Veronica shook her head. 'No,' she said. 'I mean, yes, I'm fine, thank you.'

Winsome glanced at Cù, who sat beside Veronica staring up at her. She was pretty sure she knew the spirit dog's habits now, and this meant it wasn't time to go home. This woman needed something.

'Can I have a cappuccino, please?' Veronica asked. 'And a piece of the cake I had last time if you've any?' She wasn't hungry, but it would give her a better excuse to sit here.

Right now, she thought her legs felt too weak to carry her back to the car.

What was going on with her?

First, she'd spilled long-held secrets to Erin, and now here she was, acting like a bit of a wreck. She grimaced a smile at the two women looking at her, then ducked her head.

'Today's cake is a nice, fresh, lemon cake, with whipped coconut cream and fresh fruit on the top.' Lucy smiled. 'Pure, summer perfection.'

Winsome's mouth watered. 'Gosh, that sounds good,' she said.

'It is good,' Lucy answered with a laugh. 'And with no butter, it's almost health food. I'll get you a piece too, shall I, Winsome?'

Winsome looked at Cù again, who was ignoring her completely, his gaze fixed on Erin's mother.

'That would be lovely, thanks Lucy,' she said. 'And a small pot of tea, please.' She turned to Veronica. 'Would that be all right?' she asked. 'If I sit with you and enjoy this fine June morning for a little while?'

Veronica nodded wordlessly, not knowing why she was agreeing to it, really. But the woman had kind eyes and looking at her made Veronica feel a little bit better. Steadier.

Lucy smiled. 'I'll get it all in a jiffy,' she said, then looked speculatively at Veronica for a moment. She wanted to reach out and put her hand on the woman's arm, but there was no excuse to do it. Still, she wondered what she would see, if she could. 'Right then,' she turning instead to go inside. 'Won't be long.'

There was a pause after Lucy left, and Winsome didn't

hurry to fill it, letting it stretch out a little while she looked at Veronica Faith. Erin's adoptive mother. The woman looked a little worn around the edges.

And she understood all about that.

She wanted to ask about it.

'Did you find the website easy to navigate?' she asked instead. 'I'm only just learning my way around it.' She waved a hand. 'I'm in the midst of setting up some computer classes – for when we can hold them, of course – so that those like myself, who could do with a bit extra tuition on all things digital, can get it.' She was rambling on, and she knew it, but she wanted to put Veronica at ease. 'I'm looking for funding for it too, which isn't so much fun, but it would be nice to have a couple computers set up for general use as well, especially as so many resources are only truly accessible online now. And not everyone has access to a computer.' She gave a little laugh. 'As hard as that is to believe in this day and age.'

Veronica nodded. She was only half-following the woman's chatter, letting Winsome's friendly voice waft over her instead.

'I can contribute something to that,' she said, surprising herself.

'What?' Winsome shook her head. 'I wasn't soliciting,' she said. 'Just chattering on. I tend to do that – just natter on a bit.'

'I can, though,' Veronica said, with no idea why. 'My husband has contacts. How many do you need?'

'Oh.' Winsome was taken aback. 'Erm, I was thinking two?' it was her turn to feel knocked off-kilter. 'Gosh, though – I really wasn't asking. It never occurred to me.'

'No,' Veronica said. 'I know. It's all right.' She tried a shaky smile. 'It would be nice, I thought.' She shrugged. 'Since Erin lives here and is determined to keep living here.' She trailed off.

'Well, it would certainly be welcome,' Winsome said. 'But you're under no obligation.'

Veronica dropped her gaze, nodding.

Lucy brought the food and drinks out, laid them out on the table, and lifted her eyebrows at Winsome. 'Everything all right?' she asked.

'Yes, thank you,' Winsome said. Then added, 'everything looks lovely.'

She looked back at Veronica when Lucy had gone inside. 'Is everything all right?' she asked. Then risked more. 'It must be very odd for you, to come here and see the things Erin is doing.' She gave a tiny shake of the head. 'This place took some getting used to when I came here last year, I can tell you.'

Veronica looked at her.

'It's not quite the usual little village, is Wellsford,' Winsome said, reaching for the small teapot and her cup.

Veronica was silent.

'And you'll know about Wilde Grove, of course, what with Erin being part of it.' Winsome added a good dollop of milk to her tea, looked at the sugar, then left it alone.

'What do you know about Wilde Grove?' Veronica croaked. 'Aren't you a vicar?'

'Was,' Winsome corrected, and blew gently on the hot tea. 'Parish shuffle-around means the church here is being closed, which does hurt, actually.' She smiled sadly.

'Why are you still here, then?'

Winsome shook her head. 'I can't imagine living anywhere else, now,' she said. 'I haven't been here long, but it's become home.'

'So what will you do now?' Veronica glanced around. 'I can't imagine there are many jobs here.'

'Not many jobs, perhaps, but plenty of work to be done. I'll keep ministering, in my own way.' Winsome sipped at her tea. Let the silence settle again.

'I met Morghan Wilde,' Veronica said, then clamped her mouth shut. She'd not meant to say anything.

'You did?' Winsome gave her a speculative glance, ignoring Cù still sitting close by Veronica. 'What did you think of her?'

Veronica looked down at her frothy cup of coffee. She hadn't touched it. Or the pretty slice of cake.

'I don't know,' she said at last. 'What sort of woman is she? Do you know her?'

'I do,' Winsome said. 'And she can be quite the experience upon first meeting.'

Veronica couldn't help it, she snorted a laugh and picked up her cup, finally. 'Yes,' she said. 'That is true.'

'Morghan Wilde is, however, a woman of great integrity, and many skills,' Winsome said and wanted to reach across the table and pat Veronica's hand reassuringly. She kept her hands to herself, however. 'You can trust her.'

Veronica put her cup down again. 'I can trust her?' she said, her voice little more than a croak.

Winsome nodded. 'Did something happen?' she asked gently, then gave a crooked smile.

'It often does when one first meets Morghan.'

43

Veronica pushed her coffee away and looked at her cake in dismay. 'I'm sorry,' she said. 'I can't sit here and eat and drink and talk about this like it's all normal.'

'I completely understand,' Winsome said. 'Let's walk while we chat, shall we?' She stood up, noticing that Cù was standing now also, as though he thought this was a good plan. 'I'll get our cake put in boxes for later.' She walked swiftly to the door of the cafe and waved for Lucy's attention.

Lucy came scooting over. 'What's happening?' she asked.

'We're just going to go for a walk,' Winsome said. 'You know how it is – much easier to talk about difficult things sometimes if you're moving.' She smiled. 'But the cake – can't go to waste.'

'I'll get you something to put it in,' Lucy said, and disappeared with a flick of her ponytail. She was back in a moment with two small cardboard cake boxes. 'Here you go.' She glanced at Veronica who stood by the table in something of a daze. 'Is there anything I can do to help?'

'Not at this stage,' Winsome said. 'But thank you.'

'There we go,' Winsome said a few minutes later. 'Saved for when we're hungry.' She stepped out onto the village green and smiled at Veronica.

'You must be very proud of Erin. You've seen the cards and prints Haven is selling made from her artwork? She's very talented, and hard-working. Sometimes hard-working is more important than talent, I've always suspected.'

'Yes,' Veronica said, lifting her face to the hazy warmth of the sun. 'They're quite beautiful.' She grimaced. 'I'm afraid I never encouraged her enough with her art.'

'Why do you say that?'

Veronica shook her head. 'I thought she ought to look to more important things.' She hugged the cake box to her breast. 'Now I wonder.'

'About the more important things?' Winsome asked, keeping her voice warm and sympathetic, and her body relaxed and open. She'd found right from the beginning of listening and ministering to people that it wasn't just her voice that she needed to watch, or her expression, but her whole body. Now, of course, after meeting Morghan, she understood it. The way she held her body affected her energy, and her aura, and the way other people picked up on it.

Living, she'd discovered, was a whole-body experience. Mind, body, spirit, just like they said. But even more so, because it seemed to her that her body was part of her mind, because to experience spirit, she'd learnt, you had to use the whole of your body. It was endlessly fascinating, and not a little baffling.

Veronica nodded. 'I was invested, you see, in her being the sort of person I thought it was important to be.'

'Oh?'

They came to the edge of the green and Veronica looked around. 'An influencer, you know? Successful, beautiful, someone to be admired.'

'Well, that doesn't sound too bad,' Winsome said.

Veronica shook her head. 'Erin wasn't keen on it; I see that now. She tried telling me. Said she didn't want to be a poster girl for empty consumerism.'

Winsome laughed, shook her head. 'I'm sorry,' she said. 'But kids don't tend to pull their punches, do they?'

'No,' Veronica said, and managed a small smile. 'Certainly not Erin. Especially now. Being here has given her a new...conviction.'

'She's found a place where she feels she belongs,' Winsome said. 'That's very compelling for anyone.' She looked around, drew Veronica down the street, past the small row of shops, so they could keep walking.

'I thought she would need the same things as I did,' Veronica said. 'But the very things that made me feel safe – she won't have any of it.'

'What were those things?' Winsome asked.

Veronica lifted her shoulders in a shrug, but she answered anyway. Part of her couldn't fathom the fact that here she was, strolling along the main street of this tiny place, unburdening herself to the local vicar. Ex-vicar. It wasn't like her.

But that hour she'd spent in Morghan Wilde's drawing room had...upset things.

'Money,' Veronica said. 'I was very poor as a child. There was...there was a lot of suffering.' She blew out a breath. 'Money makes me feel secure. I wanted Erin to feel secure as well.'

Winsome looked at Veronica, her face softening into a smile. 'Erin didn't have the childhood you did,' she said. 'She had one in which she was loved and cared for. Money wouldn't have the same meaning for her. She was raised in love, not suffering. That makes all the difference for a child.'

Veronica looked at her feet as they walked. 'My grandparents loved me,' she said. 'But they died, and I was lost without them.' She lifted her face and stared at the trees that surrounded the village. 'It was the greatest loss of my life. I lost part of myself when they died.' She pressed a hand to her chest and laughed a little, self-consciously. 'Listen to me – telling you all this when we've only just met. You must think I'm a basket case.'

'I don't think anything of the sort,' Winsome said. 'And you can say whatever you need to. We're all in this together.'

Veronica frowned. 'We're all in what together?'

Winsome shook her head slightly and smiled. 'Life,' she said. 'That's what we're all in together.'

'Becca, Erin's birth mother, she told me this place was a black magic cult.'

Winsome looked at Veronica, astonished. 'She did?'

'She wanted some money from us,' Veronica said. 'That's what it was, why she said that. She knew we were well-off. Gave us a big sob story so it could all be justified.'

'Ah, I see,' Winsome said.

'Is it a black magic cult?' Veronica blinked. 'Only, you know – most stories have a kernel of truth in them.'

'It is not,' Winsome said. 'And I ought to be qualified to say, as a recent woman of the cloth.'

'But what is it then?'

Veronica's question was a wailed plea. She stopped walking, abashed at her outburst. 'I'm sorry,' she said, realising she'd crushed the cake box's corners. 'I shouldn't be going on like this, taking advantage of your good nature.'

'It's perfectly all right,' Winsome said. 'You're not even at the stage of crying on my shoulder, yet.'

Veronica stared at her, blinking, then burst out laughing. 'I'm having a very crazy week,' she said.

'That's quite all right,' Winsome answered. 'I've been having a very crazy year. I've seen and experienced things I had no idea of the existence of, and frankly, it's had my head spinning at times.' She shook the head in question. 'I think coming here, to Wellsford, has that effect on some people.'

They walked again, Veronica's chin almost on her chest as she thought about what Winsome had said.

'Morghan,' she said, then closed her mouth, frowned.

'What about her?' Winsome asked.

Veronica shook her head, but she answered anyway. 'When I met her,' she said. 'Something...odd happened.'

'Yes,' Winsome said. 'I'm familiar with that occurrence. What was it? If you want to tell me?'

'I do,' Veronica said. 'I don't know why, but I do.'

'I don't think things are supposed to be carried on your own,' Winsome told her. 'So, I understand.' She smiled again. 'And I'm a good listener.'

Veronica glanced around, moistening her lips. 'Can we

walk in there?' she asked, pointing to the church grounds. 'It's just, more private.'

'And pleasantly shady,' Winsome added, trying not to stare at the shade of a couple, and older woman and gent, standing by the church. She blinked discreetly, but the spirits didn't go away.

'You said the church was being closed down?'

'Deconsecrated, yes,' Winsome said, unable to stop the sadness turning her lips down. Still, it was mostly sadness now, instead of mostly regret. 'Next month, actually.' She turned her head so that she couldn't see the middle-aged ghosts.

'It's a pretty building,' Veronica said. 'A bit grim having all the gravestones around it, though. What's going to happen to it?'

'It will be sold, I believe. I don't know under what conditions, however.'

'Huh. Well, it's pretty,' Veronica said. She swallowed, bracing herself to return to what was really on her mind. 'About Morghan?'

Winsome nodded, reaching out to touch the ancient yew growing in the churchyard. Its branches shaded almost the whole lawn.

'When I saw her,' Veronica said. 'Something...happened.' There was a bench under the tree, and she set the cake box down on it. 'We were talking – arguing really, about Erin, and then something happened.' She closed her eyes, remembering.

My darling Vera. We didn't want to leave you.

'She...' Veronica said, then shook her head. 'I don't know how to say this.'

'Fast, probably,' Winsome said. 'Just get it out. You'll feel better.'

Veronica shook her head again but forced the words out. Perhaps she would feel better. 'She talked to me in my grandmother's voice.'

Winsome's eyebrows rose. 'Really?' she asked. 'Gosh, that would have been a bit of a surprise.'

Now she was sure she knew who the spirits standing watching them were.

'A surprise doesn't cover it,' Veronica answered. 'It was so strange. This odd look came over her face. Morghan's, that is, and she said she had someone who wanted to speak to me.' Veronica sat abruptly down. 'I didn't know what she was going on about. There was no one in the room but us.' She licked her lips. 'And then she started talking to me, but it wasn't her.'

Veronica looked up at Winsome. 'It was my grandmother. She called me by a name I haven't used since I was sixteen. How is that possible?'

'All manner of things are possible, I'm afraid,' Winsome said, sitting down next to her.

'Dead people don't speak through the living,' Veronica insisted.

'Don't they?'

'I've never believed in mediums and psychics and so on. Not really. All frauds.' Veronica curled her fingers together. 'Or so I thought.' She glanced at Winsome. 'It wasn't real, was it?'

Veronica sighed. 'It was real. How would she know about my grandmother? Erin couldn't have told her. Erin doesn't even know about my grandparents, or anything about my youth.'

'She doesn't?'

'Well,' Veronica said. 'She does now because I was so befuddled and upset by everything that I told her. But she didn't when this Morghan woman talked to me.' She glanced at Winsome. 'Do you think it was real?'

'Yes,' Winsome said, without hesitation.

The spirits nodded as well, but they didn't come any closer.

Veronica sighed, rested her head in her hands, rubbing her temples. 'I feel like I'm in the middle of an earthquake,' she said. 'Like the world has literally shifted and I can't keep on being the same person I used to be. As though that person has been stripped away from me.' She straightened. 'Except where does that leave me?'

'I don't know,' Winsome said. 'Where would you like to be?'

'Back where I was before!' Veronica rubbed her eyes. 'Sorry,' she said. 'I know none of this is anything to you. I don't even know you.'

'It's all right,' Winsome told her. 'I'm here. I'm listening.' She glanced over at the spirit of Veronica's grandparents. They looked like they'd been kind people in life.

Veronica nodded. Gazed out over the graveyard, seeing nothing but the lawn and gravestones. 'I was going to go back and see her,' she said. 'Morghan. Ask her what happened, what I was supposed to do now. I was going to demand that she told me.'

'But?' Winsome asked, sensing there was one there.

'But I was too scared,' Veronica said. 'In case it

happened again, or something else, or I would just discover that the earth really had cracked open, and it was all real, all of this. Everything Erin is doing, which I don't even understand, all this Wilde Grove stuff.' She sighed. 'I don't want to have to think about any of this. I just want to go shopping. Get my hair done. Read glossy magazines. Be empty-headed and pampered.'

She shook her head. 'I didn't ask for this,' she said. 'I certainly didn't want this.'

Winsome looked over at Veronica with sympathy. 'I don't think this is the time for empty-headedness.' She smiled sadly. 'Our world needs more from us than that.'

The ghosts took a step closer. Cù left Winsome's side and went and sat beside the couple, and the man reached down and patted him.

'You mean all this climate change agenda stuff?' Veronica asked, clasping her hands between her knees.

'Up to one hundred and fifty species are going extinct every day,' Winsome said. 'And sea level rise is something we're beginning to face now.'

'I'm not,' Veronica said. 'My life continues on the way I wanted it to.' She paused. 'Or at least, it did until this pandemic thing.'

'Even if you could continue your life the way it's been the last thirty years, or whatever,' Winsome said, 'Erin won't be able to. Her children won't be able to.'

They sat silently for a long minute. Winsome watched a blackbird and his brown-feathered lady dig around in the grass for their morning tea. They were right next to Cù and Veronica's grandfather.

Veronica stared at the gravestones, most of them sitting

in damp beds of moss. This would be her one day, she thought morbidly. Staring sightlessly at the wormy ground.

'What does the world ask of me?' she said. 'What can I do that makes any difference?'

'I know,' Winsome said. 'I asked myself the exact same question – I think we all do.'

'I never have before,' Veronica sighed, looking at the grass between her feet now. She shook her head. 'I can't believe I'm sitting in a graveyard in a tiny village in the middle of nowhere, talking to a complete stranger like this.'

Winsome laughed. 'I've had that exact same thought too, a time or two since I came here.'

'I tried to give Erin her allowance back,' Veronica said abruptly. 'She wouldn't take it.'

'That's a shame,' Winsome said. 'She could do a lot of good with it, I'm sure.'

Veronica turned and stared at Winsome. 'She could, couldn't she?'

'Yes. And that could be something you could do, by extension perhaps, but nonetheless.'

'And I'm serious about those computers you need,' Veronica said, deciding suddenly that she was. 'That's another thing I could do.'

Winsome nodded.

'My Gran,' Veronica said, then ground to a halt, took a breath and started again. 'My Gran, when she was talking to me through that woman, asked what had become of me.'

She stood up, restless suddenly. Looked over at the small church sitting stolidly in its nest of gravestones, then around at the trees. So many trees.

'What do you think she meant?' Veronica asked, still

looking at the trees that rimmed the village in a green and brown belt.

She turned and looked at Winsome. Sat down again. 'What do you think she meant?'

Winsome looked at Erin's mother, at the tight lines around her eyes, the arched brows drawn together in distress. 'I hate to turn it around on you like this,' she said, keeping her gaze averted from the spirits standing with her dog on the church lawn. 'But what do you think it meant?'

Veronica shook her head. 'She doesn't like the way I turned out?'

'Why would you think she doesn't?' Winsome asked the question carefully, gently.

'I don't know – I have it all. Money, security.'

'Does money and security feel like everything to you?'

Veronica grimaced. 'It is when you don't have it,' she said.

'That's true enough,' Winsome conceded. 'But you have it, so now what?'

Veronica's shoulders slumped. 'I don't know,' she whispered. 'I'm living out of a suitcase in my daughter's spare room, my husband keeps having affairs, I can't go anywhere and do anything with this damned virus all over the place, and I...' She trailed off. Shrugged.

'Hearing my grandmother ask what has become of me has me questioning everything.'

She stood up again, rubbing her knuckles against her thighs. 'Thank you,' she said, shaking her head. 'For listening to my ravings.' Veronica made her mouth smile. She could feel tears threatening and no way was she going to turn into a blubbering mess in front of this woman. In front of anyone.

'I think I need to get going,' she said, and picked up her handbag. 'Thank you again.'

Winsome watched her stride off down the path, then stood up. 'Wait,' she called. 'You forgot your cake.'

Veronica glanced back over her shoulder, shook her head. Kept going.

Trying to see the path through a hot sheen of tears.

Winsome turned to look for the spirits, but they were gone.

Only Cù sat grinning at her.

44

Winsome picked up the two small cake boxes and walked across the churchyard to the vicarage. She supposed she ought to stop thinking of it as the vicarage, but it was going to be a hard habit to break.

She set the boxes on the table inside with a sigh then looked up at a shadow that crossed her doorway.

'Hello Morghan,' she said.

Morghan had a wide smile on her face. 'Hello Winsome,' she said. 'What's in the boxes?'

Winsome laughed. 'I swear you can sniff out whenever there are biscuits or cake around.'

'It's a talent, for sure,' Morghan answered with a grin. 'Two of them? You are expecting a visitor?'

Winsome shook her head. 'No, one of these belonged to Erin's mother. I was just talking to her.'

'I see,' Morghan said. She leant against the doorway. 'I met her just the other day.'

'I know.' Winsome gave Morghan a pointed look. 'Which was, believe me, quite a topic of conversation.'

'Ah.'

'Mmhmm.'

'She came to see me in an absolute state – wanting to take Erin away, accusing us of black magic of all things.'

Winsome put her hands on the back of a chair and gazed at her friend. 'Is that why you did what you did to her?'

Morghan narrowed her eyes, although her mouth held its smile. 'What did I do to her?'

'Tore her composure completely apart.' Winsome shook her head. 'The poor woman is a complete wreck.' She paused. 'Tell me you didn't do that deliberately.'

Morghan shifted slightly on her feet. 'I confess that Veronica Faith did bring out a little of the...less patient part of me.'

'She was just being a mother bear!' Winsome said.

'I did not channel her grandmother on purpose,' Morghan finished. She pursed her lips. 'But in saying that, I did not refuse her grandmother the opportunity to speak, either.'

Winsome stared at her silently for a moment, then shook her head again. 'It is a fine line you walk sometimes, Morghan,' she said. 'And I say that as someone who loves you.'

Morghan thought of Catrin, of their meeting in the forest. Of Catrin laughing and telling her she had inherited a lot of herself.

'It's true,' she said.

426

Winsome nodded. 'It is true. That woman's life has been broken wide open, because of you.'

Morghan shook her head. 'Because of me, or because of what her grandmother had to say to her?'

'You let her grandmother speak.'

Morghan shifted again, frowning.

'Come in, for goodness' sakes,' Winsome told her.

Shaking her head, Morghan sighed. 'This visit is just a detour, I'm afraid. I'm meeting Erin shortly. It's time to teach her healing. She has been making great strides in her travelling to the Otherworld.'

Winsome raised an eyebrow. 'Healing?'

'I will take her to the clearing in the Wildwood, and teach her there,' Morghan said. She thought for a moment. 'Would you like to come too?'

Winsome was taken aback. 'Erm, I don't know.' She put on a frown. 'I'm still mad about the way you dealt with Erin's mother.'

'Really mad, or pretending to be mad?' Morghan asked.

Surprised by the question, Winsome barked a laugh. 'You didn't lead her gently to the well, Morghan. You dunked her right in.'

Morghan inclined her head. 'Yes. But it is not often that I get a spirit so strongly wishing to speak through me. It is not something I tend to do at all, really.'

'And Veronica's grandmother was right there?'

'Right there and very insistent. In such circumstances, letting her speak seemed the right path.' Morghan shrugged. 'Obviously, I had no idea what she was going to say.'

'Were you aware what she was saying while she was

talking?' Winsome shuddered lightly. It was bad enough seeing spirits – she wasn't entirely sure she fancied the idea that they could pop in and use one's vocal cords.

'I was, but distantly so.'

Winsome sighed. 'Well, considering I saw the woman in question, and the grandfather, in spirit form, while I was talking to Veronica, I suppose I can't be too mad.'

'Aha!' Morghan said. 'You saw them – I should have thought you might.' She gave it a moment's consideration. 'Nope,' she said. 'Doesn't surprise me at all. There's a lot of healing that needs to be done in that family.'

'Is that why you're taking Erin to learn it now?'

'Part of it, certainly,' Morghan answered. 'But this is the next stage for her anyway. The fact it might come in useful at home right about now is just the way the wheel turns.' She smiled. 'So, are you coming?'

Winsome gazed down at the table, sifting through all she had to do. She wanted to keep messing around with her website, which was becoming quite the joy as Krista taught her more, and she wanted to deliberate over how, exactly to use the rooms in the vicarage for her new plans.

'Yes,' she said. 'I'm not doing anything that can't be put off for this.'

Morghan beamed at her. 'Excellent,' she said. Her gaze fell regretfully on the cake.

'Do you want me to bring it with us?' Winsome asked, seeing exactly where Morghan was looking.

'No,' Morghan said. 'We can ground ourselves back at Hawthorn House. Mrs. Palmer tries out all of Simon's recipes anyway – do you know Simon's putting together a recipe book?'

. . .

ERIN SIDLED INTO THE CARE HOME'S LOUNGE ROOM, ALREADY changed out of her uniform, and touched Wayne's shoulder. 'Good movie?' she asked. 'What is it?'

He wrinkled his nose. 'No idea,' he said. 'I slept through the first hour or so. But it looks like the guy is going to get his girl.' He frowned and shifted uncomfortably in his chair. His abdomen throbbed with pain. 'I think.'

Mrs. Sharp piped up. 'It's a time travel thing - and you, my friend, snore.' She turned a brilliant smile on Erin. 'Are you done for the day, love?'

'I am, yes,' Erin said. 'And I come on for the afternoon tomorrow, so I'll see you then.' She patted Wayne's shoulder and made her way out into the sunlight, turning up the street to nip through the churchyard and into the Grove. She'd been supposed to spend the afternoon with Stephan, but Morghan had called and changed her plans, so Stephan had simply swung by and taken Burdock.

It was dim and fragrant under the trees, and Erin hoisted the strap of her bag higher on her shoulder and wondered what was in store. It was good timing, really, because hadn't she just that morning decided she needed to talk to Morghan about the City of Shadows?

'Hello,' she called, coming up to the stone circle where she was supposed to meet Morghan. 'Oh, hello Winsome,' she said. 'Hi Clarice.'

'Winsome has decided to join us,' Morghan said. 'And Clarice will be drumming for us.'

Erin raised her eyebrows. 'Okay,' she said. 'What are we going to be doing?' She smiled at Winsome and Clarice.

'We're going to the cave, I think,' Morghan said. 'And from there, to the Wildwood. I've a place I wish to show you there, Erin. I believe it is time.'

'That sounds...daunting,' Erin said with a laugh, and fell into step behind Morghan. 'I've been wanting to ask you about a place I've discovered,' she said. 'In the Otherworld.'

Morghan glanced back at her, bright enquiry on her face.

'I went there this morning – remember how I told you Macha had taken me to this weird maze?'

'I do,' Morghan said.

Erin glanced at Winsome and Clarice, then looked back at Morghan. It was obvious that Winsome was following the conversation just fine, which meant, Erin thought, that Winsome knew more about the Otherworld than the average vicar. Obviously, she did, since Erin doubted she would have been able to seek Morghan and Blythe there so easily without Winsome's help and steady calmness.

And Clarice had been wandering the highways and byways of the Otherworld since who knew what age.

'Anyway,' Erin continued. 'There's this place at the other end of the maze, and it has this big gate, and on the other side of it, is a really freaky city.' She frowned, shook her head. 'I call it the City of Shadows. The name just kind of came to me and it fits.'

Ahead of her, Morghan nodded. 'This is why we're doing this today,' she said.

'You know about the place?' Erin asked, surprised.

'I do,' Morghan said. 'And we will talk more of it soon.'

Erin and Winsome both took deep breaths before they

ducked down into the cave the Grove used for journeying and keeping vigil. Erin added a whispered prayer.

'Mother, welcome me into your womb and hold me safe.'

'I'm never going to get used to this,' she muttered once they were inside.

'Still don't like the cave?' Morghan asked, moving around behind the firepit, and sitting down.

Erin glanced around. 'I'm not as nervous as I was the first time,' she said and looked over at Winsome. 'I was sure the hill would come down on top of me,' she explained.

'Yes,' Winsome agreed. 'I felt rather the same way.'

'Well, you'd best both get used to it,' Morghan said. 'The Otherworld is full of caves and tunnels. From what I've learnt over the years, it seems the quickest way to get from one region to another.' She looked over at Clarice. 'Isn't that so?'

Clarice nodded, and she opened the bag she'd been carrying on her back and removed her drum.

Morghan reached into her Druid's bag for a box of matches and lit one, holding it to the tinder in the pit. The flames caught and she smiled at the red tongues. 'Erin,' she said. 'Any progress making fire as Kria did?'

Erin was startled by the question. 'Um, no.' She looked at the flames. 'But then, I haven't spent much time trying, either.'

'I'm intrigued by the possibility of bringing that talent back,' Morghan admitted. 'I know from my own past experience, that such things and others are possible.'

'Wait,' Winsome interrupted. 'Your past experience?'

'Very past,' Morghan said lightly. 'Lifetime's past.'

'Oh,' Winsome said, settling herself on the other side of the fire next to Clarice. 'That makes more sense.' She blinked at the fire as Morghan threw a handful of herbs upon it. 'I wonder what I was in past lives?'

'Perhaps you will one day explore some of them,' Morghan said.

There was an overwhelming idea, Winsome thought. But, gazing around the ancient cave, and at the way the fire-light flickered upon her companions, it was very hard to disbelieve in the possibility of past lives, of reincarnation, of souls that did not perish but returned to life over and over.

She nodded.

Morghan smiled over the fire at her, then looked at Erin. 'There is a knack to travelling together,' she said. 'It is like entering the same dream, but it can be done, can it not, Winsome?'

Winsome nodded. 'It can,' she said. 'You've taken me with you several times now.' She glanced over at Erin. 'And of course, you and I have done it together as well.'

'Yes,' Morghan agreed, taking a breath. 'That is true. But now it is time that we learn this well, for as you go forward, being able to do these things will be essential.'

Erin licked her lips. 'Like Stephan is learning healing from Bear Fellow?' That was in the Otherworld.

Morghan tipped her head to the side. 'There are similarities, certainly,' she said. 'Stephan is being taught important things – but mostly to do with healing the body.' She blinked. 'Your task is to learn to heal the soul.'

'That's possible?' Erin asked, practically squeaking.

'It is,' Morghan said. 'And more than that, it is essential. You've already done some of this work, with Kria, singing her over, returning that aspect of yourself home.' She glanced at Winsome. 'Both of you saw me doing the same thing for Blythe only several weeks ago.'

Erin blanched. 'It won't be like that, though, will it?'

Morghan didn't hide her smile. 'Seldom, I hope,' she said.

Seldom. That was probably as good as it would get, Erin decided. She nodded, a lump in her throat. 'Is this healing I have to learn going to be for myself?' she asked.

'We always begin with ourselves,' Morghan said turning her head to smile at Clarice. 'But ultimately, it is for your community.'

'Really?' Erin asked, flabbergasted. 'We do this for other people?'

'When it is necessary. Do you remember when Minnie was having trouble?'

Erin nodded. 'Yes,' she said. 'Of course.'

'Winsome and I helped her then. That is, in part, the same sort of thing I will be teaching you now.' Morghan fed another piece of wood to the fire.

Erin glanced over at Winsome, wondering how Winsome had come to do so much – more than Erin had realised.

Winsome gave a grimacing smile. 'Morghan has been dragging me along on these escapades practically since the day we met.'

'You have a calling for death work, I believe, Winsome,' Morghan said.

'What about me?' Erin asked hesitantly. 'Will I be learning that too?'

'You will learn it all,' Morghan said.

For some reason, the answer shocked Erin. 'All of it?' She stared around the circle, then back at Morghan. 'All of it?' she repeated.

'Of course,' Morghan replied.

'Now, shall we begin?'

45

'How do we do this?' Erin asked, nervousness puffing up inside her and making her pulse quicken under the delicate skin of her wrist.

Morghan took Winsome's hand and reached out for Erin's. She smiled gently, already breathing slowly, deeply. 'Like this,' she said. 'The same way I have taught you to travel, except this time, when you feel yourself leaving, you are to keep holding onto me.'

Clarice knew her cue and began drumming, softly, the beat quick, insistent. Ambrose had taught her this, when she was young, and she closed her eyes now, letting the sound of the drum sing its rhythm to her.

'It's just like we did it before, Erin,' Winsome said, amazed that she felt so calm, that she was here doing this as though this was her new normal, and perfectly all right. 'When we went to find Morghan. When she was with Blythe.' The drumming quickened the pulse of her blood.

Erin nodded and slowed her breath. The atmosphere in

the cave was thicker somehow, perhaps because of the herbs Morghan had scattered upon the flames. Or perhaps because she was feeling herself shift, the cave becoming a liminal place she could step into, the sound of Clarice's drum calling to her. She held Winsome's hand, and Morghan's hand, and let herself go, travelling on her breath, on the beat of the drum, taking just a small step to the side.

The cave widened around her, grew shadows, and she looked over at Morghan, saw her sitting there, her spirit wide awake and looking back at Erin with eyes that were deep with knowledge. A wolf stood at Morghan's side, gazing at Erin as though they saw right through her.

She turned her head through the smoky air and looked at Winsome, a smile curling her lips. Winsome's spirit dog sat next to her, so similar to Burdock.

Where was Fox?

She had the thought and then Fox was there, her dainty paws glowing white in the cave's dimness.

Morghan's fingers tightened for a moment on Erin's, and when Erin blinked, she opened her eyes to find herself standing in a different world, the drumming now a singing in her ears. The forest Morghan called the Wildwood. It towered green and ancient around her, the trees breathing, sighing. Erin listened to them, and the sighing became the hum of a song they'd been singing since before she was born. She reached out and touched the rough trunk of the nearest tree and felt a surge of energy up her arm as the tree greeted her in return. Erin closed her eyes. She loved this place, she decided. Being able to step through the thinning veil between the worlds was an incredible gift.

One, she vowed, she would learn to use well.

A long, large snake slithered out from the undergrowth and looked at the group of them, before turning its strong, sinuous body along the path.

'We will follow,' Morghan said. 'The clearing is not far.'

'The clearing?' Erin asked.

Morghan nodded. 'It is the place I come when there is need of healing.'

Erin nodded, but there was more she wanted to know. And hadn't she come here to learn?

'How did you find this place?' she asked.

Morghan, walking along with one hand on her black wolf, thought about it for a moment. 'It revealed itself to me,' she said. 'This world is like that. It brings what you need to you. That is why learning to follow your intuition is so important.' She glanced back at Erin and Winsome. 'There is already a part of us, I think, that knows this world well, and we need to find that part of ourselves and wake it up.'

Erin nodded and didn't ask any more questions. She concentrated on her breathing instead, settling into herself with every outward breath, looking for the part of herself who knew her way around.

She wasn't sure that she found it, but she was calm, and that seemed a good beginning.

The path widened at last into a clearing about twenty steps across and Morghan stopped in the middle of it and turned to face the other two.

'Here we are,' she said.

It was just a clearing, Erin thought. The trees stood in a circle around the edges, their branches outstretched to form a latticework ceiling. And yet, what had she expected?

Perhaps it did not pay to carry expectations when she travelled to the Wildwood.

She glanced down and started back in horror, holding her arms out, looking down at her chest, her stomach.

'What's this?' she said, her mouth dry, throat suddenly raw. She lifted her gaze and saw that Winsome too, was covered in black crustaceans, knobbly barnacles across her shoulders and over her back. Erin leant forward, sure she was going to throw up. The sight of these things over her hurt. 'What are they?' she wailed.

Winsome looked at Morghan in horror. 'Why are these on me?' she squeaked.

'You've seen them before,' Morghan told her calmly.

Winsome nodded. 'On Minnie and Eileen,' she said and looked over at Erin. They were crowded over Erin as well, on the left side of her chest almost like a plate of armour. A black, crusty one.

'These are the accumulations of our hurts,' Morghan said. 'Hurts borne and given.'

'Get them off me,' Erin wheezed. 'Please.' She shook her head. 'Please get them off me.'

Fox gazed up at her with bright eyes as if she were finding this all very interesting.

Morghan stepped over to her and put a hand over Erin's eyes. Her hand was cool, the touch brief, but when she took it away, Erin saw that the crusty barnacles were gone.

'What happened to them?' she asked, her breath coming in short pants.

'They are still there,' Winsome said. 'I can see them on you.'

Erin's eyes widened and she looked from Winsome to

438

Morghan, then back down at herself. She shook her head. 'This is horrible,' she said. 'What are they called?'

'Intrusions, usually,' Morghan said. 'For obvious reasons.' She beckoned Winsome over. 'We are going to clear them away from Winsome.'

Erin cringed. 'We have to touch them?' she whispered. 'It hurts to look at them.'

'I know,' Morghan soothed. It pained her to see them as well. Something about the shape of them, maybe. Their unnaturalness upon the body, perhaps. 'But this is what must be done.' She knew that once they began their task of removing these intrusions, their bodies back in the cave would twitch and shudder.

It wasn't to be helped. It was part of the job.

'Why don't you have any?' Erin said, creeping closer to Winsome but looking at Morghan.

'Because I come here regularly to remove them. As you will also, from now on.'

Erin knew that was right. There was no way she wanted to walk around knowing these things were all over herself.

'And they lessen once you walk the path,' Morghan added.

Erin was glad to hear that. She made herself look at Winsome. 'What's happened to Winsome?' she asked, alarmed.

Winsome stood in the same place, but her eyes were closed.

'She is sleeping,' Morghan said, opening her arms to her friend and lying her down on the soft ground of the clearing. 'The souls you help here are usually asleep while you work on them.'

439

This, Erin thought, was sounding complicated. She swallowed, her throat still dry, and went to kneel beside Morghan.

She took a deep breath. 'Show me what to do,' she said.

And that was right. That was the right thing to say, and it was the right thing to do, and now Morghan didn't need to show her, because she knew already.

'I remember,' she said dimly, her hands reaching to loosen one of the barnacles from Winsome's shoulder. 'Have I done this before?'

'Not as Erin,' Morghan answered. 'But yourself as others.'

Erin worked it loose and pulled it as gently as she could from Winsome's skin. She hated touching it, and her insides churned as though she still might be sick, but she got it free, dismayed to see that it had roots that had sunk deep inside Winsome.

'As Macha?' she said.

'Yes, for certain,' Morghan answered. 'And likely as others.'

It was free. Erin wondered what to do with it, then followed an impulse and threw it down on the ground.

Morghan smiled, waved a hand at it, and the black mass transformed into a flower.

Erin nodded. That was right, she thought, and went back to remove the next one.

She didn't know how long it took. The trees linked their branches overhead and stood softly singing. The breeze tickled their leaves, swooped down to lift Erin's hair from her face.

· · ·

Winsome, sleeping, dreamt she was awake.

'This place,' she muttered, her hand resting on Cù as she looked around herself at the inside of her dream. 'This place.' She raised her face and saw movement shadow a far doorway. Drawing herself upright, she stepped through the rubble and into the doorway.

For a moment, the sight of herself, bent over, searching through the bricks and broken chairs, pushing aside the piles of scattered and torn papers, peering underneath overturned desks, tables, stopped the air in her lungs.

But she remembered what Morghan had said about trusting herself, and she knew a breath later where she was and why she was here.

It was the same as it had been when they'd gone looking for Minnie.

Minnie sitting at her family table waiting for her father to come home.

And hadn't she asked Morghan whether part of herself would get stuck in this dream of the vicarage in rubble around her?

She had. Part of her had broken off and was still searching through the broken rubbish of her life.

But she was there, and she was calm with understanding. She was there and Cù was with her.

The part of herself that had gotten herself stuck there looked up, saw Winsome, and stared in shock.

'Hello,' Winsome said. 'I've come to take you home.'

Her soul shard blinked, looked at her, shook her head. 'This is my home,' she said. 'It's all broken.' She glanced down at the pile of rubbish by her feet. 'I keep looking, but I can't find the way to make this okay for the children.'

'The children are both safe,' Winsome said. 'And you're safe too. The house fell, but I rebuilt it. You don't have to stay here. I've come to take you home.'

Cù stared at the shard of Winsome's soul.

Her soul shard blinked again, then uttered a harsh laugh. 'Why would I trust you to tell me the truth – or to look after me?' She waved a hand at the place. 'Look what a mess you made of things!'

Winsome let herself nod. 'I made some mistakes. I did.'

'You ruined everything!' She bent again and resumed her frantic search, scraping the table across the floor to peer under it. 'I have to find a way to keep the children safe.'

This was interesting, Winsome thought. Who were the children? She remembered this dream, remembered combing the broken house up and down, a child on her hip, another at her feet. But she didn't know who they were.

'Whose children are they?' she asked.

The other part of herself stopped searching and looked at her in disbelief. 'Whose are they?' She straightened. 'They are mine, of course. My responsibility. *Suffer little children, and forbid them not to come unto me: for such is the kingdom of heaven.*'

'Ah,' Winsome said. 'Of course.' She took a few steps closer, compassion flooding through her. Really, she'd been terribly hurt by what had happened, losing her ministry, letting down her parishioners. It was little wonder that part of her was still stuck here, searching for a way to do what she'd always thought was her calling.

She picked her words carefully. 'I know you think there is no way to rebuild this terrible mess we made of things, but I'm here to tell you that I am rebuilding it. That nothing has truly been lost – that in fact, life is just as rich and deep and full of meaning and wonder as it always was.' She paused. 'Perhaps even more so.'

The other part of her shook her head. 'We let everyone down.'

'I thought so too,' Winsome said. 'But you know what happened?'

Her soul shard shook her head.

'A group of them – not everyone, no, I can't tell you that, but quite a few – reached out to me, dragged me out of the house, and asked that I continue.'

'I don't understand.'

'They asked that I continue with the website. They asked for more lessons and exercises like we'd put on the site. They said they wanted us to continue the charity shop with them, the Men's Shed, the coffee mornings, the prayer groups, the study groups, and they want to do more as well.' Winsome spread her hands. 'More of it all. More of everything. More teaching, helping, listening, growing.'

There were tears flowing down her lost self's cheeks. 'You're telling the truth?'

'I am,' Winsome said. 'And I'm going to do everything I can to never let them down again.' She took a breath. 'Love and care, kindness and compassion, growth and community – none of these things were ever owned by the Church. We can continue them, even when we are not a vicar, when we are not dispensing the blood and flesh of Christ.' She smiled. 'Because we are part of this place, my love. We belong here. This is where we need to be and there is still so much we can do.'

'I thought it was over,' her broken piece of herself said.

443

'So did I, for a while,' Winsome answered. 'But it's not. It's really only just beginning.'

She opened her arms. 'Come to me. I need you.'

The broken piece of Winsome's self looked around one last time, then stepped over to her, into her arms.

And back into wholeness.

46

'I'VE GOT THEM ALL,' ERIN SAID, WITH A SIGH OF RELIEF.

'Yes,' Morghan replied, and handed her a pot of salve. 'Rub this on the raw skin to help the healing.'

Erin took the pot. 'Where did you get this from?'

'This is the Otherworld,' Morghan said. 'It was in my bag.'

Nodding, Erin remembered her own travelling, how she had opened her small satchel to find the necessary things to make an offering. She smiled.

'Like magic,' she said.

'Like magic,' Morghan agreed.

Erin smoothed the salve into Winsome's skin, watching as the rawness and scars faded under her hand until she couldn't tell they'd ever been there.

And Winsome's eyes fluttered open. She looked around the clearing, at Morghan and Erin, saw Cù there, and sat up, smiling, shaking her head.

'I dreamt,' she said.

Morghan nodded.

'I dreamt I was in an old dream,' Winsome said. 'And I met myself, the part of myself lost there, in my dream.'

Erin sat back on her heels.

'And I told her, that poor lost part of myself, that it was okay now. She didn't have to stay there. She could come back to me because things were different.' Winsome blew out a breath and closed her eyes. 'I'd fixed them.'

Morghan nodded again. 'And did she come back to you?' she asked, her voice quiet, gentle.

'She did,' Winsome said, tears standing in her eyes. 'She came back. I can feel her inside me, still a little fearful.' She swallowed. 'I'm going to look after her. Show her things are all right.'

Morghan smiled, took Winsome's hand and held it. 'You did well,' she said. She turned to Erin. 'Winsome has retrieved a shard of her soul that split off from her during the difficult time she went through, after losing her position in the Church.'

Erin's eyes widened and she looked at Winsome. 'What was that like?' she asked. 'How did you do it?'

Winsome shook her head. 'I dreamt a dream and there I was, needing to come home.'

'Did you go to the City of Shadows?' Erin asked, unsure why she did, except that there was a dim connection in her mind.

Morghan looked at her. 'You have been far into its streets?'

Erin shook her head. 'Just a little way.' She shivered. 'It's a scary place.'

'I didn't go to any city,' Winsome said. 'I went to a dream I had back then. And there I was.'

'What is the City of Shadows, then?' Erin asked.

Morghan touched Erin's shoulder, rested her hand there. 'Soul shards and aspects become lost in many places and situations. Some gather together, if they have been wounded or refuted in similar ways, and it is one of these places you call the City of Shadows.'

'You've been there too?' Erin asked.

'I have, and when we go there, we go quietly, carefully.'

Erin nodded and shuddered. 'I don't like it there,' she said. 'Why would Macha want me to go there?'

'Wounded in what similar ways?' Winsome asked, on her knees now, listening.

Morghan shook her head. 'Wounded from the committing of violence, usually, or the suffering of it.'

That didn't sound good to Erin. But, remembering the place, she decided she wasn't surprised.

'I don't want to go back there, then, if that's what sort of place it is,' Erin said. 'Not alone.' She shook her head.

'We never go to these places alone,' Morghan said. 'Were you alone when you went there?'

'You weren't with me,' Erin said. She looked around the clearing. 'Fox was.'

Fox pulled back her furry lips into a grin.

'Raven was too,' Erin said.

'Not alone, then,' Morghan told her.

'No,' she agreed. 'Not alone.' She paused. 'But why have me go there?'

'It is part of your learning,' Morghan said. 'Your soul's

path is to walk the worlds, learn the ways of healing.' She paused. 'In a way, I think, it is the path of all of us.'

Winsome remembered something and looked down at herself. 'They're all gone,' she said. 'Those things – they're all gone.'

Erin nodded and stood up, giving Winsome space to stand as well.

Winsome did more than stand – she spun slowly round in a circle, took a few dancing steps, then laughed.

'This is amazing,' she cried, then came slowly to a stop and looked at Morghan. 'Now what?'

Morghan transferred her gaze to Erin and nodded. 'Now you must deal with your intrusions,' she said. 'You must clear them from yourself.'

'From myself?' Erin asked. She looked over at Winsome. 'Won't you help, like we did for Winsome?'

Morghan considered it for a moment, chin tucked down. 'Yes,' she said at last. 'We will help. She stepped over to Erin, placed one arm across Erin's back, and touched her hand to Erin's eyes. 'And you will sleep.'

Erin's eyes closed at once, and she sagged back in Morghan's arms.

Morghan lay her gently down, and Winsome stepped forward to help remove the intrusions that pockmarked Erin's skin.

ERIN LOOKED AROUND, TURNING HER HEAD FRANTICALLY TO the right, then left. There was nothing there, nothing she could see. Everything around her was greyness, as though she had walked into a thick bank of smog. She thrust her hands out, seeking something to hang onto, but there was nothing. She covered her eyes and wept.

She knew this place. This was where she'd gone, so many times, away into the nothingness, seeking to escape.

This was the grey fog of her memory, of the times when things had gotten too much for her.

And here she was again. The mist whirled and swirled around her, blown by an unseen wind and she felt it cold and clammy against her skin, her hair, pushing at her, tugging her. She shook her head, peered through splayed fingers.

'Noo,' she said.

And then she remembered. She was journeying within a travelling. Things were different. She was Erin Lovelace Faith now, and she lived in Wellsford, not in this fog of nothingness. She was a Lady of the Forest. A Lady of the Grove. She breathed deeply, filling her lungs, reminding herself.

And she walked, and realised that Fox walked with her, and standing on Fox's back, Raven was along for the ride.

She wasn't alone.

She was never alone now.

She stepped forward, through the fog, walking until it thinned.

And it did, and she was standing in a room.

A room with bare walls and bare floor and no light hanging from the ceiling.

A room with only one item of furniture in it.

A bassinet.

Erin swallowed and tiptoed forward, holding her breath, her hands pressed to her thumping heart. She looked into the bassinet, and spied the small child beneath the covers, peering back at her, eyes wide.

'Sweetheart,' she said. 'Come here, my little love.'

Fox stood on her hind legs to see inside the baby's bed, and Raven fluttered to rest on the side of the bassinet. Erin reached in and touched the baby, ran a finger down the round cheek.

She scooped the child up and held her to her breast.

'Hello Erin,' she whispered. 'I've come at long last to bring you home.'

The baby gazed at her, eyes round and the colour of autumn leaves. One tiny hand escaped the blanket, starfish fingers reaching. Erin took the small hand in her own, closed her fist over it, bent down and kissed the little fingers.

'Hello precious,' she said. 'I'm here at last and I'm sorry I've taken so long.' She closed her eyes and felt the warm weight of the child against her breast. 'You'll never be alone again,' she said.

'I will take you into myself and you can grow and bloom and be at peace. I will take care of you.'

Erin closed her eyes, holding the child close, and taking long, deep breaths, tears of gratitude standing in her eyes. Here was a piece of herself she'd been missing, and she meant to take very good care of it.

When she opened her eyes again, she was no longer in the room, but standing on a green hill, looking out over a vast, high meadow, the ground curving gently, the sky close enough to reach up and touch. The child was no longer in her arms, but she touched her chest, feeling its presence inside her, another piece of herself in its rightful place.

The air was cold and clear, the breeze stiff, pushing

Erin's hair back from her face. She stood, with Fox beside her, and surveyed the surrounding hilltops, and the one she stood on. Raven flew in a looping circle, black gaze fastened upon the ground, and Erin watched him disappear behind a low hill.

She bent slightly, and touched her fingertips to Fox's warm fur, then set off in the direction Raven had shown her, and she listened to the wind as she walked, and heard nothing else – no bird song, nor any traffic noise – no sound of human habitation at all.

Just the wind, and the grass, and the hills rolling and turning upon each other in a slow dance that took millennia.

Down the slope, Raven stood on the roof of a low, long building that hunched under an overhanging roof. Erin walked up to it, looked at the blank windows and shivered.

She stepped up to the door, lifted her hand, and knocked upon it. The wood was old, unpainted under her knuckles.

The door opened and a pale face surrounded with dark red hair looked out at her with green-brown eyes.

'What do you want?' the woman asked. 'Why are you here?'

Erin looked at herself and sought an answer. 'I've come to take you home,' she said.

The eyes, identical to her own, narrowed at the answer, and the mouth beneath them twisted. 'What makes you think I would go with you?'

Erin bent her head. 'I let you down,' she said.

'You did. You put aside everything I held dear. And for what?'

'I didn't know what else to do,' Erin told her other self.

Behind the door, her shard shook her head, eyes hard in the dimness. 'You were weak. You were willing to make only piddly efforts with our drawing and making our art, just for the sake of getting along.'

The door began to close.

'Wait,' Erin said. 'I'm here to apologise.'

'I don't want your apology.'

'But you deserve it,' Erin said. 'May we come in?'

The soul shard's eyes narrowed in suspicion again. 'Who is we?'

'Fox and I,' Erin answered.

The door opened wider again, and Erin's other self gazed down at Fox's smart, smiling face.

She blinked at the orange-pelted fox, then stood back, and held the door open for them.

Inside, the room was dim, and Erin allowed herself to look around curiously. It was furnished sparsely, with a narrow bed at one end, and at the other, near a window, a small table with one chair. Upon the table was a sketchbook.

'May I look?' Erin asked, her hand near the book.

She got a shrug in response, so she picked it up and looked through it. The pictures were unfinished, begun and abandoned, the book half full.

'Do you have others?' Erin asked, holding up the sketchbook.

Her other self shook her head. 'I've only that one,' she said.

Erin looked down at the book again, her heart contracting in pain. This was herself, unwilling to compromise, unwilling to live with the decision she'd made to be only half-hearted at best about her art, because her mother discouraged it, because Jeremy didn't care for it, because it was easier to give in than to fight.

This part of her hadn't given in, however. This part of her had split off, run away, rather than give up what was important.

And yet, here on this lonely hill, here in this ramshackle place, she'd only had one small sketchbook.

Erin looked at the table.

And one pencil to work with.

She bowed her head and put the book back down.

'Things are different now,' she said. 'I am drawing and painting every day.'

'I don't believe you,' her shard replied. 'Why would you have changed?'

'Because I discovered I needed to,' Erin said, confronting the truth. 'I found that I needed more – just as you knew I did.' She looked down at her hands, so comfortable holding pencil or brush. Made for it. 'I am not complete without my art, and I am not complete without you.' She looked across at herself.

'You paint? Every day?'

'Yes,' Erin said. 'And I sell my art too, now.'

There was scepticism in the eyes looking back at her.

'It's true,' Erin said. 'I no longer live under our mother's thumb. I'm not engaged to Jeremy anymore. I'm my own person, living a life I design, and I'll never stop painting again.'

Her other self regarded her as though trying to make up her mind. Erin watched as she looked around the room, then down at the sketchbook and pencil on the table.

'Do you promise?' she asked at last.

'I do,' Erin said, heart lifting in hope. 'I promise. And I will listen to your needs, and make sure they are met, so that you never have to choose like this again.'

There was a long pause, during which the wind swept down to the house and in through the eaves, making Erin shiver.

'It's so lonely here,' she said. 'How have you been able to live here?'

'I've had my art to sustain me.'

Erin glanced again at the table, with the one small sketchbook and pencil. She shook her head. 'I know why you came here, and I can't blame you for doing so at all.' She looked over at herself. 'But this isn't good enough for you,' she said. 'You need more, and I can give it to you now.'

Again a pause, and the other looked at her. 'You sell our art?' she asked.

Our art. That seemed hopeful. Erin nodded. 'I do. A friend has helped me turn some of it into greeting cards, and others into prints for people to buy and frame.'

'A friend?'

'Yes,' Erin said. 'I have friends who are supportive now. Much has changed since you left me. I live a different life now. I have a cottage of my own, and I am happy.'

'Happy?'

Erin smiled because it was true. She was happy, and things were only beginning. There was so much to look forward to, to strive for, to be part of. She nodded.

The other looked at her, and Erin waited.

'I will come,' her other self said.

Erin beamed at her. 'I'll make sure you never regret this,' she said. 'And that you never have cause to leave again. I will make sure that the things that are close to your heart – our heart, are never neglected again.'

Erin's long-lost self nodded, and walked to the door, stepping outside into the wind that pushed her thick dark hair back from her face. 'Let us go, then,' she said.

Fox slipped outside and Erin followed. She glanced back at the sketchbook, then gently closed the door. Turning, she reached for her other self's hand.

Their fingers met, and the woman who was a shard of her own soul stepped towards her, and inside her, and Erin felt her there, turning around, melting in, coming home.

She bent down for a moment, sank to her knees in the grass, feeling both of them – the baby who was wounded by being taken from one mother and given to another, and the woman who could not bear to give up the art that was so important to her. Tears flowed from her eyes so that she covered her face with her hands.

'Blessed Goddess,' she whispered. 'I am following your path, and my heart is full of gratitude.' She let her hands fall and held her face to the sky. 'I have recovered that which was lost, and so shall never be lost again.'

She got back to her feet, and Raven fluttered down to settle on her shoulder, and Fox fell into step at her side, and together they walked back up the hill.

Back to the clearing where Morghan and Winsome waited.

47

CLARICE GAZED AROUND THE CAVE, HOLDING HER DRUM WITH one hand, keeping the beat steady, quiet but strong. A pulse to guide the travellers, a calling to the Otherworld. She blinked, feeling the dirt floor of the cave under her, seeing the shadows from the fire dancing around the rough, natural-hewn walls of the cave. She did not travel to the Otherworld on the sound of her drum, but she slipped sideways nonetheless, sitting in the cave, gazing at her companions with their eyes closed to this world.

She saw Morghan's wolf and heard the beating of Hawk's wings. The slither of Snake.

She saw the wiry fur and gleaming eyes of Winsome's Dog.

She saw the white-tipped paws and tail, the sharp, laughing snout of Erin's Fox.

She sat in the cave with the shadows dancing.

Her heart quickened in time to her drum. Her blood rushed between her ears.

Her head swam. She remembered her dreaming.

She remembered her mother, leaning close, her eyes keen, looking at her.

She requires the truth, her mother said. *You must focus.*

Clarice nodded. The truth. 'Who requires the truth?' she whispered.

Her drum carried her into the flickering dreaming and she stood, stretched, stepped in time to her drum.

'Who requires the truth?' she asked again.

She spun and the fire spat red sparks out at her. The shadows on the walls bent and stepped with her. The three sleeping women held hands beside the fire, swaying slightly, twitching.

The drum beat on. Calling Clarice into her dance, into the space between the worlds where everything existed, where there was no barrier, no veil, where everything was dream, and was real.

She focused. She drew breath, held it, let it out, danced.

And her mother came to dance with her, red hair in wild curls down her back, head thrown back so that the fire turned the skin of her neck rosy.

They danced together, eyes locking. Grainne smiled.

'Call your kin, Clarice,' she whispered. 'You are at the heart of your own home and you require the truth.'

Clarice nodded, her drum singing. She beat the rhythm and the call.

Come to me, her drum sang. Dance with me, it called.

White wings swooped silently down to rest on Clarice's shoulder. It was Sigil, and yet it was not Sigil.

'Owl,' she breathed. And danced with the bird on her shoulder.

Grainne wove a circle around her.

'We danced like this when you were a child,' she said.

Clarice nodded, remembering.

'I danced with my mother and grandmother like this when I was a child,' Grainne said, stepping on the cave floor, arms out, as graceful as Clarice's owl.

'And she danced with her mother, and she with your great, great grandmother, and she with her mother, grandmother.' Grainne closed her eyes. Spun. 'This is how I raised you. None of us alone.'

Now, the cave was full of women dancing. Clarice looked at them, red-haired, dark-haired, one or two as fair and wraith-like as herself.

Grainne smiled at her.

Clarice blinked, smoke in her eyes, and then tears to wash away the sting. She beat upon her drum and danced with the women who had come before her, who were her family, who held her in their dance, just as she held them in the singing of her drum, the stepping of her feet, the lifting of her arms, the weeping of her tears, the joy in her heart.

Then the dance slowed, and Clarice stilled, her drumming quieter now, a whisper through the dream, through the worlds. Grainne came to her, smiled up into her face.

'My blessing, daughter,' she whispered, then moved away.

Another woman took her place. 'My blessing, granddaughter,' she said.

The women smiled at her. Blessed her one by one.

Great granddaughter.

Great great granddaughter.

Child of my blood.

Child of my magic.
Child of my heart.
Walk in strength.
Walk in ease.
Walk in the world with your head high.
We are with you.
We are with you.
Our blood runs through you.
Our magic runs through you.
We carry your heart.

48

VERONICA STOOD IN THE KITCHEN, COFFEE MUG GOING COLD in her hands as she gazed out at her daughter, watching her.

She'd done this every morning for the last week or more, trying to understand what Erin was doing. She took a sip of her coffee, grimaced, wondering how long she'd been standing at the window in her dressing gown and slippers, hair in disarray. Watching Erin go through a series of exercises – dancing steps – that she knew the sequence of by heart now.

Erin was different, Veronica was realising. And the extent of the difference astounded her. How was this her daughter? The child always with her head in the clouds, turning away and retreating into a grey fog whenever anything frightened her.

Nothing seemed to frighten Erin anymore.

Instead, Veronica thought, it was she who was frightened.

Erin was happy. In love with her boyfriend. Gloriously

so. Veronica took another sip of her coffee. She'd never been in love with Vincent like that. They'd made a good team, as far as that had gone, but love?

Love like Erin felt with her Stephan?

Veronica shook her head. There had never been that.

And confidence. Erin was so much more confident. She was developing, Veronica thought, an easy grace about her that was just stunning.

It was Veronica now, who felt gauche and uncertain. They'd reversed their roles.

But every time Veronica thought about going back to her life, picking up the pieces of it, slipping its yoke back over her shoulders, she couldn't bring herself to do it.

Her grandmother's voice was too loud in her mind.

Oh my Vera, what's become of you?

Veronica's lips twisted in a pained grimace. What had become of her? She looked down at her chest and felt the same vague, puzzled surprise that it wasn't cracked wide open like it felt it was. She pressed her hand to herself and wondered at how her body could be intact when she was walking around with a gaping hole there.

'Mum,' Erin said, sweeping into the room with Burdock at her heels and leaning over to kiss Veronica on the cheek. 'Good morning – it's a beautiful one after the rain last night.' She opened a cupboard and brought down a mug. 'How are you feeling? Did you sleep well?'

They were the same questions Erin asked her every morning, but suddenly Veronica opened her mouth and told the truth.

'I don't know what I'm doing, Erin,' she said.

Erin put the mug down and looked at her mother. 'I know,' she said.

'I don't want to go back to your father.' Veronica blinked. It was true, she thought. She didn't. 'But I don't know what to do instead.' She touched her chest again.

'I know that too,' Erin told her.

'I can't keep staying here though,' Veronica said. 'You and Stephan need your space.'

'It's been lovely having you here,' Erin said. It was true as well. She and Veronica were finding their way towards each other in ways that Erin had never known or expected were possible. 'And Stephan and I have all the time in the world. You don't need to leave until you're ready.'

'I don't know what to do,' Veronica said.

Erin paused before answering, then smiled at her mother. 'Clarice is holding her first dance class today – outside, just a small group, absolutely for beginners. Would you like to come with me?'

Veronica frowned. 'Dance class?'

'You admired my dancing out there a while back.' Erin nodded at the garden outside the window. 'Movement is good,' she said. 'It'll help.'

'How?' Veronica asked. 'How can dancing help?'

But Erin just smiled. 'Trust me,' she said. 'It can. Will you come?'

'I look a fright,' Veronica said, touching her hair. Threads of grey were darkening the blonde. 'I've got nothing to wear.'

'We can find you something,' Erin said. 'I bet you have something loose and comfortable in one of your suitcases. No one is really going to be looking at you, anyway.'

Veronica opened her mouth to say no. She even went as far as to shake her head, then stopped herself. She sighed.

'All right,' she said. 'What's the harm?'

Erin smiled at her. 'No harm at all,' she said.

'I FEEL RIDICULOUS,' VERONICA HISSED, AS SHE WALKED across the village green with Erin.

'Why?' Erin asked, baffled. 'You look fine.'

'It's not how I look,' Veronica said, and waved a hand. 'This is just so weird.'

'It'll be fun,' Erin said, and waved to Clarice. She turned and touched her mother on the arm. 'I'll be back in a minute, okay?'

Her mother made a grumbling noise as Erin skipped over to Clarice. Erin ignored it and smiled.

'Good turnout,' she said. 'And beautiful weather. I'm excited about this!'

Clarice shook her head. 'I think I'm going to be sick.'

'No,' Erin said. 'You'll be fine. Just remember that everyone is here because they want to be – they want to learn what you have to teach.'

Clarice blew out a breath and was glad for once that no one could tell she was blanched pale with nerves. She pushed her sunglasses higher on her nose and sighed. 'I guess so.'

'It's going to be great,' Erin said, then shook her head. 'And now I have no excuse except to do the art classes.'

'Huh,' Clarice said, 'that's true.'

'Sorry I'm late,' Krista called out, hurrying over the grass. She beamed at Clarice and took her hand, holding on to it while she spoke. 'Do you want me to introduce you, or do you want to just get into it?'

Clarice shivered despite the warmth of the day. Krista's fingers around hers tightened. 'Are you sure you can't just play the video of the lesson we made?'

'You made a video?' Erin asked.

Krista nodded. 'It's going to go up on our website and Winsome's, so those who can't make it here in person, or don't want to, can still follow along.'

Erin turned to Clarice. 'Wow,' she said. 'That's brilliant.' Then she glanced over at Krista, frowning. 'We have a website?'

'We do,' Krista said. 'I've had one for Haven for ages, of course, but now...' She held up her hand, still linked with Clarice's. 'Now Wilde Grove is online too.'

Erin's eyes widened.

Krista shrugged. 'Ambrose and Morghan and I have been working on it all week. I'm sure you'll get the memo soon enough. And be asked what you'd like to contribute.'

That made Erin shake her head. 'Gosh,' she said. 'Things are really happening, aren't they?'

Krista grinned, lifted Clarice's fingers and kissed them. 'Sure are.' She looked at Clarice. 'Ready?'

Clarice nodded grimly and Krista squeezed her fingers one more time, then let go and moved away with Erin.

Clarice faced the small crowed, spaced out on the green, everyone watching her, waiting. She took a breath.

'Welcome,' she said, then cleared her throat and let herself remember her mother, grandmother, great-grandmother, her long line of ancestors dancing with her in the cave. She straightened, smiled.

'For any of you who don't know me, I'm Clarice Wilde, and this is the first of our classes where we'll learn ritually-inspired dance movements to help ourselves physically and energetically.'

She looked out over the rows of faces, most of them people she knew who smiled back at her, ready in the sunlight to breathe and stretch and dance with her.

She blinked, and for a moment the green was crowded with others as well, ancestors, guides, gods.

And overhead the web hummed and gleamed.

She was part of it. She was part of Wilde Grove.

And she was part of Wellsford.

'What did you think?' Erin asked Veronica as they walked across the village, the warm air heavy on their skin, Burdock trotting ahead of them, head in the air, nose working.

'I think we should have driven,' Veronica said. 'Two cars at home and we're walking.'

Erin laughed and linked her arm through her mother's. 'It's a beautiful day.'

'You say that even when it's raining.'

'I'm in love with the worlds,' Erin said, and it was true. Everything in her hummed and sang. She patted her mother's hand. 'Tell me truly,' she said. 'Did you enjoy Clarice's first class?'

Veronica wrinkled her nose, then sighed. 'I did,' she said. 'It wasn't too difficult, and all that breathing was good.'

'There!' Erin laughed. 'I thought you were getting into it.' She glanced behind them, saw Winsome and waved.

'Good,' Winsome said. 'I was hoping I'd catch you – did you enjoy the dancing?'

'We did,' Erin said. 'What about you?'

'I thought it was perfect.' Winsome smiled over at Veronica. 'I was hoping I'd see you today,' she said.

'Me?' Veronica asked.

'Yes, do you think I can borrow you for an hour or so? I can run you back to Ash Cottage afterwards.'

'Of course you can,' Erin said, unhanding her mother.

Veronica snapped a glance at her. 'You don't even know what she wants me for.'

'It's Winsome,' Erin said, as if that explained everything. As far as she was concerned, it did. 'And besides, I've things I need to do.'

Winsome beamed at Veronica. 'Please?' she said. 'I'm working with a few others to organise those computer classes and some other things, and we could really do with some extra help.'

'I don't know anything about computers,' Veronica frowned. 'Not really.' She gave a strained laugh. 'Only how to buy them.'

'That'll do,' Winsome said, unperturbed.

Veronica thought for a moment. What else was she going to do for the rest of the day? Sit around brooding?

'Okay,' she said. 'I'll help.'

'Lovely,' Winsome said. 'Perfect.' She patted Burdock, who had come to nose at her hand and say hello. 'This way, then,' she said.

Veronica fell into step with her, shaking her head as she watched Erin dash off to do who knew what. 'I really don't know anything about computers,' she said to Winsome.

'We'll learn together, then,' Winsome said, then slowed her steps as they passed Julia's house. She craned her neck over the low fence.

'Julia,' she called and waited for Julia to stand up, shading her eyes to see her. 'Your roses look magnificent.'

Julia looked around her garden, and let herself nod, walking over to Winsome. 'I think they've forgiven me,' she said.

'I'd say so,' Winsome answered. 'They look very happy.' She appraised Julia for a moment. 'And you look much happier too.'

Julia flicked her eyes towards the stranger beside Winsome, and she shrugged awkwardly. 'I am,' she said.

'Goodness,' Winsome said. 'Forgive my lack of manners. Julia, this is Veronica, Erin's mum.' She turned to Veronica. 'Julia is a good friend,' she said. 'And her garden is the envy of all of us.'

'It is beautiful,' Veronica said.

'It definitely is,' Winsome said, looking back at Julia. 'Are you coming to our little meeting?'

Julia looked down at her hands, still in their gardening gloves. 'I don't think so. Not today anyway.' She squinted back at her plants. 'I still need to see to some of these.'

'All right, then,' Winsome said. 'Next time?'

Julia flicked a glance at her. Took a breath. Nodded. 'Next time.'

'Wonderful.' Winsome waved goodbye and drew Veronica along the road again with her. They walked in silence for a moment.

'Everyone is so friendly here,' Veronica said.

'Everyone knows each other,' Winsome laughed. 'That's

a small village for you – and this one in particular likes to pull together, take care of everyone.'

'Why this one in particular?'

'Hmm. The Grove's influence, mostly, I'd say. But more than that, we're all trying to find a way to live in this world, and Wellsford is full of very determined people.' Winsome smiled at Veronica. 'And how are you getting along?'

Veronica blinked back sudden tears, glad she was wearing sunglasses. 'I'm still a bit of a mess, actually.'

'Yes?'

'I feel like I've been torn open.' Veronica touched her chest where she imagined the hole was. 'But I don't know how to knit myself back together.' She swallowed. 'The things that Morghan woman said really rocked me.'

'I can well imagine,' Winsome said.

Veronica looked at her.

Winsome shrugged. 'When I first moved here, I had some...experiences...that made it seem like the rug had been ripped out from under me.'

'Yes!' Veronica stopped walking for a moment. 'That's exactly how I feel.' She shook her head. 'How do I get it back?'

'The rug?' Winsome laughed. 'I had to install whole new flooring.'

They walked on again.

'I think I'll have to as well,' Veronica said. 'But I don't know how.'

'It's a process,' Winsome said. 'You just start living, open to the flow.'

'I want to know what to do next,' Veronica said. 'I don't want to go back to Vincent, my husband,' she added.

'Then that's what you do next,' Winsome said. 'You don't go back to him.'

'That's not doing something.'

Winsome raised her eyebrows. 'Isn't it? Every choice is an action, whether we're choosing to do something, or choosing not to do it.'

Veronica thought on this, nodding her head slowly. 'But what do I do instead?' She lifted her face to the sun. 'I can't just stay on with Erin.'

'Has she asked you to leave?'

'No. She says I can stay as long as I need to.'

'Is there somewhere else you are ready to go to?' Winsome asked.

Veronica shook her head. 'I don't know where to go next.'

'Then stay here, see what unfolds. Live and breathe one day at a time for a while. See where that takes you.'

'Will it take me anywhere?' Veronica asked dismally.

Winsome laughed. 'Sometimes,' she said, 'you just have to embrace the indecision. Clarity can take time.' She looked over at Veronica, met her eyes, smiled gently.

'You're in transition,' she said. 'That keeps its own time, and if you step into it, trusting the process, it will flow around you like a river, and take you where you need to go.'

Veronica licked her lips, nodded. A river, she thought.

'Do I get a boat?' she asked. 'Or do I have to swim?'

Winsome laughed again. 'Just float for now, Veronica. Just float.'

She smiled. 'Swimming can wait until you know you're not going to go against the current.'

49

'Are you sure about this?' Stephan asked, staring intently at Erin. 'I wish I could come with you – you don't know what you're going to find in that place.'

But Erin shook her head. 'I'm sure,' she said. 'And I trust Macha. She wouldn't send me somewhere that I'm not ready to go.'

Stephan wasn't sure. Macha was formidable. And maybe a bit reckless. 'You've only done this sort of thing once so far,' Stephan said, unwilling to budge just yet.

Erin thought about that before answering. 'I don't think it works like that, though,' she said. 'Maybe I've only done it once so far this time around, but it's different over there, in the Otherworld – you know it is.'

Stephan dropped his gaze. It was different over there. In the Otherworld, intuition and knowing was strong. He thought of Bear Fellow, their lessons together. It wasn't so much that Bear Fellow was teaching him anything new, but rather, he was waking up the knowledge Stephan already held.

Because, Stephan had realised not far into his training, that he was Bear Fellow.

Or had been, just as he had once been Finn.

And still was, if one discounted linear time.

Erin was still looking at him. 'There's a sort of flow, I think, to moving in the Otherworld. You just have to get out of your own way, follow your heart, realise that you already know a lot of what you're doing there.'

'Yeah,' Stephan said on a sigh. 'I know you're right.' He shook his head. 'It just goes against my...' He shrugged.

Erin stepped over to him and wrapped her arms around him. 'Your protective Bear instincts?'

'Exactly.'

She lifted her face from his shoulder and smiled at him. 'I love your protective Bear instincts,' she said. 'But I am light on my feet and swift and knowing like Fox.' Her smile widened and she let go of him, cupped his face instead and kissed his lips. 'I can't put this off – or I'll never continue with the initiation.' She shrugged. 'And then what am I doing here?'

'I know,' Stephan said, even though he was shaking his head.

She kissed him again. Dropped her hands and found his, linked their fingers together. 'Doing that last journey with Morghan opened something up inside me, Stephan,' Erin said. 'I know so much more about who I am.'

Stephan frowned, thinking of Morghan. 'Does she know about this?' he asked.

'I talked it over with her, yes,' Erin replied.

'And she was cool with it?'

Erin shrugged lightly. Squeezed Stephan's hands. 'This is what we do, Stephan. This is who we are. The spirits lead, we follow.'

Stephan's lips twitched. 'Lady of the Grove,' he said.

Laughing, Erin let him go, and stepped back to look at her garden. 'Not yet,' she said. 'Not even close.' She touched her hand to the warm stone of the well. 'But Erin of the Wildwood – perhaps. Erin of Earth, Sea, Sky.' She laughed again. 'Perhaps,' she said. 'Becoming, anyway, just as you are.'

'Okay.' Stephan nodded, held up his hands in defeat. 'Okay, then.'

Erin looked at him, at the sun on his dark hair, his blue, bright eyes, and her heart swelled with a joy that stunned her with its simplicity.

'I love you,' she said. 'I've always loved you, haven't I?'

'Too right you have,' Stephan said, a grin overtaking his face. He leant over and kissed her. 'And I you. For who knows how many lifetimes.'

'This one, for sure,' Erin said.

RAVEN SWOOPED DOWN FROM THE SKY AND PLUCKED ERIN UP with his strong feet. Erin had Fox in her arms, and Raven flew with both out over the far meadow towards the maze. His wings beat against the breeze and the wind lifted them, and Erin was exhilarated, Fox tucked under her arm with whiskery lips pulled back in a grin.

They flew over the maze, and Erin gazed down at it in astonishment. Didn't they need to go through it?

But Raven set her down beside the oak tree, and the deep well she'd come to think of in her head as the scrying pool.

Fox leapt from her arms. Raven settled in the branches of the oak, his bright eyes fixed on her.

Erin took a breath, turning to look at the stone wall, the gate in it that led to the City of Shadows.

There was something in there she was supposed to retrieve. She felt the truth of this deep inside her, in the knowing centre of her being.

Something. Or someone.

Erin frowned, trying to tease out more information, but shook her head. She would have to go on trust, on faith and instinct.

The gate was the same as she remembered it, and Erin reached for the latch, a sudden anxiety tightening her chest at the thought of what she might have to see and do upon entering this place. Her fingers tightened on the gate, and she stilled herself, breathing deeply, slowly.

Macha flickered into being behind her, and behind her was Kria, her hair braided with seagull feathers. Erin closed her eyes, grateful for their presence, for the reminder that she was more than just the Erin she'd always known.

She was Macha, she was Kria, she was a dozen others.

When she turned back to the gate, Macha and Kria were gone, and Fox stood looking up at her, waiting. Erin nodded, pushed the gate open, and stepped through.

Fox tucked herself neatly beside Erin's leg.

It was the same as before, and Erin looked around, blinking because even the air seemed darker here, as though clouds sat low upon the mean streets, and she imagined breathing in the greyness, the hopelessness.

Erin shook her head. She would not breathe in the despair that seeped over this place. This was not somewhere she was stuck – she walked here as a seeker, not as a resident of this sad, run-down place.

For a moment, she stood tall and felt herself shine, then dipped her head and hushed herself. This was a silent place, and under the silence, she knew it was a dangerous one.

It would not do to let herself shine so brightly here.

Drawing herself inwards as though throwing a cloak around her shoulders, Erin ducked her head and looked to the left, then the right. Which way did she need to go?

She chose the same direction she had walked before. There was something along this way she needed to find.

With Fox beside her, Erin walked and walked, past the place where she had turned and retraced her steps the last time she'd come here. She kept her head down, her shoulders and body loose, ready.

Ready to flee. Or fight.

How would she fight in this place, she wondered? She had no weapon.

The answer came to her. In a place this grubby, this grey, all she would need to do would be to stand, to let herself grow tall and strong with her shining.

But it was best to be quiet, to pass the dirty and suspicious faces peering at her from windows and doorways without meeting their eyes.

Without challenging them.

Something was calling to her. She touched her centre, the point under her ribs from which it drew her on, her knowing. Her intuition. She followed it, not looking at those who peered out at her, their lips curling. She walked quietly, unobtrusively, willing them not to pay her attention, to glance, then look away.

'Nothing to see here,' she whispered.

Fox's nose lifted, and she paused for a moment, one white paw in the air as she sniffed, keen eyes trained on a dark doorway ahead of them.

Erin looked too, and knew she had come to the place she had been seeking. She stepped silently over the road that was slick with rubbish, oil, other substances that she tried and failed to tell herself that they were not blood.

The doorway gaped at her, a dark mouth leading into a stinking belly of a building.

She had to go in there and so she did, not letting herself hesitate. Fox darted inside with her, white fur luminous in the dimness.

It was an old boarding house, Erin thought, and turned instinctively to go up the stairs, their treads littered with broken bottles, the dull gleam of needles.

On the landing, Erin faced the closed doors and picked one, following the knowing inside her.

'The pin cushion,' she murmured, and Fox glanced up at her, pulling back her lips in a grin.

There, inside the room, was what she had sought, and Erin took a breath, stunned that she had not guessed this all along.

The woman lay on a stained mattress under a grimy window, her skin dark with blood and dirt. Erin knelt beside her, reaching out to touch her, to roll her over so that she could see her birth-mother's face.

Becca was barely conscious, eyes staring at Erin, unseeing.

She was light as a feather, and Erin picked up the shadowed fragment of the woman who had given birth to her, and cradled her in her arms, turning to leave the room without a second glance.

One of the other doors opened and a man, eyes feverish and glittering, shouted at her, the words unintelligible except for the anger behind them. Erin didn't so much as flinch, but headed straight for the stairs, ignoring him, breathing calmly in and out.

In and out.

He didn't follow, and Erin heard his door slam shut. Good, she thought, and stepped out onto the street with relief. She was leaving, and she was taking Becca with her, and there would be no argument that would dissuade her.

She and Fox retraced their steps, moving swiftly, Erin's will an iron, unbending thing. She would carry this lost aspect of her mother, and she would take her out of this place.

Faces looked at her from the windows and doorways, then moved away, shrinking back into the shadows.

Then the gate was in front of her, and Erin slipped through it, Fox nipping ahead.

Erin laid Becca down beside the pool and looked at her for a long moment, then bent and placed a kiss softly on her forehead.

She did not stir. Erin sat back, realising there was more to this journey that needed to be done, and she reached into her pocket, drawing out a cloth that she dipped into the warm, dark waters of the scrying pool. She rung it out and wiped the blood and dirt from her birth-mother's face. She wet the cloth again, kept at the gentle job until Becca's face was clean, and then Erin started on her arms and legs, smoothing the cloth over Becca's skin until her skin shone.

She wet the cloth again, and washed Becca's long, dark hair, and when it was clean, she ran her fingers through it, picking the tangles undone.

Becca was transformed, and her eyes flickered open, and she groaned, standing up. Erin looped and arm around Becca's waist, supporting her, and they walked a few steps, tottering together across the grass.

When Erin looked up, they were no longer where they had been, but were walking through the Wildwood, Fox trotting in front, leading the way.

It was the healing clearing, Erin realised with a gasp. Morghan's healing clearing.

Morghan was nowhere in sight, but standing in the middle of the clearing, encased in a sort of cocoon, was another figure. A woman, Erin thought, peering at her in consternation. She shook her head, at a loss as to what to do next.

But there was nothing for her to do, because as she watched, the cocoon peeled back like the petals of a flower, and Becca stood there, eyes closed, hair about her shoulders.

On Erin's arm, the soul fragment she had just brought back cried out, then stumbled forward, arms out and reaching for herself. Becca opened her eyes, lifted her arms up in welcome and a moment later they were merged, one soul again.

Erin pressed a hand to her mouth and felt glad tears flow down her face. She shook her head. What had happened? What had she done?

Something amazing. Something wonderful.

Becca looked over at her, a smile on her lips, and Erin thought she was beautiful, unblemished, smooth, and clear and reborn.

Something rustled in the undergrowth at the edge of the clearing and Erin watched in delight as a young white hind stepped out from the bushes and walked on dainty legs over to Becca. Becca looked down at her for a moment, then laid a hand on the animal, her smile widening on her lips.

There was nothing else for Erin to do, she knew, except for one thing more. One thing more and Becca would be able to return to her greater soul, to her soul family, whole again, at peace.

She drew breath, returning to her instinct, knowing she was doing as she had before, as Macha, as others.

'May your family come to you now, to receive you and accompany you in peace and grace,' she said. 'May one who guides you in this life come to show you the way.' She pressed her lips together, waited.

Then bowed, for a Goddess had stepped into the clearing. Erin fell to one knee, head bent even while she basked in the light from the Goddess.

'I will take this one,' Brigid said. 'If she will come.'

Erin lifted her head, reached out to touch Fox's soft fur, watching them walk out of the clearing together, the white hind, the Goddess, and the transformed woman, around whom swirled a sudden dance of butterflies as they left.

There was another movement in the clearing, and Erin looked over to see Teresa standing there, gazing after her daughter. Erin pressed a hand to her heart and the tears came again.

'Teresa,' she whispered.

Teresa turned and looked at her, then stepped over and picked up Erin's hands in her own, her face beaming as she dropped a kiss upon Erin's knuckles, her eyes wet with delight.

'Thank you,' she whispered, and then let go of Erin's hands, turned, and followed her daughter from the clearing.

50

'Hello Mum,' Erin said.

Veronica shook her head. 'I thought it was the mothers who were supposed to have eyes in the backs of their heads?'

Erin set the photo of Becca back down next to Teresa and turned, a smile on her face. 'I can feel when you walk into a room.'

For a moment, Veronica wanted to roll her eyes. 'What do I feel like?' she said instead and groaned inwardly. She was getting used to this place. Too used? That, she hadn't yet decided.

Getting up, Erin walked over and hugged her mother. 'Better than you did a week or two ago,' she said. 'I've hardly seen you – what have you been busy with?'

Veronica flushed, standing in the doorway to Erin's little sunroom, where she kept her altar. 'Winsome and Cynthia have been keeping me busy – they seem to think I'm useful.'

'I'm sure you are, Mum,' Erin said. 'Don't sell yourself short.'

'I'm enjoying myself, to my own surprise,' Veronica said. She looked over at Erin's altar. 'We've got the rooms at the old vicarage all spruced up, ready for everything.'

There was a new photo on the altar. Veronica frowned at it.

'When did you put that there?' she asked.

Erin turned her head. 'Put what, where?'

Veronica's mouth was dry, and she touched a hand unconsciously to her chest, to the hole she still felt there. 'The photo,' she said. 'Of me.'

'Oh.' Erin looked at the little black and white square showing a small Veronica – or Vera, as she had been back then – with her grandparents. She stood between the adults, holding their hands, and they were both smiling down at her as the photo was taken.

'I love that photo,' Erin said. 'And it just seemed right to put it there.' She looked at Veronica. 'You don't mind, do you?'

Veronica shook her head slowly. 'I should have a larger copy made,' she said, testing out the idea, tasting it on her tongue as she said the words. 'Put it in a frame.' She stumbled over a laugh and wiped her eyes. They were damp.

Erin was watching her, reached up and touched her mother's soft, wet cheeks. 'The loss of your grandparents is still a hole inside you, isn't it?'

Veronica winced, almost didn't answer, then let herself sigh and nod. 'Part of me got lost when they died,' she said. 'I was on my own after that.'

Erin thought of the soul retrieval she'd done – inadvertently, perhaps – for Becca. 'We can get that part of yourself back,' she said.

'What?' Veronica's eyes narrowed at her daughter. 'I don't know what you mean.'

'There's a ritual we can do,' Erin ventured, thinking it was probably too soon to suggest things like this to her mother. 'To retrieve the lost parts of ourselves, bring them back home so we can feel whole again.'

Blinking, Veronica was speechless for a moment. 'There is?' she squeaked at last. She cleared her throat. 'I've been dreaming of them,' she said. 'My grandparents.' She sighed, backing out of the room, and turning for the kitchen. 'I need a cup of tea and to get off my feet for five minutes.'

'You've been dreaming of them?' Erin asked, following Veronica.

Veronica nodded. 'A lot.' She paused with a cup in her hand. Shook her head. 'It's so real,' she said. 'The dream, that is.'

Erin sat down at the table. 'Do you want to tell me about it?'

'There's not much to tell, really.' Veronica put the cup down and reached over to feel how hot the kettle was. Then busied her hands spooning tea into the pot. 'We're at the seaside – that's where they took me for a holiday once.' She smiled, sniffed. 'That's where Grandad won me my teddy bear. It was the best week of my life – of my childhood, I mean.'

Burdock wandered over at sat down next to Erin. He licked her hand, and she patted him.

'Part of you is probably still there at the seaside,' Erin said.

'What do you mean?' Veronica laughed, but it was a little too high-pitched and she shut her mouth.

Erin tipped her head, gave her mother an apologetic look. 'I mean, that the shock of losing them would have made you lose part of yourself.' She gave her mother a pointed look. 'Didn't you just say that you lost part of yourself when your grandparents died?'

'Well, yes, but I didn't mean it literally.'

'But it's actually a thing, Mum,' Erin said, warming to the subject she'd done quite a bit of research on over the last several days. 'Traumatic events can splinter us.'

Veronica looked dubious.

'At its worst, the splintering can result in dissociative disorder.'

'Like your fugues?'

'Yeah, similar to that. Most people probably still know dissociative disorder as multiple personality syndrome.'

'I don't have that.'

'No,' Erin said. 'I'm not saying that you do – that's when it's at its worst.' She took a breath, not sure any longer that she should have brought up the subject. But how could she not have, she asked herself?

She shook her head. 'Anyway, the gist is that when something goes wrong in our lives like that – something that is so important to us – part of us splinters off. It's a protective thing, something we do to protect ourselves.' She tried to smile. 'But it means we're walking around not quite whole, if we don't take care of it.'

'Is this what you've been learning in the Grove?' Veronica asked.

Erin nodded. 'One of the things, yes,' she said, looking safely down at Burdock's shaggy head.

Veronica turned away, picking up the kettle and thinking furiously. She didn't know what to make of what Erin was saying. It all seemed a bit far-fetched. And yet...

And yet, she did feel like part of herself was missing. And now that she'd recognised the feeling, she knew it had been like that for a very long time.

She only hadn't noticed because she'd been busy filling the hole with other things. Possessions. Meals out. Friends and gossip.

But she didn't have any of those anymore. Or not to speak of, anyway. She was living out of suitcases at her daughter's house. Veronica drew breath, set the kettle down. Her own house seemed a long way away.

She didn't want to go back to it.

The knowledge that she didn't had come on slowly. It had been full of comfort, her previous life, but she realised now how lonely she'd been. Even her friendships had never seemed to touch any deep part of herself.

She was making new friendships now, and they seemed of a different type.

Better.

Veronica carried the teapot over to the table. 'How do you do this thing?' she asked. 'This ritual?'

Erin stared at her. 'Oh,' she said. Then blinked. 'Well, I don't really know.'

'You don't really know?' Veronica frowned. 'But you just said you did.'

'I don't really know how to do it when the other person is with you,' Erin said. She chewed her lip for a moment, thinking. Then brightened. 'But, if you're dreaming about it, I'd say we just go into your dream.'

That made Veronica laugh. Here she had been taking it seriously for a moment. She shook her head. 'That makes no sense.'

'No, wait, Mum. It does, I promise.' Erin nodded, seeing it now, how it could be done. How Veronica could be part of the doing. She didn't have a drum like Clarice did, or Ambrose, but with a start, she realised she had something else. 'Just a minute while I get something,' she said, leaping up and going for what had been in Teresa's leather bag.

A branch made of silver, golden bells hanging from its twigs.

She drew it out of the cupboard where she'd tucked it away, unwrapped it from its velvet cloth and felt the same sensation she'd felt each time she'd handled the small item. A sort of tipping, as though the world tilted and slid slightly around her.

This would do perfectly.

'What's that?' Veronica asked. She was almost ready to shake her head over Erin's suggestion, but something, some small, insistent part of her told her to wait, to be open to it.

It spoke to her in her grandmother's voice.

Erin shook the branch and the bells tinkled in their golden tongues.

'That sound makes me shiver,' Veronica said, reaching protectively for her mug of tea and holding it in front of her chest.

'Me too,' Erin admitted, lying it down carefully on its cloth on the table. She looked at it and nodded. 'It will help us travel to your dream.'

Veronica stared at her. 'You're serious, aren't you?'

'Yes,' Erin said. 'And something's keeping you here, staying in my cottage, in my village, so maybe that something is a part of you which knows you need what can be found here, done here.'

'That's a presumptuous thing to say. And it's not your village.'

'I know,' Erin sighed. 'I'm sorry – I don't know where that came from.'

Veronica looked down at the little gold and silver jingle-jangle Erin had put on the table and pressed her lips together.

'I don't have anywhere else to go,' she said. Trying to refute Erin's statement.

Erin shrugged though. 'You have the flat in the city,' she said. 'Or the house – wasn't Dad saying he wanted you back?'

'I don't want to go back to him,' Veronica said. It was a truth that had settled gradually over her like the shadows of a long summer dusk.

'The flat, then.'

'Maybe,' Veronica said, then lifted her head and looked at her daughter. Erin was so lovely, she thought. She glowed. Not just because she was fit from all the walking she did, and healthy from all the home-cooked food, but there was something else. The light came from inside her, Veronica decided. An effervescent joy and peace.

Veronica wanted some of that.

Was some of that to be had?

She thought of her dreams. Night after night it seemed, the same dream.

She nodded before she could change her mind. 'I want to do it,' she said.

A different voice spoke up in her head then, and this one jeered at her for buying into the same mumbo-jumbo Erin had.

Erin's eyes widened. 'You do?'

Veronica nodded again. 'Yes.' She paused. 'Now, before I lose my nerve.'

'Oh,' Erin said, then looked around the room, flabbergasted.

'We can do it now, right?' Veronica asked. 'Or do we have to fast for three days or something?'

'Um.' Erin rubbed her head, flustered. 'Not as far as I know.' She wished suddenly she could run to Morghan to ask her what they should do. She took a breath, slowed the thoughts that dashed hither and thither inside her head. Remembered the conversation she'd had with Clarice after their time together in the cave with Morghan and Winsome. The five of them had talked back and forth for some time, going over their experiences.

Clarice had talked, haltingly at first, her hair covering her face like a curtain, then lifting her head, she'd spoken clearly, reverently, sharing her experiences with the dream rituals Morghan had set for her, and what had happened for her in the cave.

'It needs to be a ritual,' Erin said. 'We'll need some time to prepare.'

Veronica tightened her grip on her cup. 'A ritual?'

But Erin nodded, the plan firming in her mind. 'Tonight,' she said. 'We'll do it tonight, if you still want to.' She looked at her mother, then got up and moved around to the back of Veronica's chair, leaning down to put her arms around her.

'I love you,' she said simply. 'I'm glad you took me into your home, and your heart.'

It was true. This was the way the wheel had turned, she realised. This was the life she had lived, and the life that had brought her here. It was no use pining for it to have been different, for Teresa to have raised her, or Becca, even.

Her heart sang. She was here, in Ash Cottage. Becca was safe and whole. Teresa was eased of the burden of having lost her daughter, and Erin was here with the woman who had raised her as best she could, despite not having had a loving mother of her own.

Thus was she singing healing into the threads of her life.

She stood up, patted Veronica on the shoulder. 'Tonight,' she said. 'I'll get things ready.'

Veronica looked at her through a haze of tears. She still didn't know what she was doing, or where it would lead.

But she was treading that water, she thought.

And maybe after this, she'd float, and the river would carry her.

51

'I FEEL A BIT SILLY,' VERONICA WHISPERED.

'Well you look lovely and smell divine,' Erin said, glancing over at her mother, freshly out from a cleansing soak in the tub and now dressed in her nightwear.

Veronica cleared her throat and inched closer to where Erin sat at the dressing table, her face lit with the yellow glow of the candles that reflected in the mirror.

'What do we do next?' she asked, blinking at the small array of things Erin had organised in front of her.

'We are going to make a pin cushion,' Erin said.

'A pin cushion?' Veronica was completely discombobulated by the answer. 'What on earth?'

But Erin just smiled at her. 'Sit down,' she said. 'I'll tell you the story – or a bit of the story.'

Veronica gazed at her a little while longer, then sat down on the bed. She fought the urge to tell Erin she'd changed her mind, that they'd be better off going downstairs and having a mug of warm milk, or something else equally innocuous.

She frowned. She hadn't had a mug of warmed milk since she was a child. It was what her grandfather had used to make her every night before bed, when she stayed with them.

Veronica closed her eyes. Opened them. 'What do we do?' she asked.

Erin smiled at her, handed her two pieces of fabric barely bigger than her palm, and a needle threaded with red thread.

'In the forests of faraway Russia, there is an old woman,' Erin said, dipping her needle into the circle of fabric. 'A witch,' she said. 'Baba Yaga, feared and loved far and wide, and she lives in a house that stands on chicken legs.' Erin blinked, pulled her thread through the cloth. Red thread, just as Clarice had said, and it reminded her of following the thread back to Kria, and the loch.

Red thread, she thought, for life and death and the endless expanse of time.

'The fence that surrounds Baba Yaga's house is made with bones, topped with lanterns made from human skulls,' Erin said and smiled at her mother as their faces flickered in the candle's uncertain light. 'And she rides through the air in a mortar, guiding it with a pestle.'

Veronica stared at her, brows knitted, then looked back at the pieces of fabric in her hands. She swallowed, and sewed.

'Baba Yaga's faithful servants are three horse riders, one dressed in white, one in red, one in black. These are the day, sun, and night, and Baba Yaga, if you approach her carefully, answer her questions properly, perform the chores she sets you, and show her the proper respect as one who controls the waters of life, will give you the magic you ask for.'

Erin glanced up at her mother, smiled, then tied off the thread in the tiny circular case she'd made. She smiled, then quoted the lines Ambrose had said in the story he had told months before.

'Little cot turn around, on thy foot turn thou free,
To the forest set thy back, let thy door be wide to me.'

She shivered slightly as though she'd just said the words of a spell.

Erin took a breath, continued. 'The gift of magic might be a pin cushion she gives you, that when thrown down, shows you the way you must travel to find what you seek.

'This you must throw in front of you and follow whithersoever it goes.'

Veronica, listening, clipped off her thread, turned the case in the right way and took the dish of dried herbs Erin passed her.

'Lemon balm,' Erin said. 'To ease wakefulness. Lavender, to rock us to sleep. Mugwort for dreams and visions.'

She'd collected the dried, fragrant herbs from Stephan.

They filled their pincushions and stitched them closed. Erin stitched the wheel into hers, pulling the thread through from the middle and around the outside. Veronica watched, then did the same.

Erin nodded, satisfied. 'We will tuck these under our pillows and follow them into your dream.'

Veronica, eyes wide in the candlelight, wanted to ask how they would do this, but something about the sewing, the story, the old witch Baba Yaga, had her feeling she was already in a dream.

She looked around the room for a moment, at the two narrow beds, covers turned down ready. She would sleep in one, Erin in the other.

Perhaps it was the tinkling of the gold bells as Erin shook the silver twig, or the lazy light from the candles, or the herbs that Erin had burned earlier, her lips whispering something – a prayer? To whom? – or perhaps it was simply that she was warm from the bath still, and tired from the day, but Veronica wanted to lie down, rest her head upon the pillow, the strange pin cushion in her hand, the fragrance from the herbs following her into sleep.

As she followed them into dreams.

Erin looked down at her mother, then drew the blankets over her, and leant down to place a silent kiss on Veronica's forehead, as if she were a child.

She stood up, looked at the line of candles in their jars, seeing the bright wicks of light for a moment as the glowing skulls surrounding Baba Yaga's house on its chicken legs.

Someone had mentioned the Yaga to her recently, she thought, reaching for the memory. Who had it been?

The old woman, she thought. The old woman in her travelling. The one who threw the twigs and stones and bones and gave her the runes. Erin closed her eyes for a moment, then went to the other bed and climbed in beneath the covers, her pin cushion tucked in her palm.

On the edge of her dreams, the golden bells still ringing, Erin threw the pin cushion, and the wheel-shaped pocket of herbs spun off ahead of her, the red thread unspooling into a web to catch her mother's dream.

Erin squeezed her eyes shut as cold water caught her ankles. For a moment she wondered where she was, who she was; was this the loch?

She opened her eyes, found herself on a stony shore, the water in front of her not lake but sea, lights glittering upon its waves. She turned and waded from the water, seeking her mother.

'Erin?'

Veronica stood on the shore, gazing around herself. 'Am I dreaming?' she asked, looking down at her hand. She opened her palm to find the pin cushion.

Veronica closed her fingers around it.

'Yes,' Erin said. 'You're dreaming.'

Veronica stared at her. 'But this isn't how it usually goes,' she said. 'And you're here.'

Erin smiled at her. 'I'm here because we're doing this together.'

But this was odd, Veronica thought, gazing past Erin towards the sea, the moon and town lights making the waves gleam. 'It's night,' she said. Then shook her head. 'It's not supposed to be night.' She looked down at herself. 'I'm me,' she said, then lifted her gaze to Erin. 'I'm me,' she repeated.

Her mouth was dry. Was it possible to have a dry mouth when you were dreaming? She looked at her hands again, at the pin cushion with its spokes of red thread.

'Why is it night?' she asked. 'When I dream of being here, it's always daylight.' She turned and looked away from the beach, up to the boardwalk. Pointed. 'My grandparents take me for a walk along there,' she said. 'We stop for ice cream. I'm six years old.'

Erin put her hand out, touched her mother's arm lightly.

Veronica nodded. 'It's hot.' She frowned slightly. 'We were lucky with the weather the week we came here. My grandparents said so, every morning we got up to find the sun shining.'

'Where did you stay?' Erin asked, linking her hand with Veronica's.

'In a small, shabby hotel well back from the pier,' Veronica said. 'We walked down to the water each day.' She blinked. 'I had my photo taken with a monkey.'

Erin gaped at her. 'A monkey?'

Veronica smiled. 'It was quite the done thing, back then.'

Shaking her head, Erin tugged on Veronica's hand. 'Let's go and find you.'

Veronica looked at her in consternation. 'Find me?'

'Yes,' Erin said. 'Where would you be if you weren't with your grandparents?'

'Why wouldn't I be with my grandparents?'

'Were you always, during your stay?'

Wordlessly, Veronica shook her head. 'I always had to have a rest in the afternoon before teatime.' She nodded and let Erin lead her over the beach and up to the road. 'Gran and Grandad would go downstairs, and he would have a glass of beer and she would have a small sherry.'

'That's where you'll be, then,' Erin said, 'Waiting for them.'

THE HOTEL WAS SHABBY, BLACKENED WITH SOOT AND Veronica stared up at the blank windows in dismay. This was where she had stayed? She was sure of it, and yet...

'It doesn't look like it's in business anymore,' she said.

Erin didn't reply, instead she led her mother up the steps and pushed the door open.

Veronica was relieved to see there was a light burning in the lobby. She nodded toward the stairs, feeling a pulling inside. 'Up there,' she said.

Erin nodded.

Veronica drifted up the stairs in a daze. This was a dream, she told herself. And it felt like a dream, but how did you think about dreaming while you were in a dream?

And then it didn't matter because she stood outside the door to the rooms she'd shared with her grandparents when they'd come to stay, when she was only a little girl.

'I don't want to go in,' she said. 'What's in there?' She winced. 'Who am I going to see?'

Erin touched her mother's arm. 'We have to go in,' she said. 'You've been in there waiting for long enough.'

Veronica's eyes widened. 'I've been in there waiting?'

Was this what she'd come here for? It was, wasn't it?

Erin nodded and took something out of her pocket, held it up so Veronica could see it in the jaundiced light of the hallway. 'You might need this,' she said.

The teddy bear's little black eyes seemed to wink in the dimness.

Veronica reached out and took it, then turned and pushed the door open.

'Gran? Is that you?'

Veronica's eyes filled with tears at the sound of the small, piping voice. She shook her head, unable to speak.

The bedside light was on, and a small girl looked up at her, a frown scrunching up her face.

'You're not my Gran,' the child said. 'Where's Gran and Grandad? Will they be angry I'm sleeping in their bed? I've been waiting for them to come back.' The little girl looked down at her hands. 'I got frightened.'

Veronica gulped and stepped further into the room. She flung an anguished glance back at Erin, who nodded and prodded her forward.

'It's me,' Veronica said. 'Can I sit down here?' She hovered over the side of the bed, staring at herself as she'd been all those years ago.

'Who are you?' little Veronica asked.

But Veronica couldn't speak straight away. She sat down, tears streaming down her cheeks. She held out the bear.

'Ted!' Little Veronica snatched up the soft toy. 'I've been looking for you everywhere,' she said, hugging the bear to her scrawny chest and looking at Veronica with eyes too big for her face. 'Where did you find him?'

'I kept him,' Veronica said, wiping her tears away.

The little girl frowned. 'But he's my bear.' She looked down at the teddy and examined him. 'He looks old,' she said disgustedly. 'He's not my bear – Grandad won my bear for me. He's perfect.'

'He won him on the pier,' Veronica said, glancing over at Erin who stood by the door, eyes wet and shining. She looked back at the child. Her own little self. 'After we had our photo taken with the monkey, do you remember?'

Little Veronica nodded. 'Darling – that's what the monkey was called.' She turned and scrabbled under her pillow, pulling out a photograph. 'Here it is,' she said, then ducked her head. 'It's all creased.' She knelt on the mattress and pointed to it. 'Look,' she said. 'Gran and

Grandad are in it with me. I'm holding Darling – that's the monkey.'

Her face had lit up while she was talking, but Veronica watched the pleasure seep from it a moment later.

'Where is Grandad?' little Veronica asked. 'And Gran? I keep waiting for them to come back, but they don't.' Her slender throat jumped as she swallowed. 'Have I been bad? Is that why they don't come back?' Her shoulders shook as she began to cry. 'I try not to be bad,' she said. 'Gran always says I'm a good girl.'

It was too much. Veronica's tears flowed again, and she shook her head, putting out a tentative hand to touch the small child. 'You are a good girl,' she said. 'You're the best girl ever.'

But little Veronica shook her head. 'Then how come no one comes to get me?' she asked.

Erin put her hand over her mouth. She was crying too.

'I've come to get you,' Veronica said. 'I'm sorry I made you wait so long.'

The girl looked at her. 'Are you my auntie or someone?' she asked.

'Something like that,' Veronica said, looking over at Erin for a moment then back at the child. She brushed little Veronica's hair back from her face. 'I'm you,' she said. 'But all grown up.'

Little Veronica gazed up at her, tears forgotten for a moment. 'Is that how you have Teddy?' she asked.

There was a knot in Veronica's throat, and she nodded, spoke around it. 'Yes,' she said. 'I've kept him all this time.'

'How long?' the child demanded, then peered closer. 'You look old.'

Veronica gulped a laugh. 'I am old,' she said. 'I'm sorry it's taken me so long to remember you.'

Little Veronica looked at her, a frown puckered between her brows, mouth pulled down. 'Are you taking me to my gran and grandad?' she said.

'No,' Veronica replied. 'Not yet. I want you to stay with me first.'

The child looked at her, still frowning, thinking hard. 'Can I bring Teddy?' she asked. 'And my photo?'

'Of course.'

'And you'll look after me?' She blinked solemnly. 'Properly, I mean.'

'I will, yes,' Veronica told her.

'And we can do things I like?'

Veronica nodded, remembering the things she'd liked to do. 'We can do colouring,' she said. 'I can get some brand-new colouring books.'

'And can we have ice cream?'

She'd only ever had ice cream when she was with her grandparents. Veronica nodded, deciding she didn't give a damn about her waistline. 'Lots,' she said. 'All the different flavours.'

'I like chocolate best.'

'Chocolate it is, then,' Veronica said, and opened her arms to the child.

Little Veronica climbed into them, onto her lap, and Veronica closed her eyes at the weight of the child settling into her chest, filling the hole there, making her complete.

'Thank you,' she whispered.

52

AMBROSE WOKE HER WITH A KISS. 'IT'S TIME,' HE SAID.

Winsome blinked sleep-laden eyes and pressed hot fingertips to her lips where a moment before Ambrose's had been.

'It's time?' she repeated.

He sat on the side of the bed and turned to smile at her. 'The night was short.' His smile widened. 'Too short for some things.'

'They will be lengthening,' Winsome said, returning the smile. It was, after all, the summer solstice. She glanced at the uncurtained windows, at the greyness of the pre-dawn. 'I hope it will be fine,' she said.

'The night was cool, the sky clear,' Ambrose said, heading to the bathroom. 'Fortune smiles upon us. It should hold.'

Winsome lay back down and felt the heaviness of her body. Contentedness had weight, she decided, her lips curving again. She murmured Ambrose's words as though they were a prayer. Perhaps, for all that, she thought, they were.

'Fortune smiles upon us. It should hold.'

ERIN ALL BUT SKIPPED DOWN THE STAIRS, BURDOCK ON HER heels. She let him out and left the door open, the last dregs of the shortest night of the year seeping in through it as she turned and looked at her mother.

'It's time,' she said. 'Are you ready?'

Veronica looked back at her, eyes wide in the dim kitchen. She gave a coughing laugh. 'Is it possible to be ready for this?' she asked.

Erin shook her head, delighted. 'No,' she said. 'We just go and do it anyway.'

Burdock came clattering back in, toenails clicking on the flagstones. He looked at Erin, eyes bright. There were goings-on outside, he wanted to tell her, but he didn't have the words, and she probably knew anyway. She smelt as though she knew. He turned his head and looked at the other woman. She'd been mean and salty when she'd arrived, but lifting his nose, Burdock gave a good sniff and snuffled to himself. No vinegary, shadowy stink from her now. She smelt like smiles and even – he checked, nostrils flaring – a little bit of magic. Burdock squinted at the air beside the Erin-mother and wrinkled his lips.

Yes. There it was beside her, bright eyes peering out from its masked face. A spirit Raccoon.

There was a shadow at the open door and Burdock leapt up.

'Stephan!' Erin beamed at him. 'You're here.'

Burdock put his front feet on Stephan's shoulders and licked his cheeks.

Squirming, Stephan hugged him, then pushed Burdock gently down. 'I'm here,' he said. 'Are you ready?'

'GRANDMA,' MINNIE SAID. 'YOU LOOK BEAUTIFUL!'

Rosalie looked down at her new dress and blushed. 'I feel a bit silly all dolled up when the sun isn't even up yet,' she said. She brushed invisible lint off her skirt and looked over at Minnie.

'You look beautiful, too,' she said.

Minnie twirled and grinned.

'What about me?' Tiny asked, dancing into the room in her own new dress. 'And Mum – she's really pretty today.'

Natasha sidled self-consciously into the kitchen, Robin on her hip.

'We all look wonderful,' Rosalie declared, then took a breath, raised her eyebrows. 'Now,' she said. 'Are we ready?'

JULIA STOOD IN HER KITCHEN, GAZE FIXED ON THE ROSES SHE'D cut and readied. Her heart thumped loud enough that she couldn't hear anything over the rush of blood in her ears.

There was movement at the corner of her eye, and she turned her head. The cat stood by the door, tail high, a little kink in the end of it, and it stared at her, obviously waiting.

Julia shook her head.

'I'm not ready for this,' she said.

. . .

'You look gorgeous,' Ambrose said, outside on the spot where the paths through Wilde Grove diverged.

Winsome planted her palms against his warm cheeks and smiled back at him. She could see him only faintly in the glow of the dawn. 'You can barely see me,' she laughed.

'I can see you just fine,' Ambrose corrected her. 'Winsome,' he said. 'You shine.'

Erin looked over at her mother. They were outside in the garden now and above them, there was still a whole swath of sky blue with night, bright with stars.

'Will you be all right?' she asked.

Veronica nodded, laughed, unable to fully believe she was doing this. Was part of this. 'I'm driving,' she said. 'It should be me asking you if you'll be all right.'

'We could walk these paths in our sleep,' Stephan said.

Erin nodded. 'See you soon, Mum,' she said.

They arrived in ones and twos, appearing between the trees like wraiths, their white shirts and robes glowing in the first reachings of dawn.

'Blessed Litha,' Erin murmured, nodding to Clarice, Krista, her headdress of summer blooms rustling.

'Solstice blessings,' Krista answered, then touched Clarice on the arm. 'Are you ready?' she asked.

Clarice's hair was loose under her crown of summer flowers, and she was clothed, like the rest of them, in white. White with solar symbols embroidered down the front of her dress in red thread. She bared her teeth. 'As I'll ever be,' she said. She blinked. 'What about you?'

Krista, resplendent in her own robe, grinned at her. 'Are you kidding?' she asked, then smiled over at Erin and Stephan. 'I feel like I've been waiting all my life for this moment.'

'I'm almost shaking with nervousness,' Erin admitted, holding up a hand that trembled slightly. 'I was just getting used to things.'

On the other side of their loose circle, Ambrose picked up his drum and began a slow, sure beat.

'Where's Morghan?' Erin whispered.

'She's not here yet,' Krista answered.

Erin nodded, drew a breath, looked at Stephan. 'What if I forget my words?' she asked.

He shook his head. 'You won't.'

The drum beat was insistent and Erin fell quiet, listening to it.

When someone passed her a lantern, she held it in front of her, under the spell of Ambrose's drum, the flickering circle of lights. She swayed slightly, realising she was part of this space they were creating, this liminal space, between shortest night and longest day, between the Waking and the Wildwood, between inhale and exhale, between thought and prayer.

She stepped to the right, finding that everyone stepped with her, and they moved in a circle, then a spiral, then a circle, and a spiral again, lights weaving through the growing dawn.

A flute lifted its voice above the beating of the drum, then swooped and dived between the beats and she picked up her feet again, moved, danced, swirled, a glowing ember in the dawn.

The music grew and swelled around them, and Erin lifted her gaze as she moved, sweeping it over the trees, seeing those who had come out of the forest, out of the Wildwood to join them. She glanced over at Clarice, who stared at the beautiful, glowing figures of the Fae as they stepped closer to the circle to dance with them.

Clarice danced and watched, bowing as she met those who had come to celebrate with them. Maxen's dark eyes smiled at her as she passed, and then she turned, looking for Krista. They joined hands and continued their spiralling, circling dance.

And then the shining crowd of Otherfolk parted, and Erin glanced over at Stephan, who nodded and smiled, and she drew her breath in, letting it out slowly, and holding her lantern, she led the members of Wilde Grove between the Shining Ones and onto the path between the trees.

Down the path they went, their steps sure over the soil and roots, and then they were in the graveyard of Saint Bridget's, and out onto the road of Wellsford, lanterns swinging gently with their silent steps, Ambrose's drum coming with them, slow, insistent, the deep, dreaming voice of the world.

Past the silent straggles of villagers out early in the dawning to watch their procession.

Onto the village green, the villagers falling in behind them, beside them, some carrying lanterns of their own, wearing solstice crowns of their own.

The grass was springy under Erin's feet, the dew soaking into the hem of her dress. She stepped lightly over it, leading the Grove back into their circle, back into their dance that wound and unwound and wound again so that there was beginning and ending and beginning again, onwards, inwards, outwards.

Her lantern lit the faces of those who had risen early from their beds to come watch them. She smiled at a curly-haired child as she passed.

She smiled at Veronica as she passed.

And Winsome.

And Rosalie.

And Cynthia, and a dozen, two dozen, three dozen people whose names she didn't know.

Little Robin ran from the wide-spread crowd, and danced alongside her for a minute, feet stomping to the beat of the drum, before running giggling back to Natasha, crown of bright orange dahlias askew.

Erin slowed her steps, bringing the circle to stillness. They stood, listening to the drum's heartbeat and Erin let go of her breath, raised her voice.

'We sing the worlds together,' she called. 'We come together here to do this singing to bring peace to the heart of our beloved community, so that our song vibrates ever outwards and inwards.'

She closed her eyes, swallowed. Then the circle moved again, slowly, lanterns swaying, their lights already paler with the faraway, growing strength of the sun.

Erin took another breath. Lifted her voice again.

'Hail and welcome to all who call this land home, to all in this circle, to all in this community. Hail and welcome to all the gods we serve, with whom we walk our paths. Hail and welcome to our honoured Neighbours, with whom we are grateful to share this land. Hail to our ancestors, who have walked this circle before us, treading a path that we might follow, and whose love and tears we carry in our hearts, burden and blessing both. Hail to all those here, seen and unseen, remembered and forgotten, known and unknown.'

She subsided and smiled across the circle at Stephan.

'Hail and welcome!' Stephan called. 'To all those who come in peace, be welcome to our singing. Hail and welcome!'

The circle danced again, sunwise around the green.

A gaggle of children ran giggling into the centre of the circle, lifting their arms and spinning, hands towards the lightening sky.

Erin took a breath. 'We call peace into this space. We call for peace so that inside that peace we may hear the voices of our souls and our gods and sing the strength and glory of the sun and the season so that the wheel may continue to turn.' She lifted her hand and touched her forehead where Stephan had drawn the symbol of the sun in red across her skin.

The drumming continued, and they lifted their feet with it, humming in between the beats, weaving in and out the song of their flesh and blood and spirit.

Erin spread her arms out and danced, tipping her head towards the sky.

The children in the centre of their circle laughed and spun.

'In peace may the voice of spirit be heard,' she called.

'May there be peace in the east. May there be peace in the south. May there be peace in the west. May there be peace in the north.'

She drew breath again. The words came to her as if she'd always known them.

'May there be peace throughout all the worlds. May all who gather here with us at the dawning of this longest day, seen and unseen, be blessed by the growing light. May we walk blessed by the spirits of sea and sky and soil. May the worlds always be known, and may we walk in each, honour each, receive the blessings of each. May we sing the truth season to season, may our singing turn the wheel and bind the worlds together.'

Stephan answered her. 'World upon world upon world,' he called.

'World upon world upon world,' the circle answered.

Minnie stepped forward, face shining with the morning's birth. She lifted her arms. 'I call the spirits of the south,' she cried. 'Those who reflect the fire of our hearts, our passions, because we burn and keep the world alive. Spirit of Dragon, guardian over the bright gold that is our own treasure, the gold of our eternal souls, whose purpose never dulls nor tarnishes. I call you to be with us, to surround us with your protective breath of fire. Hail and welcome!'

There was a low murmur from the crowd, and the children in the centre of the circle stopped their dancing and listened, wide-eyed, crowns askew.

Charlie stepped forward, smiled at the children, took a dancing step, skirt sweeping around her legs, and lifted her voice to make the next call.

'I call the spirits of the water! You who hold the memory of the ages within you. I call the spirit of Whale, who dives to the deepest depth, whose songs bind each to the other, who swims in community and love and knows the memories and secrets of the worlds.' She lowered her head for a moment, seeing as always, the bulk of Whale swimming beside her, one wise eye turning to look at her. 'We are blessed,' she cried, 'we are blessed by you. We call you – hail and welcome!'

Simon, heart beating to the sound of Ambrose's drum, took his place, made his call. 'I call to you, spirits of the north, of earth, of the ground upon which we walk, the Earth that sustains us, gives us life, growing us from seed. I call upon the spirit of Bear – bless us, Great Mother, with your calm wisdom, your fierce love, your great power of healing. Hail and welcome I call you!'

Clarice stepped forward, lifted her voice into the still air of the dawn. She closed her eyes as she made the call, seeing herself in the circle of her Grove mates, in the circle on the green of her village, in the circle which her ancestors had danced before her, and still danced with her.

'I call to you, spirits of the east.' The dawn air was cool in her lungs. 'Spirits of air whose breath fills us, who offers wings to our prayers. I call to you, spirit of Owl, who knows the secret paths through the worlds, who comes to guide us as we find our way.' She paused a moment, head cocked, then smiled, carried on. 'I call to the spirits of the eastern wind, who blows upon me, the breath of the world, the wind under my wing, the song of the world.'

And she came then, Sigil, ghostly white in the dawn and silent on the breeze. Clarice lifted her arm and Sigil reached for her, legs outstretched, wings like an angel's, and landed, her great, golden gaze looking around the circle.

The children gaped at Clarice and Sigil, then laughed

and tumbled in delight. *A bird*, they called to their mothers and fathers. *See the bird!*

The circle moved again, lanterns held high to lend strength to the midsummer's sun, to herald its coming. The drum quickened, grew louder, and the children ran and ducked in and out of the dancing circle.

Morghan stepped into the space between Erin and Stephan, and they walked her to the centre of the circle, their Grove mates following them, then leaving her as they peeled off and reformed the circle. Morghan stood, dressed in red, the solar symbol in white on her dress, in red upon her cheeks. Her hair was loose down her back, silver threaded through with braided red thread.

On her head she wore a crown of oak leaves.

The crowd hushed their murmuring, the dancers paused, stood still, the drum beat quietened, became a whisper.

The children scattered, sank down in the grass, staring raptly.

'We are at our strength under the rising midsummer's sun,' Morghan said, lifting her face for a moment from the watching crowd to the sky.

'We are at our strength here, united today, Grove and village, Wilde Grove and Wellsford.' She blinked, lips curving in a slow smile. 'For who is not strong who has so many by their side?'

She saw Winsome, her dress the colour of sunlight, and smiled, nodding to her.

And beside Winsome, the men and women of Wellsford, spread out upon the green, more in number than she had hoped for.

'This is the season of our coming together,' she said, her voice clear on the morning air. 'This is the season of celebration, the dancing of our spirits before we retreat into the quietness of our solid companionship. Long have been the months to get to this place. Hard and well have we worked, have we settled differences, have we become allies.'

She swept her hands out at the circle. 'For here in the height of summer we look forward to harvest, to the fruits of our endeavours, to the sure knowledge that together we shall provide for ourselves and one another. None of us shall be hungry, none of us shall be weary, none lost, none lonely, for we have each other now, and when you suffer, I suffer, and when you suffer I shall seek to ease you.'

Morghan lifted one hand, holding it out, head bent, waiting.

On the outside of the Grove's circle, Winsome took a deep breath, glanced at those beside her, smiled weakly at their nods, then stepped forward, through the circle, and walked towards Morghan. She took Morghan's hand in her own and Morghan bowed to her.

'Lady of Wellsford,' Morghan said. 'Hail and welcome.'

Winsome blew out a quick breath. 'Lady of the Grove,' she replied, and bowed in return.

Winsome turned, her hand still in Morghan's, held up to the sun, and saw that she had not entered the circle alone. Cynthia, Emily, Rosalie, Natasha, Fiona, Melody – they had arranged themselves in an inner circle, their faces bright under their headdresses, their clothes the colours of the sun and summer and flowers.

Julia was there, her face pale, lips set, a garland of roses on her head.

Outside the Grove's circle, the rest of the villagers spread out, encompassing them all.

Circle upon circle upon circle.

Tears stood in Winsome's eyes.

Ambrose's drum beat louder.

From the village, a fiddle-player struck up a tune that wove in and out of the drumbeat.

Morghan smiled at Winsome, then turned slightly and looked at the sun-streaked sky. 'The sun rises upon us,' she called. 'The wheel turns, and this,' she said, turning back to gaze at the crowd.

'This is our Singing.'

53

ERIN DUCKED HER HEAD DOWN, GLAD OF THE TREES' SHADE from the heat of the July day, and watched Morghan's bare feet as she walked the path in front of her.

The sunlight through the canopy cast speckled shadows upon Morghan's green tunic and Erin blinked, reached out, and touched the folds of cloth lightly, before dropping her hand down again.

Here they were again, she thought, walking as they had so many times, along the same path, she and Morghan, Macha and Ravenna, she and Morghan.

How things spun and turned.

Her hair was heavy on her shoulders, and she drew in a deep breath of warm air. Behind her, she could feel Stephan, and the others behind him. Ambrose, Charlie, Clarice, Lucy, Krista. They snaked their way along the path to the cave.

She remembered her dream of the night before and shivered, even in the warmth, remembering how Stephan had leant over her, shaking her awake, quietening her shrieking.

'You're dreaming,' he'd whispered.

She'd dreamt that she and Stephan were sleeping the night in a house she hadn't recognised and before climbing into the bed, she'd closed all the doors out in the hallway, and to the bedroom. The house was haunted; the doors needed to be closed.

In the dream, Stephan had watched, shaking his head, and told her everything would be all right.

But in the dream, she'd woken and climbed out of bed, going out into the hallway and opening all the doors, as if she were still sleeping, sleepwalking. Ghosts came crowding out of the open rooms, pressing against her, and terrified, she'd run back into the bedroom – or tried to, it had been like running through syrup.

In the dream, she'd screamed out to Stephan, her voice choked, frightened. She'd turned to look at the bedroom door and there, hunched over, all strange angles and humps, a dark shadow, was a fox, and Erin had howled again, utterly terrified.

On the path, safe in the light of day, Erin shook her head. Why would she have dreamt of Fox like that? Fox had never frightened her.

The entrance to the cave loomed over her and Erin pushed the dream aside.

Because this was the day of her formal initiation into the Grove. This day, if she passed the spirit's test, would be the day from which she was formally acknowledged as the successor to Morghan. The next Lady of the Grove when the time came.

Erin whispered her prayer, ducked into the coolness of the cave. *Mother, welcome me into your womb and hold me safe.*

And then they were all assembled, the fire burning, Morghan's offering scenting the cave, Ambrose's and Clarice's drums calling the worlds together.

Erin closed her eyes. Thought of the shining form of Elen of the Ways, and her gift of diamonds. Prayed to her for courage.

May the strength of your heart be with me where I go.

May you guide me through the wilderness,

Protect me through the storm.

May I follow your path through the eternal forest.

Fox met her on the track through the Wildwood, and for a moment, Erin shrank back, her dream still inside her, but then she chided herself – this was Fox. This was her dearest companion, the kin of her spirit.

Fox led her through the forest, paws flashing in the green-gold light from the sun between the leaves, ears twitching.

Erin hurried after her.

They burst from the trees and Erin fell to her knees, turning her face away, panting, gasping for her breath.

It was too much. The sight of it was too much. The world tilted around her, and she dug her fingers into the dirt.

She was on the edge of a great, deep bowl in the earth. Flattening herself to the ground, Erin could only cast side-long glances at it.

Whatever she'd expected on this travelling – it hadn't been this.

At the bottom of the enormous crater was a pool, a

perfectly circular lake, the water a clear, pure turquoise. Erin, taking deep breaths, found her knees, then her feet, and stood, wobbling, unsteady, staring down at the water.

The World Pool, she thought, the name coming unbidden to her.

She twisted her head to look for Fox, who stood on the edge of the great bowl, gazing down at the World Pool.

'We don't have to go down there, do we?' Erin croaked.

But of course they did, and Erin followed Fox on shaking legs, and down, down, down they went, down the steep side of the bowl in the earth until at last they stood beside the lake.

And Erin looked at it, hoping she did not have to swim in it.

Fox trotted away, skirting around the shore, all the way around to where the lake tipped from its earthen bowl in a long, streaming waterfall, and they climbed down spray-covered steps in the rock beside it.

Fox disappeared, and Erin looked after her in consternation, then realised what had happened, and took a breath, and ducked under the waterfall, stepping into the cave behind it.

Fox padded forward into the dimness, and Erin followed, and behind her, Macha stepped silently into place. Erin glanced back at her, eyes wide at her sudden appearance.

But Macha just blinked at her, lifted her chin.

Keep going.

The dark tunnel opened out into an eerily-lit large chamber, and Erin stopped walking to gaze up at the stained-glass ceiling, staring at it open-mouthed, realising it was not stained-glass at all, but the bottom of the World Pool, where large shadows crossed and recrossed, swimming in the pool above. The floor beneath the pool was coloured tile, spreading out from a central design under the pool in a widening circle.

Erin, feeling as if in another dream, touched the centre of her ribs, and feeling her intuition flare into knowing, stepped onto the tiled floor and walked to the centre, and stood there, looking around, apprehension rising inside her, making her heart thud.

She stood in a huge chamber, and around the sides, Erin saw there were arched tunnel entrances. They were dark, except for eyes glowing like pinpricks of light, staring out at her.

Macha walked over to Erin, producing a sharpened spear and handing it to her. Erin took it and gazed down at it in horror, before lifting her eyes to Macha who merely looked back at her, face impassive, then turned and walked back to her place beside Fox.

Erin's hands were sweaty on the wooden shaft of the spear, and she gazed around, waiting, heart in her throat.

A shape tumbled out of one of the tunnels and ran, lopsided and deformed, stumbling over itself, but still swift.

It circled the tiled area where Erin stood.

Erin stared at it, gripping the spear tightly. She watched the creature run around and around her, a tumbling, stumbling, awkward and unnatural thing, sharp-toothed, glint-eyed.

She took a breath, raised the spear, closed her eyes for a moment, then flicked them open and walked across the tiles to where Macha stood.

She gave her the spear back.

The deformed creature had the heart of a fox.

It gleamed and glowed within the tangle of dark limbs, bright and fox-like and Erin watched it go around and around, tripping on itself, righting itself, running, stumbling, a whirl of limbs and patchy fur.

It was a thought Fox, Erin realised, misshapen through the error and ignorance, and perhaps even the darkness, of the person who had thought it into life. She stood in the centre of the circle, the World Pool a great, coloured weight over her, and came to the knowledge that many thoughts in her world grew these misshapen forms, that this was the way people made them, because they did not know that their thoughts could have form, that things were birthed and grew from that which was dwelt upon long and hard enough.

She caught the poor fox as it dashed past, and held it, stroking its red russet fox essence, tucking it under her arm as she stepped out from under the massive ceiling of the pool and walked towards one of the arches and through it into the tunnel, following the path her shuddering heart told her to take.

Erin stepped slowly, carefully, her lips pressed together to keep herself from howling in pain. Hideous things were being born in the tunnel, some hatching from mottled eggs, others being knitted from the darkness.

She stroked the fox, breathed, and passed on.

The tunnel widened and Erin sighed in relief. Then lifted her face in astonishment.

Her way was blocked, an enormous Elephant God peering down at her, with no intention of letting her by.

Erin stared up at him, then looked down at the fox-form in her arms. Regretfully, she kissed it on its soft forehead, then set it down on the floor of the cave.

This, she knew deep inside where all was knowing and being and singing, this was what came next.

Whatever it was.

She stepped forward, hands empty at her side, and looked up at the great Elephant God, waiting, her chest rising and falling as she breathed.

The Elephant God stared back at her, and then moved, his swiftness belying his great size, reaching out and grasping Erin.

He pulled her heart from her chest and flung it away into the darkness of the tunnel.

Then, as she collapsed, eyes staring at him, he tore her limbs from her body and threw them down upon the ground, and her head from her neck, until she was in pieces there on the dirt.

Erin, still conscious, lay in shock, her eyes swivelling to look around at all the bloody pieces of herself.

The sight was gruesome, a great dismembering slaughter of herself.

But she sat up, her spirit body shining, unharmed, and then she stood, and gathered up her heart, replacing it inside the split-open ribcage of her torso, slipping it back into place.

She retrieved her limbs and knitted them back together, singing the bones and flesh back to wholeness.

Finally, she was in one piece again, and breathing. Erin stood, looking down at herself, at the job she had done, then walked back to stand in front of the Elephant God once more.

'Show me your heart,' he said, his voice a harsh, beautiful gusting of wind and sound.

Erin moved without hesitation. She pulled open her ribs and showed him her beating heart.

The Elephant God grasped hold of it and tore it from her chest once more, throwing it away. Erin stood there for several beats, her chest an open wound, then walked over to retrieve it, and she replaced it in her chest before returning to her position in front of the God.

She would do this as often as he deemed necessary, she knew. Because there was something else she knew – whatever was torn apart could be woven back together.

Whatever was broken could be mended.

Whatever died lived again.

But the test was over, the Elephant God turning away, closing his eyes, ignoring her.

Erin stayed still a moment longer, then turned with a quiet breath and retraced her steps to the cavern with the pool as its ceiling. Fox and Macha, casting glances her way, walked to the exit, back to the waterfall to take the steps up to the surface.

But Erin went to stand underneath the pool and looked up at it. She reached a hand up to touch the ceiling, then turned to the others and waved them on.

Her attention was taken by the pool, and she touched it again, her hand passing through the membrane that was the ceiling, which was the bottom of the pool. She touched the water.

It drew her upwards, until she was in the water, swimming, deep in the bottom of the World Pool. The water was a cloudy aqua and she blinked her eyes, breath bubbling.

There were animals swimming in the pool.

Whales. Gigantic as the Elephant God, and as beautiful. A whole pod of them swimming together in a dance around and around the World Pool.

Erin swam with them, her face broken wide in a laughing, wondering grin, breathing easily, around and around in their great singing circle to the surface.

In the Wildwood, she knew the test was over, that she had done what she had come for, and that Fox was leading her home, back to the cave, back to her friends and companions, to her life walking the worlds with them.

But she blinked in the sweet sunlight that streamed drowsily between the singing trees and shook her head, calling Fox to her.

'I want to know what my dream meant,' she whispered.

Fox looked at her, searching her gaze, and then, coming to some sort of decision, turned, and led her again, deeper into the woods.

They stopped at a building and Erin gazed at it, out of place amongst the trees, makeshift as though put hastily together for just this purpose, and Fox glanced at Erin, lips pulled back in a grin as though to say – here it is. Here is your dream.

There was a door, and Erin pushed it open, stepping onto the set of her dream, as if it were a play and this was the stage. She shook her head in wonder, for there were all the characters of her dream, waiting in the wings.

How though, to find out what she wanted to know?

Stephan, she thought. Stephan would know.

She beckoned him to come forward.

'What does my dream mean?' she asked him, knowing he would have the answer. She cleared her throat. 'Even though I have just seen for myself that many spirits are thought-forms that come from people, I still want to know why I ran from them, why they chased me.'

She held her breath, waiting for the answer.

The Stephan from her dream smiled at her. 'You have opened the doors,' he said. 'Opened the doors to dealing with spirits. You did that yourself, of your own volition, so now you must not be afraid that they come to you.'

He paused and reached for her hand. 'We must not be afraid of the work we want to do,' he said. 'We must deal with our fear and then turn and do our work.'

He smiled.

'This is the way we sing the wheel to turn.'

Erin nodded, spoke the next words with him.

World upon world upon world.

PRAYER OF THE WILDWOOD

May the strength of your heart
be with me wherever I go.
May I be guided through the
    wilderness,
protected through the storm.
May I follow your path
through the eternal forest.
May healing and blessing be mine.
May compassion be in my heart
and in my hands.

AFTERWORD

The Singing is the culmination of over a year's work and I'm honored and humbled that the books have touched so many hearts and stirred so many spirits.

I've plans to go on writing about new and old characters from Wilde Grove and Wellsford for quite some time yet, so please have a look for the next book in my recommended reading order. It's Wilde Grove Series 2: Selena Wilde, and it's called Follow The Wind.

Do keep up with me via newsletter or social media to see my upcoming release schedule.

May healing and blessing be yours.
May compassion be in your hearts and
move your hands.
May there be peace in your heart.
May you sing the beauty of the world.

ABOUT THE AUTHOR

Katherine has been walking the Pagan path for thirty years, with her first book published in her home country of New Zealand while in her twenties, on the subject of dreams. She spent several years writing and teaching about dreamwork and working as a psychic before turning to novel-writing, studying creative writing at university while raising her children and facing chronic illness.

Since then, she has published more than twenty long and short novels. She writes under various pen names in more than one genre.

Now, with the Wilde Grove series, she is writing close to her heart about what she loves best. She is a Spiritworker and polytheistic Pagan.

Katherine lives in the South Island of New Zealand with her wife Valerie. She is a mother and grandmother.

Printed in Great Britain
by Amazon

44246042R00303